THE BOY IN THE CANVAS

CHRISTOPHER SWEET

OTHER DOOR PUBLISHING

For Annie

A WORD TO THE READER (AND A SPOILER-FREE CONTENT WARNING)

In the 1970s, at thirteen, my dad was incarcerated in what, in its day, was referred to as a training school—a correctional facility for "incorrigible" youth—for three years of his life. While there he was subjected to a prison-like lifestyle, subject to the whims of the abusive clergy who oversaw the students. He doesn't talk much about it but when he does, he's quick to say there were others who suffered even more than he did behind those walls. In 2018, almost fifty years later, he broke his silence about the experience, giving voice to many more who were abused in the same institution and places like it.

I found out most of the horrific details of his and others' experiences in "training schools" and places of their ilk along with much of the rest of the world; printed in black and white ink in the paper. I was justifiably disgusted with what I read, from my own dad's accounts to those of the many people who came forward after him. Of course there were countless others to speak up before him but these stories often get pushed to the bottom of the news pile.

It was difficult to know how to react when my dad first suggested to me that I should write something inspired by his experiences. I didn't want to bring them to life. I wanted to bury them. Not because I didn't care or wasn't sensitive to them; quite the opposite, in fact.

Shortly after my dad made that suggestion, my writing mentor, Thom, gave me a bit of advice that I'll never forget; something that keeps me up at night.

"Write what scares you," he said.

And the accounts of those who were held in training schools did scare me.

Cut to a year or so later and the idea for *The Boy in the Canvas* manifested itself in my psyche. I had the whole story laid out in a flash of inspiration but was stuck on a setting for it. I knew early on that I wanted it to be set in the 8os but that was about it. If you put a gun to my head and cocked the hammer, I still wouldn't be able to tell you what it was that made me decide to subject young Joseph to a nightmarish place like St. Theodore's Academy. I certainly didn't want to write about such things.

But the story demanded to be told and the more I tried to think of other, better places to set it, the more St. Theodore's rooted itself in my mind, demanding to be filled with troubled kids and despicable adults. Places like that come with baggage and it was a heavy task sorting through it all.

This brings us to your **content warning.** There are some rough scenes with descriptions of abuse in this book. They were tough to write and, I imagine, they can't be pleasant to read about, but they serve to tell Joseph's story honestly. I considered glossing over some of these scenes and actually did, in some regards, in an earlier version of the book. Some early readers who had experience with being subject to childhood abuse pointed out that they felt cheated when the icky parts were removed. Not because they were proud of them but because they felt they deserved an honest representation of the horror involved in such a situation. I had a good amount of sleepless nights thinking over that and eventually found what I hope to be a respectable middle ground.

St. Theodore's Academy is a fictional place but some of what goes on within its walls comes close to reality and, in cases, pales in comparison to what so many suffered through only a few decades ago. None of this is based on actual accounts.

I wrote this with the utmost respect and compassion for those who have suffered in these nightmarish "schools".

May they find peace and justice.

-Christopher Sweet
January 2022

TALLAHASSEE, FL - 1974

"Keep up, child."

The girl, ten-years-old just yesterday, looked up from the frog she'd been chasing. Her mother held the door to the gallery open, tapping one foot in a vain effort to conduct her daughter's tempo.

"I seen a frog," the girl shouted, sprinting the rest of the way to the door, light rain misting her face, feet splashing in small puddles just enough to dampen the hem of her skirt.

"You're embarrassin me," her mother hissed at her as she darted through the door.

The gallery, Colorata, bustled with activity. Men and women in expensive-looking suits and cocktail gowns chatted and cackled, threw back cocktails, and plucked hors d'oeuvres from platters bussed around by tuxedoed servers. The girl's mother disappeared into the fray, indifferent to the activity of her child as long as she was under the roof of the gallery.

One of the servers knelt down next to the girl and presented a silver tray. "Good evening, Miss Hasty."

The girl plucked a sausage roll from the tray and popped the entire thing in her mouth.

"It's Hast*ings*," she said around her mouthful.

"I think Hasty is catchier," the server said as she plucked another roll from the tray. "Are you excited for the debut of your mother's newest work?"

The girl shrugged. "I seen it. I don't like it much."

The server patted her on the head and stood to make his rounds. "See you around, little Hasty."

"Hast*ings*," she corrected again, bits of sausage roll falling through her wide grin.

She wandered through a sea of tailored trousers and slit gowns, plucking a prize from any tray that was carried low enough for her to reach. She worked her way to the back of the hall with an ease that spoke of many previous visits. As she meandered down a long, empty hallway, the babble of the art crowd faded out behind her. She wove through the exhibition rooms. One housed a display of porcelain busts. In the next was a still life exhibit, and the next, walls of abstract paintings. She stopped dead in the middle of the last room.

She may have been catatonic for how still she stood. She stared at the painting in front of her, hypnotized as though it were the flickering light of a TV set.

On the wall before her hung an unremarkable painting that depicted a swan gliding over the crystal surface of a pond surrounded by reeds. The girl took a step toward it then looked over her shoulder, her face a mask of guilt, as though she were a cat burglar who had just tripped the alarm. She had the room to herself. She took a step closer. And then another. Within fewer than a dozen paces she stood directly in front of the painting, nose almost touching the canvas. Her eyes traced over the work as if she was looking for something or, perhaps, following something with her gaze.

A smile materialized on her face, full of wonder, as though a unicorn stood in front of her instead of the painting of a swan. She reached out a hand, pulled it back. Another glance over her shoulder. She stretched her hand out once more and placed her palm flat on the surface of the painting.

And then she was gone.

Hours later, her mother, along with the help of the server who had greeted the girl at the beginning of the night, searched every room in the gallery. Police arrived on scene when no sign of the girl could be found. A county-wide investigation was conducted and soon made state news. Nobody had seen anyone suspicious looking or who may not have belonged at the showing. The best guess of everyone involved was that the girl had become bored and wandered off into nearby swamp-land where she could easily have become stuck or drowned or, God-forbid, been killed by one of thousands of gators that roamed those swamps.

Of the girl, her mother never saw another sign.

The painting of the swan sold to an unknown buyer the next day.

1

PHILADELPHIA, PA - 1984

JOSEPH WARD WATCHED AS THE REST OF HIS CLASS FILED out of the room ahead of him. He remained at his desk, a wobbly thing with the seat attached by a steel arm, and ran his finger along the grooves carved into its surface; initials of the desk's former occupants, the exception being the depiction of a pair of enormous boobs. As one of the few twelve-year-old boys at Roosevelt Middle School who did not possess a pocket knife, he was unable to add his own initials. He had asked for a knife for his tenth birthday and was told by his father, who had been uncharacteristically sober-in-mind (if not in blood) that day, that he would sooner lob off the boy's pinky finger himself so that he could at least be sure there would be a clean cut. Joseph gave up entirely on the notion when his birthday passed without so much as a hug from either parent, let alone a knife. By his twelfth birthday his expectations were more reasonably set. It didn't bother him, it was all he knew to either be invisible or an overwhelming burden to his parents.

Out of nowhere, someone shoved his head from behind.

He'd been holding it close enough to his desk that it smacked off the wood surface. Paul DiMarco howled laughter and danced past Joseph, high-fiving his entourage as they left the classroom together. Paul's attitude far outmatched the boy's actual size. He was a full head shorter than Joseph, and scrawny to-boot. He compensated for this with all the spit and noise of a Rottweiler. The boy was vicious and would not hesitate to brandish his switchblade, handed down to him by his older brother, at the slightest provocation. To avoid ending up on the business end of that blade, Joseph did his best to give in to whatever amused Paul the most that day.

Ignorant of Joseph's torment, his teacher, Ms. Hendrix, tidied her desk then turned to the blackboard, brushing away the day's lessons in broad sweeps of her arm. Joseph watched as she procured a handkerchief from the top drawer of her desk, dipped it in a chipped mug of water, and used the damp cloth to clean the blackboard from edge to edge, humming a soft tune to herself. Finished with the board, she dropped the used kerchief into the mug, straightened the back of her dress, and took a seat behind the desk.

"Come sit up here, Joseph." She gestured to the desk directly in front of her own.

Joseph picked himself up, grabbed his knapsack by its one remaining strap, and marched to the front of the classroom. He dropped his bag and plonked back down into the frontmost desk.

The clock ticked away the seconds. Ms. Hendrix stared at him with kind brown eyes. A ringlet of black hair fell across her forehead and she brushed it behind her ear with the rest of the curls. She was a pretty lady, younger than his mother, and one of the kindest grownups he had ever met. He was oblivious as to why she had asked him to stay behind after class, mortified that he had, apparently, done something to upset her. He met her gaze with his own, pale, grey-blue eyes.

"Always look them in the eye," his grandfather had said one night, over a game of chess.

"Who?" a ten year old Joseph asked, moving his bishop into what he'd thought at the time was a strategic position.

"Your opponents, your superiors, your friends." His grandfather's big, wrinkled hand slid his rook into Joseph's bishop. He used the castle to flick the bishop off the board. "Anyone you respect or who you want to respect you."

"Why?" Joseph stood up the fallen bishop and put it in line next to its eight defeated comrades.

"For one thing, it's respectful. Maybe look at where your queen is." His grandfather sat back and puffed his clay pipe. Cherry Cavendish smoke streamed out his nostrils and over the board. "For another thing, you can tell a lot about a man, or a woman, by watching their eyes. When you're paying attention, you can tell if they mean you good or harm, whether they're lying or telling the truth. You can tell your friends from your enemies."

Jeremiah Fisher died of heart failure later that same year. It was the most devastating time of Joseph's life to date.

Joseph remembered his grandfather's words and stared into Ms. Hendrix's eyes. He even imagined he smelled a ghost of his grandfather's pipe tobacco. He'd lost that game, as he'd lost every game against the old man. But he learned.

Ms. Hendrix cleared her throat. "Do you know why I asked you to stay behind?"

Joseph shrugged. It was as close to an accurate answer as he could give.

She smiled and said, "You're not in trouble, Joseph. I want to help you if I can."

He shifted in his seat. "Help with what?"

"Is everything okay at home?"

He felt blood rise in his cheeks and looked away. How could he tell someone he barely knew what things were like at home?

"Joseph?" She waved a hand in front of his face.

"Everything's fine."

"Would you like to talk about your last test?"

"What about it?"

Instead of answering, she leaned over, bouncy curls falling over her face. She rummaged through the bottom drawer of her desk, brought up two sheets of paper, and placed them in front of her, side-by-side.

"At the beginning of the school year we had what I called a general aptitude test." She looked up from the papers and held his eyes with her own. "Do you remember that?"

Joseph shrugged. He understood where this was going.

"You did well on that test. Top of the class, in fact."

"Oh yeah," he muttered.

He remembered that test all too well. Ms. Hendrix, with intentions he was certain were as pure as gold, had called him up to the front of the room after announcing he'd been top of the class; almost perfect score. She'd led the rest of the students in a round of applause, had even cheered for him. He remembered feeling a deep sense of pride in that moment. Nobody except his grandfather had ever shown him that level of appreciation before. His pride swiftly gave way to shame when he sat back down at his desk and heard the snickers of Paul DiMarco and his pals.

"Fucking nerd," Paul had whispered from behind him.

Ms. Hendrix held up the sheet of paper on her left. "This is that test. You got all but one question right. I might add that it was a question none of your classmates answered correctly. In fact, at the beginning of the year, my expectation was that none of you would pass that test with more than a B."

"Okay."

She held up the other sheet of paper, the one on her right; the most recent test they had taken, he suspected. Ms. Hendrix confirmed this.

"This is the test we took at the beginning of this week." She slid the paper forward so that Joseph could see the D minus scrawled over the top of the page. "You are the only student who not only showed no significant improvement, but who also did much worse on the second test than the first. Almost like you were *trying* to fail."

Joseph stared at her, an average looking boy of average height in secondhand clothes, with mousy brown hair clipped just above his ears, and a welt forming on his forehead where Paul had slammed it on the desk. He *had* tried to fail that test. He could never make Ms. Hendrix, nice as she may be, understand why.

He had no real friends to speak of. As far as he could figure, the reasons for this were two-fold. One reason was because of where and how he and his family lived. The other was that he was actually a pretty bright kid. He was no genius but he was bright enough that he could be at the top of his class if he applied himself. He took no pride in this, it was embarrassing that learning came so naturally to him. Before Ms. Hendrix, his grandfather had been the only person to ever point this out to him. He'd been proud of his intelligence when

Jeremiah Fisher had acknowledged it, as he had been the first time Ms. Hendrix celebrated it. His peers did not think it was so cool. He could've lived with it if it was only Paul DiMarco and his cronies who made fun of him but, of course, all children are capable of cruelty, even if they don't know they are being cruel. For weeks after that initial aptitude test, Joseph had been referred to as *Nerd* or *Brains* by everyone in his class. It was silly to let it get to him but twelve-year-old hearts are vulnerable to even the slightest injury.

"It might be best if I spoke to your parents about this," Ms. Hendrix said, not unkindly.

"No!"

"We can work something out together, a learning plan that is a little more up to your speed."

He didn't know whether to be more worried about the special learning proposal or about bringing his parents to the school. Not that he thought they'd actually show up. The one thing he'd been able to keep from his schoolmates, the thing he knew would cement him in the role of outcast for an eternity was his parents. He didn't even like to think about them while he was around other people. He would have to stop coming to school altogether if the kids in his class were to find out what kind of people they were. His father would be drunk, and would most likely hit on Ms. Hendrix, while his mother sat and swayed in her chair, staring out the window or scratching at her arms.

Ms. Hendrix leaned back in her seat and let out an exasperated sigh. They stared at one another for a long minute.

Finally she said, "I want to help you, Joseph. I know you can do better in my class."

Not trusting himself to speak, he turned his attention to

the window. Outside the classroom, kids chased each other around the playground. Some lined up for buses. Others walked home in pairs or groups. Nobody waited for Joseph or wondered what was taking him so long. Why this woman was being so kind to him, he felt he would never know. Why did she care so much?

"Do you get paid more?" he asked.

"Excuse me?" She blinked at him.

"Like a bonus or something. For having good students. Is that why you want me to do well in your class?"

"I don't want to see you fail."

"Am I failing?"

"Joseph..."

"Am I?"

She stared at him for another long moment, like she was trying to see into him. She let out another one of those sighs.

"Not yet," she said.

"So why me?"

Her normally gentle face hardened, her lips pressed tight together. She was upset and he had no idea why. He could completely understand the feeling though, he wanted nothing more than to bury his face in his arms and sob, out of frustration more than anything.

Ms. Hendrix sniffed, snatched the papers off her desk, and shoved them back into the drawer.

"You're free to go, Joseph."

He stood slowly. This might be some kind of ruse, the kind of trick adults played on kids to test them. He slid the strap of his backpack over his head so it fell diagonally across his chest and trudged toward the door. He had just grasped the doorknob when she spoke again.

"If you decide you want my help, or if you want to talk, about anything, I'm here."

He stood at the door, hand on the knob, back to her. He felt like he should say something but didn't trust his voice not to shake. He yanked the door open and stepped out into the hallway.

He speed walked through the hall and shoved through the double doors into the welcoming spring sun. The day was clear and warm, perfect after school weather. A group of a dozen or so kids kicked a soccer ball in the field next to the school, their bags abandoned at the periphery of the pitch. Three girls played hopscotch on a grid drawn in chalk on the asphalt. School buses loaded with kids trundled off in a parade of yellow steel.

Joseph surveyed the yard, looking for Paul DiMarco or any of his gang but it seemed like they had taken off. They usually didn't hang around on school property unless they were waiting to harass someone, often himself.

The school buses didn't run to Joseph's end of town and he typically took the city bus to get to school. He was never in a rush to get home though. On nice days like this, he opted for the hour long walk back to his apartment. He enjoyed walking through the city and it still afforded him enough time to get his homework done, especially since he didn't go out to play in the evenings.

The sun beat pleasantly down on his hair, warming his head and provoking beads of sweat to break out on his neck as he strolled the city streets. High rises, boutique shops, and fancy restaurants gave way to bodegas and corner stores, which gave way to single-story houses and low-rise apartments, all in varying degrees of disrepair. Beyond these, soot-covered factories and warehouses loomed over him, blocking out the sun's light. His father worked at one of these though Joseph was never sure which one. Just beyond the industrial sector was his neighborhood, if it could be called that. His was an apartment building in shambles on the corner of an intersection that was home to two other such buildings, with McLaren's Sports Bar, a dive bar Joseph had heard his mother call it, occupying the fourth corner. The dump was only a mile or so from their building and on hot days the stench was so bad that it wasn't uncommon to see people walking around with bandanas tied over their noses. It wasn't too bad today but, like an aromatic welcome mat, the funk still reached his nostrils as he approached his building.

Joseph let himself in the front door and checked the mail slot before stepping into the lobby. The building used to require a key to get in but the lock had been damaged in an incident Joseph could only imagine the details of. All he knew was that it resulted in the building being swarmed by police cars and two ambulances. Since whatever had happened that night, the door remained bent out of shape and unable to lock properly. There was also a dark brown stain on the carpet in the lobby that he tried to convince himself was not blood.

The elevator was down again so he took to the stairwell, trying to breathe through his mouth to avoid the thick smell of urine and cigarette smoke that hung in the air and pressed around him. At the eleventh floor, he pushed through the door to his hallway, relishing the relatively clean air. The smell of cigarette smoke still persisted but at least the piss smell was gone, replaced by a foreign but pleasing aroma of spices his parents never used.

He let himself into the apartment with a key he wore on a

string around his neck and was greeted by the sound of the television blaring from the living room. His mother was probably watching one of her soap operas; a man and woman were arguing about who loved the other more.

He poked his head into the living room and saw he was right about the program. His mother, Anita, wasn't so much watching it as much as she was dwelling in the ambiance of it. She sprawled on the couch, faded pink bathrobe draped loosely over her skeletal frame, strands of limp blond hair hanging over her face, a cigarette dangling from the corner of her mouth. She was a wraith of a woman, who spent her days drifting listlessly from her bedroom to the kitchen to the living room, where she would take her medicine and watch endless hours of television, the one luxury their family had afforded themselves.

His mother sucked on her cigarette and, as she parted her lips for the smoke to escape, a long tube of ash tumbled from it and landed in a dark pile on her leg. The floor and couch around her were black from months of sitting in this same spot and spilling ash around herself. The only place on the couch that wasn't blackened was the spot she sat in, darkened by a V shape where her legs parted slightly. His father was on her constantly about the mess she made on the couch and carpet but once he had a few beers in him he was just as bad with his own cigarettes in his chair. He at least used an ashtray almost compulsively, flicking his cigarette half a dozen times between each drag.

"Hi, Mom," Joseph said, standing at the threshold.

If she'd heard his greeting, she didn't give any indication. He hadn't expected her to respond. It looked like she had already taken her medicine; even from here he could see how red her eyes were. At least she had made an effort to conceal the evidence this time. Sometimes he would come home to find a needle next to her on the couch or her old, cracked rubber tube still tied around her arm. On these occasions he would untie the tube for her and allow circulation to flow back to her hand. He never touched the needles, never even looked at them if he could help it. They scared him. Like venomous snakes coiled and ready to strike should he get too close. His mother called the stuff medicine but it never actually fixed anything in her, only made her worse. He didn't even know what it was supposed to be for. His father only really spoke about it when he complained about how expensive a habit it was. Joseph didn't think taking medicine counted as a habit.

He took his backpack to his bedroom, by far the cleanest room in the house, then went to the kitchen to make some spaghetti. If his mom had already taken her medication by the time he got home it wasn't likely he'd be getting supper unless he made it himself.

His father, Alan, came in, announced by the slamming of the door, just as Joseph was straining the noodles. Heavy footsteps as he tromped into the living room were accompanied by the rattle of empty aluminum cans rolling around in his lunchbox; he typically packed a small bottle of liquor or a few beers for the way home. Fridays were the exception, when, instead of coming home, he would go straight to McLaren's Sports Bar and stay until the fluorescent Open sign clicked off and he was tossed out.

"Clean up this fucking mess, Anita," he heard his father say from the next room.

If she responded, Joseph didn't hear it.

His father stomped into the kitchen and dropped his steel

lunchbox on the small dining table they seldom used for eating. He was a tall, heavyset man with greasy black hair that was always pasted to his scalp with sweat and grime from the factory. For the most part he wore a sardonic smirk at one corner of his mouth that could just as easily have been a grimace. His nose and cheeks were red from broken blood vessels and a permanent heat rash from work.

He fished in the refrigerator for a beer, cracked it, drained half, belched, and stomped out of the kitchen into the living room.

"Not too much sauce on that," he called over his shoulder.

"No, sir," Joseph said, slopping the noodles from the strainer back into the pot.

Once he'd tidied up, he brought a bowl of spaghetti to his father, who took it without a word and immediately started slurping up noodles. He brought a second bowl to his mother, who still didn't seem to realize he was there.

"Mom?" He held the bowl in front of her.

Her eyes remained glued to the TV screen.

Joseph cleared a space on the end table next to her, set the bowl down, and gave her a kiss on the cheek. He went back to the kitchen and spooned the rest of the pasta into his own bowl, which he took to his room.

He sat at his desk, a small wood table his father had found at the curb outside their building, and did his homework while he ate. When he was finished, he lay back in bed and stared at the stucco ceiling. He imagined different shapes in the white bumps and fissures. Sometimes he could make out faces of people or monsters. Sometimes it was animals, earthly or imaginary. Today he imagined the ceiling was all one great landscape, like the surface of a distant planet. He pictured a white planet floating undiscovered just outside their solar system. He imagined himself flying through its valleys, between great white mountains. It was a planet utterly devoid of life. A world just for him, where he could be whoever he wanted. He drifted off exploring his alien ceiling.

2

———

HE DREAMED HE WAS BACK IN HIS CLASSROOM AT SCHOOL. He stood at the front of the class and lectured his peers about the topography of the planet Ceiling. A girl at the back of the room raised her hand and Joseph pointed to her with a piece of chalk. She stood to ask her question and he saw it was Ms. Hendrix.

She smirked at him and said, "Why are you such a nerd? There's no such thing as planet Ceiling. Your mom's a zombie. Your dad's a drunk. You're a nerd. Why do you bother coming to school?"

Joseph asked her to sit down. Instead she grabbed a handful of her own hair and tugged it upward. The flesh of her face stretched up with her hair and still she continued to yank on it. The skin around her neck stretched taught then pulled apart, like taffy stretched too far. She pulled her face entirely off, like it was a Halloween mask. Underneath, glistening with Ms. Hendrix's blood, was Paul DiMarco's face, sneering at him. He still wore Ms. Hendrix's blouse and dress, which

Joseph might have found funny under any other circumstances. In this case it horrified him.

"Why are you such a nerd?" Paul jeered.

He raced at Joseph, hands outstretched, Ms. Hendrix's dress billowing behind him, and tackled him, pinning him to the floor. He grabbed the edges of Joseph's shirt and shook him so that the back of his head smacked on the linoleum.

Joseph woke up with a jolt and clawed at his throat to free himself of Paul DiMarco's hands. He was covered in what he hoped was sweat and had kicked his blanket onto the floor. He lay in bed, catching his breath, the details of the dream already escaping him. He could remember that he had been in class and that Paul had attacked him for some reason. He tried to recapture the memory of the dream but it slipped out of his grasp like a live fish.

Fully awake, he slid out of bed and padded out of his room in his underwear, up the short hall to the bathroom. His father muttered something from the living room. His parents frequently slept in their respective spots in front of the television, his mother more often than his father. She rarely left her couch. Sometimes, after they'd both passed out in the living room, Joseph would sneak in and sit next to her. He'd watch whatever was on TV and pretend they were a normal family.

He peed, flushed, and washed his hands. As he rinsed, he looked at himself in the dingy bathroom mirror. He had dark circles under his eyes and crow's feet at their corners. He splashed cold water over his face and scrubbed. A crash from the other room startled him. It was immediately followed by his father shouting something he couldn't make out.

Joseph tiptoed down the hall toward the living room, beads of water running down his face, onto his chest. His father was berating his mom for something. Joseph almost went right back to his room but curiosity got the best of him, carried him to the end of the hall where he could spy around the corner.

"I told you," his father said, "I told you this would happen. I told you. Stupid bitch."

The words stung Joseph, as they always did when his father directed such language toward his mother. When he was ten, Joseph's father had called her a worthless whore. Joseph, in a fit of chivalry that must have come from his mother's side, stood between his parents and commanded his father not to speak to her that way. His father had punched him so hard that he'd blacked out for a full minute. When he woke up he had a fat lip and a welt under his left eye. His father had stormed out, leaving his mother to cry silently on the couch. Ten-year-old Joseph crawled up there and lay with her until they'd both fallen asleep.

Now he watched as his father swayed over his mother, who was sprawled out on the sofa. He grabbed at his hair with one hand in a gesture that was almost comical but that Joseph recognized as a sure sign that he was both drunk and angry. In the man's other hand was a beer can, which he threw at his wife with such ferocity that Joseph cried out.

His father spun around to face him and Joseph was stunned to see tears in his eyes. This picture of his father was so absurd to him that he all he could do was gape. His father stared back, mouth hung open as though he was waiting for words to just make themselves happen. His eyes were red rimmed and drops of spittle clung to the stubble around his lips.

The thrown beer can had landed on the floor and Joseph's father bent to scoop it up then slunk across the room to his chair. He collapsed into it and stared at the crumpled can as though it were some holy artifact that had fallen from the sky. He seemed to have forgotten Joseph was there at all. He turned the empty over in his hand, examining every side of it.

Joseph turned his attention to his mother. Gasped. Her skin, normally slightly yellow, had gone completely pale— almost grey. A brownish goo covered her mouth and had spilled over her chin, onto her chest and the cushion. One hand dangled off the couch, her fingertips, nails chewed down to the skin, barely touching the yellowed carpet of the living room floor.

"Mom?"

He drifted toward her and wondered in the back of his mind if he might still be dreaming. If it was a dream, the detail was something to marvel at. From his mother's fingernails to the perpetually dry, flaking skin around her scalp, to the cracked rubber hose still tied above her elbow. A hypodermic needle protruded from her arm and hung at an angle. She'd never passed out like that before. As forgetful as his mother could be, she'd never actually left a needle in her arm. And why hadn't she bothered to wipe her face off after vomiting? Why hadn't his father insisted she clean herself up, as he normally would when she forgot to bathe or change her clothes for a few days?

Joseph knelt beside her and placed a hand on her forehead. It was cold and dry to the touch. This close, he could see that the brown mess she had spewed on herself had streaks of red running through it. Her lips were a deep purplish-blue.

He looked over at his father, who still turned the crushed beer can over in his hand.

"Is she okay?"

His father didn't seem to have heard him. He kept turning that can over, as if looking for some piece of advice that may have been written on it. The man was never at a loss for words, especially when he'd been drinking. It was this silence, more than his mother's blue lips and cold skin and bloody puke, even more than the needle sticking out of her arm, that told Joseph everything he needed to know.

He wanted to shake her and shout her name. He wanted to lift her up to a sitting position, instead of the crumpled recline she was in. He grabbed the thin blanket she always used from where it was bunched up at her feet and wiped at the brown gunk. It had partially solidified and only the top layer came off her skin, leaving behind a smeared mess of red and brown. How long had she been like this? How long had his father sat here drinking while she lay with a needle sticking out of her arm and dried puke on her face? Did he really sit there and drink a beer, *enjoy* a beer, while his wife lay dead or dying just across the room? Did he know she was dead when he threw the can at her?

Joseph had never felt much more than a cautious regard for his father. Now he was flooded with overwhelming hatred toward him. The selfish, worthless, alcoholic bastard had watched his own wife die. Joseph wanted to scream at him, to hit him over and over, but he found himself unable to move or speak. He swiped again at the smear of brown but it was caked to his mother's skin. The smell of it invaded his nostrils and he felt like he might vomit if he stayed too close. The idea of puking didn't bother him but the idea of doing it on his mother, on her body, was enough to bring a choked sob to his throat. He pushed himself back from her and collapsed in the middle of the living room floor, between her and his father, and wept.

3

———

THE FUNERAL WAS A SIMPLE AFFAIR THAT HAD BEEN PAID for in full by Joseph's grandfather before his passing. There were fewer than a dozen people in attendance and Joseph knew only one of them, his mother's brother, Edgar Fisher.

Joseph had only met his Uncle Edgar once before and knew very little of the man except that he lived in California, where he sold real estate to movie stars. The man was the complete opposite of Joseph's parents; tall and handsome, with a square jaw and a head full of wavy blonde hair. Joseph had no trouble imagining him jogging into the spray of the Pacific with a surfboard under one arm. His mother had boasted to him that her brother had met and shown houses to Harrison Ford. For Joseph, who was obsessed with *Star Wars*, this practically made Edgar a movie star himself. He'd always idolized the man and had pestered him nonstop about the nature of his work when they'd met a year ago. Edgar told him about the enormous houses famous people moved into, about the beaches, the constant sun, and the beautiful people everywhere. He'd promised Joseph that he'd fly him and his mother out to visit him sometime soon. They'd even discussed the possibility of Joseph spending a summer with him.

Now Edgar gave the eulogy for his departed sister and Joseph listened as his uncle spoke tenderly of her, recalling memories of their childhood together and lamenting her descent into addiction.

"She deserved someone to look out for her," Edgar said from the pulpit, casting an unmasked glare at Joseph's father. "My sister was the kindest, most generous person I knew. Given half the chance, she could have done something great with her life. Sadly, as we all know, life doesn't always work out the way it should. Sometimes we wind up in places where we are held back and made to stagnate. Anita wasn't given much of a chance. The only freedom she knew was the fugue brought on by the chemicals she shot into herself. I sincerely believe she could have made a real difference in this world, if she'd made other choices earlier in life."

At those words, Alan Ward stood from where he was sitting, next to Joseph, and stormed out of the sanctuary. Joseph felt no inclination to follow. He kept his eyes on Edgar while he finished the eulogy. His uncle looked satisfied that he had managed to banish his brother-in-law from the rest of the service.

Hymns were sung and the reverend, a small man in his sixties with the whitest hair Joseph had ever seen, said a benediction over the congregation. The reverend announced that Anita's will dictated she be cremated. At this Joseph stood, ready to protest that no one would be burning his mother. A warm hand on his shoulder stayed him and he looked up to see Edgar, wet-eyed, looking down at him. Joseph was overcome and hugged the uncle he barely knew. It was the closest he could come to hugging his mother anymore. Edgar wrapped his arms around him.

"Take me to California with you," Joseph pleaded, his face buried in his uncle's torso. "Please. I won't be any trouble and I'll make all my own food and get a job."

Edgar pulled back, prying Joseph's hands from around him. "You know I'd love to, kiddo."

"You can't leave me here with him."

"Your old man wants what's best for you. He tries."

"No he doesn't. All he cares about is his stupid beer and if the Pirates make it to the World Series."

Edgar knelt down in front of him. Joseph refused to look him in the eyes until his uncle took him gently by the chin and turned his face toward him.

"Maybe once you've finished high school we can talk about it. I'd love to have you out to visit sometime but I can barely take care of myself. And your old man needs you."

"Don't you hate him for what he did to Mom?"

Edgar gazed up at the ceiling and rubbed his face. He stood abruptly.

"Anita...your mother had her own problems. It's not fair to blame it all on your dad. They both made choices that weren't very healthy." He reached out a hand and mussed Joseph's hair. "You ever need anything—to talk, or you need some advice on your homework or something—you call me. Tell your old man you can reverse the charges to me if he's worried about the long distance."

Without waiting for a response, Edgar strode to the exit, shook hands with the reverend, and disappeared through the doors. Joseph's father walked in at the same moment. The two men barely glanced at each other.

Before his father could see him, Joseph ran in the opposite direction, through a door at the front of the sanctuary, and down a flight of stairs into the church basement. The stairs ended in a long hallway. Noise came from one end of the hall; voices and the clanking of dishes, accompanied by the strong aroma of coffee. He turned in the opposite direction and wandered deeper into the church. His stomach knotted and his heartbeat picked up; that familiar sensation that came with being somewhere he shouldn't be. He passed nearly a dozen doors, all open. One of the rooms had a table in the center with orange plastic chairs all around it. Along the back wall of the room were shelves lined with books, Holy Bibles and hymnals. Another room had a table set up in similar fashion with cloth backed chairs arranged around it. At the front of this room was a chalkboard with the words *Fundraising Committee* scrawled across it in white chalk. At the end of the hall stood the only closed door in the basement. Naturally, he needed to know what was behind it.

He stood in front of the door, undecided, as the unintelligible babble of the ladies in the kitchen drifted down the hall toward him. He couldn't help but feel as though he was trespassing. He realized he was holding his breath and blew the air out of his lungs at the same time that he grasped the cold, steel doorknob. Confident it would be locked, he gave it a jiggle. The knob turned easily. He glanced over his shoulder to make sure none of the church ladies had snuck up on him. The coast was clear. He nudged the door open. And felt immediate disappointment.

It looked like little more than a storage room. In the light spilling in from the hallway, he could tell the walls on either side were lined with shelves. These held various texts as well as the obligatory Bibles and hymnals but were also stacked with folders, boxes, and a variety of other items that would no doubt be the victims of the next yard sale the fundraising committee put together. Lamps with their cords wrapped around them, an old record player under a plastic cover, porcelain Jesus figurines, and old rotary phones were scattered haphazardly throughout the shelves. Stacked on the floor in the corner closest to him were towers of those orange plastic chairs. Joseph barely registered all of this, his attention drawn to the back wall of the room. He felt along the inside of the doorway until his fingers touched a light switch. He flicked it on and stepped inside.

Hanging on the far wall, dead center, and at his eye level, was a canvas painting, held within a worn, wooden frame. He crept up to it until he stood no more than a foot away. He realized he was holding his breath again and let it out slowly. He had seen art before, in black and white photographs in school books, but that had been the extent of it. The walls of his house were unadorned by anything but an outdated National Geographic calendar that hung on the wall of the kitchen. His mother had brought that calendar home from a grocery trip one day and the two of them had flipped through the pages, ooh-ing and ah-ing at the photos of wildlife within. Now, out of date and ignored, the calendar was stuck perpetually on September's photo of a grey wolf. The memory brought an ache to Joseph's heart but the sentiment quickly moved to the back of his mind as he stared at the picture in front of him.

The painting was striking in its realism. It depicted a small lake in front of great, snow-capped mountains. A river snaked its way from the lake into the distance and Joseph figured it fed the lake, that somewhere in the distant mountains was a waterfall or a greater lake spewing out crystal clear water that travelled all the way out to form this body of water. Where in the world could such a beautiful place be? The water in the lake was a deep, clear blue that shimmered in the sunlight. The green grass surrounding it grew wild and free but Joseph could make out dimples in it, close to the shore, where deer or some other form of wildlife had stood to drink. In the distance, the mountains stood as sentries over the scene, their rocky slopes perfectly topped with pure, white snow. Between these mountains, a far-off, harmless cloud had formed. The way the artist had depicted the sunlight was so realistic that it actually irritated his eyes the longer he stared at it. He leaned closer, felt himself drawn into the painting. He wanted to study every detail, every blade of grass, and keep the memory of this work in his mind. He'd never been inclined to any sort of creative work before, and was hardly capable of even drawing a passable stick figure, but this tugged at something deep inside him. Perhaps it had to do with the loss of his mother.

Time stood still. Was this how art critics discovered their calling?

Someone flitted past the frame.

Joseph jumped back so fast he almost fell into the stack of chairs behind him. He must have been staring at the picture in the dim light for too long; it had looked almost as though the painting was a camera lens and someone had walked through the shot, mere inches from it. He knew that's not really what happened, that a shadow had passed over the room from the hallway. Never mind that he hadn't heard anyone behind him.

He inched closer to the painting.

Nothing. He'd imagined it.

Something disturbed the water and caused a gentle ripple to move through the surface, which was impossible. And then the person in the painting walked back into the frame. And looked directly at him.

It was a young woman, maybe in her early twenties. She wore modern clothes that didn't go with the rest of the painting; jeans and a dark t-shirt with a denim vest. There was a patch on the breast of the jacket that Joseph could swear was for the band Iron Maiden. He didn't have any tapes of his own but Matthew Grey had brought his boom box to school a few months ago with *The Number of the Beast*. He'd allowed the kids out on the playground to pass around the cassette case to check out the artwork. Joseph had been fascinated with the cover art; Eddy the Head looming over the Devil himself, seeming to control him with marionette strings. Joseph was certain the lettering used to spell out the band's name on that cassette cover was the same as that on the girl's jacket in the painting.

She waved.

He screamed and ran from the room, flew down the hall toward the voices he'd heard when he'd first come downstairs. He burst through a door at the other end of the hall and skidded to a stop in a huge kitchen full of old women plating Peek Freans cookies and sandwiches cut into triangles. None of them appeared surprised by his presence.

One of the ladies, a plump woman who reeked of flowery perfume, held a platter of cookies out to him.

"Take as many as you like, you poor thing," she said with a sympathetic smile.

He ignored her. "There's a painting in the other room and

a girl is in it and she's moving like she actually saw me looking at her and she looked back at me and there was water and it moved too you have to come see it! Please!"

The women continued their assembly of the platters of food. A taller lady smirked at him and tutted but that was the only response he got.

"Someone help me!" he shouted.

The plump woman put an arm around him and led him out of the kitchen. "We're a little busy for games, dear. If there's a girl looking at you, maybe she likes you. Try saying hi."

She gave him a gentle shove down the hall, disappeared into the kitchen, and closed the door.

He was on his own. There was no way he could tell his father about this. If his mother was here he'd tell her. He missed her more than ever in that moment. She might tell him the same thing the plump old lady in the kitchen had, that he should say hello. He decided then that he would be brave for his mother, it was just a painting after all.

He stood outside the closed door to the storage room for a few minutes, listening. Had he shut it on his way out? He couldn't remember. Finally he told himself he was being silly. He was upset and had imagined something in the painting. He nudged the door open.

At first, all he could see was the painting hanging on the wall at the back of the room, completely free of girls in Iron Maiden vests. Reassured, he stepped halfway into the room before he realized she was still there. Only now she stood *outside* the painting, off to one side of the room, inspecting a porcelain Jesus figurine.

They spotted each other at the same time. Joseph froze, terrified.

She gave him a huge, toothy grin.

"You saw me," she said in a twangy southern accent.

"Where did you come from?" Joseph asked.

She put the Jesus figurine back. "You first. You could see me? In there?"

He nodded.

"And you saw me movin around?"

Joseph nodded again. "Is that an Iron Maiden patch?"

She grinned and stuck her chest out so that he could get a better look. He was a little embarrassed to be alone with this strange girl who was sticking her chest out at him. The stark, red lettering of the band's logo was indeed ironed onto the jacket. He found his gaze lingering on the rise of her breasts beneath the thin fabric of the shirt she wore under the vest. Something stirred just below his belly button, a feeling he was beginning to get more around girls and, lately, around Ms. Hendrix.

"You a Maiden fan?" the girl asked.

"Yeah!" Joseph lied, unsure why he wanted to impress her. "Number of the Beast."

She raised her eyebrows and grinned at him again. "Dickinson sure made that band what it is."

Joseph had no idea who Dickinson was, nor did he care. A girl, up close she looked more like eighteen or nineteen, had just popped out of a picture and now they were discussing Iron Maiden and a guy named Dickinson. What would his father think if he happened to show up at this moment? He would probably be really nice to her and smile at her a lot, which is what he did around pretty women that weren't his wife.

"How did you get here?" Joseph asked.

The girl put a hand over her chest in mock outrage. "You don't even wanna know my name?"

He blushed. "I'm sorry. What's your name? I'm Joseph. Joseph Ward."

She offered her hand out to him as though she expected him to kiss it. "Deborah Hastings is my name but I go by Hasty. Some folks call me Deb. Nobody, but nobody, calls me by my full name."

Joseph took her offered hand and gave it an awkward shake. "Pleased to meet you."

"What a polite little guy you are," Hasty said as she strolled around the room, inspecting its contents. "We in a church?"

"In the basement, yeah."

"It's Sunday then?"

"Tuesday."

She smirked at him. "You a preacher's kid? Nothin wrong with that, mind you."

He looked at his feet. "It's my mom's funeral today."

Before he realized what was happening, she grabbed hold of him and squeezed him in the tightest hug he'd ever received. She was taller than him and he was very aware of his chin resting atop her breasts. She pulled him even tighter and he inhaled her scent; a heavy, musky aroma, like she hadn't showered in quite a while. Mingled with it were odors of the outdoors; grass, fresh air. That stirring sensation started up again followed by a far more embarrassing reaction. He pulled away from her before she could feel him stiffen.

"I'm so sorry I showed up like this. If I'd known, well, how could I have? Anyhoo, I'll leave you to grieve." She turned to the picture.

"No!" he half shouted. "I mean, you're nice to talk to."

She smiled at him and turned to the shelf with the porcelain Jesus. Joseph took the opportunity to adjust himself under his pants.

"What city we in?" She turned back to him just as he pulled his hand from his waistband.

"Philly. Philadelphia. Pennsylvania."

She raised her eyebrows and Joseph couldn't tell whether that meant she was impressed or just the opposite.

"How did you do all that with the painting? Do you live in there?" He had a hundred questions that wanted to spill out of his mouth.

She shrugged and sighed. "I honestly do not know. It's something I discovered I could do, I guess when I was around your age. How old are you?"

"Twelve years old."

"Ok, I was ten," she ran both hands through her dirty blonde hair. "My God, I've been doing this for nine years now."

She was nineteen. He was alone, in a basement with a nineteen year old girl. He tried to think about unsexy things. He imagined his dad bursting through the door and that cooled him down. For now at least.

She looked at him. "Nobody's ever been able to see me move around in a painting before. At least, nobody who I've noticed. Funny enough, I haven't been able to see anyone as clearly as I saw you while I was in there. Usually people appear all muddy-looking."

Joseph's mind whirled. "You can do that in other paintings?"

"Oh sure," she waved a hand as though it was nothing. "Not every painting, mind you. I think it has something to do with how much feeling was put into a piece. Or how much a painting means to the artist. I haven't quite figured it out."

"I'm not sure I know what you mean."

"It's okay, little man. I've never talked to anyone about this, at least not since I was a little girl. I'm probably not explaining it very well. You've seen *Star Wars*, right?"

He nodded with enthusiasm.

"Well, imagine C-3PO painted a picture. I don't know for sure, but I don't think I'd be able to jump into his painting. There wouldn't be any soul behind it. Not least of all cause he's a fictional character and whatnot."

"Paintings have souls?"

"Maybe. The people who create them sure do. At least, some part of them bleeds into their creation. Might as well call it their soul."

Joseph's mind reeled with all this information. He wanted to refute all of this, wanted to tell her she couldn't trick him into believing this baloney but he had seen her moving around in the picture with his own two eyes. He pinched himself on the thigh as hard as he could. Nothing changed.

She put a hand on his shoulder. "It's a lot, I know. I had to discover it all by myself."

"Did you see someone in a painting?"

She rubbed her chin. "No, I don't recall seeing nobody in any painting. When I was a little girl we went to an art gallery in Tallahassee, my momma and me. While we were there I wandered off to browse the artwork while she got drunk. I found this painting of a swan in a pond and it was the most beautiful thing I'd ever seen. As I watched it, this swan began swimming around the pond. The whole scene came to life! Then I just sorta slipped into it. I still go back to visit that bird sometimes."

"What did your mom say?"

A sad smile crept across Hasty's face. "I don't think she ever knew what happened."

"You never told her?"

"Never saw her again. She died a little while later."

"I'm sorry," he said with a tremor in his voice. And then, after what he hoped was an acceptable pause, "I don't understand. You stayed in the painting?"

"Not that one, no. It's really hard to explain." She rubbed at her eyes, looked at Joseph, and sighed. "I'm no expert in all this, I just kind of roll with whatever happens."

"Can you try to explain?"

"Only because if you saw me, you might wind up being able to do the same thing and I don't want you to have to learn the hard way." She took a deep breath. "Apparently all of an artist's creations are tied together somehow and apparently, for people like me, it's possible to travel between those creations. I wandered away from that pond to explore the rest of the park it was in and wound up on this rainy city street and couldn't find my way back. I wandered around and asked people how to get back but none of them knew what I was talking about or made any sense. I was in another painting by the same artist. I found my way out and wound up in someone's living room in Toronto. That's in Canada."

Joseph, who knew full well where Toronto is, had even

more questions than before. "You said I might be able to do the same thing."

Hasty shrugged as though this wasn't the most exciting thing to ever have happened.

"How do you do it?" Joseph pressed.

She shrugged again. "It's just like walkin for me. Give it a shot. I'll come in right behind you so you have someone to show you around."

Joseph approached the picture, eager to impress this girl. He raised a hand, closed his eyes, and touched the painting. When he opened his eyes again, his hand was placed flat on the canvas. Nothing moved within it, no part of him passed into it. It was just a picture.

Hasty stepped up beside him and put an arm around his shoulders.

"Maybe you just need practice," she offered.

"How do I practice?"

"It just happened for me. Maybe it's not the same for you. Or maybe it's just a fluke that you were able to see me."

He shook his head so hard his neck cracked. "I'm going to figure out how to do what you can do."

"Listen," she said, "In nine years I haven't come across anyone who can do what I can."

"I really hope I'm able to."

"I hope so too, but listen." She grasped his chin and turned his face so he was looking right at her. "It can be dangerous. You never want to stay in a painting for too long. Something happens when you do, the paint degrades or something. I think being in there destabilizes it or something like that. Anyway the whole world starts to fall apart if I'm in any one painting for too long."

"How long is too long?"

"Depends on the painting, I think. I haven't come up with a way to figure it out until it's too late. I try to limit my stay to less than a day."

"What's the longest you've stayed in a painting? Can you eat stuff there? Where do you live?" Joseph fired off the questions with barely a pause between them. There was so much he wanted to know about this mysterious girl's ability.

Before she could answer, his father's voice echoed up the hallway, shouting his name.

Hasty's eyes widened at the shouts. "He doesn't sound happy."

"He never does," Joseph said, "We have to hide you."

She chuckled. "There's nowhere to hide in here. I'm gonna disappear."

"That's it? You're leaving?" He couldn't believe this magical visit was already coming to an end.

She ruffled his hair, just as his uncle had done not even an hour before. "I got a feeling maybe we'll run into each other again. You're a special guy, Joseph Ward."

"Joseph!" his father shouted from much closer.

Hasty darted to the door and swung it shut. She grabbed him by the shoulders.

"You've gotta listen to me a second," she said, her face suddenly serious. "If you can do what I do, you're gonna find out not every painting is nice. Be careful about which ones you visit and which ones you jump to."

His father's footsteps echoed through the hall beyond the door. They sounded close.

"Joseph?" He was right outside.

Hasty put her hands on the sides of Joseph's face. "Watch

out for the eels most of all." She read his panicked confusion. "Paintings are magical. They're a reflection of the artists passions, dreams, and loves, but also their fears and doubts. I think there might be some things out there that thrive on that stuff. You'll know what I'm talking about when you see them. You mind them."

He opened his mouth to say something else but she turned his head and planted a soft kiss on his cheek, then stood and stepped toward the painting.

He grabbed the back of her vest. "Can't you take me with you?"

She turned back and offered him a sad smile. She blew him a kiss then stuck her hand directly into the painting. It shimmered and then she disappeared into it, almost like a noodle being sucked between someone's lips.

The moment she was through, the door to the room burst open. His father stood there, red-faced.

"Who were you talking to?" he barked.

"Nobody. Myself."

"Bullshit."

Joseph looked around the room, arms out at his sides.

"We're going home." His father grabbed him roughly by the shoulder and pulled him out of there.

4

They rode the bus home in silence. Joseph's father sipped from one of six beers he'd purchased on their way to the bus stop. The beer was part of a package that included a bottle of Wild Turkey, a carton of filterless Camels, a tin of coffee, and a loaf of bread. They were out of milk, eggs, butter, and pasta but let the man find that out for himself. Joseph had no desire to speak to his father, and, in some distant part of his psyche, wanted him to find out on his own that there was nothing to eat. Perhaps it was so that his father would need him, ask him to help out with groceries. Maybe it was so that he would miss his recently departed wife.

When the bus let them off in front of their building, his father fished another beer and a pack of cigarettes out of the paper shopping bag then handed the rest of the groceries to Joseph.

"Take this stuff upstairs," he said. "Going to McLaren's."

Joseph's first instinct was to throw the paper bag and its

contents to the ground. He was on the verge of doing just that when his father swiped the back of his sleeve over his eyes. It was the most emotion Joseph had ever seen him express. Unable to face the man any longer, he turned and marched into the building with his father's groceries and the loaf of bread that would be a staple of the next three or four meals.

In the apartment, Joseph dropped the bag on the coffee table in the living room, doing his best to avoid looking at the couch where his mother passed away not three days ago, then went to his bedroom and flopped onto the bed.

The day was a massive beast clinging to his back, weighing him down, spewing hot breath on his neck. His mother's funeral was a blur of faces he barely recognized expressing their "deepest condolences". He tried not to think of her laying in the casket. The notion of some stranger closing the lid on her, sealing her in that box forever, and then setting the whole thing on fire made him want to scream and claw at his own face. He was powerless to deal with his grief, couldn't decide if it was more outrage or anguish. He fought against tears but they ultimately won out and he cried himself into a dreamless sleep.

A harsh buzzing woke him an hour or so later. Visitors to their home were so scarce that at first he didn't recognize the sound for what it was. He glanced at his Mickey Mouse watch, a gift from Uncle Edgar that he wore at all times, except when he bathed, and saw it was just past supper time.

Another buzz. His father was obviously still at McLaren's. Joseph didn't expect him home until well after the bar closed.

He dragged himself out of bed and trudged to the callbox. Stood in front of it, finger hovering over the Answer button. He waited for a minute then assumed whoever it was must have given up. Just as well. He had no friends who would be visiting him at home. He'd done a good job of making sure the few kids who spoke to him had no idea where he lived.

Yawning and rubbing at his eyes, he padded across the carpet to the kitchen, intent on scraping something together for supper. He scooped up the paper grocery bag from the coffee table in the living room on his way by and let his eyes drop to his mother's spot on the couch.

A dry, brown patch crusted the side of the couch cushion where she had taken her last breath. The couch bore a permanent imprint in the shape of her body, more pronounced on the side closest to the door, the spot she would sit up in when she was feeling active. The imprint was thin, as she had been. She was so vulnerable in life.

Joseph's chest tightened up. Rage surged in him as he recalled the sight of his father tossing the empty beer can at his wife. Such a wasted life. Such neglect. How could someone treat a person they claimed to have loved, at one point anyway, with such cruelty? How could his father live with himself knowing that, in all likelihood, it was his fault she had died? Tears prickled at Joseph's eyes, threatened to fall. A light rapping on the door put an end to them, if only for the moment.

The knock, gentle as it was, sounded like firecrackers going off in the silence of the apartment. Joseph dropped the bag of groceries and they hit the ground with a dull thunk. He idly hoped one of the beers had burst and soaked his father's cigarettes.

Another knock. He had forgotten the lock on the main entrance was busted. But who would visit them? Surely someone who wished to offer condolences for the passing of his mother but Joseph couldn't imagine who that might be. Pretty well everyone they knew had been at the funeral; all ten of them. It was possible that it was a friend of his father's but he'd never spoken of any friends at the factory. The only person from work he'd ever talked about was the foreman, and the words he had for him were never nice.

He stood in front of the door, torn. It could be someone who knew he was alone in the apartment. But even then, what could they want? There was nothing in here that anyone could possibly desire, nothing worth committing a crime for anyway.

"Mr. Ward? Joseph?"

He recognized the voice.

He opened the door to reveal Ms. Hendrix standing in the hall, looking over her shoulder as though she expected to be mugged at any moment, which was a reasonable concern in this building. The tight curls of her hair fell over the shoulders of the green turtleneck she wore. She held a bouquet of yellow daisies in one hand and an orange Tupperware container in the other. Joseph caught himself staring at her breasts, even as surprised as he was to see her standing at his door. She turned toward him and he redirected his gaze to the floor, cheeks growing hot, certain she had seen him peeking.

When he looked up at her, the sympathy in her eyes was so apparent it made his chest tighten and his throat bunch up all over again. She knelt, placed the flowers and container on the floor, and hugged him. He was mortified that in spite of his grief he was hyperaware of her breasts pressing against him.

He pulled away from her before his body could react, as it had with Hasty and swiped at his eyes so she wouldn't see the tears that had formed there. A tornado of emotions swirled within him. He batted them all away and tried to play it cool. He realized he loved Ms. Hendrix, wished she could have been his mother. Immediate guilt followed that thought and his heart grew heavy all over again.

"You poor child." She stroked his hair.

He looked down at what she was carrying, more to avoid eye contact than anything else. She followed his gaze and smiled.

"I thought you two could use a nice home-cooked meal." She scooped up the flowers and the container and stepped into the apartment. "Is your father home?"

He shook his head but she had already stepped past him and gone to the bag on the floor. Transferring the Tupperware to the hand holding the flowers, she stooped and picked up the groceries.

She peered into the bag and looked up at Joseph. He averted his gaze and found himself staring at that crusted spot on the side of the couch cushion once more. How many times had his mother thrown up in that exact spot? She got sick frequently, whether from the medicine itself or from her butchered immune system, he would never know.

"Where's your father, Joseph?" Ms. Hendrix's voice startled him out of his thoughts.

He shrugged. Why burden her with his family's problems? As if they were a family anymore.

"Well why don't I stay with you until he gets back? I'll warm up this casserole for us. There will be plenty left for your father when he returns." She carried everything into the kitchen without waiting for permission.

Joseph followed wordlessly, wondering if he should tell her his father probably wouldn't be home until after midnight and would be very drunk when he got in. What would she think of him when she found out what kind of man his father was? He thought back to the man ripping him away from that magical painting in the church basement. He hadn't even bothered protesting when he was pulled away from it; what was the point? His father had no patience for the fanciful imaginings of a twelve-year-old. In fact, he had no patience for Joseph whatsoever. He hadn't asked Joseph to explain why he was in that room or what he was doing staring at a painting in the basement.

Ms. Hendrix would've asked me.

He imagined her as his mother, asking him about his days at school, helping him with his homework, and sharing his celebrations and sorrows. He thought of his mother and the few moments of tenderness she'd offered him, during her rare bouts of lucid sobriety. Rubbing his back when he had a stomach bug and couldn't stop vomiting, watching a movie with him while his father was at the bar, laughing with him when she'd spilled chocolate milk all over them both and the board game they'd been playing at the time—the last board game they'd ever played together.

He realized he was leaning in the kitchen doorway, staring at a spot on the floor where part of the linoleum was peeling. Ms. Hendrix was looking at him expectantly, apparently having had asked him something.

"Hm?"

"I asked if you have a microwave I can use to heat up this casserole?"

He turned away from her. "Uh, no. It's busted."

A lie. They had never had a microwave. Joseph's father, if asked, would go on about the radioactive beams that shot out of them and fried your sperm. This was likely little more than an excuse to keep his dad from admitting that they couldn't afford one. Unless maybe he gave up drinking, and nobody wanted to have *that* conversation. What did it matter now, anyway?

"Well," Ms. Hendrix said, "I'll just pop it in a baking dish and warm it in the oven. You can go watch TV if you'd like, Joseph. I'll let you know when it's ready."

He was so overwhelmed by her hospitality that he didn't know how to react. He drifted out of the kitchen, to his room. He lay on his bed and daydreamed about what his father would say when he came home to find his teacher here. If he came home at all. The thought sent a shiver of excitement through him. He realized that he hoped his father didn't come back. He didn't care if he wound up in a foster home or an orphanage. Anything would be better than the situation he was in now, stuck with his dad to take care of him. How old did he have to be to emancipate himself?

"Joseph! Supper!"

He'd never heard those two words strung together like that, with nurturing and tenderness behind them instead of anger and impatience. His throat tightened again. He told himself not to be such a baby, that he'd already let Ms. Hendrix see him cry once and that was more than enough. He took a deep breath, slid off his bed, and headed to the kitchen.

The casserole was the best he'd ever had. It was loaded

with cheese and had a crunch to it that took him a minute to place.

"Are there potato chips in this?" he asked between bites.

Ms. Hendrix winked at him. "Old family recipe. My momma used to tell us 'ain't no point havin no casserole if y'ain't gonna put tayta chips in it.'"

Joseph laughed at the put-on accent. He'd never known her to behave so casually, like a friend instead of his teacher. One who put chips in casseroles at that.

Once they'd eaten (Joseph had three helpings of the casserole, exclaiming each time that he'd never had one so delicious), he cleared the table and washed the dishes. Ms. Hendrix packed the leftovers into the Tupperware container, stuck it in the fridge for Joseph's dad, then found an old vase for the flowers she'd brought.

"Are you sure you'll be alright on your own?" she asked as she put on her coat at the front door.

Joseph had explained to her that his dad was working the late shift and wouldn't be home until after midnight. He tried to make it sound like it was a regular occurrence, which was at least a half truth.

Ms. Hendrix hugged him tightly before stepping out the door.

"We'll see you back in school when you're ready, Joseph," she said from the hallway.

He thanked her again and closed the door on her. Then he went to his room where he shoved a sweater, two chocolate bars he'd stashed under his bed, and a few dollars he'd saved over the years into his backpack.

He'd made up his mind to sneak out while he and Ms. Hendrix were eating together. Not that he could really call it sneaking out when there was no one to care if he was gone.

Over dinner she'd asked him about his hobbies, but beyond reading or watching TV with his parents, he had never really had a hobby that was worth talking about.

"What about you, Ms. Hendrix?" he had asked between mouthfuls.

He recalled her eyes lighting up as though she'd been waiting for someone to ask her just such a thing.

She had placed her fork down, folded her hands together under her chin, and looked up at the ceiling as though she was watching an exotic bird fly through the kitchen. She had stared like that for a long moment before answering, long enough that Joseph almost followed her gaze to see what was so interesting.

"I've always loved to paint," she said.

His heart skipped a beat. He was immediately brought back to the church basement, to the painting and the landscape with its blowing grass, the lake with its rippling surface, and whatever untold beauty was hidden in the mountain ranges. He longed to be with Hasty, brimming with adventurousness, representing a potential life full of wonder.

"It sounds silly but there's almost a magic to it," she had said, still staring at the ceiling, her eyes wide. "As though I'm creating an entirely new world with my paintbrush. I don't mean that to sound as boastful as it does, I'm no Rembrandt, but even the simplest of paintings can feel as though they contain life, if they're painted with the right feeling, the right emotion. Does that make sense, Joseph?"

He had only been able to nod, lost in his thoughts. Maybe she was more right than she knew. Maybe there was something more to art than just a picture painted on canvass. He needed to see the painting in the church basement again. The rest of his life depended on it.

"Do you think they really contain life?" he'd asked, casserole forgotten for the moment.

She'd smiled at him kindly. "Not literally, of course. But some *appear* to more than others. Do you know who Norman Rockwell is?"

Joseph shook his head. He didn't miss the look of pity that flashed across her face.

"He was a very famous painter who died not too long ago. He painted a lot of scenes from everyday life, families at supper, children playing, that sort of thing." She gave him a look that said she knew that these things weren't exactly everyday family life for Joseph.

"And his paintings had life?" he'd asked, more to get her to stop staring at him than to hear about Mr. Rockwell.

"They certainly appeared to. He captured emotion and painted things that everyone, most people, could relate to. Not only that, he was passionate about the subjects he painted and I think that's what gave them such a lifelike quality. And there are many other artists who paint things that are entirely unrealistic who are also able to imbue their work with that sort of life. It's difficult to explain. It's more of a feeling."

"I think I get it," Joseph had said.

Less than fifteen minutes after she left, he stepped out into the hallway and locked the apartment door behind him. He needed to see that painting again for himself. Would Hasty still be there? She'd told him that she tried not to stay in any one painting for more than a day. Had she mentioned how long she'd been in that painting? He couldn't recall. He only hoped that she hadn't left yet.

What if he had imagined his encounter with Hasty, though? He was aware that grief played a role in how some people interpreted the world around them. Perhaps he was setting himself up for disappointment. But he had to see it again. Had to know for himself. Desire tickled in the back of his mind like an insect rooting for a place to call home. Breaking into a church was probably a sin that God would forgive without too much fuss. After all, didn't God want him to go to church? He wasn't going there to steal anything. Just to visit and look.

The second part of his plan is what scared him the most. He had no intention of returning home after his visit to the church. He was going to California. His Uncle Edgar wouldn't turn him away if he showed up on his doorstep. He had no idea how he'd find the man once he got to Los Angeles, phonebook maybe, but he'd deal with that when he got there. First he had to figure out how to get across the country.

He decided to take the stairs down, afraid that, if he took the elevator, he'd get to the lobby only to find his father standing in front of the doors. When he reached the main floor, he inched the stairwell door open and gazed across the lobby, to where the elevator doors stood closed. He stayed where he was for a full minute to make sure his father wasn't coming through the front entrance. Each second he remained hidden in the stairwell was another blow to his resolve. What if his father walked in just as he was leaving? He glanced at his watch. Only 10:30. Unless his father was kicked out before closing time, he wouldn't be home for at least a couple of hours.

A heavy sadness stole over him and he almost changed his mind about the whole thing. His dad was a mean alcoholic, sure, but did he deserve to be abandoned? And so soon after the death of his wife? Joseph's thoughts drifted to the memory of his father shouting at his mother's corpse. The brown vomit with flecks of red. His father throwing that beer can, that *trash* at his mother. His sadness evaporated as quickly as it had come upon him. If anything, his dad would be happy to be rid of his only other burden.

He took a breath and stole across the lobby, past the elevator doors, through the broken main doors, and out into the night. The air was cool and still. His nerves jangled inside him, making him shake and, funny enough, feel like he had to poop. Across the street, the neon Open sign in the window of McLaren's buzzed and cast a red glow on the sidewalk in front of the bar. The street was empty save for an elderly man in a long coat across the street, pushing a shopping cart full of tin cans, plastic bags, and a dented boom box. Classical music issued from the speakers and wafted across the street to where Joseph stood. The music was melancholic, dominated by a deep-sounding string instrument, perhaps a cello. It drifted away with the man as he pushed his possessions further up the street, around a corner.

Joseph caught movement at the door of McLaren's and took off up the street, away from the bar. He resisted turning around to see if it was his father stepping outside. Would it make a difference if it was? Odds were the man would be too drunk to recognize him in the dark and from so far away. He ran for three blocks before allowing himself to slow down, assured that he was out of sight.

He detoured slightly so that he could pass his school and see it for one last time before moving on. He'd opted against taking the bus, choosing to save the small amount of money he'd brought with him for things like food or, hopefully, transportation west. He stopped in front of the building and marveled at how ominous it appeared in the dark. Normally this was an inviting place that he was happy to be entering, if for no other reason than to be away from his parents for eight hours. A bitter sadness stole over him. How often had he avoided his mother in the past? Would he have spent more time with her if he'd known the end would come so soon? Or would he have come to resent her even more?

"Goodbye, Ms. Hendrix," he said.

Of all that he was leaving behind, she would be the one he missed the most. He thought of her appearing at his door and his heart swelled with gratitude. He blew a kiss to the building, intending it for her, then looked around, his cheeks burning at the idea that someone may have seen him. But the street was empty, he was utterly alone in the night. That brought on another wave of melancholy but this was quickly replaced with excitement. He imagined himself as a rogue from one of the fantasy novels he liked to read. Emboldened by this, he turned away from the school and continued on his way.

It took him a lot longer than he'd anticipated to reach the church. According to his watch, it was well after midnight by the time he arrived.

A chill went through him as he stood before the building. It was old, traditional, built of heavy stone blocks with great oak doors that lead directly into its sanctuary. An iron gate surrounded a small graveyard to the right of the church. Silhouetted within the confines of the graveyard, leafless trees stood watch over the dead. Headstones, rounded and square, lined the rows like giant teeth. A small mausoleum stood at the back of the cemetery. He shivered, glad he did not have to go in there. The church was spooky enough, its stained glass windows black in the night, their pictures indiscernible. The building's gables appeared bigger, more pointed than they had in the light of day. He realized he was a little frightened.

"It's just a church," he told himself.

His voice echoed back to him off the walls and he winced at the sound. He glanced around to make sure no one had heard or noticed him. He couldn't just keep standing in front of the church forever so he forced himself to move.

On the other side of the church was a parking lot that wrapped around to the rear of the building. He remembered seeing a side door that led inside from the parking lot; he'd try that first. There were blessedly few streetlights around and he was able to stick to the shadows as he crept around the church. He approached the side entrance, a steel door painted dark green, and pulled on the door handle. Locked, as he'd expected.

This part of the plan was only partially formed in his mind. He intended to try each door to see if one had been left unlocked. It was a church after all. If anyone would leave their doors unlocked, it would be churches. What if someone really wanted to talk to God in the middle of the night?

He snuck around to the back, a rogue once more, the hood of his sweatshirt pulled over his head. Edged up to the back door, old and wooden, with a brass doorknob. Grasped the cool metal in his hand, twisted, and gasped when it turned. His resolve began to slip so he turned it the rest of the way and shoved the door open before he could convince himself to chicken out.

It was pitch black inside but he knew this door led into the church's foyer. From here it would be a short walk down the hall to the stairs leading to the basement. His guts climbed up into his throat. He shook his hands out, pulled the hood back off his head, and stepped inside.

He grabbed the door to close it and all at once the room was illuminated, his shadow growing huge and long on the floor and wall in front of him. He spun around and squinted against the blinding light being shone directly at him.

"Alright son," said a deep voice from behind the beam, "Step out of there and let's have a chat."

5

———

JOSEPH SQUIRMED IN THE CONFINES OF THE POLICE cruiser's back seat. The cop who'd arrested him, Constable Dawson, was a black man built like a line backer. He sported a thick mustache that made him look like he was perpetually frowning.

Joseph had been shaking when he'd stepped out of the rear door of the church to see the silhouette of the huge man commanding him to come out of there. His imagination had placed a gun in the officer's hand, pointed directly at his head. When the officer stepped into the light, Joseph had to fight from bursting into tears. Constable Dawson had been nice enough once Joseph had stepped outside with hands held over his head, as he'd seen convicts do in the movies. He'd expected the cop to throw him against the car, yank his arms behind his back, and frisk him. Instead he'd had only asked what was in Joseph's backpack and then told him to toss it in the front seat.

Now Constable Dawson kept both hands on the wheel, piloting the cruiser through the night. He glanced in the rearview mirror and locked eyes with Joseph, who was struggling to get comfortable in the confines of the back seat.

"Just be glad I decided not to handcuff you," he said, "It's much less comfortable back there with your hands stuck behind your back."

Joseph quit squirming and folded his hands in his lap. Dread closed in on him like the lid of a coffin, his father was going to flip. He feared what the man would do once he got Joseph home and away from the eyes of the police. Maybe if he confessed to a much worse crime, they would simply throw him in jail and he'd never have to worry about his father again.

"Where do you live, son?"

"Past the factories," Joseph mumbled.

"Little far from home, aren't you?"

Joseph shrugged though he had no idea whether or not Dawson saw him.

"Want to tell me what you were doing in that church?"

What could he say? He had met a super cool, heavy metal cowgirl who could travel through paintings and who had suggested Joseph might be capable of the same thing? Perhaps instead of escaping his father in prison, he could get himself sent to a nut house. Spend his days thumping his head against a padded wall.

"My mom's funeral was held there."

Constable Dawson kept his eyes on the road. "How long ago?"

"This morning."

"Your old man?"

"He's busy."

The car was silent for a long time, except for the occasional fuzz and squelch from the radio.

Dawson shifted in his seat. "I've got two kids. Son and a daughter. She's your age. He's seven. Their mother is the light of my world and if anything ever happened to her I'd be a wreck. But I'd never be able to live with myself if I lost her and then something happened to one of my kids on the same day we buried her."

"You've got a lucky family," Joseph muttered.

"Your old man misses you. You may not know it and he may not show it, but he probably needs you right now as much as you need him. Here we are."

Constable Dawson guided the cruiser into the parking lot of the police station. The place looked deserted and spooky, like everything did at this time of night. They parked close to the front doors and the big cop opened the back for Joseph and led him inside.

Dawson held up the backpack. "Gonna hang onto this while you're here. You'll get it back when you go home."

Joseph was too tired, too bummed out with how this whole thing had gone to care. He hadn't even made it through the first step of his plan to get away before blowing it. How did he expect to make it all the way to California on his own if he couldn't even sneak into an *unlocked* church? He'd overestimated his ability to take care of himself.

The fluorescent lights of the station hummed overhead as he was led across the linoleum floor to a row of plastic chairs. Another officer lounged behind the counter reading a paperback.

"Constable Isaacson," Dawson said to the other cop, "This here's Joseph Ward. Found him looking to get some extra prayer time in at St. Anthony's."

Constable Isaacson nodded in their general direction without taking his eyes from his book.

Dawson guided Joseph to one of the chairs, told him to sit tight, then disappeared around the reception desk and into a back room.

While Dawson did whatever he was doing in the back, the desk officer glanced over the top of his book every minute or so, apparently to make sure Joseph didn't slip out the front door.

Joseph's stomach rumbled and he desperately wished for one of the candy bars in his backpack. He sat for an eternity on the hard plastic seat, listening to the buzz of the overhead lights before Constable Dawson reappeared from the back room. The cop lowered himself into the seat next to him, the chair creaking and groaning as he settled into it.

"I've spoken to your father," he said. "He's on his way to pick you up."

Joseph's heartbeat quickened. He felt nauseous at the idea of his father walking through those doors and dragging him all the way back home. How would he even get here? He'd probably have to take a cab. He'd be livid about having to spend money on something other than booze or cigarettes.

"Come on," Dawson put a hand on Joseph's shoulder. "You can watch TV in the back until he gets here."

He led Joseph around the counter and through a door that led into what looked a lot like the staff room at Joseph's school. A formica topped card table stood in one corner, surrounded by worn out vinyl-backed chairs. A huge ashtray in the rough shape of a police shield sat overflowing in the center of the table. Joseph took a seat, pushed the ashtray to the other side of the table, and turned his attention to a TV that hung in the corner playing *The Great Escape*, which Joseph had seen a couple of times already. Before he knew it, his eyes grew heavy and he was drifting off in the seat.

A commotion woke him some time later. It sounded like a heated exchange coming from the reception area, where he'd first come in. A man was shouting at the top of his lungs in a way that reminded him of his parents' arguments. For the first time since her death, Joseph thought that perhaps his mother had received a bit of mercy. Or taken the easy way out. Though no one said it to him directly, Joseph had overheard two of the attendees at the funeral, men he didn't recognize, musing about how her death could have been a suicide. They spoke about her *habit* and Joseph knew that had something to do with her medication and the addiction that Edgar had alluded to. He would never accept that his mother would deliberately abandon him but the thought that her death could have been deliberate haunted him. *Would* she leave him like that? Alone with his father? He'd give anything to hear them fight again.

A crash came from outside the lounge, making him jump. Sounded like they had a real upset criminal out there. He had never watched someone being arrested or tussling with the police in real life and was compelled to peek in on the action. Might as well get something positive out of this experience since he clearly wasn't on the road to his uncle or doing something ridiculous like trying to relive what must have been a hallucination brought on by grief over his mother.

He crept to the lounge door and inched it open. From here

he could see behind the reception desk; stacks of forms and office supplies occupied the shelves. Boring.

The ruckus came from beyond the desk, just out of his line of sight. He slid out of the lounge and crept around the counter, careful not to be spotted; he didn't want one of the officers sending him back to the lounge out of concern for his safety or anything. Grown ups never wanted young people to watch the exciting things they did.

The shouting turned into grunts of exertion. What if the criminal had gotten the best of the officers? He made himself move as slow as he could so as not to attract attention. As he rounded the corner of the desk, he spotted the feet of someone on the ground. Looked like the cops had managed to get the guy down. With a little less caution he stood upright, stepped out of cover, and groaned.

"Dad?"

His father twisted his head around and sneered through bloody teeth at Joseph, as though a big joke had been played on him, then spit a glob of blood onto the floor.

"They sah you brobe ina a chursh?" It was impossible to tell if his father's speech was slurred more from being drunk or the damage that had been done to his mouth during his fight with the police.

Constable Dawson had his knee squarely in the center of his back. Isaacson was sitting back against the wall holding his nose, blood seeping from under his hand. Dawson regarded Joseph with sympathy in his eyes as he snapped a set of handcuffs on his father's wrists.

Joseph was suddenly livid, full to bursting with anger. Not just at his father but at all these people who looked at him with such pity in their eyes, like he was a starving dog on the street.

"Go on back into the lounge," Constable Dawson said to him, "I'll be in there to chat with you about all this in just a minute."

Joseph ran into the back room and slammed the door behind him. He stormed to the formica table with its goofy ashtray and kicked one of the chairs. It wobbled on two of its feet but didn't go down, which only added to his wrath. He grabbed the chair by the back and threw it to the ground, where it clattered impotently against the linoleum. Not good enough. He'd wanted it to crash. To break! He picked up the stupid looking ashtray and hoisted it over his head. Ashes rained down around him and for a moment it was like being in a gothic snow globe, one with snowflakes as black as death. Then two powerful hands grabbed his wrists and slid up them to take the ashtray from his hands.

"Sit down, son," Dawson said from behind him.

Joseph dropped into a ragged cloth couch set against the far wall with as much attitude as he could muster. Already his anger was evaporating, replaced by embarrassment. He'd thrown a tantrum like a little child.

Dawson picked up the chair Joseph had thrown and dragged it in front of the couch. He eased his bulk into it and leaned forward, fingers tee-peed under his chin.

"Your father is being arrested for drunk and disorderly behavior, for assaulting a police officer, and for destruction of private property."

Joseph stared hard at his hands. No way was he going to look this man in the eye and give him the satisfaction of seeing him cry. Because that's exactly what would happen if he looked at Dawson, who had been kind to him when he deserved to be locked up just like his father.

The cop cleared his throat. "This puts us in an awkward spot as far as you're concerned."

"I should be locked up too," Joseph muttered.

"Maybe," Constable Dawson said. "I got a feeling you're a good kid though. I think you might've had a rough go of things up until now."

"You say that like things are getting easier."

"Very little in life is easy, Joseph." He cleared his throat again. "Your father is not likely to be getting out any time soon. Do you have any family in the area we can call?"

Joseph shook his head. "I have an uncle. Edgar Fisher. He lives in L.A. He was here for the funeral but he had to fly back home right after."

"Here's what we're gonna do then," Dawson said. "I'm going to make up a cell for you to sleep in since it's," he glanced at his watch, "Lord almighty, three in the morning. Which means it's midnight on the west coast. So you're going to get some sleep and I'll call your uncle once it hits around seven a.m. his time."

Joseph's heart lifted. He was going to live with Edgar after all! It wasn't exactly fair to his uncle, but what was he going to do, turn Joseph away now that he had absolutely nowhere to go? Surely he wouldn't let Joseph become an orphan. He could teach Joseph the ins and outs of real estate and, when he was old enough and Edgar was ready to retire, Joseph could take over the business. Things might actually turn out even better than before.

"How's that sound?" Constable Dawson asked.

Joseph sniffed. "Do I have to sleep near my dad?"

The big cop smiled. "We've got him a little deeper in the

station where he won't disturb anyone. I can put you in a holding cell close to the front."

"Thanks."

Dawson stepped out of the lounge and Joseph must have dozed off almost immediately because, a few minutes later, the cop was shaking him awake. He led Joseph to a cell next to the reception area. A steel cot had been outfitted with a thin mattress, simple sheets, and a small pillow.

"I'll keep it unlocked so you don't feel like a criminal," Dawson said as he held the cell door open.

Joseph fell onto the mattress. "I am a criminal."

"I got a feeling there won't be any charges laid. Could be a fresh start for you." Dawson pulled the cell door closed then inched it open a crack. "Sleep tight."

Joseph was already drifting off again even before the cop was out of sight. He lay back on the cot and let his eyes slip shut. Stiff and uncomfortable as the bed was, he was asleep seconds after his head hit the pillow.

⁂

He woke to raised voices coming from down the hall. It sounded like an argument. He turned over and pulled his pillow over his head. His parents were fighting again. About what, it didn't matter. Probably something to do with the cost of his mother's medicine. That was often what the arguments boiled down to.

He shifted on the thin mattress and remembered where he was. The funeral the day before. Being arrested. His father. So who was arguing? He pulled the pillow from his head and made himself open his eyes.

A familiar pool of dried, brown vomit in the far corner of the cell caught his eye. Had that been there last night? He sat up to get a better look and was relieved to see it was what looked like an old rust stain. For a moment, it had been the exact shape and color of the mess he'd seen on his poor mother. That vomit would haunt him for the rest of his life.

He stood from the metal frame and stretched. A dull ache pulsed at the back of his head, probably from too little rest combined with sleeping on a steel shelf. The pillow he'd used was thin and had barely provided cushion between his head and the frame.

He pushed at the cell door, half convinced it would be locked. It wasn't. The door swung open easily on its hinges. He crept up the hall and looked in on the reception area. Constable Dawson stood behind the desk arguing with an officer who hadn't been here last night. This man was old and white and wore a much more heavily decorated uniform than Dawson. He seemed to be in charge.

"I don't care who he is," the older officer said, "He's not our problem."

"We just need to give the uncle a couple of days to get things sorted and get back here," Dawson pleaded.

"We're not a hotel, constable. St. Theodore's Academy will take him. I've already spoken with Headmaster Lachlan."

"Come on, Chief. We can't send him there. Aren't those creepy priests under investigation?"

"Friars, technically. And they were," the man, who was apparently the Chief said. "Obviously, since they remain in operation, there was nothing to investigate."

"There's a reason they're shutting those places down."

The Chief slammed his hand on the desk. "Process the father. Get the kid ready to go."

"You're sending him now?"

"We have a bus leaving for the penitentiary this afternoon. I'll have them detour to the school on the way."

"You're going to stick him on a bus with those—"

The Chief raised a hand to silence Dawson. "He committed a crime. That school is exactly where he belongs. He broke into a church, man."

"His mother's funeral just happened. He's grieving."

"That's no excuse. You know how many people we'd have to turn loose if loss of a loved one was justification for breaking the law? He leaves this afternoon. Get him something to eat and get him ready."

Joseph darted back to his cell before anybody could look his way and catch him spying. They were talking about him. The Chief had said he wanted to send Joseph to a school, which, the way they were speaking about it, sounded more like a prison. Of course the Chief was right. He *was* a criminal. He'd broken the law. Dread filled his insides like a bowling ball leaking battery acid.

Constable Dawson appeared at the cell door about half an hour later. The smell that accompanied him was familiar and wonderful and made Joseph's tummy utter a loud, painful growl. He didn't have to see the gold arches on the front of the paper bag Dawson carried to know what that smell was.

"I don't know what you like," he said as he laid the contents of the bag out on Joseph's cot. "So I got a bit of every-thing. Eat as much as you like. More if you can manage it."

There was more food than Joseph had ever had at his disposal. Three Egg McMuffins, one with sausage, four hash browns, and a stack of hotcakes steamed on his bed accompanied by a plastic cup of orange juice sealed with a foil lid. Dawson crumpled the bag and tossed it under the cot.

"We'll clean that up after," he said with a wink.

Joseph was too hungry to manage much in the way of manners.

"Thanks," he said as he tore into one of the McMuffins. "I heard you talking to the Chief."

Dawson sighed heavily and sat on the cot. It made so much noise under his weight, Joseph feared the whole thing would collapse.

"I'm sorry, kiddo."

Joseph swallowed a mouthful of egg and english muffin. "And my uncle will pick me up there when he gets into town, right?"

"That's the idea."

"Can't I just go home?"

Dawson sighed again. "Can't do that. There's no one to take care of you there. And I know you're a bright kid and you can probably take care of yourself but that's not how the law works. And technically you did commit a crime."

"What are they under investigation for?" Joseph asked. "The school, I mean."

The cop stood and stretched. "Don't you worry about that. The investigation didn't turn anything up and you'll be out of there in no time. Just keep your nose clean and your head down, you hear me?"

Joseph nodded. "Yessir."

"Someone'll be around to gather you in an hour or so," Dawson said as he stepped out of the cell.

6

———

JOSEPH TOOK HIS TIME EATING THE REST OF THE FOOD Constable Dawson had brought him. When he'd finished, he peeled the foil off his orange juice, drained the cup in two big gulps, and belched loudly. He fished the crumpled paper bag from under the cot and stuffed it with the garbage from his meal; he had been able to finish all but one of the hotcakes, which he left in the styrofoam container, thinking that maybe whoever cleaned up would want it. He paced his cell, counting the steps it took to walk around it. He counted forty one. Confused about where the odd step came from, he went back around, making sure to take ten steps for each wall so that he came out at an even forty, which comforted him for some reason. After another couple of walks around his cell he realized he had to go number two. Bad.

From the corner of his cell, the stainless steel toilet appeared to laugh at him through its wide open toilet bowl mouth. He was suddenly very self-conscious, which made him have to go all the more. He'd used a staff bathroom last night, maybe they'd let him use it again. He shoved the cell door to open it and smashed his hand against the unmoving steel. He wrapped his hands around the bars and yanked on the door. That bastard had locked him in! Was this because he'd snuck out and eavesdropped on his conversation with the Chief or because they finally decided to start treating him like the criminal he was? He felt like a caged animal. Trapped. Last night he hadn't even considered himself a prisoner. Amazing what a locked door could do.

"Hello!"

His voice echoed down the hall but that was the only sound that returned to him. He danced a jig, squeezing his butt cheeks together.

"Please, I have to go to the bathroom!" he called.

Nothing. It was either do it in the can or in his pants. He shot another glance at the toilet. Not even a proper seat for him to sit on. The appliance looked more like a medieval torture device than something for him to crap in. But between doing it in his pants and risking someone walking in on him pooping, he had to go for the toilet. He shot another glance up and down the hallway, thankful there was no one in any of the other cells (and *very* thankful his father wasn't being kept in this section), and dropped his pants over the toilet. He got his business over with as quickly as possible, wiped with what felt like fine-grain sandpaper, and flushed the evidence.

A door at the end of the hall opened as he was doing up his pants. Moments later, a young officer, who barely looked old enough to be out of high school, appeared in front of the cell. His head was buzzed short underneath his uniform hat and spots of acne dotted his thin face. His name badge said *Bolson*.

If he smelled the ghost of Joseph's bowel movement, he didn't let on.

"Ward?" Bolson asked, even though Joseph was confident there weren't any other twelve-year-old boys hanging out back here.

Joseph nodded, too nervous to say anything.

Bolson unlocked the cell and opened the door. Joseph had barely stepped out when the officer stepped in front of him and shoved an arm into his chest, knocking him back into the cell. He fell into the cot, barking the backs of his legs on it.

"What the hell do you think you're doing, boy?" Bolson's face had gone red enough that his acne disappeared.

"I'm sorry," Joseph managed to stammer. "I thought maybe you were letting me out."

Bolson smirked. "I'm escorting you to your prison transport, punk. Who do you think you are?"

"I'm not going to prison, I'm going to St. Theodore's."

"What did you think that place is?"

Joseph suddenly felt sick. The hotcakes turned over in his stomach.

"I'm only going for a couple of days," he said. "Until my uncle comes for me."

The officer unclipped a pair of handcuffs from his belt. "Turn around and put your hands behind your back."

He was going to cuff him! Even Constable Dawson, who had been the one to bring Joseph in, hadn't put handcuffs on him. He tried to protest, to tell this new officer that he had the completely wrong idea about what he was here for. He'd barely committed a crime! The doors to the church had been open and Constable Dawson had been so nice to him. Was all that an act?

He had barely turned around when the pimply cop yanked one of his arms behind his back so hard that Joseph was certain he had broken it. He screamed in agony and tried to pull his arm back, which only made Bolson pull it harder. He grabbed Joseph's other wrist and yanked it back just as painfully. Shoved Joseph against the back wall of the cell. Kicked his feet apart. Removed his watch.

"Why are you—?"

"Speak again and I'll give you a fat lip, kid." Bolson patted down his legs and arms as though he really expected to find a weapon concealed somewhere.

Joseph's eyes burned. He squeezed them shut to keep his tears at bay. He did not want this guy to see him cry. Had a feeling it would only provoke more roughness.

Bolson led him out of the cell and down the hall. They passed the reception desk, where a female officer now sat doing some kind of paperwork. She didn't even look up as Joseph was escorted past. He wanted to ask her for help but judging from the way she kept her head down he had a feeling his plea would be in vain. He wanted to shout for Constable Dawson to come and intervene. He was even tempted to call for his father, for what little good that would do.

He was led down a long hallway with cinderblock walls painted powder blue, which Bolson's heavy footsteps echoed off of. Did he deliberately stomp his feet like that? Joseph's father would stomp in a similar way when he was angry about something, to make sure Joseph and his mother knew what sort of mood he was in. So they would fear him. Bolson shoved open a steel door at the end of the hallway and Joseph was momentarily dazed by the bright daylight that streamed in. Had it only been a day since he'd last seen sunlight? His eyes felt like they'd been dealing with the gloom of the police station for months. The whole experience was so surreal that even now he questioned whether he may be having an intensely vivid dream.

A slate-grey bus idled in the middle of the parking lot, PRISON TRANSFER stenciled in black paint on the side. Within the bus, silhouettes of men's heads swiveled to watch Joseph being led toward it. More than a few of them hammered on the windows. Joseph kept his eyes straight ahead; he'd been bullied enough in his life to know that any reaction he showed would only make things worse for him.

The bus door squealed open and he stood frozen in front of it, fear bubbling up in his guts like poison.

Bolson huffed behind him. "Get on the bus, kid. Or I could let one of those guys escort you."

The bus driver stared ahead, expression blank, as though he couldn't care less whether the bus left in three minutes or three hours. Sitting just behind him was a police officer who looked about the same age as Officer Bolson, only with a much cleaner complexion. The look on this new officer's face conveyed a lot less patience than the driver's. This guy's name badge said *Riley*. When Joseph didn't immediately climb aboard, Riley came forward, grabbed him by the arm, and yanked him up inside. Joseph's shoulder popped with the force and his ankles smashed against the ridged, steel steps leading into the bus. He cried out and the bus filled with roars of laughter and mock imitations of his yelp.

Riley put his mouth against Joseph's ear, so that his mustache prickled against his earlobe. "Don't look at these guys. Don't talk to these guys. Go straight to the back and take the seat on the left. They're all chained up, they can't hurt you. Any of 'em try and I'll beat the piss out of them. It's a five hour drive to St. Theodore's. Just keep your head down. Try to sleep if you can." He shoved Joseph along the aisle.

Joseph stumbled and, only when he caught himself on one of the seats, realized this new officer had removed his handcuffs. One small favor in the middle of a nightmare.

Dozens of pairs of eyes stared at him from faces that ranged from indifferent to downright hungry. Jeers barraged him from all directions, swirling around his head as he trudged to the back.

"It must be Christmas."

"Saved you a seat, pal."

"Careful, I seen that dude off a dude."

"Kid, let's play G.I. Joes."

"Hey, kid. You gonna be my new roommate?"

"Naw, he's a mail-order bride."

"Riley, you bring your little sister to work today?"

Joseph inched forward, eyes on the filthy floor. Tried not to listen to anything being said or shouted, which became easier as the jeers turned into shouts at one another and eventually into what sounded like total chaos.

"Shut the fuck up!" Riley's shout filled the bus and put an immediate stop to the racket.

Joseph took the back seat, grateful there was no one in the seat across the aisle. The man sitting in front of him, a tall skinny guy with a shaved head, craned his neck to stare at him. Joseph avoided his eyes and prayed silently that the man wouldn't say anything to him. His wasn't a religious family by any stretch of the imagination but he needed every bit of help he could get. The bus rumbled out of the parking lot and the guy with the shaved head lost interest in him for the time being.

The ride out of the city was louder than any school bus Joseph had ever been on—though he never rode the bus to school, he'd been on his share of field trips and those trips were never quiet. It seemed like every man on this bus had something to say about every corner they passed. *I kicked so-and-so's ass right there* and *That's where I got busted* and *I fucked your momma in that alley*. It was strange how a bus of grown men could be rowdier and more foul-mouthed than a bus of kids. Men, he'd learned, either grew up to be bigger children or animals that preyed on those weaker than themselves. Few exceptions seemed to exist; Uncle Edgar, Grandpa, perhaps even Constable Dawson.

Joseph closed his eyes and tried to shut out the noise.

He must have drifted off because when he opened his eyes again they were out of the city and coasting along a hilly road surrounded by dense forest. The sky was a deep orange and the sun had sunk below the tree line. He'd slept for most of the ride. It was a bittersweet feeling. He'd be off this bus and away from its passengers soon, but would be stepping into the confines of what Constable Dawson had referred to as a reformatory, and what Bolson had referred to as a prison. He'd only heard of such places in movies and books.

He scanned the scenery outside his window; all trees and brush. He had no idea where they were. He'd been out of Philadelphia only a handful of times in his life, and even then, no more than an hour outside the city limits. He shifted his gaze and saw that the man in the seat ahead and across from him was staring his way. The guy was heavy set with short hair ending in a long, greasy rat-tail that he had draped over one shoulder. He twirled it around his fingers absently as he stared at Joseph, who tried to pretend he didn't notice.

"They're taking you to St. Teddy's."

Joseph didn't respond. He looked out the window and tried to focus on the trees going by. It was impossible to ignore the reflection of the big guy still staring at him, twirling that disgusting length of hair through his fingers and around his hands.

"Kid."

Joseph looked over.

Rat-tail grinned, pleased with himself for successfully getting his attention.

"That true?"

"What?" Joseph asked, more annoyed by than frightened of this man.

"You're headed for St. Ted's."

Joseph nodded.

Rat-tail leaned his face against the back of his seat. "That's too bad, pal. For you. That's not a nice place."

"How do you know?" Joseph asked.

"Been there myself." He gave a proud smile. "Age fifteen to eighteen. Then they let me go. Then I robbed a gas station and broke the owner's face and I got sent to real prison."

"Oh."

"Them guys did a good job getting me ready for jail life." He was wrapping his rat-tail around his fingers so tightly that they were going red at the tips.

"What do you mean?" Joseph asked, trying not to look as the fingers turned a shade of purple.

The guy watched his fingers. For a moment it looked like he'd just let them go dead and fall off—Joseph's mother had told him that could happen when he'd wrapped a rubber band around his finger until it went numb. Rat-tail blinked and unwound the hair from around his hand. He shot a look up at Riley then leaned closer to Joseph, as close as his cuffs would allow him.

"They're all scumbags," Rat-tail said. "Those bastards. The stuff they done to me and some of my friends. I heard they were shutting all these places down but the pieces of shit running Teddy's got deep pockets, I guess. I don't know how else they keep the feds outta there."

"What did they do?"

Rat-tail seemed not to hear Joseph, had apparently forgotten about him altogether. He just stared at his hand, wrapping and unwrapping it with his hair.

The trees stayed just as thick as the bus trundled down a smaller gravel road that looked like it might be a private drive. The sky was darkening and Joseph's stomach rumbled to remind him he hadn't had anything to eat since breakfast. He was suddenly very grateful for Constable Dawson feeding him so much that morning.

Across from him, Rat-tail swayed back and forth and stared straight ahead, muttering something to himself.

The bus rounded a bend and a huge iron gate with stone pillars on either side loomed ahead of them, blocking off the entire road. Chainlink fence extended from the outsides of the pillars and ran endlessly into the depths of the forest, presumably around the entire property. The bus came to a stop in front of the gate and the driver hopped out and strolled up to a steel box affixed to one of the pillars. He pulled a handset from it, said something, then replaced the phone and got back behind the wheel. A moment later the gate rumbled open and the bus pulled through.

As soon as they were through the gate, Rat-tail started smashing his forehead on the seat in front of him.

"Bitch, stop smacking my seat!" the guy in front of him, shouted.

Rat-tail raised his voice. "Not here. Not back again. Not here. Not back again. I ain't going back. I ain't going back." He pulled hard on his hair.

"Shut the fuck up!" someone shouted from the front of the bus.

"I'm trying to sleep, asshole," another guy said.

"I ain't going back! Not here! Not again! Not back!" Rat-tail shouted as a chant. He continued to smack his head on the seat in front of him, in time to his chanting.

Riley stormed back from the front of the bus, finally annoyed enough to do something about the noise.

"Hey tubby, shut your fuckin trap and sit still. I won't tell you twice." He looked at Joseph. "This is your stop."

It was as though the words were a trigger for Rat-tail. He screamed at the top of his lungs and yanked on his hair with both hands. There was a soft rip and suddenly the rat-tail was no longer attached to Rat-tail's head. Blood swelled out of the back of his scalp. He wailed and swung the cord of hair around in the air.

"Not here! Not back here!" He threw the hair like a bola, directly at Riley.

There was a bit of flesh still attached to the rat-tail and it was this that hit Riley in the forehead, above his right eyebrow, with a wet smack.

Everything went still for a moment. Even the bus itself

seemed to freeze in time. All eyes were on the cop. Rat-tail had gone silent. He looked around as though confused about what had just happened. The bloody clump slid down Riley's face and hit the floor with a dull splat. It would have been hilarious if not for how obviously furious he looked.

Riley's eyes narrowed. "You mother—"

Rat-tail freaked out. He leapt up and fell into Riley just as the bus came to a halt. The momentum brought both men to the ground. The big guy writhed on top of Riley, still screaming at the top of his lungs. The cop jabbed his elbow into the Rat-tail's jaw five or six times before he managed to scurry out from underneath. He shot to his feet and brought one of his boots down directly on the screaming man's face. Something, probably his nose, crunched and his head bounced off the floor. Rat-tail was out cold.

Joseph stared in horror at the mess of the man's face, the mound of bloody hair laying next to him. Riley caught his breath and looked down at Rat-tail with disgusted rage. Joseph had seen that look before, in his father's face, usually when he was speaking to his mother. The cop raised his boot again.

"Man, he's out," someone shouted.

"Shut the fuck up or you'll be the next one on the floor," Riley snarled.

The bus driver's soft voice called back to them. "We're here."

Riley lowered his foot. The wrath evaporated from his face though the disgust remained. He looked to Joseph and made no attempt to soften his expression.

"Let's go." He stormed back up to the front of the bus.

Joseph got out of his seat on shaking legs. Tiptoed over the unconscious man on the floor, the guy who had been here before. The guy who had warned him. The man was clearly crazy though. He'd yanked out his own hair. Sane people didn't do that. What if his time in this place had done that to him? He'd been pretty freaked out about even being close to St. Theodore's.

Jeers mixed with words of encouragement mixed with phrases he didn't want to know the meaning of followed Joseph as he made his way to the front of the bus. He stopped in front of Riley, hoping against all odds that the man would tell him there'd been a big mistake and that they would bring him right back home.

The cop jerked his head at the door.

"I don't have a change of clothes," Joseph said, fighting to keep a tremor out of his voice.

Riley reached down and for a moment Joseph was sure the man would hug him and tell him it would all be okay. Then he grabbed Joseph by the shoulders and spun him around roughly.

"They'll give you everything you need at St. Teddy's." He pushed him forward.

Joseph stumbled and caught himself on the railing. He looked back at the other passengers as though one of them might offer to take his place, then went through the door. He thought about running as he stepped off the bus but quickly banished the idea. No doubt they were ready for him to do just that and he was certain Riley would quite easily be able to overcome him, even if he did make it to the tree line. And then there was that gate and the fence that extended out from it. Escape was not an option. Not yet.

7

———————

Joseph stared up at St. Theodore's in awe. It was like something straight out of a horror classic, like Hill House from that black and white movie with Vincent Price, especially in the dying light of the day. He stood on a cobblestone pathway that wound around a marble water fountain bearing the carved likeness of a man knelt down in prayer at its center. The school itself was enormous, made of huge blocks of stone and ancient beams of timber, the windows all covered by thick iron bars. Identical wings with gabled turrets on their ends walled in the massive central structure. Above the ominous looking front doors loomed a great stained glass window, lit from behind. The window depicted who Joseph assumed must be St. Theodore, hands together in prayer, a rosary dangling between them.

The bus door squealed shut and before he could react, the vehicle was heading back up the driveway. He watched it rumble around the laneway, toward the gate. The truth hit home; they were actually leaving him here. He jogged after the bus and made it as far as the tree line of the surrounding woods before it disappeared around a bend.

A low growling came from within the darkness of the trees and at first he took it to be an echo from the engine of the bus. This sound was a lot louder than the bus though. Much closer. He held his breath and listened. The sound intensified. Joseph took a step toward the house. Another bestial growl from somewhere to his left joined that of the one in front of him. He was going to be eaten by monsters before even seeing what the inside of this place looked like!

A branch snapped from somewhere in the trees. He imagined a hulking beast with fangs the size of carving knives watching him from within the brush. It was just dark enough that anything could be standing a few feet in front of him, concealed by tree and shadow.

He ran.

He darted around the fountain, full of water that looked almost black in the darkness. Images of glistening swamp monsters with webbed hands and gills on their necks invaded his imagination. He raced up the huge stone steps leading to the enormous double doors of the school. Claws scratched against the cobblestone path behind him. He slammed into the doors. Pounded on them.

"Help me!"

As though triggered by his cries, the doors swung open. Joseph stumbled into a tall, robed figure, bounced off, and fell hard on his back end. He shut his eyes and waited for the monsters to eat him alive.

A shrill whistle pierced his ears. He opened his eyes and looked up. The figure he'd run into was a silhouette against the ceiling lights. Behind Joseph, the growling and scratching of claws gave way to a heavy panting.

"Sit," the robed figure said in a crisp, lilting voice.

Joseph looked around for a chair before realizing the man spoke to his pursuers. He looked over his shoulder and saw an enormous German shepherd sitting inches behind him, tongue lolling. Just behind it sat another, slightly smaller than the one closest to him. Both looked like perfectly happy dogs, not the snarling beasts that had chased him across the grounds.

"Julius and Hilda are quite docile unless provoked," the man, in what Joseph now saw was a black friar's cassock, said. "They are trained to keep trespassers at bay. And to keep anyone from wandering off the grounds."

"My name's—."

"Joseph Ward." The man smiled at him through a thick, dark beard. "Of course, we have been expecting you. I trust you'll be on your best behavior during your stay with us."

Joseph nodded.

"'Yes, Brother' is the appropriate response."

"Y-yes Brother," Joseph stammered. "Have you spoken to my Uncle Edgar? He's picking me up in a couple of days."

"Everything has been arranged for."

The robed man snapped his fingers in the air.

A figure stirred at the top of a great stairway rising up from the center of the room.

"My name is Brother Lachlan Kelly," the man said as the figure came down the stairs, toward them. "I am headmaster of St. Theodore's these days. I'm sure we'll get to know each other better over the duration of your stay."

The figure from the top of the stairs approached them. He was a wiry, red-haired boy of fourteen or fifteen, wearing a white, short-sleeve, collared shirt with a blue tie and brown trousers. He sneered in a way that made it look like he was sucking air through his tiny, crooked, and severely stained teeth.

"Mr. Avery will take you to your room," Brother Lachlan said, adjusting round bifocals that, in the light of the great chandelier hanging above them, made his eyes look like white orbs.

"This way." The older boy, Mr. Avery, gestured at a nearby hallway and started off in that direction without waiting for him.

Joseph ran to keep up, giving an awkward half-wave to the headmaster as he left. This place didn't seem all *that* bad. The dogs had been scary, sure, but they were obviously very well trained animals.

"My name's Joseph," he called ahead to his guide, still struggling to keep up.

"Daniel," the other boy said without turning around. "I'll give you the nickel tour and then you're on your own. How long's your sentence?"

Joseph jogged to fall in step with Daniel. "I'm just here for a couple of days until my uncle comes to get me. There was a mix up."

"Lucky you."

"My mom died and my dad got arrested," Joseph said. He realized that might come across as a little depressing and added, "The headmaster, Brother Lachlan, he seems nice."

Daniel chuckled. "He's nice alright. Everybody here is very nice."

That made Joseph feel a little better about his stay. He couldn't help but think that the other boy was mocking him for something, but older kids were always mocking younger ones; that's just the way life went.

They reached the end of the hallway and Daniel shoved open a door leading to a twisting staircase that took up one of the turrets bookending the school. They mounted the stairs, which spiraled upwards into shadow. In spite of the circumstances, it was sort of cool. Like being in a castle.

"Why'd they send you here just to wait for your uncle?" Daniel asked as he led Joseph out of the turret and down a narrow hallway lined with doors bearing brass numerals.

"I broke into a church."

Daniel stopped in front of a door marked 432 and held it open for Joseph.

"So you do belong here."

The door opened into a small bedroom that was about the size of his room at home. It was outfitted with a simple cot, a writing desk, a narrow dresser, and a small, barred window. The only decor was a wooden cross on the wall over his bed. Daniel flicked the lights on and Joseph saw that a bundle of clothes and books were stacked neatly on the mattress. A pair of simple, brown loafers sat on the floor, which, like the floors in the rest of the manor, was made up of ancient hardwood. The air was heavy and damp, only slightly cooler than it was outdoors. He took a step into the room

"Keep your clothes neat and your shoes polished," Daniel said in a rehearsed tone. "Make your bed every morning. You missed supper by about an hour. Breakfast is at seven-thirty sharp. Don't be late or you don't get to eat. Uniforms have to be worn at all times. Your class schedule is in the first page of your workbook. Bathrooms are at the end of the hall."

"Probably won't need most of this. I'm leaving again as

soon as my uncle gets here. He's taking me to live in Hollywood with him."

"Right." Daniel turned to leave.

"What room are you in?" Joseph asked.

"Seniors are on the third floor."

Before Joseph could ask another question, Daniel stepped out into the hallway and pulled the door shut, leaving him to adjust to his temporary quarters.

Compared to the prison cell he'd spent the previous night in, this place was the Ritz. He was surprised to find his exhaustion outweighed his hunger, though he wished he'd thought to bring that last hotcake with him.

He was sure he'd have a hard time falling asleep, if he'd be able to at all. The last two days, without a full night's rest, had worn on him though; he was snoring softly just minutes after his head hit the pillow.

8

———

He woke the next morning disoriented but feeling more rested than he had in days. He rolled out of bed and glanced at the clock hanging on the wall.

Just after seven.

Daniel, his tour guide, had said breakfast is at seven-thirty, not a minute later.

Joseph was halfway to the door when he remembered the uniform folded neatly on the bed. He changed quickly. Or tried to. He'd never tied a tie before and he fumbled with this one, which he assumed was a non-negotiable part of the uniform. He struggled with it for several minutes before deciding it was better to be on time than well dressed and settled for looping the tie in a loose knot around his neck.

He cracked the door open and surveyed the hall. Empty. Where was everyone? He shuffled to the bathroom, counting the doors along the way; there were eight on each side of his stretch of hallway. There was no way they were all occupied if it was this quiet first thing in the morning, and so soon before breakfast.

When he finally found his way to the main hall, he heard voices coming from behind a set of double doors toward the rear of the manor. The doors were partway open and the bewitching smell of bacon wafted out to him. His stomach growled, loud and painful.

The main hall itself, he found, was much less ominous in the light of day. Whereas last night he'd felt like he was stepping into a haunted house, today he could very clearly tell that this was an educational facility, even if it was one with bars on the windows. A big German shepherd, presumably one of his pursuers from the night before, sat at attention near the front entrance. Its tongue lolled out of its mouth making it look like just another happy dog.

An enormous clock donned the wall above the front doors. The big hand barely touched the belly of the six at the bottom of the clock. The numeral looked to be as tall as Joseph himself from where he stood.

His stomach rumbled once more and this time he obeyed it, hurrying toward the double doors of the dining hall. The aroma became overwhelming as he got closer and drool pooled in the corners of his mouth. The noise from behind the doors grew along with the smell. It sounded like a regular school cafeteria in there. Whatever he'd been so nervous about before, whatever had made Rat-tail freak out on the bus, was obviously nothing more than dumb rumors. Maybe he'd even make a friend or two here. He shoved the doors open and the chatter came to an abrupt halt.

Hundreds of eyes stared at Joseph as he stood in the doorway. A clank came from his right. An older woman, clad in kitchen whites, stacked dirty plates from the end of one of two dozen long dining tables.

"You're late," a guy, called from somewhere in the hall.

The entire cafeteria erupted in laughter. It died out quickly and returned to regular chatter as several friars and nuns went around to the tables with fingers raised to their lips. Soiled, empty plates littered every table. Only a few people at each table were eating and even they were on their last bites. Was his clock slow? Impossible. The clock in the main foyer had the same time.

The room was split in half by gender. On the left, a dozen long tables full of girls, maybe eight to a table. On the right was the same amount of tables but closer to a dozen boys crowded around each one.

Daniel Avery sat at the end of a nearby table. He picked bacon off the plate of the boy next to him and crammed it into his mouth. His tiny teeth gnashed at it, spraying bits of meat onto his chin. Joseph scurried over and bent next to him.

"You said breakfast is at seven thirty," he whispered, fighting to keep his voice from shaking.

Daniel wiped his chin with his sleeve. "You musta heard me wrong."

A few other kids at his table laughed. Joseph stormed away, face burning. He stood at the back of the dining hall and looked around for a place to sit or for an adult to provide him with food—the kitchen staff member who'd been collecting plates was nowhere to be seen. His face grew hotter by the second. Most of the kids in the room seemed to have forgotten about him but he still felt ashamed standing there, imagining they were all talking about him and would continue to laugh about the new kid who got no breakfast.

It was more than he could take. His whole experience at St. Theodore's so far had been miserable and it would only continue on that way. Forget breakfast. He'd go to his room and suffer until lunch. He bolted for the double doors. And ran directly into Brother Lachlan.

"Mr. Ward," the headmaster said, "I won't tolerate you running into me a third time."

Joseph stammered and searched his mind for an explanation. He didn't want to cause any trouble during his stay. He wished Edgar would hurry up and get here already so that they could be on their way to L.A. Thinking of living with his uncle boosted his spirits a little. He could get through this, no problem. He'd been mocked and laughed at before, by people he had to see every day. What did it matter if he had to endure a bit of teasing and be the victim of some harmless pranks while he was here?

"You're late for breakfast," Lachlan said.

Joseph heard no anger in the man's voice, which comforted him. He glanced over his shoulder at the red-haired kid, who was turned around in his seat, watching them.

"Yes, sir, I mean, Brother."

Brother Lachlan held his hands up and looked around as though he was waiting for someone to deliver the punchline.

Joseph said, "I guess I heard the time wrong."

Brother Lachlan folded his hands in front of him. "Let's make sure that doesn't happen again, Mr. Ward."

"Yes, Brother."

Lachlan sniffed. "You'll spend morning mass cleaning up after breakfast with the staff. You understand, of course. There must be some consequence for our actions. We are, first and foremost, a correctional facility after all. Even if we do, at times, appear to be just another well-run educational institution."

Joseph stared at the floor and muttered his understanding. He started off to find a member of the staff to tell him what to do when Brother Lachlan put a gentle hand on his shoulder.

"That doesn't mean you get to miss Friday assembly," he said. "Find a seat."

Joseph turned to face the hall once more. Again, all eyes were on him. Most looked fearful, as though the headmaster had reacted in a much stronger fashion. He took deep breaths and wandered down the rows of tables, searching for an empty spot. Anytime he found a space he thought he could squeeze into, one of the boys sitting next to it would shift over so that the spot disappeared. He pleaded with his eyes as he passed by the tables but those who met his gaze did so with hostility. He was ready to cross the hall and ask to join one of the girl's tables when he spotted a boy with some of the darkest skin he'd ever seen sitting near the end of one of the tables at the back of the hall. This boy nodded at him then at the space next to him, closest to the end of the table. Joseph upped his walking speed and plopped down next to the kid before anyone else could see where he was going and try to foil him again.

"Thanks," Joseph kept his eyes on the table, afraid to meet anyone else's gaze.

A messy dish slid into his field of view. Half of an egg was mangled on the plate, its yolk spread across the surface. A full piece of toast sat soaking in the yolk. Next to it was a full strip of bacon.

Joseph looked up at the boy next to him.

The kid smiled, showing his teeth. He nodded down at the plate.

Joseph didn't need to be told twice. He gobbled the food in seconds, using fork and toast to scoop up the egg and devour it in two bites. The strip of bacon didn't last any longer. His stomach grumbled appreciatively then immediately growled for more.

He wiped his mouth with the back of his sleeve and turned to his savior.

"Thanks. I'm Joseph."

The boy held out his hand, his skin appearing even darker against the white fabric of his shirt. Joseph grasped it firmly, the way his grandfather had taught him to, and shook.

"My name is Odilon Mercier," the boy said.

Joseph recognized the strong Haitian accent right away. There was a Haitian girl in the grade below him at his real school. She'd gone around to all the grades and given a presentation on life in Haiti. Joseph had been enthralled. It fascinated him to know that there were places out there so different from the world he lived in and knew.

Even sitting down Joseph could tell that Odilon was a short boy with a delicate frame to match his height. Odilon's tightly curled hair was cropped close to his head. When he smiled, it lit up his entire face and made him appear taller, fuller.

Odilon said, "Try not to attract any more attention to yourself. The boys here are bad enough but the brothers are the worst. They are bad people with short tempers."

"Except Brother Lachlan," Joseph added. "He seems really nice."

Odilon only grunted.

"How did you wind up here?" Joseph asked. This boy

seemed nice, well-mannered at least. He had a hard time picturing him as wayward, or even mischievous.

Odilon opened his mouth to speak but before he could get a word out, an ear-splitting clanging filled the room. One of the older boys, a hefty kid sporting a crew cut on top and a yolk stain down the front of his shirt, whipped a large metal bell back and forth in the air. The mallet barely struck one side of the bell before it was jerked back in the other direction. The result was a jarring noise which more than served its purpose.

The room went silent—there was an audible smack as everyone closed their mouths at the same time. Not even a fork could be heard clanking against a plate when finally the large boy up front put the bell down. Job done, he silently made his way back to his seat.

Joseph was about to ask Odilon what was supposed to happen next when everyone in the hall rose to their feet in unison. Odilon grabbed Joseph's arm and yanked him into a standing position. Everyone's eyes were turned to the room's entrance. Joseph directed his attention that way in time to see Brother Lachlan come through the doors and strut to the front of the room. Had the headmaster left the hall after chastising him just so that he could make his entrance? The notion brought a smirk to his face and he quickly fought it back, fearing Brother Lachlan would look his way at that moment.

The headmaster stood at a podium and raised his arms while two others joined him up at the front. On Lachlan's right, on the girl's side of the dining hall, stood a nun with severe features. She stared out at the dining hall with barely-veiled contempt, her bottom lip jutting out just slightly as she surveyed the room. On Lachlan's left stood another friar, almost as tall as the headmaster and at least twice his weight.

This other man kept his hands folded over the front of his cassock, resting on his protruding belly. He stared out over the heads of the children with a dazed expression.

Lachlan brought his hands down to his side and everyone in the hall took their seats. The nun and the friar seated themselves in chairs on either side of him and gazed up at him with open reverence.

"The Lord's blessing upon you all." Lachlan's voice projected effortlessly over across the hall.

"And also on you," said everyone except Joseph.

"We have a few items to address before we make our way to morning mass." Lachlan's eyes searched the crowd. "The sign up sheet for spring cleaning is still incomplete. Might I remind you that if we do not receive enough volunteers, I will be forced to assign the tasks. Unlike the students who volunteered, any student who is assigned spring cleaning duty will not receive any sort of lenience for the completion of their school work."

This was the sort of thing Joseph would normally sign up for if he was at a regular school. Even in this place, though he was only going to be here a couple of days, he was tempted to volunteer if for no other reason than to let the staff know that he could be counted on to stay out of trouble.

Brother Lachlan went on, "I want to remind you all that the dogs are not to be fed by students under any circumstances. If you are caught doing so, punishment will be immediate and severe."

Many of the students looked around, trying to pinpoint the guilty party. Next to him, Joseph felt Odilon shift in his seat. Joseph himself did not want to take his eyes away from the front lest he be accused of not paying attention. He knew well enough how to keep himself off the radar of teachers and authority figures. He'd dodged most of his father's attention all these years after all. The ghost of guilt embraced him as he recalled how often his mother had been the brunt of his father's tantrums because Joseph himself wasn't brave enough to stand up to the man, to endure his fury. As far as he knew, his father had never hit her, but hitting someone wasn't the only, or even the most effective way of hurting them.

"Lastly," Brother Lachlan said, raising his voice only slightly to overpower the low murmur of voices that had been stirred up, "It seems as though there may be some confusion as to what time breakfast occurs."

All eyes turned to Joseph. He had an idea that even the students who weren't staring at him knew who the headmaster was talking about. He felt his neck and cheeks grow hot. Lachlan's gaze bored into him. Joseph maintained eye contact, fearing what would happen if he should look away.

Brother Lachlan shifted his attention away from him, focussing on the back of the room.

"Daniel Avery, stand."

All eyes, including Joseph's, snapped to the back of the room where the red-haired boy who had shown Joseph to his room stood, eyes cast downward.

Brother Lachlan strolled down the middle of the hall, eyes locked on Daniel.

"Mr. Avery," he said, "What time does breakfast occur?"

"Seven AM, brother." Daniel's cheeks were almost as red as his hair.

Brother Lachlan snapped his head around and locked eyes with Joseph. "Joseph Ward. Stand."

Joseph forced himself upright. His legs became Jell-O and he had to hold the table to steady himself.

"Mr. Ward, what time did Mr. Avery tell you breakfast is served?"

This had to be a nightmare. Joseph actually pinched his own thigh to be sure this was happening in real life. How could things go so sour when he'd been here less than twenty-four hours? Lachlan wanted him to fink on Daniel. Did he want them to hate each other? It was an impossible situation; Joseph could be even further on the hook for tardiness if he didn't tell the headmaster what he wanted to know. He wished with all his might that something would happen to distract the man's attention. An explosion in the kitchen would do.

"I must have heard him wrong," Joseph said, doing his best to avoid looking at Daniel.

"Humor me, Mr. Ward," Lachlan said, "What time did you think he said?"

"Seven-thirty. But—."

Lachlan silenced him with a raised hand. He turned his attention back to Daniel.

"Surely, Mr. Avery, having been here for as long as you have, you would have been utterly clear with our new ward, pardon the pun, knowing the importance of punctuality in my institution. Am I incorrect in assuming that?"

"Yes, brother," Daniel stammered, "I told him seven sharp."

"So it is safe to assume that Mr. Ward's tardiness was deliberate? To assume that perhaps he believes meals are served to whomever wishes to have them at the precise time they wish to eat?"

Daniel was nodding furiously.

Joseph didn't know what to say. The accusation came out of left field. What kind of grudge could Daniel already have against him that would make him want to put them both in such a situation? Perhaps it wasn't in his best interest after all to try to protect the boy. He'd tried and still Daniel had insisted on throwing him to the wolves. If that was how the game was to be played, then so be it. He'd be gone soon anyway.

Lachlan looked at him expectantly. Out of the corner of his eye, he could tell Daniel was staring at him too. Everyone in the dining hall was.

Joseph took a deep breath. "He told me seven-thirty sharp. That if I was a minute late, I wouldn't get to eat."

Brother Lachlan smiled.

Joseph finally allowed himself to look at Daniel. The other boy's eyes burned as he stared at him. He mouthed something but Joseph was unable to make it out. He caught the gist anyway.

"Three stripes," Lachlan said.

"No, brother," Daniel cried. "Please. I swear I told him the correct time."

"Each."

The word dropped out of Lachlan's lips like an icicle from an eave. Joseph's heart jackhammered in his chest. He felt sick. He searched Brother Lachlan's eyes and found them devoid of any identifiable emotion. Was his plan all along to have Joseph publicly snitch on Daniel, only to have them both punished? The good feeling he'd had when he woke up was nowhere to be found now. Even thoughts of his uncle soon coming to whisk him away from this place did nothing to dispel the fear that bloomed in the pit of his stomach and spread upward, into his heart, like venom.

"Approach," Lachlan said. "Come and accept the consequences of your actions."

Daniel shook his head and collapsed into his seat, gripping the end of the table with both hands. A short, stout friar appeared behind him and lifted him effortlessly. Daniel kicked and struggled but was easily brought to the front of the room, where he cowered in front of Brother Lachlan, held in place by the other friar.

Joseph didn't need to be told he'd receive the same treatment if he didn't approach on his own. This, thankfully, was not a new routine to him. He'd been striped by his father plenty of times in the past, both bare-assed and with his jeans on, depending on how angry or drunk his father was, regardless of his crime. He calculated that the punishment was deserved approximately twenty five per cent of the time. The other occasions were typically due to blame being shifted to him for something that was otherwise entirely out of his control.

He thought of last year's Good Friday, a day celebrated even more than any other in the Ward household because, for Joseph's father, it meant the start of a four-day weekend. His father would wake up early in fine spirits. He'd eat breakfast and drink coffee at a leisurely pace with the newspaper spread out on the table in front of him. He would stretch his meal out until eleven in the morning, when McLaren's opened. When he was finished eating, he'd bid Joseph and his mother a good day before leaving for the bar. He would stumble in after midnight, have a nightcap, and pass out in his chair in the living room. The process would be repeated all weekend.

Last Easter had been no different and, Joseph recalled with a bitter sort of sweetness, his father had even kissed his wife goodbye before leaving. Joseph could remember maybe half a dozen occasions that he'd witnessed his parents show affection to one another. That Good Friday had been one of the best and, now that his mother had passed on, Joseph held the memory even closer to his heart. The two of them had watched an old movie on TV together, sipping hot cocoa (made with water instead of milk because milk was expensive and took away from the beer budget), and eating cookies his mother had made—and burned. After the movie, they were both hopped up on sugar and got it in their heads to play hide and seek in their tiny apartment. There was no place for either of them to hide, of course, that the other wouldn't find as soon as the count was up but it was the most fun Joseph could remember ever having with his mother.

Everything would have been fine if he hadn't insisted on just one more game. He'd just thought of the perfect hiding spot; he figured he could cram into his laundry hamper in his closet and pile enough clothes overtop of himself that he might just fool his mother. He did just that while she counted and it worked for about two minutes. Once she'd checked the rest of the apartment, she circled back to his room. She checked under his bed as Joseph watched her through a crack in the hamper. It would be a matter of seconds before she turned her attention to the closet so he sprung out and sprinted through the door. She lunged after him but he just managed to escape her grasp. He raced down the hall and around the corner. His mother was hot on his tail as he slid into the kitchen, socks gliding easily on the linoleum. Then came the crash. He ran back into the hallway to find her kneeling in front of a broken frame. On the floor, amid shards of glass, was a heart-shaped piece of metal with a purple ribbon attached to it. His own heart sank at the sight.

Joseph's father was not the least bit sentimental and took pride in very few possessions. His own father's Purple Heart was one of those few things he owned that he cherished more than even his precious beer. He spoke about it as though he'd been the one to lose a leg in enemy territory. Joseph watched him take it out of its frame and polish it every year on Veteran's Day.

His mother held the golden medal in her hands and wept over it.

"Can't we just get a new frame for it?" Joseph had asked.

She had looked at him with pity in her eyes.

His father returned from McLaren's early that night, just after ten. The glass had been cleaned up and the Purple Heart sat on the kitchen table. Joseph's mother was semi-conscious on the couch, medication coursing through her veins. She'd taken it immediately after cleaning up the glass, showing no more patience for a holiday alone with her son. Joseph had been sitting up in his bed, reading, when his father burst through the bedroom door, his face scarlet with rage.

"What did you do?" his father had hissed at him.

He'd answered without thinking. "I was running in the hall and I bumped into it. I'm sorry, dad."

Joseph had no idea how many times his father had whipped his exposed buttocks with his belt that night, only that it was a lot more than three. The welts had covered his thighs, ass, and back and had bled for two days after. He was glad for the long weekend from school because he couldn't bear to sit with any amount of cushioning, let alone on the hard plastic seats of the chairs in his classroom.

Now Joseph stood in front of Brother Lachlan, looking him straight in the eyes, as his grandfather had taught him. The chubby friar, who had been stationed at Lachlan's side, approached and held out a leather-wrapped flail, which the headmaster took from him with reverence. He held it in front of him with two fingers so that Joseph could see the whole thing. The handle was flexible and wrapped in brown leather. The business end of the flail was made up of thick strands mingled with knotted laces of leather. It didn't take much imagination to figure out how much damage those knots would do; he'd been hit with the buckle-end of a belt in the past. His father had claimed it was an accident at the time. Joseph never quite believed him.

"Community," Lachlan said, "Is something we strive to achieve here at St. Theodore's. How can we have community if we do not cooperate with one another? The book of Galatians tells us, 'Bear ye one another's burdens, and so fulfill the law of Christ.' In a community, we share each other's joys *and* burdens, trials *and* successes, rewards *and* punishments. This institution will not tolerate any offense to the idea of community. As such, I find it only fitting that each of your punishments be administered by the other."

Daniel looked triumphant. Was he really going to enjoy this? Joseph couldn't manage to feel much more than humiliation. And betrayal. Not from Daniel, he'd come across dozens of boys like him—guys who got off on watching people smaller than them suffer. Brother Lachlan, on the other hand, had seemed so nice when Joseph arrived. Even now the man spoke as though they were having a friendly conversation. His gentle voice hadn't risen in the slightest this entire time. He simply stated how things were to be and expected that everyone and everything around him would fall into step. He had disarmed Joseph by making him feel welcome and now he was blindsiding him by pitting him against a vicious older boy.

"Mr. Ward," Lachlan held the flail out to him, "You may draw first blood. The punishment is three stripes. And I do not encourage you to actually draw blood."

Joseph stood there stupidly holding the flail by the business end. How could he strike another person with this thing, knowing the damage it could inflict?

"Mr. Avery, please drop your trousers."

Daniel looked up at Brother Lachlan with tears in his eyes. "Everybody's watching."

Lachlan indicated the table next to him. "Nobody will see anything you don't want them to. Bend over this table and face your peers. I'm sure they would much rather witness your remorse as opposed to your rear."

Daniel looked to Joseph with pleading in his eyes and shuffled around the table. He faced the rest of the dining hall and slid down the back of his pants. The room was completely still, as though everyone held their breath. Joseph was frozen in place.

"Mr. Ward, if you do not get on with it, I'll have Brother Stuart administer the punishment three-fold to you both." Lachlan nodded toward the stout friar who had dragged Daniel out of his seat.

Joseph made himself put one foot in front of the other and step to where Daniel bent over the table. Excited murmurs bubbled up from the other kids in the dining hall. Brother

Lachlan silenced them with a hiss that sounded like a soda bottle being opened.

Daniel had an angry red pimple on the side of his left buttock and it was all Joseph could look at as he approached. It quivered as the other boy trembled, clearly fearing the worst. Joseph grit his teeth and smacked Daniel's rear with the flail. Daniel yelped though Joseph had barely touched him—there wasn't even a red mark to show for it. He wound up again but Brother Lachlan grabbed him by the wrist.

"I won't have you holding back, Mr. Ward. Last chance before I lose my patience and have Brother Stuart take over." He threw Joseph's hand back down with enough force to hurt his shoulder.

"I'm sorry," Joseph whispered.

He struck Daniel hard, three times in the same place. He knew from experience that it was better to have the stripes in the same area so that you only had one sore spot. After the third strike, Daniel yanked his pants up and snatched the flail from Joseph.

"My turn," he said with wet eyes and a vicious grin on his face.

Joseph didn't expect Daniel to hold back, nor did he expect the assault that took place as soon as he was prone.

He slid his trousers down and bent over the table before he could be told to do so. Every eye was on him and he felt a strange kind of intimacy as he leaned over and met the eyes of those nearest him. He would not be seen as a coward.

He'd barely got his drawers down when Daniel began thrashing wildly with the flail, shouting with each strike like a tennis player on the court. The stripes came hard and fast, all over Joseph's backside. He grit his teeth and squeezed the edge of the table with both hands as Daniel struck him over and over.

Most of the kids in the dining hall wore shocked expressions, mouths hanging open, as Joseph endured the beating. He thought he even heard some of them crying but couldn't be sure it wasn't his own whimpers.

He'd lost count of how many times he'd been hit by the time Brother Lachlan placed a hand on Daniel's wrist, stopping him mid-strike. He heard the boy grunt as the flail was wrenched from his grasp. Brother Stuart led Daniel out of the dining hall while Joseph pulled up his pants.

Lachlan stepped in front of him and addressed the dining hall. "Morning mass starts in six minutes and I will not excuse any tardiness, as I hope has been proven today." He turned to Joseph and said, "As I said before, in lieu of attending mass, you will be assisting the staff with cleanup."

Joseph could barely stand after the thrashing. The thought of having to move around and clean made him want to cry. He gave Brother Lachlan a stiff nod and waddled toward the swinging double doors that he assumed led into the kitchen. With each step, the fabric of his pants slid against the raw flesh of his rear and thighs, reminding him of his punishment and humiliation. The waist of his pants hugged a particularly sore spot and he had to adjust them frequently to relieve the pain.

9

———————

CLEANUP TOOK JUST OVER AN HOUR. JOSEPH'S FIRST TASK was to gather leftover dishes from every table. Then he scrubbed down each table down with a solution of white vinegar and water. After washing the tables, he was made to sweep the floors, then to take the trash to the dumpster out back. All two dozen bags of it.

By the time he was finished with his duties, blood had begun to soak through his pants. One of the friars who worked in the kitchen sent him to the infirmary to have himself cleaned up.

The infirmary was located just off the main hall and was run by a no-nonsense nun named Sister Nina. She recognized Joseph as he stumbled through the door.

"I wondered when I'd see you down here. 'Twas quite the beating you took," she said in a light Scottish accent that Joseph may have found endearing in any other place.

"I had to help clean up," he murmured as she guided him to an examination table.

"Don't make excuses, boy. Accept the consequences of your actions and the Lord will bestow upon ye great wisdom."

As Sister Nina applied iodine and bandages to Joseph's rear, he wondered if everyone here was as intense as the rest of the faculty he'd met. He was not keen to find out. For the rest of the day he would heed Odilon's words and keep a low profile. He couldn't trust a word out of anyone in this place except, maybe, Odilon himself. The Haitian boy seemed nice enough and did, after all, make sure Joseph got something to eat. He decided he'd try to sit next to him again at lunch.

When she was through with his backside, Sister Nina said, "They'll be expecting ye in your next class. What do ye have before lunch?"

Joseph shrugged. "I'm only here for a couple of days, until my uncle picks me up."

She chuffed. "Just passing through, are ye? Well then it's off to your room until lunchtime. Straight there, mind ye. Even priority guests aren't permitted to be wanderin round the halls while classes are in session."

Joseph had no intention of missing anymore meals so he asked Sister Nina about other important times and, unsurprisingly, there was much that had been left out of his tour with Daniel. Breakfast, as he had learned the hard way, was served at seven. Lunch was at noon, supper at six. Morning mass occurred every day after breakfast, except for Saturdays when mass still occurred in the mornings, at seven, but was much longer and was conducted prior to breakfast so that students might more clearly focus on God's Word. Joseph had an idea there was something a little more sadistic to it than that but kept his opinion to himself, relishing in the knowledge that he wouldn't be here to see more than one Saturday mass. Sundays were for chores, which were completed in the times between meals. This was backwards to Joseph, who came from a Protestant background, not that his family was very religious. He had always figured Sundays were for church and rest. There was very little allowance for outdoor time, no more than an hour a day except Saturdays when they got two hours.

He hobbled straight back to his room after the infirmary visit. There was well over an hour until lunch and he needed a rest. A clock hung on almost every wall, which he was grateful for since his watch, along with his backpack, had been confiscated by the police. He hoped his belongings would be waiting for him when he got out of here. He and Edgar would have to detour to his place anyway to get his stuff—they could stop by the police station on the way to claim his watch and his backpack.

He shut himself in his room and belly-flopped onto the bed. Just one day in here was enough of a prison sentence for him to never again even think about trying to sneak into any place he didn't belong. All because he couldn't keep his curiosity in check. He thought about the painting in the church basement for the first time since he'd been put in the back of that police car and scolded himself for having been so foolish as to think he'd actually experienced something as outrageous as a living painting, for not recognizing that he'd been upset and that of course his mind would've conjured things that weren't there. What about Hasty though? Sure, he could imagine a little bit of movement in a painting, especially when the light was dim. He could remember being eight years old and thinking his teddy bear was moving on its own in the dimness of his room. But to imagine an entire person, someone he had never seen before, standing directly in front of him?

Touching him? He'd had fantasies about girls before, some real doozies too, but none of them came anywhere close to what he could remember so clearly happening in that church basement. How could that possibly have been an illusion? Maybe he was going crazy.

At eleven-thirty he heard footsteps pounding up and down the hall outside his room. They were surprisingly muffled; the rooms were pretty sound proof. He was starving but made himself wait. The last thing he wanted was to face any of the other students in this place until it was absolutely necessary. He hoped that by being on time to lunch he wouldn't draw any more attention to himself. At ten-to-twelve, he pulled himself out of bed and limped his way down to the dining hall.

Odilon waved to him from the same place he'd been at breakfast and Joseph made his way over to join him. The majority of the kids were still finding their seats, which Joseph was grateful for, since no one really paid him any mind. The last thing he wanted was to be the center of attention in this place ever again.

Sitting wasn't something he'd thought about having to overcome until he dropped onto the bench next to Odilon. Sharp, burning pain exploded in his backside. It took the discipline of a Tibetan monk not to yelp. He yanked his butt off the bench as though it was full of hot coals, then, still determined not to attract attention, eased himself back down onto it. It was agony.

"It's fine," Joseph said in response to the look of grave concern Odilon was giving him. He tried to sound dismissive though he could feel sweat prickling his forehead. "Better than not eating, anyway."

Odilon said nothing but shot continual looks his way.

Joseph was touched by the concern, glad to at least have one ally during his short stint in this place.

Lunch was Chef Boyardee spaghetti, a slice of buttered white bread, and a fruit cup. They made small talk while they ate and Joseph got the impression that Odilon didn't have many friends here. The boy was kind but also very reserved in a way that struck Joseph as being guarded.

He learned that Odilon was the same age—just six months older, having been born in December while Joseph's birthday was in June. He also learned Odilon had been at St. Theodore's for a full year. He'd become a ward of the state and sent here when he was caught stealing at a downtown grocer's. Odilon's mother had fled with him to the United States when her husband had become mixed up in what sounded a lot like a Satanic cult and had tried to force her and their son to come live in a commune. When she had refused, his father had come at her with a knife. He'd apparently planned to kill her and make off with Odilon. She appealed to her sister, who had managed to become a US citizen years earlier, and agreed to have them to stay with her for a short time. Odilon's mother secured them passage on a ship headed to Boston. Odilon was eight at the time but he remembered little of the journey except that his mother became deathly ill. She died shortly after they'd arrived in Boston. He lived with his aunt, who made it very clear she was not happy to be stuck with him, until she took her own life when he was ten. He managed to fend for himself for almost six months after she died. Nobody asked any questions when her body was taken away, all assuming there was another parental figure somewhere who would step in and continue to provide for the crying boy in the apartment. Odilon didn't know why his aunt had taken her own life. He assumed it had to do with being burdened with a child she hadn't asked for. After her death, he continued to go to school, and even excelled in his class. He survived on what little money his aunt had stashed away until the landlord got tired of waiting for a rent payment. When he discovered Odilon surviving on his own, he offered to call the police. Odilon, being a black boy in Boston in the eighties, had a severe distrust of the police and had run off. He lived on the streets for several months; working for food when he could, panhandling when he couldn't, and stealing when he had to. He'd lived under a bridge in the middle of the city with a dozen other derelicts who, as a community, made it their business to look out for him. Odilon learned a lot of hard lessons but also found great love among the homeless in the city. When he was finally arrested and sentenced to St. Theodore's for stealing a can of soup, his biggest regret was that he wouldn't have a chance to say goodbye to the family he'd made while living on the streets.

Joseph took Odilon's story in without interrupting, barely tasting his food. The noise in the dining hall had become a dull background roar. Only when the story was done did he realize he'd finished his meal. He looked at Odilon's plate and saw it was untouched. When Odilon saw him looking he smiled and shrugged.

"You get used to not eating three square meals a day." Odilon folded his bread into his napkin and shoved it in his pocket, pulling another bunched up napkin from his other pocket as he did so, and laying it on the table. Joseph made a note to ask him about that later.

The rest of the afternoon passed uneventfully for Joseph. When he inquired about what he should be doing with his time, he was told that Sister Nina had recommended he be regulated to bedrest in lieu of classes to allow his posterior some time to recover. It was a little late for that, but he decided that he could do with a day to himself to get used to the new environment.

He managed to sleep for an hour immediately after lunch. He hadn't planned to but by the time he got to his room, his backside was on fire. He flopped belly-first onto his bed as soon as he stepped through the door and fell into a thin, dreamless sleep. When he woke, he felt more groggy than rested.

He padded down to the washroom, where he peed then washed his hands and face. Stepping out into the hall, he realized there wasn't anything or anyone keeping him in his room. There must be some form of security, other than the dogs, to keep him confined to the school. For now, it seemed, he was free to wander.

The fourth floor, which housed his room, was deserted, its residents no doubt in their various classes. He walked the length of the hall, which bent around the boy's wing in a U-shape. The walls were adorned in a plain wallpaper of burnt-orange which, along with the dark wood floors, lent the place a gloomy look. The halls were devoid of any sort of decor.

The ancient wood door to the turret was propped open, letting a cool breeze waft in from the stone column. He looked up as he stepped through the door and spotted an iron hatch leading up to a fifth level of the turret. He'd have to remember to ask someone about that.

The third level of St. Theodore's, the senior's floor, according to Daniel, was much the same as the fourth. He stole into their bathroom and discovered the biggest difference between the two floors was that the senior students had much larger facilities.

The second floor was split between faculty dorms and classrooms. He stepped out of the turret into a hall of closed doors that he knew from his tour were dorms belonging to the friars. The muffled murmur of voices echoed from up the hall. He stepped around the corner and here the hallway opened up. The doors here were windowed and spaced much farther apart. Joseph stepped up to the closest one and peered inside. A friar he didn't recognize had his back turned to the door and was writing something on the blackboard. The students looked as though they were a bit older than himself, likely seniors. A pimple-faced boy with short black hair spotted him staring into the classroom, sneered, and raised his middle finger. Joseph slipped away from the door before he could be discovered by the teacher.

The first floor consisted of more classrooms, the library, the gymnasium, several offices, and, of course, the dining hall. Joseph drifted out of the boy's wing and into the main hall, which was just as quiet as the rest of the school. The hall was resplendent in the daylight. Beams of sunlight shone through the stained glass windows. The iron bars in the lower windows cast lines of shadows on the floor, serving as a reminder that there was no actual freedom in here. This was one of the only places in the school that did not have wood floors; Joseph's shoes clicked on great slabs of grey stone, his footfalls echoing throughout the hall. The ceiling was wide open, creating impressive acoustics that echoed back even the slightest sound. An enormous crystal chandelier hung over the center of the hall, suspended by four herculean chains fastened to the ceiling with rings that looked like they were designed to imprison a dragon. The great staircase led up from the center of this hall to the second floor.

Joseph looked down the hall of the girl's side of the school. It appeared identical to the boy's. Were the hallways on their side wallpapered in the same rusty orange color as the boy's hall? He considered sneaking into the other side of the school to find out but swiftly reigned in his traitorous curiosity. He needed to keep a low profile from here on out.

Bored with his self-guided tour, and nervous about being caught out of his room, he headed back into the boy's wing and up the turret stairs, which he was more fond of than the main stairway. Being in the turret, he felt shielded from the rest of the world and, more importantly, from St. Theodore's. He stared longingly at the hatch leading up to the fifth level of the turret as he stepped through the door onto his floor, yearning to make it past that hatch and find out what secrets that fifth level held. He yawned and squinted at the clock hanging at the other end of the hallway. Three o'clock. Still a few hours until supper. He decided to take advantage of the free time while he could and headed back to his room for another nap.

10

———

HE MADE IT TO SUPPER WITH PLENTY OF TIME TO SPARE and sat in the same place as before. Odilon didn't wave him over this time but he did shuffle to make space for Joseph when he saw him coming. Nobody else at the table offered any conversation to either of them while they ate. Probably just the way new guys, along with anyone who was nice to them, were treated. Or maybe Odilon had already been an outcast. It didn't take much looking around to see that the majority of the kids, and all of the faculty, were white. He had no doubt Odilon had suffered for it. In fact, as Joseph surveyed the dining hall, he realized Odilon was the only black kid on the boy's side. An Asian boy, who sat at one of the senior tables, was the only other non-white boy Joseph could spot. Several black girls sat on the other side of the dining hall. Odilon probably found little solidarity with them. Boys and girls were never really allowed to interact except during outside time and even then it was under strict supervision. Joseph added it to his list of things to ask Odilon about when they had a chance to speak out of earshot of a dozen other kids.

After supper, one of the nuns, a tall, gangly woman, stepped up to the front of the hall and held her hands over her head as though she was signaling a plane flying overhead. The room fell silent and the nun introduced herself, staring directly at Joseph, as Sister Petra. She announced that there would be a movie shown in the dining hall at seven-thirty that evening. Attendance was not mandatory but if students wanted to opt out, they would be confined to their rooms, except for senior students who could spend their time in the library if they wished. The cheers at the announcement of a movie led Joseph to believe this was not a weekly occurrence.

He leaned closer to Odilon and whispered, "You going to the movie?"

Odilon nodded without taking his eyes off the nun. Joseph took his cue from him and turned his attention back to her as well.

Sister Petra let everyone know that the dining hall would still have to be cleaned and set up for the movie and that everyone was to return to their dorms in the meantime. There were a few groans of protest at this but a sharp look from her silenced them immediately. They were dismissed to their rooms until showtime and the hall emptied out in a bustle, with students bumping each other excitedly and gabbing about what movie it might be.

Joseph looked for Odilon in the crowd as they processed out of the dining hall but had lost him almost as soon as dinner was let out. He lingered behind the crowd to see if he could spot him but had no luck. He must have been one of the first ones out of the hall.

"Joseph."

Hearing his name made his balls shrink up into his stomach—what had he done now? He turned to find an old, weathered friar standing near the door and beckoning him over. The man stood only an inch or so taller than himself and looked to be in his seventies, wispy grey hair brushed haphazardly to one side. He wore tiny, square spectacles that he fussed with as he spoke.

"I'm Brother Oswin," he said with the ghost of a German accent, "Headmaster Lachlan asked that I provide you with your class schedule."

The friar handed over an index card with a schedule typed out on it.

"The work you have missed so far this semester will be averaged out based on the grades you receive for the balance of the term. I trust that sounds fair to you."

"Oh, I won't be here much longer," Joseph said, offering a sheepish grin. "My uncle is coming to pick me up soon."

The old man peered at Joseph over the rim of his spectacles. "Maybe that is something you wish to discuss with Brother Lachlan. In the meantime," he shoved the card into Joseph's hand, "It would be best to do what is asked of you."

Joseph accepted the card without another word. He glanced over it; geography, history, English, math, and physical education. All the heavy-hitting courses loaded into this semester. The next one would be a cinch. Not that he would be here to find out.

He turned away from Brother Oswin without another word to the man. It might have been his age or the slight accent but this guy gave Joseph the heebie-jeebies. He looked over his shoulder as he left the dining hall. Oswin stared after him, holding the tips of his fingers together, looking nefarious. He reminded Joseph of Emperor Palpatine from the *Star Wars* movies, albeit in a cassock instead of the hooded cloak from the movies.

Joseph made his way through empty halls toward the turret. They had about half an hour until the movie and he decided to use that time to brush up on what was being taught in his classes. He didn't plan on trying to impress anyone here but he also didn't want to cause further trouble for himself by being dismissive of instructions. He'd gotten into enough trouble allowing himself slip up out in the real world and, thanks to Daniel Avery, was already on the outs with the staff of St. Theodore's.

He thought about Ms. Hendrix and how she had tried to help him with his grades. He'd deliberately allowed them to drop and had assumed that would make him popular with the other kids, or would at least make him less of a loser. Now he felt foolish, ashamed of such thinking. How could he think someone like Paul DiMarco was capable of being anything less than an abusive brat? Why would he want the approval of someone like that anyway? For the first time since arriving at St. Theodore's, he thought that all of this could have been avoided if he'd not allowed himself to care about what other people's opinions of him were. Would he still have tried to break into the church if he'd not allowed himself to slide down this path of rebellion? It didn't matter. What mattered was getting out of here. He'd talk to Brother Lachlan tomorrow and find out if he could get an idea of when Edgar would be arriving.

He stepped out of the stairwell to find the fourth floor hallway utterly abandoned. It seemed no one would risk missing out on the movie by not going directly to their rooms. He was just opening the door to his quarters when he heard a low murmuring coming from around the bend in the other direction. It was a kid's voice, heavily accented, and familiar to Joseph by now. He crept down the hall and peered around the corner.

Odilon was crouched with his back turned, talking to himself.

"What are you doing?" Joseph asked.

His friend jumped. One of the big German shepherds lay on the floor in front of him, belly exposed. Odilon tossed something and the dog snatched it out of the air before running off. The boy looked like he'd been caught murdering the animal instead of petting it. He glanced up and down the hall, as if worried Joseph had brought a squad up here to bust him doing whatever it was he looked so guilty about. Joseph couldn't help but smile at the idea. Seeing him smile, Odilon appeared to relax a little bit.

"The dog seems to like you," Joseph said, "Was that Hilda or Julius?"

"Please," Odilon said, eyes huge and fearful, "Do not tell anyone."

"You're not allowed to pet the dogs?"

Odilon lowered his voice. "We are not allowed to *feed* the dogs."

Joseph remembered Odilon folding his bread up in his napkin and swapping it with an empty napkin in his pocket. He also recalled Lachlan's warning about such behavior.

"You bring the dogs some of your food every day?"

Odilon shook his head. "Just Hilda. I think Julius eats her

food. And he won't come near students unless he is chasing them down."

Joseph remembered all too well and said as much.

It turned out Hilda had taken to Odilon soon after he had been brought here. On his first day, he told Joseph, he was chased and beaten by the senior boys for no better reason than him being black. He'd hidden down a hallway and balled himself up in a corner. Hilda had found him there, crying. She'd stuck her nose under his arms and licked the tears off his face. The two had maintained a secret friendship ever since. When no one was around, she would come to him for affection or for whichever scraps he was able to save for her. She didn't seem to prefer one over the other.

Joseph swore himself to secrecy. He was horrified that someone as kind as Odilon could be punished for such a thing.

He nodded at a clock hanging on the wall. "It's almost movie time. Want to head down?"

The movie was *Wizard of Oz*, which was one of the few movies Joseph had seen more than once. The boy's side groaned almost unanimously when the movie was announced. The girls all cheered. Joseph was happy with the selection; he'd always enjoyed the magical transition between the bleak, monochromatic world of Kansas and the vibrant land of Oz. As Dorothy opened the door to Oz for the first time, Joseph's heart skipped a beat. The Technicolor, the new world, it all spoke to him in a voice that was familiar, tempting, and terrifying.

That night he dreamt of Oz.

One moment he was in his bed thinking about California beaches, and the next he was spinning. He accepted this with the submission that came with most dreams. He stood in a familiar little cabin, in color instead of black and white. No Toto. The single window showed the outside world as a swirl of debris. No old ladies on bikes or broomsticks.

As the place twirled within the cyclone, the interior changed and Joseph found himself standing in his apartment. He was in the living room and, though the window had disappeared, he could feel the apartment spinning in the wind.

"You're in the way."

His father reclined in the chair he had spent most of his life in and waved an arm at him.

Joseph took a step to the side and looked behind him, to where the TV sat in their apartment. Except instead of the TV, a painting stood upright on the floor. It was the same painting as in the church basement—same lake, same fields, same mountain range.

"It's the only way out," his mother said from behind him.

Joseph's heart caught in his throat. He turned to see her laying on the couch, in the same position she had always lain, the same position she had died in.

"Get out of the damn way," his father barked.

Joseph knelt in front of his mother. Her eyes were closed. A smear of brown vomit caked to her chin.

He shook her, whispered to her. Encouraged her to get up.

Her eyes shot open. She grabbed him by the shirt and pulled him close. Her breath reeked of something sour and old.

"It's the only way out!" she shrieked.

She shoved him and he flew backwards into the painting. When he hit the floor, he was no longer in the apartment. He knelt on a bright yellow surface, gleaming in sudden sunlight. He stood and immediately recognized the village of the Lollipop kids; the endless, yellow-brick road winding off into the horizon. This place was different than the Oz in the movie in that the yellow-brick road lead across a green field into a mountain range, similar to that of the painting in the church basement.

"Where are you tryin to get?" a familiar voice asked from behind him, prompting him to turn around.

Hasty stood in the middle of the road, dressed in Glinda's pink gown. She wore her Iron Maiden vest over top of it. The combination was perfect.

He hugged her tightly and relished the low cut of the gown. His face smooshed into her cleavage and he felt that all familiar stirring low in his belly. He stood back from her, embarrassed even in his own dream.

"I'm going to California. To live with my uncle," he said.

She shook her head. "Not that way, you ain't."

He looked up the yellow brick road, which no longer led to a mountain range. Now it wound its way around a fountain and up the steps to St. Theodore's Academy. The sight of it panicked him, made him feel like a caged animal. His chest tightened.

"How do I get out?" he pleaded.

"You know how."

She raised a silver staff and pointed it at Joseph's feet, which were suddenly clad in glistening ruby slippers.

"Click my heels?"

Hasty chuckled and shook her head. "You know what shoes are for and you know what you've gotta do."

"Run away?"

As soon as the words were out of his mouth, the sky darkened. Thunder boomed from the direction of St. Theodore's. The school appeared closer. Bigger. The doors at the top of the stairs flung open to reveal the silhouette of a tall figure. Brother Lachlan.

"He won't let you do that," Hasty said.

Joseph turned back to her. "Then what do I do? Hasty, help me!"

She floated up and away from him.

"See you soon," she called.

And then she was gone.

The thunder resolved into a deep, throaty cackling. Joseph faced the school again and screamed. It had grown to the size of a mountain and he stood at the foot of the giant staircase leading up to the door. Lachlan stepped through the open doors and glowered down at him. He looked enormous from where Joseph stood.

The headmaster held something square and flat in his hands; a canvas painting, the one from the church basement. He raised it up to his face and chomped into it as though he was eating a sandwich. The frame splintered and rained wood chips on the stone steps. The canvas made a horrible tearing sound as he chewed through it. In seconds the whole thing had disappeared down his throat.

Joseph woke himself up screaming and thrashing in his bed. By the time he scrubbed his face in the bathroom, next to half a dozen other boys going through their morning routine, he couldn't recall any of the dream though he was pretty sure Hasty had been in it.

11

———

Monday came and Joseph was awake to see its sunrise. He had barely slept since his dream the other night, not because of the nightmare, but because he expected his uncle any day now. He was disappointed Edgar hadn't shown up on Sunday but he was certain he would show up today.

He practically skipped into the dining hall, ignoring the annoyed looks he got from faculty and fellow students. Brother Lachlan stared him down as he made his way to his seat. Joseph avoided making eye contact with the headmaster, refusing to give him the satisfaction of acknowledgment.

"Don't look too excited to be leaving," Odilon said as Joseph took his seat next to him. "You are upsetting Brother Lachlan."

"Let him be upset. I can't wait to be out of here."

Odilon looked down at his plate and stirred refried beans around with his fork.

"I'm gonna miss you, though," Joseph told him, putting a hand on his shoulder.

Odilon smiled. "It was very nice getting to know you, Joseph."

They finished their breakfast in relative silence. When they were dismissed, Odilon left quickly, maybe so that he didn't have to say goodbye again to the only friend he had in this place. Joseph felt guilty about leaving him but what was he supposed to do about it? Refuse to leave? This place wasn't a holiday resort anyone could just choose to stay at. Even if he had the option, there was no way Joseph would spend a minute longer than he had to in this place.

It was the longest morning of his life. Even on his dullest school days, he couldn't remember time dragging like this. Of course, he mostly enjoyed school, not least because it had given him a break from his parents. Now he'd do anything to have his mother back. Even living with his father was better than this.

His first class, geography, crawled by. His eyes were drawn to the clock as if by magnetic force. Each time he looked, it was like a minute had gone by at most. The friar teaching the class, Brother Lewis, an irritable man roughly the same age as Joseph's father, droned on endlessly about various types of forest. Coniferous this and deciduous that.

When finally the class had finished, Joseph ran out of the room and into the main hall, fully expecting to see Edgar standing there with his arms open, ready to take him home. He was met only by students parading to their next classes and faculty shepherding them along. Joseph remained in the hall, watching for his uncle, until Brother Stuart snapped at him to get to his next class.

The day dragged on like this and by the time supper rolled around, anxiety burned in him like a hot stone in the pit of his stomach. How long did Edgar plan on taking to come get him? Didn't he realize the kind of place this was? That Joseph was being held in a prison while he took his time? Joseph felt hurt and betrayed by his uncle's apparent apathy.

Odilon was very obviously happy to see Joseph at supper, though he tried not to show it. Joseph ate his dinner without really tasting it while his friend prattled on about his classes and something about pulling a tick off Hilda. He was sad to be leaving him, wished he and Edgar could bring him with them. Maybe they could meet up when Odilon was released. The idea brightened Joseph's mood a little bit. He offered this idea up to his friend.

Odilon gave him a sad smile. "That would be nice."

"Don't look so happy about it."

"It will be a long time before I'm allowed out of here," Odilon said.

"Can't be that long. How long do you have? Another year?"

"Joseph, I am a homeless orphan."

"So?"

This time Odilon didn't try to hide his misery behind a smile. "I will be here until my eighteenth birthday."

"What?" Joseph almost shouted. "They can't do that! They just take your life away because your mom died?"

"I committed a crime."

"That's bullshit, Odi."

Neither boy spoke for several minutes. Around them the din of the dining hall carried on—hundreds of voices merging into meaningless babble. Joseph crammed dry chicken into his mouth while Odilon sequestered a portion of his own for Hilda.

After a while Joseph said, "It's just not fair that they can keep you like that."

Odilon put an arm around him. "They can only keep me as long as God lets them."

"Crappy thing to let someone do."

"Maybe it's for a good reason. I might be meant to do some good here. Maybe I would have done something very bad out there," Odilon mused.

Joseph nudged him with his shoulder. "Sometimes you talk like you're thirty."

After supper they took their time walking back to their rooms. They walked side-by-side up the turret staircase to their floor. At the top of the stairs, Joseph grabbed Odilon's arm and pointed to the hatch above them.

"What's up there?"

Odilon shrugged. "Storage?"

"I want to find out before I go."

Joseph grabbed a rung of the ladder and managed to hoist himself up one step before Odilon yanked the leg of his pants, pulling him down. Joseph had to hold onto him to keep from losing his balance. There was a long second during which it felt like they would both tumble down the stairs.

"What the hell did you do that for?" Joseph hissed.

"You may be leaving tomorrow," Odilon said, "But if we get caught, I will be the one to pay for this. I do not want to suffer anymore than I already have to."

It was frustrating but his friend was right. Of course it would be huge trouble for Odilon if they were to be caught here. For both of them. The fact that Joseph was leaving tomorrow wouldn't absolve him from punishment either. He wasn't sure where the sudden bravado had come from though he recognized it as the same thing that had driven him to break into the church. His curiosity screamed at him to go back up the ladder but Joseph made himself pull open the door to the fourth floor and step through with Odilon close behind.

"See you at breakfast," he said as he pushed into his room.

From up the hall, Odilon gave him one of his trademark grins and disappeared around the corner.

If Joseph dreamt that night, he wasn't able to recall any of it the next morning. Nor did he attempt to. Today was the day. It had to be. Though it had been less than a week, it already felt like he'd spent a lifetime in this place. Certainly it felt like he'd known Odilon for much longer than only a few days, maybe because he'd never had a friend who he'd been as close to as he was with him. He'd never shared so much of his life with anyone. Before his time at St. Theodore's he'd done his level best to hide as much of himself as possible from everyone he met. It was a bittersweet feeling to be leaving this place, his friend. Just last night he wouldn't have considered that he could feel anything less than absolute joy at being free from here. Knowing he was leaving the best friend he'd ever had made him sick to his stomach.

When Joseph came down to breakfast, Odilon greeted him with a grin as he did every day. How could this boy be so happy when he knew he was going to spend the rest of his childhood behind these walls, with people like Brother Lachlan minding him?

Breakfast was oatmeal and fruit but Joseph could hardly bring himself to eat more than a few bites of either. Odilon either didn't notice or chose not to comment on Joseph's mood. He acted as though there was nothing different about today than any other day. He certainly didn't appear upset that

Joseph was leaving. That was just fine. It would be easier for Joseph to leave this place knowing there wouldn't be anyone missing him.

When the meal was over, Joseph shoved up from his seat, ready to storm out of the hall and leave his one-time friend behind for good. Odilon grabbed his arm before he could get more than a couple of steps from the table. Joseph whirled on him, biting words on the tip of his tongue. He caught himself when he saw Odilon was holding something out to him.

"What's this?" Joseph said as he took the item; a small something bundled in string.

He unraveled it and saw the string, twine really, was part of the package. It was a homemade necklace. At the end of the string was a cross made out of two old, rusted nails fastened together with wire.

"A cross?"

"A going away present," Odilon said. "I hope it is not too sharp. I made it myself."

Ashamed for being so bothered by his friend's natural optimism, Joseph couldn't bring himself to look up from the cross. Tears pricked the corners of his eyes and he worked to get them under control lest anyone else in the dining hall see them. He draped the twine over his neck and tucked the cross into his shirt, enjoying the coolness of the metal against his skin.

"Thank you," he said through tight vocal cords.

The class bell rang.

"I hope to see you again one day, Joseph." Odilon grabbed him in a big hug, tighter than Joseph would have thought the slim boy capable of.

"Bye, Odi." He hugged his friend back, then watched him leave the dining hall.

Joseph lingered for half a minute, trying to get his emotions under control. He hadn't expected to be upset about leaving. If it wasn't for Odilon, he wouldn't be feeling anything but pure joy at this moment. At least he'd had a friend during his short stay.

He strolled out of the dining hall at a leisurely pace, getting one last look at it. No doubt Edgar would be here before lunch. Might as well go gather his things so he was ready. He headed up the turret stairs, popped out onto the fourth floor and stopped dead.

Brother Lachlan leaned against the wall leading into Joseph's room.

"Mr. Ward," the man said, standing up to his full height. "Why aren't you in class? I heard the bell ring not minutes ago."

Joseph made himself look the headmaster in the eyes. He reminded himself that this man wasn't in charge of him anymore.

"I'm packing up my stuff. My uncle will be here soon."

Whether Edgar would be here this morning or this evening, Joseph didn't really know. Regardless, he planned to wait outside until his uncle's car came through the gate. Then he would get in and wouldn't even crack a window until they were off the property.

"Don't talk nonsense, young man, or you'll discover my patience is a lot thinner than I let on."

Why the headmaster was trying to get a rise out of him on his last day, Joseph couldn't understand. If Brother Lachlan didn't like him, wouldn't it make more sense to just let him go in peace? He decided he didn't need anything out of his room after all. His stuff had all been confiscated back home and he really had nothing worth going back for in his room except perhaps the clothes he came here in.

"Actually, I've got everything I need." He turned and pulled the door open to the stairs.

Before he could get a foot over the threshold, a searing pain shot through his shoulder and he was stopped dead in his tracks. Lachlan's hand clamped down on him in an iron grip. He dragged Joseph backwards and shoved his back against the wall so hard that Joseph's head snapped back and cracked against it.

He cried out. In a flash, the headmaster's hand was over his mouth, pressing his head back into the wall.

"This attitude of yours is going to stop," Lachlan hissed. "You think you're above reproach? You think you get a pass out of here? That you don't have to pay for your crimes?"

"Let me go." Joseph struggled uselessly in the man's grip.

"I'll do no such thing, Mr. Ward." Lachlan threw him into the door to his room.

"I'm leaving!" Joseph shouted. "My uncle is on his way. I'll tell him what you did to me."

He squirmed out of the headmaster's grip and darted to the stairwell. He burst through the door and flew down the stairs, barely keeping himself upright, taking them two and three at a time. He stumbled through the door on the first floor and sped down the long hall that led to the foyer. Once out of the hall, he sprinted for the doors. And skidded to a halt.

Julius stood sentry in front of the exit, staring directly at him.

Joseph inched closer and a growl rose from within the

depths of the beast's chest. Julius lowered his head and bared his huge teeth.

"Good dog, Julius." Lachlan's voice came from behind him.

Joseph turned to find the headmaster coming down the main stairwell toward him. Obviously he'd taken his time coming around the other way, knowing the dog would stop Joseph.

"Mr. Ward," Lachlan said, "If you would please join me in the main office, we can sort this out." He gestured to a door Joseph had never been through, next to the main entrance.

Allowing himself to feel defeated only for the moment, Joseph stormed across the hall, through the door, which had the word OFFICE in block letters across its glass window. A young, pretty nun he'd never seen before smiled up at him from a desk immediately inside the door. Her smile faded as the headmaster stepped through the doors behind him. Lachlan nodded to her and led Joseph to an empty desk in the corner of the room.

"Is this phone connected, Sister Tina?" he asked of the receptionist.

"Yes, brother," came her reply in a quiet, mouse-like voice.

"Do you have your home phone number memorized, Mr. Ward?"

The fine hairs on the back of Joseph's neck prickled. Why would Lachlan want his home phone number? The only person there was his father *if* he'd been let out of jail. Joseph was going to live with his Uncle Edgar so there was no reason to be speaking to his father.

"Mr. Ward?"

"Yes."

Brother Lachlan smacked Joseph in the ear. It came so quickly that Joseph didn't even see his hand move. One second he was standing there fine as can be and the next, his head was snapped to one side and a stinging pain was shooting through his ear.

"Yes, *brother*," Lachlan said. "Dial."

Joseph picked up the receiver and, with a shaking finger, dialed his home phone number from memory. His finger shook as he held it over the holes for each digit, twisting the rotary and feeling his guts liquefy with every ratcheting spin.

There were three rings before the line was picked up on the other end.

"Yeah." His father already sounded drunk and it wasn't even lunchtime yet.

"Dad."

There was a long silence on the other end. His father sniffed and Joseph assumed that he at least had the man's attention. His story came out in a ramble. He told his father about what had happened, how Constable Dawson had called his uncle, that he was waiting for Edgar to pick him up and this mean guy Lachlan wouldn't let that happen. He begged his father to understand. To tell this guy to let him go.

Another long silence.

His father said, "S'okay Joseph. You belong there."

"What? No! I just told you, Uncle Edgar's coming to get me."

"I told him to stop."

Joseph almost screamed. "What? Stop what? Why would you do that?"

"Not your father," his father slurred.

For a brief second, Joseph's heart went out to the man. Of

course he was upset someone else was going to take his son from him.

His father went on and Joseph's sympathy for him evaporated.

"You're gonna stay there," his father mumbled. "They'll take better care of you. Better than I can. Don't need Edgar."

"No, dad. Please." Joseph clutched the phone receiver in both hands. "You can't leave me here. I'll come home. I don't need to go stay with Edgar. I'll live with you. I'll get a job."

"Shouldn't've snuck out."

The line clicked dead. Not even an *I love you*, not that the phrase was something Joseph had come to expect to hear from his father.

Brother Lachlan, who Joseph had almost forgotten was standing just behind him, plucked the receiver from his grip.

"That takes care of that, I suppose." The headmaster replaced the receiver and put a hand behind Joseph's back, ushering him out of the office.

On the way past the desk, Sister Tina gave Joseph a sympathetic half-smile. He hardly noticed. His vision had gone dark around the edges. For now he saw only his feet moving one in front of the other as he was piloted toward the door and out into the foyer of what had suddenly, cruelly become his new home.

The slamming of the office door behind him snapped Joseph out of his fugue enough to notice Brother Lachlan was saying something to him. He looked up at the man with a blank expression, not caring one way or the other what he had to say. Lachlan had somehow tricked his father into giving custody of his only son over to him. To this man who had proven to be crueler with every day that passed.

Brother Lachlan darted toward him with ghastly speed and grabbed him painfully by the shoulders. "I understand you're a little upset so I will grant you my last ounce of leeway. You are officially, fittingly enough, a ward of the state. Your father has signed court documents remanding you into the custody of St. Theodore's Academy. Into my custody. You will remain in my custody until you reach the age of adulthood which, if I am not mistaken, is eighteen years old."

The words closed around Joseph like a shackle. His head swam, guts roiled. This couldn't be reality. He was dreaming. He closed his eyes and willed himself to wake up. When he opened them, Lachlan was staring down at him with an amused half-smile showing through his beard. Five years. Joseph turned thirteen this summer which meant he was stuck here for *five years.* It wasn't possible. He refused to accept it. If this wasn't a dream then it was certainly a huge misunderstanding.

"Can I call my uncle?" he asked, trying not to sound upset and failing miserably.

"Telephone privileges are reserved for seniors on their best behavior. Sadly, you've got a couple of years before we can even consider such a thing."

Joseph opened his mouth to protest. Before he could even take a breath, Lachlan wound up and cuffed him, open-handed, across the mouth. He fell to the floor with the force of the slap. Bloody drool dripped from his mouth.

"I've about had it with your talking back, young man," Lachlan said, voice even, never rising a decibel. "You will return to your room until lunch. After that, I expect you will be in each and every class on time. Tardiness, disrespect, or any other sort of misbehavior will no longer be tolerated from you. You are not a guest in this institution. You belong to me. Clean up that blood and return to your room."

Having damned Joseph to spend the rest of his youth behind these walls, the headmaster marched off, no doubt to torment some other kid.

Joseph stared at the little pool of blood he'd left on the floor as Lachlan's footfalls disappeared down the hall. He swiped at it with his tie, caring not in the least how he would get the stain out. He remained there on his hands and knees for several minutes, staring at the smear he'd just made. He blinked and the smear was no longer his spit and blood—instead he stared at a familiar brown patch of puke. Up close he could see those red streaks laced throughout it. He could even smell the aroma coming off the mess. It carried a faint tinge of what his mother's breath smelled like when she'd forgotten to brush her teeth for a couple of days, which had happened more and more in the last year. It was a sick, sour smell—and he relished it. He squeezed his eyes shut and wished with every fibre of his being that she were here. He begged God to make this a dream and to let him wake up in bed at home in their apartment with his parents arguing in the other room. He opened his eyes and regarded the smear of his own spit and blood in the foyer of St. Theodore's Academy.

He swiped at the mess once more, but the blood was already drying. One of the dogs would get it. He made himself stand and return to what would be his room until he was eighteen. Unless he had something to say about it.

12

———

Joseph had half a mind to skip lunch. Almost did until he recalled Lachlan's words to him about being on time for every meal and class. The headmaster was no doubt capable of doing a lot more than just slapping around disobedient students and Joseph had no desire to see what the limits of the man's patience were. At the same time, he had no intention of staying here of his own free will. He felt like a caged animal slamming itself against the bars of its prison. As he stepped through the door into the turret staircase on the way to his room, he was struck by inspiration. There might be a way out of this place after all. He would need to check on something first. And maybe borrow a couple of things. He took the rest of the stairs two at a time, excited by the plan that formed in his mind.

Odilon's eyebrows raised when Joseph sat down next to him at lunch. He didn't seem surprised.

"I thought your uncle would be here by now. Are you expecting him soon?"

In spite of his escape plan lifting his spirits, Joseph's heart ached at being reminded that Edgar wouldn't be coming. If only Lachlan had let him call his uncle instead of his father, he might've been able to convince him to come get him anyway.

He took a big bite of his sandwich; spam and mustard.

Through his mouthful he said, "Looks like I'm going to be here a bit longer than I thought. Not by much though."

He told Odilon what had happened in the last few hours; finding out he wasn't going home, speaking to his dad, getting belted by Lachlan. Odilon looked the least surprised about this last bit, which only confirmed Joseph's suspicion that the head-master was capable of crueler things. Odilon didn't seem very concerned about any of what Joseph had to tell him, at least until it came to his escape plan.

"I can't let you do that," his friend said when he'd finished explaining.

"I don't need your permission."

"I could refuse to give you the things you need."

Joseph wanted to strangle him. "Don't be like that. Do you want to come with me? Is that what this is about?"

Odilon's eyes grew comically wide. "I know what will happen if we are caught, which you will be. I would never attempt such a foolish thing. I hope you change your mind, Joseph."

"Not gonna happen," Joseph said. "Will you help me?"

Odilon stared down at his plate. "Of course. But I am helping you only to get yourself hurt."

"Let me worry about that," Joseph said, cramming the last bite of his sandwich into his mouth. "Just bring that stuff to supper. I'll find out during outdoor time if I can use it."

Outdoor time for the juniors came immediately following lunch. During his first few days here, Joseph had spent his outdoor time sitting on the stairs with Odilon, chatting about their lives before St. Theodore's. Mostly it had been Joseph doing the talking. His friend had wanted to know about everything he'd been missing in the outside world. These conversations had mostly revolved around Joseph telling Odilon everything he could remember about *Return of the Jedi*. Odilon had seen the first two movies in the franchise during movie nights at St. Theodore's. He'd never been to the cinema, which Joseph found to be more criminal than anything else that had happened to the boy.

Today Joseph struck out on his own and walked the perimeter of the property. It was a nice day and he found himself actually enjoying the stroll. All manner of birds, many that he had never seen in the city, flitted through the trees, criss-crossing over the grass. Their songs overlapped with one another and it was some of the most beautiful music he had ever heard; so different from the engines and bustle of the city. He hadn't even allowed himself to notice until now how much better it smelled around here. The blend of trees gave the air a fresh, natural scent he wasn't used to. Many of them, like the birds, were foreign to him. He recognized a few maples and a bunch of Eastern hemlock but that was about it. He only knew the hemlock because they had just recently learned, in Ms. Hendrix's class, that it was Pennsylvania's state tree. He could almost start to enjoy himself out here if it wasn't for the prison school all these trees stood sentinel around.

Julius, who Joseph was convinced could read his thoughts, prowled along behind him. The dog kept a respectable distance but stayed on his tail the entire time. Joseph had the irrational fear that it would go back and tell Lachlan about what he'd been up to. He hoped it looked like nothing; he couldn't be sure who else was keeping an eye on him.

He walked around the building twice. During the second pass he pretended to admire the architecture, in case someone was in fact watching him. He paid especially close attention to the peaks of the turrets on either side and, when he'd passed by the turret on the boy's side, he spotted exactly what he was looking for. When he saw it, he became certain that someone looking at him would be able to figure out exactly what was going through his mind. He took a mental snapshot of the turret and continued on his path around the school until he was back at the front steps. He'd taken his time and by now the students had begun to trickle inside. Math was his next class and Joseph headed upstairs to grab his books, assessing the interior of the turret as he climbed the stairs.

Throughout Math class, Joseph found his attention drifting helplessly to his escape plan. If all went as he'd hoped, he would be out of this place before breakfast. The idea thrilled him and helped him forget about the morning's upsetting news. Though he'd never expected much from his father, the sense of betrayal he felt hurt more than anything else he'd gone through that day. Even his disappointment at finding out Edgar wouldn't be coming paled in comparison to the fact that his father had willingly given him up.

Did you do anything to help me in the police station? His father's voice spoke up in his mind, clear enough that Joseph caught himself looking around for him. *Did you vouch for me?*

Tell them to stop hitting me? Did you even speak to me? Why wouldn't I offload you? I'm free now.

The voice was right, of course. What kind of a son was he to have just walked away from his father in that situation? A good son would have stuck up for his dad, no matter how the man had treated him in the past.

The bell rang, snapping him out of the cyclone of guilt he'd caught himself in. He scooped up his books and followed the tide of students out the door and into the hall. Guilty feelings aside, there was no chance he would ever willingly go back to his father. If it meant dying on the street, he would do that before returning to the man who had left him to rot in this prison for the rest of his youth.

He stopped by his room where he quickly changed into his gym clothes, blue shorts and a plain white t-shirt, before heading to phys-ed. His guts roiled as he made his way down to the gymnasium. He needed something from the storage room to help with his plan for escape and hadn't yet figured out how he'd go about getting it.

They were playing basketball, which he was normally pretty good at. Today, with his mind on his escape plan, he frequently fumbled the ball and missed every shot he took. The phys-ed teacher, Brother Trenton, a slender, distracted man, called out half-hearted encouragement to him. Joseph barely noticed.

During the game he'd figured out how to get what he needed.

After class, the students filtered out of the gym while Brother Trenton held the door open for them. Joseph lingered so that he was one of the last out. While the other students bustled through the door, he slipped the necklace Odilon had given him off his neck and stuffed it into the waistband of his gym shorts. He stepped through the door, smacked his head with the palm of his hand, and spun around.

"Sorry, Brother Trenton," he said, walking back into the gym. "I took my necklace off and forgot it in the equipment room."

"That's a strange place to put your jewelry, isn't it?" Brother Trenton raised an eyebrow at Joseph.

"I didn't want anyone to take it." Joseph made himself look him in the eyes, hoping he came off as sincere.

The friar chuckled. "Fair enough. Next time give it to me to hold onto. You're just lucky there's not another class waiting to get in here."

And then Brother Trenton simply walked away.

Joseph darted back into the gym, directly to the small equipment room. For all the sneaking, he probably could have just waited until the teacher had gone. Better to be in here with permission than to be caught without it though.

It only took him a moment to spot what he needed. He concealed it as best he could under his clothes, offered up a silent prayer that no one would notice anything amiss, and left the gym. He had to force himself not to run back to his room—the last thing he wanted at this point was to draw any attention, especially from Brother Lachlan, who would no doubt be able to tell he was up to something. He just had to hope Odilon would come through with the things he'd asked him to get.

The hours until supper dragged. Joseph sat in his room, on his bed, too excited to do anything else. There was no guarantee his plan would work even if Odilon managed to get him what he needed. And if he did escape the school, there was still a whole forest to get through. Sure, a road ran through it but it would still be dark and he intended to stay in the trees in case anyone drove past. He had no idea how far the closest town was, or in which direction. He had nothing to carry water in and would have only what little food he would be able to sneak off his dinner plate. He wished he'd thought to save some of his lunch but he'd still been reeling from learning he was officially a prisoner here. For breaking into an unlocked church. It was silly and embarrassing and frustrating. Such a stupid little thing for such an insane idea. He was lucky they hadn't sent him to an asylum instead of this place.

He looked up at the clock for the hundredth time and saw that it was close enough to suppertime for him to start making his way downstairs. Finally.

Odilon looked miserable when Joseph took his seat at the table next to him.

"Don't worry, Odi," Joseph reassured him. "Nobody's gonna know you helped me."

"I am not worried for myself," Odilon whispered.

"Did you get what I need?"

His friend nodded.

"You left it where I told you?"

Another nod.

"You could come with me, you know."

"No, I can not," Odilon shot back. "This will not work and you will be caught. If I am caught with you the punishment will be more severe for both of us."

Joseph laughed. "That's stupid. Why would it be worse if you were with me? If anything, we'd split the punishment."

"You are a smart guy," Odilon said with a smirk, "But you can also be very thick."

"What's that supposed to mean?"

Odilon held his arms out. "Look at me. What do you see?"

"What? Because you're black you think they're gonna be harder on you? It's 1984, Odi. People aren't racist anymore. Especially not priests, even if they are mean."

"They are called friars," Odilon muttered. "And you are not as bright as I thought you were if you really believe that."

Neither boy spoke for several minutes. The chatter of voices and the clanking of silverware on ceramic was a white noise between them. Odilon picked at his food and snuck a slice of ham into his pocket. Joseph did the same with all of his meat and his dinner roll. The ham was warm and wet in his pocket. How did Odilon deal with that feeling every day, for the sake of feeding a dog? It was completely selfless, as were many of the things he did.

"Hey," Joseph nudged his friend. "You're right. I'm an idiot. I'm sorry. I guess I should put myself in other people's shoes sometimes."

Odilon gave him a half smile. "I don't think you would be able to walk very straight."

They finished their meals in comfortable silence and, as supper drew to an end, Joseph's heart ached. He'd said goodbye to Odilon once already today but it had become more difficult over the last few hours. They'd grown closer in that short span of time. Odilon had done so much for him in the brief time he'd spent here and all he'd done is give him grief.

He clapped Odilon on the back. "You're a good friend, Odi. I'm gonna miss you."

"You have more faith in your plan than I do. I will say goodbye but I don't think you will be leaving tonight. I hope you do but I have a bad feeling."

"Keep your bad feelings to yourself until I'm out of here. I need all the positive thoughts I can get."

They left the dining hall amid the crowd of students heading to their rooms or to the library. Joseph let his friend go on ahead; he needed to linger a bit so that he could pick up the stuff Odilon had left for him in relative privacy. He watched Odilon walk away and, once more, his heart ached. And then, with absolute certainty, he knew his plan wouldn't work. He would be caught and punished. He should call it off right now and try to enjoy the next five years in relative peace. Five years. Right. He shook those thoughts from his head and ambled down the hall toward the turret.

In the stairwell he glanced up the spiral staircase to ensure no one was coming down, then felt around underneath the landing until his hand touched a cloth bundle. He snatched it up, tucked it under his arm, and sprinted up the steps. He snuck a glance through the door at the top of the stairs; the coast was clear. He slipped out of the turret and into his room.

He had to wait until well after lights out before he could do anything else and thought it would be a good idea to rest up in the meantime. He was afraid to set his alarm clock in case he woke someone else up with it so he padded down the hall to the bathroom and drank from the tap until it felt like his tummy would explode. Now there was no way he'd be able to sleep for any longer than a couple of hours before having to get up to pee.

The water in his stomach sloshed as he waddled back to his room. He fell back onto his mattress and there was some relief as the water spread out in his tummy. He figured he would be too excited to sleep but the day had taken an emotional toll on him and he soon drifted off into a thin doze.

13

———

His first thought when he woke was that he'd overslept. He panicked and leapt out of bed so fast he almost wet himself. He squeezed his thighs together and glanced up at the clock; just after midnight. He'd slept a lot longer than he figured he'd be able to. He stole into the hallway, trying not to make a sound. No one else was around but that didn't mean there weren't friars or dogs patrolling.

Bladder emptied and back in his room, he pulled out Odilon's care package and the skipping rope he had snatched from the gymnasium supply closet. There had been a huge, hempen tug-of-war rope in there that he would have loved to have used but there was no way he could sneak it out; the thing was the size of a fire hose. The skipping rope, on the other hand, while not being as long or thick as the hemp rope, was easy enough to tie around his waist and conceal under his clothes.

He unraveled Odilon's things and laid out the spare belt and tie his friend had given him. Odilon had also torn what looked like his own bedsheet into strips and included it in the package. The thoughtfulness was touching. He wished his friend had been willing to come along with him, they would have stood a better chance together.

He spread out his own tie and belt and set to tying everything together, testing each knot to ensure it would hold. The sheets were thin so he doubled them up to prevent them from tearing. He made sure to put all of the strongest material at one end of his make-shift escape rope to keep it from breaking and dropping him several dozen feet, which seemed like the biggest risk with this plan.

Rope finished, he went over it, testing each knot once more. His grandfather had taught him half a dozen knots that he was confident tying and these ones held true. He took off his shirt and wrapped the rope around his torso and waist, spreading it out as much as possible. It wasn't far to the stairwell and he didn't anticipate running into anyone but there was no sense risking his plan at this point. Rope secured around his body, he pulled his shirt back on and glanced in the mirror. He couldn't help laughing at himself. It was obvious there was something underneath his shirt; it made him look like he had strange muscles all over his upper body. He tucked his shirt in and turned away from the mirror—time to focus.

He made it the few feet to the stairwell without running into anyone. Still, he moved as silently as he could, inching the door open slowly, wincing at each creak it issued.

In the stairwell he eased the door to the turret closed behind him and paused to listen. The wind whistled through whatever cracks and crevices existed in the structure of the tower and swirled up the stairs, like a physical presence rushing at him. The more he listened to the howl of the wind, the more human it sounded. Thoughts of ghosts and angry spirits flooded his imagination.

"Ghosts aren't real," he whispered to himself.

The howling disagreed but he didn't have time to be delayed by spectres, real or not. The thought bolstered his courage a bit and he turned his attention to the closed hatch above him. He had no doubt it would be sealed or barricaded from the inside; it didn't make sense to have such a place be accessible to students, assuming there was anything beyond the hatch. What if they'd simply filled the space in? If that was the case, his whole plan would be shot. The only way to find out was to try.

He hoisted himself up the short ladder leading to the hatch and grasped the handle. A jagged spider scurried off the door and into a nearby web, where it turned around to face Joseph, as though it was as curious as he was to see what existed beyond the small door.

He uttered a small prayer of hope, and twisted the handle. The latch turned easily, screeching as the tarnished metal scraped against itself. He shoved the door open and was immediately suffocated. Grey dust rained on him in a cloud, getting into his eyes and clogging his lungs. He fell from the ladder and landed on his back, coughing and struggling for air as the dust filled the hallway around him. He couldn't open the door to let air in, on the off chance someone was wandering the halls. The only way to escape the cloud of dust was up.

He pulled himself to his feet, hacking up the dust he'd inhaled, and spit out a mushy grey substance that looked a lot like cement. Holding his breath, he scrabbled up the ladder and pushed through the door, which slammed shut behind him, shaking the whole floor. All he could do is hope nobody heard. He was more concerned with clearing the dirt from his lungs, which he did gradually in great, hacking coughs. It was musty up here but at least the dust wasn't swirling around like it had been in the stairwell. Eventually it became easier to breathe.

Across what looked like an attic, a dim square of light came through a window. The starlight did little to illuminate the attic, only served as a beacon for him to walk toward. He shut his eyes to acclimate to the gloom and, when he opened them, could make out vague outlines of some of the things that had been stored up here—mostly boxes. He wished he'd thought to bring a flashlight, not that he knew where to get one.

He took a step toward the window, stumbled, fell hard onto the musty wood floor. As he pushed himself up, something hard shifted underneath one of his hands; a small glass bottle. He shook it, sniffed. The smell of whiskey was immediately familiar and brought memories of his father with such clarity that he feared the man might appear from out of the shadows at any second. The thought, however absurd, paralyzed him. He held his breath. Listened. Clutched the bottle to his chest like a talisman.

Of course there was no other sound from within the attic, least of all from his father. He eased his breath out and set the bottle down. He got to his feet and shuffled along the floor toward the window, careful not to trip again. One foot banged against a crate full of more bottles that rattled in the dark. With all the noise he was making, it would be a wonder if he got across the floor without attracting the attention of the entire faculty. Where had those bottles come from? They may simply have been put up here and forgotten long ago by one of the faculty. Or perhaps this had, at one time, been a place where brave students had come to sneak a drink or a smoke, or both.

He tugged at the window. It was stuck fast in its frame after what must have been years of neglect. He jiggled it and thumped on the edges with the heel of his hand until finally it shifted and allowed itself to be lifted open.

The cool night air on his skin invigorated him. The next part would be difficult and would likely be what got him killed. He unwound the makeshift rope from around his waist and peered around for something to fasten it to. On one side of the window was a large, iron eye bolted into the stone wall. It must have been part of some ancient pulley system used to pull supplies up into the turret. Maybe that was how the delinquents of yore had snuck the case of booze into the building.

He tied the strong end of the rope, his stolen skipping rope, into the ring and knotted it several times for good measure. After testing his weight against it, he tossed the rest of the rope out the window and prayed that no one was on the ground to see it come down. He wiped the sweat from his hands onto his pants, gripped the rope as tight as he could, and swung a leg out the window.

He'd never been bothered by heights before but his guts roiled as looked over the slant of the turret's roof, down the five story drop to the ground below. He rested with one foot in the attic and one out on the roof. He could break an arm or a leg or any combination of those things, not to mention the very real possibility of death. He didn't prefer death over spending any more time at St. Theodore's but the risk was well worth his freedom. Before he could talk himself out of it, he pulled his other leg out of the attic and onto the roof. He held the rope with both hands and leaned back out of the window like he'd seen Batman and Robin do so many times on TV. Except they were always climbing up a building. And the buildings were always flat, with friendly Gothamites sticking their heads out of the windows. This was a rounded, pointed tower with very few windows and no friendly people to speak of. Sweat formed in his palms. He'd better get a move on before they became slick with perspiration.

Facing the window, he inched backwards, feeling behind him with each step for the ledge of the roof. He stuck a toe into empty air and his resolve dwindled, heart leaping into his throat as though he'd just fallen the full five stories. He took a deep breath, lowered himself to his stomach, and slid backwards off the roof, gripping the rope hard enough to hurt.

As soon as he was over the edge, panic set it. He swung helplessly over a drop that looked more like a mile than five stories.

He spun one leg around the rope to give his arms a bit of support, using his other leg to pincer-grip the rope to alleviate a bit more weight, and his arms felt the relief right away. Hanging there, with his weight properly distributed, his courage came back to him. The mile-long drop turned back into a mere five stories. He shimmied down the rope, slowly at first, picking up speed the closer he got to the ground. When he was flush with the first floor windows, he let go and plummeted the rest of the way down, landing on the soft grass and rolling to break his fall. He made it! He'd just scaled down a building and had no one to brag to. All that remained was to escape the actual grounds.

He left the rope dangling from the turret and darted straight into the trees bordering the property. There must be a gap somewhere in the fence, even a section with a climbable tree close enough that he could scale it and simply drop over to the other side. Once more he wished he'd brought some sort of light with him. The trees blocked most of the starlight, making it almost pitch black out here. He had to walk with his hands in front of his face and only saw the steel fence reflecting what little light there was back at him when he was a few feet from it. It was much taller than he remembered.

He grabbed a section of the fence and shook it. It was solid, like it had been newly installed. If the rest of it was as strong as this section, he would definitely need to find a way of going over rather than under or through. Keeping one hand on the fence and shaking it every few feet, he trudged toward the rear of the school.

He was somewhere behind the school when he heard the crashing in the trees behind him. Or was it off to the side? It was impossible to tell. One second, the only sounds were his footsteps and the rattling of the chainlink against its posts as he shook it. The next, a crashing and cracking of branches sped toward him. He had no idea where it came from, only that it was getting closer.

Then he saw the light bobbing around in the trees, from the direction of the school. Someone was out here! The crashing came again; a lot closer this time. By the time he heard the snarling it was too late to do anything.

The dog, Julius of course, burst through the trees, eyes glistening in the moonlight. There wasn't even a warning bark before the beast lunged at him and latched onto one of his legs, teeth digging into his ankle. Julius yanked him back and he crashed to the ground, landing on something sharp that dug into his back. The dog shook his leg back and forth.

And then they were both bathed in light.

"He's here!"

It was a familiar voice that shouted. Not a teacher. This was the voice of someone much younger.

Joseph kicked out at the dog with his free foot, doing little more than angering it. He grabbed hold of a nearby tree and tried to pull himself away.

The light was directly in his eyes, blinding him. Something struck one of his hands as it grasped the tree. It hit him so hard that Joseph forgot all about the dog, who only seemed to be holding him in place. Blinding pain as that same something smashed into his face. Joseph rolled onto his back, shielding himself with his arms. He was struck in ribs and coughed out a painful whoosh of air. His chest was suddenly tight and he couldn't breathe, a heavy weight pressing down on him.

"Ward, you piece of shit." Daniel Avery shone the light up into his own face.

He was the weight on Joseph's chest. He'd been the one attacking him. How had the older boy gotten out of the house and managed to command Julius? He bounced on Joseph's chest, squeezing out whatever air he'd managed to suck in. He slapped Joseph.

"Where did you think you were going?"

Another slap.

"Answer me."

Slap.

"I can't believe you actually climbed down that tower. You ever hear of a front door?"

Slap.

Joseph could only wheeze. Daniel finally lifted some of the pressure from his chest. Joseph gasped for air at the same time Daniel pointed the light at his mouth. The beam glistened in the golf-ball-sized gob of phlegmy spit the older boy let hang from his mouth. It happened in the space of a fraction of a second but Joseph got a good look at the viscous loogie right before it plopped into the back of his throat. It hit his mouth just as he inhaled. The spit filled his entire mouth and throat at once. It was like a bag was held over his head—the air was just cut off. He gagged and retched, writhing underneath the weight of his tormentor. Daniel bounced on him, the one bit of mercy Joseph would receive that night; the older boy's weight worked like the Heimlich and forced the loogie out of his throat. He turned his head to the side and spewed.

Daniel bounced harder, apparently trying to make him puke again, slapping Joseph with each bounce. He stopped abruptly and punched Joseph square in the mouth.

The pain was bad but, worse, Joseph was certain all of his teeth had been smashed in. His tongue ran over them instinctively, to make sure there were all there. It was bad timing. The next punch smashed his tongue into them. Joseph screamed and threw up his arms again, seeming to only remember now that they were there. He was dimly aware that Julius still held onto his pant leg.

Another punch to the side of his head. Then another. He felt the last one a lot less. Another may have followed it but he didn't notice. He was too focused on the second beam of light that had joined them.

"Thank you, Mr. Avery," Brother Lachlan said.

How many times he was struck again, Joseph couldn't have said. Darkness was all he knew after hearing the headmaster's voice. Darkness and defeat.

14

———

He woke an unknowable time later in his bed at St. Theodore's. Sunlight shone into his face, which meant it was still fairly early in the morning. He tried to get up and pain lanced through his ribs, forcing him to lie back down. This awoke him to the rest of what his body was feeling from his adventure the night before. His head throbbed, one shoulder hurt, and his legs felt bruised. He opened his mouth and winced at the pain from even that small movement. His tongue hurt where it had been punched into his teeth, his upper lip swollen. He looked down at himself, sprawled on top of his sheets. He was filthy and one of his pant legs was in tatters, the flesh underneath miraculously unscathed.

"Julius is quite disciplined when it comes to how much pressure he applies with those teeth of his." Brother Lachlan's voice came from right beside him.

Joseph turned to find the headmaster sitting in the desk chair, pulled into the corner of the room. He sat there with one leg crossed over the other, polishing his spectacles with his cassock—dark eyes, unfiltered, boring holes into Joseph's soul.

"Unfortunately," Lachlan went on, "Mr. Avery is less refined in his approach. You'll be in a good deal of pain for a few days, I imagine. Sister Nina had a look at you and assures us you've suffered no broken bones or lasting injuries."

Joseph pushed himself up to a sitting position, in spite of the pain it caused him. He couldn't bear to be laying down, vulnerable, while this man occupied his room. He'd come to see Brother Lachlan as more than just a mean-spirited head-master. He was dangerous. There was something in the way he looked at Joseph, a half-smirk that lingered under the thick tangle of his beard, the way he appeared to enjoy watching children suffer. At first Joseph had likened Lachlan to his father; mean and angry. He was beginning to see the only thing the two men had in common was the mean streak. Lachlan rarely showed anger, was always in control. He truly enjoyed punishment. He'd loved watching Joseph call his father only to find out he'd been abandoned to this prison. Joseph thought of Rat-tail freaking out on the bus on the way up here. It seemed that things could happen within these walls that stayed with a person for life. And he was stuck here.

Lachlan stood. "I don't imagine I need to tell you that what you did is wrong. You knew that from the start. I'd be lying if I said I was surprised you tried to get out of here. Many boys, even a few girls, do attempt to flee during their first few weeks with us. They are, as you've probably learned, swiftly discour-aged from indulging that urge. No child has escaped my watch, Mr. Ward."

Lachlan lowered himself onto the edge of the bed, folded his hands in his lap, and stared at Joseph.

Joseph pressed himself back into the headboard, wanting to be as far from the man as possible. It took every ounce of his will to keep looking him in the eye.

"I think we can agree that what Mr. Avery did to you is punishment enough," Lachlan said. "He was much more thorough than I would have been for a first escape attempt."

Relief flooded through Joseph. For a moment he forgot the pain he was in. Physical pain was something he was used to dealing with.

The headmaster stood once more and strode to the door. "You have time to make it to breakfast, Mr. Ward. I'd recommend being on time to avoid any further trouble."

With that, Brother Lachlan was gone.

Joseph looked up at the clock and saw he had less than ten minutes to get to breakfast. He changed his clothes as quickly as he could, in spite of the pain it caused, and hustled to the dining hall.

Odilon was not in his usual spot when Joseph arrived. When breakfast was served and still his friend hadn't shown up, he grew concerned. Odilon was early for every meal and, as far as Joseph knew, for every class. He ate and hoped his friend hadn't done anything stupid. What if he'd changed his mind about joining Joseph? What if he'd escaped and made it past Lachlan and his attack-boy? Odilon could be out there at this very moment, looking for him in the woods. As unlikely as it was, Joseph found himself worrying about his friend dying of starvation all through breakfast.

When the meal was over, Brother Lachlan took the podium. The room fell silent the instant he stepped up to it.

Joseph gave the man his attention, knowing he would be singled out and punished if he did not. When he looked up to the front of the room, where the podium stood, his guts took a nosedive. Standing behind Lachlan, head down and hands folded in front of him, was Odilon. The back of Joseph's neck tingled.

"Last night," Brother Lachlan's voice boomed across the room, "We almost lost one of our own. If he had been successful in his escape attempt, he surely would have perished from lack of nourishment, wandering around in the woods."

The room filled with murmurs, which Lachlan allowed for a moment. Clearly he relished the drama he was creating.

He raised a hand and the room once again went silent.

"The Lord gives us family and friends to look out for and so they may look out for us. Therefore it is our obligation to watch out for each other. To be our brother's keepers. If we allow one of our own to step into harm's way, are we not culpable in their demise? Do we not shoulder the burden of a loved one who we've allowed to turn to crime or addiction?" He surveyed the room, finally making eye contact with Joseph.

Joseph felt nauseous. He knew what was coming. It was entirely his own fault and there was nothing he could do to stop it.

Lachlan reached a hand back and yanked Odilon forward. He threw the boy into the nearest table, prompting the kids sitting there to shove back from it.

"Pants, Mr. Mercier."

Odilon, eyes still cast downward, lowered his pants and bent over the table.

Brother Casper appeared from behind the headmaster and handed him the switch that Joseph was already all too familiar with.

"Mr. Ward," Lachlan said, "Please pay close attention. I hope you will understand now that your actions beget consequences that impact those around you. Perhaps going forward your outlook will not be so self-centered."

He wound up and cut the switch through the air so fast that the whoosh it made was as loud as the smack of the impact. Joseph shut his eyes. Odilon didn't make a sound.

"Mr. Ward, if you are not watching, the exercise is meaningless," Lachlan said. "We'll start again."

Joseph opened his eyes and forced himself to look.

Odilon's eyes remained impassive. His mouth twitched only in the slightest each time he was struck. It went on forever. Joseph hadn't been counting but he was positive his friend must have endured at least a dozen stripes at the hand of the headmaster.

The room was silent enough that Brother Lachlan's heavy breathing could be heard all throughout it as finally he threw the switch down on the table next to Odilon. The headmaster leaned over and muttered something to him. Odilon yanked his pants up and scurried out of the room, avoiding everyone's gaze.

Joseph worried about his friend all morning. He kicked himself for having caught him up in the whole mess. The one person who cared about him at all in this place and he'd managed to get him whipped. His guilt made the minutes drag.

A couple of kids whispered to each other as he walked past or as he entered a classroom but nobody appeared that impressed or surprised by Joseph's actions last night. Apparently escape attempts were just as commonplace as Lachlan made them out to be. Why hadn't they sealed off that fifth floor before last night then? Obviously no one had tried to scale the tower from five stories up. This gave Joseph a small sense of pride. He had to admit to himself that it was a ballsy thing to have attempted. He spent the morning reliving the climb down the tower and imagining where he might be right now if he'd managed to escape. In his daydreams, Odilon was at his side. They were like Tom Sawyer and Huck Finn.

When finally lunchtime rolled around, Joseph came down to the dining hall to find Odilon sitting in his usual place at their table. He sat with his head down, staring at his fingers. He didn't look up when Joseph took his seat.

"How's your butt?" Joseph asked.

He was still very sore from his beating at the feet and hands of Daniel Avery and lowered himself gingerly. His torso was covered in bruises from being kicked around. Each one of them screamed out for attention anytime he sat.

"I told you not to do it," Odilon said, eyes still on his hands.

"Sorry, Odi. I had to try though. I shouldn't be here. Neither should you."

"Where I am supposed to be is not for you to decide," Odilon snapped. "You only thought of yourself and I paid the price for it."

"Hey, I got beat too," Joseph said, aggravated that his friend wanted to turn this against him and all the more frustrated knowing the other boy was right.

Odilon slammed a palm on the table. The other kids around it, who normally ignored the two of them, went quiet for a second before returning to their chatter.

"It's never just a beating." Odilon's voice shook.

"Okay, geez." Joseph threw his hands up in defeat. "Sorry for wanting my freedom."

"You should think about the cost of the things you want." Odilon shoved up from the table and stormed out of the dining hall.

He was right, of course. What was Joseph supposed to do though? Rot here and take the abuse? Allow himself to be wrongfully imprisoned for the rest of his childhood? He wanted to be angry with his friend, to hate Odilon for making him feel this way. Bitter shame filled his heart instead.

One of the other kids at their table, a dark-haired boy whose name Joseph was pretty sure was either Eric or Aaron, nudged him on the arm.

"Hey, Alcatraz."

Joseph looked up. All the other boys at the table were looking at him. Probably they wanted to pick his brain about how he managed to get out.

"I think you're the first escape attempt to not even make it past the fence." Eric or Aaron snickered. "You know they keep the front door unlocked, right?"

He and the rest of the kids at the table burst into laughter.

15

———

THE NEXT COUPLE OF MONTHS PASSED IN A BLUR. JOSEPH kept his head down, careful to avoid drawing unnecessary attention to himself, especially from Brother Lachlan. He was cautious with his grades so that he never dipped below or rose above the class average, an easy enough trick for him since he'd been doing the same thing back at what he still thought of as his actual school.

Though St. Theodore's operated year-round, classes came to a close at the end of June. Over the summer months, students would spend their days either in quiet reflection or completing chores around the manor. Joseph signed up for as many outdoor duties as possible, mainly to avoid being tasked with anything too revolting within the school. Odilon was frequently assigned bathroom duty and he wanted no part of that. Joseph relished each opportunity to spend time outside of the musty halls of the school—it was no doubt the closest to freedom that he would get.

His main task was brushwood removal, a job he was

delighted to have been assigned to do on his own. He started with the lawn around the school. When that was clear, he moved to the edge of the tree line and, before long, he was working in the thick of the trees, clearing out loose branches and debris.

He no longer entertained illusions of being able to escape. Between the dogs, the barbed-wire fence surrounding the property, and the constant patrol of the faculty, he knew it was impossible. It almost felt like freedom though, being in the shade of the trees, out of sight of the school even if for only a short time. Having grown up in the city, there wasn't much opportunity to explore wooded areas and he found the property surrounding the school to be almost magical. He took joy in the solitude of the task, marching by himself through the trees and picking up errant sticks and branches to be added to the burn pile. Students never got to participate in the weekly burn but Joseph enjoyed building the pyre and would watch from a barred window as one of the faculty, usually Brother Calvin, lit the whole mess on fire.

Then the storm came, bringing harsh change and all manner of trouble.

It was the first day of August and the heat and humidity had reached almost unbearable heights. Joseph came in from gathering brush that day with his clothes soaking wet, sweat dripping from his brow and beading his skin, which had developed a deep tan from all the time spent outdoors. By the time he'd showered and marched downstairs for supper, the sky had gone nearly black with thunderheads. Wind howled through the halls, especially loud in the turreted staircase. Through the windows he watched as the great evergreens surrounding the property bowed back and forth in the wind like zealous worshippers of some great, outraged god in the clouds.

The heavens broke as the students ate supper. Rain came so fast and sudden that, when the immediate cacophony of raindrops hammered on the roof and walls, several of them screamed and jumped in their seats. The wind picked up with the rain and branches flew off trees, striking the school and adding to the percussion of the storm. Thunder boomed and shook the foundation. More than one student was reduced to tears before the lightning started. When it did start, flashes came in blue explosions that lit up the school. Power went out during dessert and students were escorted back to their rooms by brothers and sisters brandishing oil lanterns kept at the ready for such occasions.

In Joseph's bedroom, wind shrieked through the night, making sleep difficult. But the storm invigorated him. The squalling was like the music of some colossal woodwind instrument. He hoped and prayed that one of the big trees would be blown through the wall of his room. He imagined climbing down the trunk of such a tree while rain pelted him and lightning flashed around him. He imagined running through the forest and coming across a place in the fence that had been toppled by another one of the trees, which were working together to help him escape. It was indulging in this fantasy that finally put him to sleep in the wee hours of the morning.

16

———

Joseph came down to breakfast the next morning feeling groggy and desperate for a boost. Thanks to the storm, he'd had little more than three hours sleep. He helped himself to two cups of coffee over breakfast, loading both with extra sugar and ignoring Odilon's raised eyebrows. He'd never been one to drink the stuff at home, never would have been allowed if he'd wanted to. St. Theodore's was bringing out a different side of him, forcing him to grow up faster than any child should.

Sunlight shone through the dining hall windows, for which he was grateful. A nice day would make his chores that much more enjoyable. There would no doubt be lots to keep him busy outside for days to come after a storm like the one they'd just had. It would be muddy but the sun would dry things up soon enough.

Before they were dismissed from breakfast, Brother Lachlan took the podium at the head of the room and announced that all but the most essential cleaning chores would be postponed so that extra help could be given to cleaning up the property surrounding the school.

Joseph slumped in his seat.

"Aren't you happy to have help?" Odilon asked, folding his bacon into a napkin and shoving it in his pocket.

Joseph shrugged. "I liked having the property to myself. Now it'll be so crowded out there I'll hardly have anything to do."

"At least I won't be in your way," Odilon said, clapping him on the shoulder. "I am on bathroom duty again."

"I'd rather you were outside. At least I'd have someone to talk to."

"Maybe you'll get the chance to speak to Blue."

At the mention of her, a frenzy of butterflies took flight in Joseph's stomach. *Blue* wasn't actually the girl's name, but, since neither of them knew what it was, they'd adopted the nickname based on the color of the ribbon she wore in her bouncy, dark blonde hair. Joseph had first noticed her during his second week at the institution. She sat facing them, across the dining hall, and was always smiling, in spite of her imprisonment. Joseph assumed that things were a little less intense in the girl's wing but still couldn't imagine anyone being happy here all the time. He'd watched her every day without bothering to hide it until, during supper a few weeks ago, the girl sitting next to Blue nudged her while he was staring. Blue had looked up from her plate and made direct eye contact with him. She'd smiled and then quickly put her face down when one of the sisters drifted past her table. He had not allowed himself to get caught looking at her since. But she *had* smiled.

"Are you crazy?" Joseph felt himself blush. "She doesn't even know who I am. And, in case you've forgotten where we are, I wouldn't be allowed to talk to her for more than a minute without us being yanked apart."

Odilon leaned close and murmured in his ear, "But it would be a minute with her."

Joseph laughed and shoved his friend off him. Odilon was right though. Even a minute with her would be worth it. But what would he say to her? In a minute he could learn her name. And then what? Tell her he'd been watching her from across the dining hall since he got here? What was she even doing at St. Theodore's? She didn't look like the kind of girl who would get into trouble with the law. Maybe she was a case like Odilon or himself; misunderstood or caught fending for herself.

Odilon slapped him on the back and said, "I'm off to get my chores done so I have some time to read before lunch. Good luck, Joseph."

He pushed up from the table and strolled out of the dining hall, arms swinging at his side, looking like he had not a care in the world. Joseph wished he could share his friend's attitude. Odilon was always in a good mood, even when things weren't going his way, which was often. Joseph had asked him about it months ago.

"God provides for me," Odilon had told him with a big smile. "Why would I not be happy?"

"Because," Joseph had offered, "You're stuck in a prison disguised as a school. One that's run by abusive friars and psycho nuns."

Odilon had put a hand on Joseph's shoulder and said, "I have a bed to sleep in, a roof to keep me dry, and more food than I need to survive. I am blessed."

Joseph had wanted to argue with him, to point out that the

price to pay for those things was, at best, his freedom. He wanted Odilon to be as angry with being here as he was. In some ways though, he understood where his friend was coming from. Odilon did, after all, live on the streets before coming here. He'd shared stories with Joseph about it, but tended to gloss over or leave out the really bad parts. He rarely spoke about having to find an inconspicuous place to take a dump when no one would let him use their bathroom, or about the days that could go by without a single scrap of food, or about drinking out of gutters or almost dying of a common cold or having to clean out rat bites while hoping he hadn't picked up some exotic disease. Joseph decided that, if Odilon was happy here, he wouldn't be the one to take that away from him.

In total about twenty students wound up being assigned to outdoor cleanup. They were split into teams and assigned different zones on the property. Joseph, who had been used to working at his own pace, in whichever area he deemed most appropriate, was not impressed. It was bad enough being told where he had to work, he was also stuck working with people who would only get in his way.

The students stood facing the stairs of the manor as a tanned, thirty-something man, Brother James, presided over them from the top step and broke them into teams. As far as Joseph could tell, he was the nicest of the friars.

Joseph stared at his feet as the teams were made, looking up only when Brother James said his name and assigned him his zone. He and his team were to tackle the wooded areas and the rear of the property. He started off toward the back of the school without bothering to wait for anyone else on his team, or even to check and see who they might be. He could do this on his own, had been doing as much up until now, and didn't need an entire team to help him. His plan was to keep his head down and do the job as though he was working alone. He was sure the other kids would be more interested in goofing off anyway, which was fine with him as long as they left him alone.

The whole property was a mess of leaves, pine needles, branches from various trees, and garbage that had been blown from the trash bins. Joseph couldn't help but feel slighted by the destruction the storm had caused after he'd spent the entire summer making these grounds pristine. One night of wind and rain had undone all of his hard work. He kicked branches and debris out of his path as he made his way across the back yard and into the trees that bordered it. He had just stepped into the woods when someone shouted for him to wait up. That voice. Upon hearing it, his frustration evaporated.

Blue.

She walked toward him with another girl and two boys. She smiled at him and Joseph felt his ears catch fire and his jaw lock up. He had no idea what to do. Hadn't even considered that he might be paired up with her. He searched for something cool to say.

"So," Blue said, "What do we do?"

"Uh, trees the clean up. I mean—pick up tree branches," Joseph stammered.

He hated himself in that moment. He couldn't make his brain work with his mouth to say anything remotely smooth. Or coherent.

"I'm Taylor," one of the two other boys said.

Taylor looked younger than Joseph, a small kid with longish, cornsilk hair and skin so pale it was almost translucent. Joseph felt bad the boy had been sent out here for work that was obviously out of his comfort zone. His own frustration, having lessened at seeing Blue, disappeared entirely. He had to remember he loved this work while all these other kids probably hated that they had been sent out here.

Everyone else introduced themselves. The other boy was Connor. He was fifteen and stood with his arms crossed and his bottom lip stuck out, looking like he wanted to be out here even less than Taylor. Yuna was Japanese, and spoke only broken English. She was thirteen and looked as happy to be out here as Connor did.

"I'm Caroline," Blue said.

Except, of course, her name wasn't Blue. And now that Joseph knew her name, she was even more beautiful than before. Caroline. He hadn't yet spoken it out loud but he imagined it would just roll off his tongue.

It turned out Caroline was the same age as him. And she was eager to pull her weight, which made Joseph like her all the more.

He realized they were all looking at him. Had he been staring at her? Had they noticed? If he wasn't blushing before, now he felt his cheeks tingle as blood filled them. It was getting to be a familiar feeling.

"What now?" Connor asked.

Joseph had no idea what to say. Was he talking about Caroline? The other boy must have read the confusion in Joseph's face.

"You're the only one who's worked out here," Connor explained. "What's up?"

Joseph was baffled. He'd never led anyone in any sort of activity before. Connor was fifteen. If anyone was going to take the lead, Joseph had assumed it would be him.

"Um, okay," he tried, "Why don't we start at the fringes and make a pile just outside the tree line, on the grass here." He indicated a spot at his feet. "Basically just grab handfuls of branches and stick them in a pile. Try to keep them straight so we can bundle them easily."

And just like that they were working as a team, with Joseph as their foreman. He took charge of bundling the sticks in twine since he'd been doing it for over a month already and had become pretty good at tying them into tight, easy-to-carry stacks. The other kids worked efficiently, keeping up to him, and managing to clear out an impressive area within the first hour. Joseph supervised, helped break down larger branches, bundled sticks, and watched Caroline as she picked her way through the trees collecting debris.

It was while he was watching her that he sliced his hand open. He'd been tying together a pile of sticks, wrapping them tight with twine, and staring at Caroline's profile as she worked. She constantly had a little smile across her lips and Joseph thought it was the prettiest thing he'd ever seen. He was staring at her mouth and thinking about making her laugh when his hand slipped and the jagged end of a dry branch sliced a deep, ragged cut through his palm. In an instant his hand, and the woodpile, were soaked in blood. He gritted his teeth and hissed air through them, refusing to allow himself to cry in front of his crush.

"Oh no!" Yuna screamed.

The rest of the group looked his way. Taylor somehow grew even whiter. He swooned and Caroline caught him by the shoulders. She gaped at Joseph's hand in horror.

"You guys keep going," he said as he wrapped his wound in

the handkerchief that was a part of everyone's uniform. "I think I have to go see Sister Nina."

"Will you be okay?" Caroline asked, still holding Taylor by the shoulders.

"It looks worse than it is," Joseph said, hoping he sounded tougher than he felt.

In the infirmary, Sister Nina chided him for not being more careful. She doused his hand with iodine and it took every ounce of his willpower not to scream in agony. The stick had cut a jagged slash in his hand that continued to bleed, so Sister Nina placed a strip of gauze in the cut and wrapped his hand tightly in a cloth bandage.

"We'll need to change this a couple times a day for the next few days or so," she said as she pinned the bandage in place. "And you'll be staying indoors the rest of the day. You don't need an infection setting in."

Joseph flexed his hand and winced. "I could go out there just to provide moral support. I won't lift anything. Promise."

He was thinking of Caroline and the time he was missing out on spending with her. This might be the only chance they'd have to get to know one another. What if Connor was out there, trying to horn in on her with his fifteen-year-old muscles? The notion made the butterflies in his stomach turn into hornets.

"Nonsense," Sister Nina said, "You'll go straight to your room until it's time for lunch, after which you will come right back here to have your bandage changed. Is that understood?"

"Yes, sister," he muttered.

"Off with ye then."

She shoed him out and he meandered his way to the main hall, inspecting the bandage wound around his hand. He considered sneaking back outside. Nobody would know Sister Nina had told him to stay indoors. He was about to try it when Julius sauntered into the hall and sat directly in front of the main doors, as if the beast had known exactly what was in Joseph's mind. The dog stared at him, mouth closed.

"You're a scary dog," Joseph said.

Part of him expected Julius to growl in response but the dog only continued to watch him, not seeming to care what he said or did as long as he didn't try to get through the doors. Joseph wasn't even sure that the dog would try to stop him if he did try to go outside, but he didn't want to come anywhere close to finding out. Instead he changed direction and marched down the hall leading into the boy's wing.

As he shoved the door open from the turret into the fourth floor hallway, he heard a whimper and then a cry come from around the corner at the end of the hall. He eased the door shut and heard the low murmur of a man's voice followed by what was very obviously a slap and then another cry.

"I said English!" the voice commanded.

Joseph recognized the voice as that of Brother Lachlan and the skin on the back of his neck crawled. He hurried toward his room, eager to get inside without the headmaster noticing that he was up here.

"I'm sorry brother! I am trying, I promise you."

Joseph stopped partway through his door. That was Odilon's voice. He sounded like he was upset or in pain or both. If what Joseph heard was indeed the sound of his friend being slapped around, he had no doubt he was also crying in fear.

Brother Lachlan muttered something again, which Odilon replied to in a murmur of his own.

Joseph almost went into his room and closed the door the rest of the way. He was stepping his other foot over the threshold when the next slap came, followed by a pummeling, thumping sound. Odilon cried in obvious pain. Joseph left his door open and crept up the hallway.

Peering around the corner, he could only see Brother Lachlan's back; a tall, black robe. Lachlan had his head bent, making the cassock look like a black, headless ghost.

"Say it again," Lachlan hissed.

A whimper.

"So I can hear you."

Odilon spoke slowly. "I am sorry, brother. I will continue to work on my English."

His words came out sounding muddled and strange. It took Joseph a second to realize his friend was trying to speak without an accent.

Brother Lachlan was obviously not sold on his progress. He delivered a swift kick and, though Odilon was obscured from view by the man, Joseph could tell the boot connected. He heard air *whoof* out of the boy's lungs with the impact. Odilon was weeping and trying to catch his breath at the same time. The sound was horrible. Outrage washed away Joseph's sense of self-preservation. He didn't even realize he was moving until he stepped around the corner.

"Leave him alone," he said with as much authority as he could muster, shamefully aware he still sounded like a child.

Brother Lachlan straightened and spun around. Joseph caught a glimpse of Odilon curled up on the floor just beyond him.

Lachlan's eyes narrowed at Joseph. He stepped to the side, allowing him a clear view of his friend.

Odilon's face was smeared in blood and tears. He lay on his side, sobs spraying a mixture of bloody spit onto the floor.

"You can't hit him like that," Joseph said, his voice shaking as his resolve began to melt. "It's against the law."

Brother Lachlan was a blur of black cloth. In an instant he had Joseph by the back of the neck and was pressing his face into the burnt-orange surface of the wall. Lachlan bent Joseph's arm around his back, grabbing his bandaged hand and digging his thumb into the fresh wound.

Joseph screamed at the top of his lungs. His vision dimmed with the pain in his head and hand. He writhed in Lachlan's grip but the man was too strong and he could hardly budge.

The headmaster brought his head alongside Joseph's, breath hot on the side of his face.

"I own you," he whispered. "You are my property and I will do exactly as I please with you."

He strode back toward Odilon, dragging Joseph's face along the wall as he did, the friction of the rough wallpaper burning against his cheek and ear.

Lachlan kicked the prone boy. "Back to your room. Work on your accent. If I can't whip the black out of you, I swear by God that I'll beat you blue until you speak proper English."

Odilon pulled himself up, using the wall to hold himself steady. He stared at Joseph through blurry eyes, one of which was half-closed with swelling.

"Joseph."

The moment the word was out of Odilon's mouth, Lachlan swung a fist around, striking him in the side of his head. Odilon's face smacked off the wall and he yelped, a high-pitch sound that made Joseph's heart hurt.

"Now or you won't eat for a month," Lachlan said.

The two of them stared at one another for a full ten seconds before Odilon limped off in the other direction, steadying himself with one hand on the wall.

Brother Lachlan shoved Joseph up the hall. Joseph stumbled and just barely managed to keep himself from going down.

"March," the headmaster barked from behind him. "You and I are going to have a long discussion in my office about expectations."

"I'm sorry, Brother," Joseph said, more in desperation than remorse.

Lachlan kicked him in the backside, the toe of his foot landing squarely between Joseph's buttocks. The pain was excruciating and he crumbled to the floor. He would have stayed there if Lachlan hadn't yanked him to his feet by the sleeve of his uniform. The fabric ripped as Joseph regained his footing, a huge tear running down the side of his shirt from his armpit. As soon as he was standing, Lachlan delivered another swift kick, not nearly as hard as the last but Joseph caught the point.

Lachlan herded him down the hallway and Joseph prayed silently that someone would see them and intervene. He didn't even want to know what the inside of the headmaster's office looked like, let alone spend any amount of time in there.

As they approached the double doors of Lachlan's combined office and quarters, the man grabbed a handful of Joseph's hair and yanked him to a stop. He produced a huge ring of keys from somewhere in his cassock and inserted the largest of the bunch into the brass lock in the door.

"Welcome," he said as he nudged the door open, "To my home."

17

JOSEPH STARED THROUGH THE DOOR, UNMOVING. BROTHER Lachlan gave him a shove and he stumbled over the threshold.

The headmaster's office was enormous. A huge oak desk took up one end. Behind it were rows of books on shelves built into the walls. The books bore titles from the likes of *Post-Secondary Administration* to *Understanding the Old Testament*. The desk was empty save for a leather blotter that covered most of it, an actual feather quill, and a small in-box. A large wingback chair occupied the space between the desk and the shelves. Along the far wall rested a modest couch with a low coffee table in front of it. To Joseph's right was an armoire and, next to that, a smaller cabinet. At the end of the office was another set of double doors which Joseph presumed led into Lachlan's sleeping quarters. The office was sparsely decorated with some sort of potted tree bearing long leaves in one corner and, above the couch, a framed painting of what looked like a farm nestled in a green valley.

"Sit," the headmaster said, shoving Joseph toward the couch.

Joseph stumbled again, narrowly avoiding tripping on the coffee table. He lowered himself onto the couch and was surprised by how comfortable it was, especially given that his backside was still in a good deal of pain from the kick he had received earlier.

Brother Lachlan pushed the door closed and turned the deadbolt. It clicked into place with a heavy *thunk*. He glided across the room to the cabinet next to the armoire, looking like a bearded and bespectacled Nosferatu in his dark robes, and pulled open the doors to reveal a collection of bottles that would have been at home in Joseph's father's liquor cupboard. These looked a good deal fancier. Lachlan took his time selecting a bottle, plucked a glass from one of the shelves, and poured himself a small portion of amber liquid. He brought the glass to his nose and waved it underneath his nostrils, closing his eyes as he did so. He drained it in one swallow and immediately poured himself another.

He turned to Joseph and said, "You'll soon learn that there are very few things in life that can not be cured by an exceptional whiskey."

"I'll never drink alcohol," Joseph said in a small voice.

Lachlan laughed. "Of course you believe that now. Any child with an alcoholic parent will make such a claim. Do you know what each of those children all have in common?"

Joseph said nothing.

"They all turn out to be just like mommy or daddy. Or perhaps both. Your mother had her own special indulgence, didn't she?"

The mention of his mother sparked something in Joseph,

an anger that felt unfamiliar and all consuming; worse even than what he had felt toward his father on the night she had died. He realized he was grinding his teeth together and forced himself to relax his jaw. Lachlan watched him carefully but Joseph refused to give him anything to go on, he knew the man was trying to get a rise out of him. Joseph wanted to leap up and hit him over and over but he didn't stand a chance against him. He'd learned Lachlan was both strong and ruthless.

The headmaster took another sip from his glass and stared at him. A smirk had worked its way over his lips and his cheeks had gained a touch of red. He drifted to the couch and seated himself close to Joseph. Too close. He slung an arm over Joseph's shoulders and pulled him close, holding him tight enough to hurt.

"You strike me as a proud boy, Joseph," he said, his breath carrying the reek of whiskey. "You know what the Bible says about pride?"

Joseph shook his head.

Brother Lachlan pulled him closer. "Pride goeth before destruction."

Joseph startled as Lachlan placed a hand on his thigh, rubbing it in slow circles. The touch felt almost affectionate. Was the man already drunk? The hand on Joseph's thigh slid higher and Lachlan pulled him even closer, squeezing his shoulder painfully.

Joseph leaned away from the headmaster and suddenly the man's fingers were digging into his shoulder. Lachlan pulled him almost onto his lap, his other hand sliding the rest of the way up to Joseph's crotch. The hand lingered there, cupped his privates, and squeezed. Hard.

It was too much. Joseph shoved Lachlan back, somehow

managing to catch the headmaster by surprise. He leapt up from the couch and backed away until he bumped into the enormous desk.

Lachlan's glass had been knocked loose in the melee and landed with a dull thunk on the rug in front of the couch. The contents disappeared into the ugly burgundy pattern, leaving only a slightly darker patch of burgundy behind.

"I'm sorry," Joseph heard himself say.

He wasn't sorry though. Why would he say such a thing?

Because he was afraid.

Lachlan flew up from the couch and was on him in an instant. He shoved Joseph backwards into the desk, hard enough that the edge dug into the small of his back. One powerful hand wrapped around his throat, squeezing just enough to make it difficult, but not impossible, to breathe.

"Insolent whelp," he hissed, face bright red. "I own you."

Lachlan tightened his grip around Joseph's neck, cutting the air off entirely from his lungs. Joseph's vision went dim.

And then, the sweetest sound in existence. A knock on the door.

The hand released him at once. Lachlan leaned forward and pressed his mouth to Joseph's ear. His beard tickled against it, like a thousand spider legs.

"Compose yourself and sit on that couch," the headmaster muttered.

Joseph gasped and limped back to the couch, eyes cast to the ground. The headmaster, a man of the church, had touched his privates. Squeezed them. He felt like he might puke. It was hard to believe what had just happened. The strangulation was one thing, and not even very unexpected. Sexual abuse, on the other hand...

"Look at me, Joseph."

He forced himself to look Lachlan in the eye, as his grandfather had taught him. He saw no remorse, no pity, no excuse. Only cold malice.

"I know I don't have to tell you to keep your mouth shut," Lachlan said in a low voice. "Nonetheless, your pain with be a hundred-fold if you decide to break the confidentiality of my office."

A muffled voice spoke from behind the door. Joseph couldn't tell what was said or who was speaking. Lachlan yanked the door open to a friar, thin, balding, and middle-aged, cowering at the threshold.

"What is it, Brother Casper?" Lachlan said, impatience clipping each syllable.

Brother Casper stole a look over Lachlan's shoulder and spied Joseph on the couch. He murmured something, obviously not wanting Joseph to overhear.

"How?" Lachlan demanded. "The brush should have been soaking wet."

Brother Casper didn't raise his voice but Joseph caught the word "kerosene". Had someone started a fire? He reigned in the hope that blossomed at that word. He wasn't yet out of the woods, which were apparently ablaze.

Lachlan spun around and caught Joseph watching them.

"I'm sorry to say, Mr. Ward, that our discussion will have to wait."

Joseph rose to his feet.

Lachlan raised a hand. "Sit down. You will wait here for me while I attend to this." He turned to Brother Casper. "I presume the fire department has been called."

Brother Casper nodded. "Of course, Brother."

"Then I'll worry about the students," he said, ushering the friar out the door. "Brother Casper, I'd like for you to stand outside my office and ensure the tenacious Mr. Ward doesn't get it in his head to sneak off while I'm dealing with this nonsense."

Lachlan gave Joseph a sharp look and pulled the doors closed. A heavy metal *clunk* came from them; the deadbolt being locked from the outside. Lachlan clearly did not entirely trust Brother Casper to babysit.

Joseph burst into tears as soon as the lock clicked into place. He allowed himself to cry for a couple of minutes before forcing himself to stop. No doubt he was not the first to receive this sort of treatment from the headmaster. Had Odilon ever been treated like this? Sure he'd been beaten but beyond that? There was no way Joseph could ever ask him. No way he could ever discuss this with anyone. He couldn't imagine describing the experience. Never in his life had he felt so powerless. What else would Lachlan have done if they hadn't been interrupted?

The clock on the wall told him it was half an hour until lunch. Would the headmaster be back by then? Not that Joseph thought he'd be able to eat anytime soon.

He poked around the office, avoiding the desk. The liquor cabinet had been left open, though he had no desire to even taste any of its occupants. He wanted to smash every one of the bottles but feared what the consequences of such an action would be.

He was so angry at what had just been done to him. Such things, and worse, were joked about on the playground but Joseph had refused to believe they were based on reality. He would never kid about that stuff again, that was for sure. Was it the whiskey that had driven Lachlan to act so aggressively? So sexually? Could what was done to him be called sexual? It certainly hadn't felt that way. Lachlan had seemed different than usual. Eager. Hungry.

He examined the bottles in the liquor cabinet but didn't recognize any of the labels, didn't think any of them were even English. They had names like *Dailuaine* and *Lagavulin*. They all looked like whiskey to him, his father's liquor of choice when he really wanted to tie one on. These were all probably much too expensive for him to afford. Joseph turned from the cabinet, disgusted.

His attention was grabbed by the painting above the couch. It was of a small farm in a grassy valley in the mountains somewhere and reminded him of *The Sound of Music*. Tall, green hills sloped down toward the farm, the sun shining down from the far side of the valley. A red barn with a fenced in pen next to it, and a larger corral just beyond that, stood across from a whitewashed house with a huge apple tree in the yard. Next to the farmhouse, a bright red rooster perched atop a wooden chicken coop. In the pen just outside the barn was a chestnut mare being groomed by a girl in a white skirt and blue blouse. Out in the corral, a man in a straw hat milked one of half a dozen cows. A woman in a beige dress stood on the front stoop of the house with a steaming pie in both hands. A pond glistened out back.

A ripple disturbed the stillness of the pond, as though something had broken the surface of the water.

Joseph blinked. There was no way he'd just seen what he thought he'd seen. He looked from the pond to the farmhouse.

The woman on the porch waved at the man or the girl, or maybe both.

The painting came to life before his eyes. Exactly like the painting in the church basement at his mother's funeral.

Joseph had put that experience, the thing that had landed him here in the first place, almost entirely out of his mind. He'd hidden it far back in his subconscious and only seldom allowed himself little glimpses of it, tried to convince himself it was all a dream. He had only allowed himself to think of Hasty late at night, when the rest of St. Theodore's was asleep. It was all coming crashing back and suddenly it felt as though it had only been yesterday when the girl with the Iron Maiden vest had popped out of a painting in the church basement. He suddenly missed Hasty. Wished she would appear now.

In the painting, the farmer stopped his milking and the girl put down her brush. Both started toward the house as the woman disappeared back inside. The farmer jogged to catch up with the girl and put an arm over her shoulders. They were a real family getting ready for supper after a long day working on the farm.

Joseph extended a hand toward the painting. He came within an inch and pulled back. Took a deep breath. What he was hoping for was an impossibility, Hasty had been a dream. He had imagined the whole thing in the church basement and his eyes were playing tricks on him now as a way of dealing with what had just occurred with the headmaster.

He shook his head at himself for getting so worked up about a fantasy. Even as his mind was made up, he reached his hand out the rest of the way and touched the painting.

It felt like regular canvas and, though he had expected as

much, his heart sank. He rested his palm on it and the canvas gave out underneath him, his hand pushing right through. He had a brief moment to wonder how Brother Lachlan would react to a hole in the painting.

And then he was falling.

18

———————

JOSEPH LANDED HARD ON HIS SHOULDER AND TUMBLED downward. He just barely got his heels underneath him, managing to dig them into the grass to bring his descent to a skidding stop. Dazed, he sat up and cradled his injured hand, which was attached to a shoulder that was now throbbing, in his lap.

His first thought was that he had fallen off the couch, it had been that instant. But the carpet in Lachlan's office was burgundy and woven, not green and, well, grass. If there had been a window in the office, he may have been able to convince himself he'd fallen out of it—until he looked around.

He sat midway up a grassy hill overlooking a quaint, familiar little farm. Smoke puffed out of the chimney of the farmhouse. A woman stepped through the front door holding what Joseph knew to be a freshly baked pie. He turned his attention to the barn where, sure enough, the girl, who must be the farmer's daughter, was running a brush along the flank of the chestnut mare. The farmer himself was already on his way toward the house, eager for a slice of pie.

"Hasty, I made it," Joseph said.

He brushed his palm over the grass, which was a vibrant, unreal shade of green, then lay back in it so the sun could warm his face. It was the most comfortable he'd been in months. The gentle sounds of lowing cattle floated up to him, through the still air. He leaned up on one elbow to watch the cows meander around their corral, scooping up mouthfuls of grass, chewing eternally. The rooster fluttered down from his perch and strutted into the coop. There was a sleepy feeling to the place though the sun still beat down from almost directly above them.

He made himself stand, favoring his injured hand, and turned back to where he'd tumbled from.

The hill rose to an intimidating height before him and would have been one hell of a task to climb. The whole valley was surrounded by such hills, which gave way to snow-peaked mountains. He turned in a circle, scanning the horizon as far as the mountains would allow. Aside from the small plantation below, there didn't appear to be any sign of civilization. He searched the hill above him for any indication of where he'd fallen from.

He had to allow his eyes to slip out of focus to see it. A shimmering, square-shaped space floated over the hill a short distance above him, distorting the view of the grass beyond. It blended in with the scenery so that it appeared more like a heat mirage than anything else. He climbed a few feet toward it and pieces of Lachlan's office began to resolve within the space. He could barely make out the liquor cabinet directly across from him. What would happen when

Lachlan came back into his office to see that he was missing? Would he spot Joseph standing there? Would he even look at the painting?

He turned his back on the shimmering space. It didn't matter what Lachlan thought when he returned; he couldn't touch Joseph here. Joseph had half a heart to stay and watch the office until the headmaster came back just to see his reaction, but the smell of fresh apple pie wafted up the hill and invaded his nostrils.

He tore a strip from the part of his shirt that had ripped when Lachlan had grabbed him. *One* of the times Lachlan had grabbed him. His anger at the man simmered as he tied the white strip of fabric around a young tree in front of the shimmering space. He'd been tossed around before, plenty of times, by his father. But that was his own flesh and blood. And his father had never touched him the way Lachlan had.

Joseph slid down the hill toward the farmhouse. After several dozen feet, he turned around and was pleased to see the piece of shirt he'd tied to the sapling was clearly visible. He shouldn't have any trouble finding his way back to the space he'd come from. Not that he was eager to go back there.

He had no idea what he was going to do when he got to the bottom of the hill. What would he say if someone came out of the house at that moment? The whole setting was so warm and inviting, it was hard to imagine that anything unpleasant could exist in this valley.

On level ground, he crept to the left, around the cattle corral, keeping a close eye on the farmhouse. The cows paid him no mind; they cared only about the next mouthful of grass. Their tails whipped across their backsides, slapping at flies that weren't there. Joseph would have thought this world devoid of any sort of insect life were it not for the occasional bumble bee that buzzed over the grass.

He approached the barn and the horse whinnied a greeting. It wore a light bridle fastened to the pen. Did the farmer's daughter ever actually ride the horse or merely brush it every day? Did the farmer milk endlessly? Was their life a permanent loop of the same actions day in, day out? He muted the questions that continued to spring up in his mind, wanting to enjoy this place, needing to believe it was nothing more or less than a quaint farm with a nice family. Everything else about this picturesque little valley was certainly pleasant. Mean people wouldn't live in a place like this. Just the same, it would be best to play it careful and try to figure out what sort of people these were before revealing himself to them. They probably never got visitors. Not like him anyway, unless Hasty had been here in the past. What were the odds though?

He made his way to the other side of the barn where he could peek around and spy on the house. From within the chicken coop came the babbling of dozens of hens clucking at one another.

After crouching there for what felt like an hour, his legs grew tired and he allowed himself to sink into the grass, leaning his back against the side of the barn. He stole glances around the corner every so often to see if there was any activity but the family remained indoors. Heavy under the heat of the sun, his eyes drifted closed. The warm wood of the barn felt good against his weary head and he allowed the tension to slip out of his body. With the sun warming him, he fell fast asleep.

He was startled awake by the crowing of the rooster. Rubbing sleep out of his eyes, he saw the bird had returned to its station on the roof of the coop. The sun was in the same spot it had been when he'd fallen asleep though he could have sworn he'd been under for hours. He squinted against it as he pulled himself to his feet.

On cue, the front door of the house swung open. Joseph was just able to press himself against the wall of the barn as first the farmer and then his daughter stepped outside. The farmer sauntered straight into the barn, oblivious to Joseph's presence. His daughter turned her face up to the sun and smiled at it.

That pleasant stirring, the feeling that came to him when he was close to a pretty girl, tickled low in his belly. She was stunning. From here she looked to be a couple of years older than himself, maybe sixteen at the most. She had golden blond hair that danced around her shoulders in loose curls. Her dress clung tightly to her body, accentuating every curve and angle. She spun in a circle and he almost expected her to start in on the first few bars of *The Hills Are Alive*. As though his thoughts had prompted her, she did start to hum to herself. The song, nothing he recognized, carried across the yard to him as she sashayed her way to the other side of the barn, where he presumed she would set to grooming her horse.

Joseph's tummy rumbled but he forced himself to stay where he was for fear of being discovered. He hadn't yet decided how to approach the family. Or if he should at all.

He waited for what must have been hours. Every so often he would stand and march in circles to keep himself from dozing. His stomach complained the entire time. He was even tempted to start eating handfuls of grass. At some unknowable time of day he roused himself from a light doze, worried he'd slept through the work day.

He poked his head around the barn just as the farmer's

wife popped out the door with a steaming pie in her hands. She was as beautiful as her daughter, hair a slightly darker shade of blond but with the same gentle curls. The smell of the pie hit Joseph and his stomach reacted so strongly that he actually doubled over in pain.

"Rupert," the woman called from the door, "Time for supper! I've baked a pie for dessert!"

Joseph heard a muffled call from around the barn and the farmer's wife disappeared back into the house. The farmer, Rupert, and his daughter appeared moments later, walking toward the house together. Rupert held the door open for his daughter and followed her inside. As he pulled the door closed, he looked directly at Joseph, though his expression showed no sign that he'd seen anything out of the ordinary.

That sealed it. If the farmer saw him as an intruder, surely he would've chased him off right then. At this point, he was hungry enough that he didn't care if the family were a bunch of murderous psychopaths, he needed to eat. He broke cover and crept toward the house.

He stepped up to the screen door separating the yard from the house and peered through the mesh, into the kitchen. Rupert sat with his hands folded, facing the door at the round wooden table that took up much of the kitchen's floor space. His daughter was seated beside him, looking fondly up at her father. His wife set a steaming platter on the table and joined them. Together they bowed their heads for a few seconds, then started in on their supper.

Joseph rapped on the edge of the door just as Rupert lifted a spoonful of what looked like mashed potatoes to his mouth. The man's hand stopped, his mouth gaping in anticipation of the incoming spoonful. He remained still like that for several minutes. The whole family was frozen in an awkward supper-time tableau.

He should have thought this through. He recalled all those reruns of *Star Trek* and the importance of the Prime Directive; never to interfere with another civilization. He hadn't been here long and already he'd messed up this whole family by interrupting their dinner.

Rupert pushed his chair back, stood from the table, and plodded toward the door.

The relief Joseph felt was immense. It would do to mind his inner Captain Kirk from now on though.

"I'm sorry to have disturbed you," Joseph said, stepping back to avoid the screen door as it opened onto the porch. "I'm sort of lost and I'm really hungry. Can you spare any food?"

The farmer glowered down at him, seemed to look right through him, hearing his voice but not actually seeing anyone there. Then his bearded face turned up in a big grin and he wrapped an arm around Joseph's shoulders, guiding him into the house.

A fourth chair had been added to the table, with clean place settings, though Joseph hadn't seen anyone move and would have sworn there were only three chairs a moment ago. The women smiled at him as he inched toward the empty seat. Rupert had gone straight back to his chair and had started up eating again, not bothering to wait for him.

The aroma made it impossible for Joseph to open his mouth without drooling. Huge roasted drumsticks were piled on a platter in the center of the table, next to a giant bowl of mashed potatoes and a platter of corn on the cob. The kitchen was old fashioned, with a big wood stove against one wall and an enormous counter along the other. The countertop looked like a single chunk of roughly hewn wood, planed flat but given little else in the way of decorative flair. A steel basin sat on the floor next to the counter and Joseph had no trouble imagining the dishes being cleaned in it after supper. He could make out a wooden rocking chair and what looked like the edge of a piano in the next room over. None of this was visible in the painting. How had they come into being? Did the artist's imagination place these things here without actually adding them in? The thought made his head spin and he put it out of mind for the time being—an easy task given the meal spread out before him.

He took his seat across from the farmer's daughter, in between Rupert and Mrs. Farmer. As he took his seat, Mrs. Farmer leaned over and poured milk into his glass from a large clay pitcher. They all smiled as though a pleasant conversation was being had and enjoyed by everyone present.

Mrs. Farmer broke the silence. "Please eat. There's plenty more where that came from."

Joseph dug in, helping himself to two juicy drumsticks, a healthy scoop of potatoes, and a cob of corn. Manners were far from his mind as he ate, stripping one of the drumsticks to the bone in a minute flat and following it with heaping spoonfuls of potatoes. He kept his head down while he ate. Plate cleared, he looked up sheepishly, embarrassed at his own table manners. But the family didn't pay any attention to him, or each other. They all appeared to be in their own little bubble as they ate.

Finally, Rupert dropped his fork and pushed back his chair. He slouched in his seat and patted his belly, a satisfied smile across his face.

"Catherine," he said, looking at his wife, "You've outdone

yourself." He looked to his daughter. "Bring me my pipe, if you would, Delilah."

His daughter sprung up from the table and dashed out of the room, returning a second later with a small, latched wooden box. Rupert took this from her with another big grin and popped it open, withdrawing a corncob pipe and a sack of tobacco. He packed the pipe, lit it with a wooden match, and puffed out smoke smelling so familiar to Joseph that he actively had to fight against tears. He hadn't smelled pipe tobacco like that since his grandfather had been alive.

Catherine, meanwhile, had already cleared the table and was setting the apple pie, still steaming, in the center of the table. She cut giant pieces for each of them, serving Joseph first and herself last.

He dug his fork into the crust of the pie, another cloud of steam billowing out as he did so. He took a small bite, cautious of the heat, and was surprised to find the temperature to be absolutely perfect. He had no idea pie could taste so good; buttery, flaky, with a soft sweetness to the apples inside. He cleared his plate in seconds flat then leaned back in his chair and belched without having a chance to do anything about it. He covered his mouth, murmuring an apology. Again, nobody noticed his table manners.

"Thank you so much for supper," he said to Catherine.

The farmer's wife stood and gathered plates. "There's plenty more where that came from."

Joseph yawned and caught Delilah looking at him as he did so. He covered his mouth and smiled apologetically at her. It occurred to him that he had no idea where he was going to sleep tonight. He supposed he could try to break into the barn and find some hay there. He'd been lucky so far though. It couldn't hurt to push his luck once more.

He turned to Rupert. "Do you have a spare bed, or a couch I could sleep on?"

The farmer gave him his trademark grin and blew a thick stream of pipe smoke out his nostrils. "My wife will make up the guest bed for you."

At this, Catherine bustled out of the kitchen.

"Come lend a hand, dear," she called to her daughter.

Delilah gave Joseph another smile and left the table to help her mother. Rupert puffed his pipe and grinned at Joseph. Smoke swirled through the beams of sunlight shining through the window.

"Does it ever get dark here?" Joseph asked, glancing outside.

Rupert was silent for a long time. When Joseph looked at him, the grin was gone and the farmer had a far off look in his eyes. He held the pipe in his mouth, bottom lip pooched out every so often to let out a bit of smoke. After a long, silent minute, the farmer stood and tromped out of the kitchen. Joseph heard the creak of the stairs under the man's heavy steps and then the house was silent.

He waited in the kitchen for a long while before figuring no one was coming back downstairs. Thankful he didn't have to navigate the house in the dark at least, he crept out of the kitchen. The next room over, apparently the only other room on this level, was a simple living room. The rocking chair he'd seen took up one corner, and it was indeed a small piano resting against the wall next to it. A small sofa, more like a bench with a cloth covering over it, sat against the far wall. Beyond the living room were stairs leading to the upper level of the house. Joseph took these up slowly, trying his best not to disturb the silence.

The second floor was little more than a hallway running the length of the house. Four doors, two on each side. One of the doors was open, likely the guest bedroom. He hoped there were dark curtains. The floorboards creaked under his feet as he tiptoed down the hall to the open door. Everything else was completely silent. No one stirred, nobody snored. Joseph was thankful they kept their bedroom doors shut when they slept. Something felt off about these people. It was like they were… hollow. Hasty had told him that part of an artist bleeds into a painting. Perhaps these people's existences were shallow extensions of that. Maybe their inner workings only existed as much as the artist imagined at the time they created their paintings. Whoever painted this could have imagined the family as a happy, simple farming family. He or she may have daydreamed about little details about them, like the pipe. If that was the case, what other possibilities might exist in this sort of world?

The open door was indeed the guest room. At least, it was an empty room with a bed. There turned out to be no need for blinds as the room had been built without a window. Did the artist imagine it that way?

The room was spartan with a plain bed, a small dresser, and a simple desk with a wooden chair. It was more than Joseph expected and felt much more welcoming than his room at St. Theodore's. Underneath the bed was a tin chamber pot that conjured memories of his night in the prison cell. Since coming here, he'd had to pee twice and had done so against the side of the barn, which is exactly where he intended to keep going. If he had to poop, there was no way he was doing it in a pot. He'd dig a hole next to the barn if he had to.

The bed was more comfortable than it had any right to be and, in the pitch black of the room, Joseph found himself drifting off as soon as his head hit the pillow. What was happening at St. Theodore's? How did Brother Lachlan react when he came back to his office to find it empty? These thoughts led to what had driven him into the painting in the first place. The need for escape. There was no way he was going back to Lachlan's office. Or the school. He'd have to find a way off this farm and into another painting, the way Hasty said she did it. He would make that his task for the next day.

His eyes grew heavy and he and recalled Hasty's warning about staying in a painting for too long. So far this place had been okay. Perhaps not every painting degraded as she'd theorized, or at least not as quickly. No sense taking any chances though—he'd find a way out of here in the morning. He was free. His excitement at the thought should have kept him awake but he found himself unable to keep his eyes from slipping shut and before long, he was fast asleep.

19

———

He woke up disoriented and needing to pee. The room was still completely dark and Joseph had to grope around the walls to find his way to the door. He smashed his thigh into the dresser and yelped in pain. He expected to hear someone call out and ask if he was okay but the house was silent. For all he knew, it was still what passed for night time and everyone was still in bed.

At long last he found the door and yanked it open. The room flooded with light, dazing and blinding him. He shut his eyes against it and then eased them open again, allowing them to adjust. He stuck one foot out the door and froze.

At first glance it looked like someone had decided to paint the upstairs hall and had given up shortly after starting. That idea evaporated swiftly. It was obvious what had happened here. Sort of.

A thick, crimson stripe ran the length of the hall toward the stairs. Splashes of it spotted the walls along the way. He made himself look the other way, up the hall, and saw the streak of red came out of one of the other rooms. The door stood open.

Joseph was frozen in fear and panic. His bladder loosened a bit and he decided he should empty it before he wet himself. All squeamishness around the chamber pot having vanished, he slid it out and peed without taking his eyes off his bedroom door. He heard some urine splatter on the floorboards next to the pot and corrected his aim without looking. He felt absurd peeing in a bedpan while someone could be bleeding to death downstairs.

Business finished, he crept back to the door. Maybe someone had seriously hurt themselves. Just because there was blood didn't mean a crime had been committed. Whoever the blood had come from, it must have been the result of an accidental injury. This did little to quell his fear but it steeled him enough to investigate the other room. He inched up the hall, afraid to do much more than shuffle his feet for fear of triggering a squeaky floorboard and giving away his position. It occurred to him that he shouldn't be afraid of making noise if someone had been hurt in an accident. But also, what sort of bedroom mishap could cause so much blood loss?

He glanced around the edge of the doorframe and slapped a hand over his mouth to keep himself from shouting, or vomiting, or both.

The room must have belonged to Delilah. It looked similar to his own—single bed, dresser, desk—except this one was covered in gore. It looked like someone exploded and all that remained of them was spread around the room in a thick, red paste. How had he slept through this? There must have been *some* noise. He tore his eyes away from the room, unable to look at the aftermath of whatever had happened any longer. He pulled the door closed behind him with shaking hands.

He held his breath in the hallway, listening for any indication that someone else might still be in the house. The two doors on the other side of the hall were shut tight. For the first time since arriving on this farm, he wished that he had never slipped into the canvas in Lachlan's office. He wished he'd never met Hasty or even seen her in that stupid painting hanging in the church basement where he'd said goodbye to his mother.

He had to get out of here. He'd obviously overstayed his welcome and things were going sour in this painting. He regarded the two closed doors. Couldn't leave without first checking what was behind them. Someone could be hurt.

In spite of his age he had seen quite a few horror movies in his time; the benefit of being raised by inattentive parents. He thought of *Halloween* and of Michael Myers prowling through the houses of his victims, unseen and unheard until he was ready to strike. He had no trouble imagining that same expressionless mask over the face of some psychopath as he dragged the carcasses of this nice family behind him.

"Stop it," he whispered to himself. Exacerbating his own fear wasn't going to get him anywhere.

He took a deep breath and shuffled across the hall to the furthest closed door. He placed his hand on the knob, said a silent prayer, and pushed it open. The room was the same size as the last two but with a bigger bed and a wardrobe as well as a dresser. No desk. No blood either. He leaned against the doorframe, relief deflating a small amount of the fear and anxiety that had built up in him since waking. He realized he'd been clenching his injured hand and made himself ease it open. He was supposed to have had the bandages, all bunched up and crusted with his blood, changed several times by now.

The last closed door beckoned to him. At least this last one was close to the stairs and he could make a run for it if a crazed murderer—or something worse—was indeed lurking in the room.

As he approached, some kind of muttering became audible from behind the door. His breath froze in his chest. Gently, he placed his ear against the door and listened. It sounded like mumbling; muted, as though whoever was doing it had tape over his mouth. He was pretty sure the voice belonged to a male. A new narrative formed itself in his imagination. Farmer Rupert had been bound in this room while his family was murdered and taken away. Joseph found himself staring at the streak of red running along the floor. He tiptoed away from the door and followed the blood trail to the stairs, where he peeked around the corner and down into the main level of the house. The only thing visible was the trail of red, which tracked down the stairs and out of sight on the downstairs floor. He breathed as silently as possible and listened. Nothing. Even the mumbling couldn't be heard over here.

He steeled himself and crept back toward the closed door. This family had given him a meal and a place to sleep, he couldn't abandon them when they needed help. What could he do though? It wasn't like he could call the police. He needed to get out of here. He realized he was putting himself in further danger for what were ultimately imaginary people. Was that noble or stupid? Either way, he was already at the door and might as well check.

He twisted the doorknob as slow as possible, nudging the door open. The room was so dark he at first had trouble making out what he was looking at. Light didn't flow into this room the way it did in every other bedroom in this house. Dark shadows obscured what he could tell was a bed with some sort of writhing lump on top of it. The mumbling came from the mass on the bed and had grown louder, more frantic, when he'd opened the door.

Joseph put a finger to his lips. "Shh."

Whatever was on the bed thrashed and flailed in the dark. It was as though the person, or thing, was screaming behind a sock that had been crammed into his mouth.

"I'm here to help," Joseph whispered from the door. "You have to be quiet."

He, or it, settled a bit and quieted down so that the voice was a whimper. Joseph crept closer. Whoever or whatever was on the bed was covered by a blanket. It shuddered and Joseph used all of his willpower to stick his good hand out and tear the blanket off.

Confusion. Sickness. Horror. Each sliced through him like a cold knife when he saw what the blanket had been covering. He couldn't take his eyes off it. In the dim light, he could make out what might be a head though its shape was not recognizable as such; it was more like a crescent, the way it was shaped. The only features that gave it away as a head was a shock of hair sticking out of the top of it, a malformed eye that stared out at him from one curved edge of it, and what looked like half a nose, roughly in the center of what could be a face. There was no mouth, but the whimpering sound continued to issue from where it may have been. The thing's misshapen eye widened and pleaded with Joseph. The rest of its body followed the same horrible nature as the thing's head. It was a twisted lump of flesh, limbless except for what could only have been an arm protruding from its chest. A thin, twisted hand flailed at the end of the limb, unable to grasp at anything. It slapped uselessly against the thing's torso.

"I see you've met my son."

Joseph screamed and spun around.

Rupert stood in the doorway of the bedroom. He held a sickle down at his side. Something dark dripped off it. The farmer was dressed in a one-piece undergarment, similar to what Joseph had seen cowboys dress down to in the westerns he sometimes watched on TV. This garment might have been white at some point, perhaps not too long ago in the past. Now it was splattered with dark stains. It didn't take much imagination to figure out what the stains were and what dripped from the end of the curved blade of the sickle.

"We're not complete," the farmer muttered.

Joseph struggled to find his voice. "What do you mean?"

"Inside. We're unfinished. Like him, but on the inside." Rupert gestured with his sickle at the thing on the bed; the thing he'd called his son.

Rupert stepped into the room, which was all Joseph could handle. He raced past the farmer, barely squeezing past him, and out into the hallway. As he sprinted toward the stairs, he heard the muted moans of the farmer's twisted son rise into a close-mouthed shriek. The sound cut off abruptly as Joseph took to the stairs.

He pounded down the steps, into the living room. Followed the bloody streak on the floor through the living room and into the kitchen. The blood trail continued through here and out into the yard. He headed for the door but made himself stop before going outside. He held his breath and listened. Hearing nothing from upstairs, he opened the nearest cupboard to him, hoping to stock up on provisions before leaving the farm. The cupboard was empty. He ripped open the doors of every other cupboard in the kitchen to find that they were all completely barren. Not a scrap of food to be found anywhere, not even a utensil. What did Catherine use to cook with? Did food just appear when it was time to eat? Dwelling on the strange logic of this place was distressing and disorienting him. He'd have to find food elsewhere—he needed to go.

He followed the red path out the door and into the farm-yard. The blood continued through the yard and into the barn, the door of which had been left open a crack. Joseph couldn't be certain whether it was a desire to help or morbid curiosity that propelled him toward the open door but he found himself walking toward it instead of racing into the hills, as he'd planned. None of the farm animals were outside today. He glanced over his shoulder at the chicken coop—it was as still as the rest of the farm. A hard knot formed itself in his stomach as he reached the threshold of the barn. He shoved the door open before he could convince himself to walk away.

Blood. Death. It was too much. He vomited. Puke mixed with the blood already soaking the dirt, creating a vile mud mixture. A wave of dizziness overtook him and he forced himself to lean back against the outer wall of the barn. It was all too familiar, seeing his own blood-streaked vomit. He missed his mother. He hated that this puddle of nastiness reminded him of her, loathed himself for associating it with her. Wished something pretty like flowers or birds could invoke her memory.

The barn was a horror show. The animals from the yard

had been wrangled inside, chickens included. They had all been hacked to pieces. There was something about them...

He surveyed the yard. All clear. He took a deep breath, wiped his mouth, turned back to the barn, and took a step inside. Delilah's horse was closest to him, hacked open on the floor. The poor beast's throat had been slashed. Its abdomen was flayed. The peeled back flesh should have given Joseph a gory view of the horse's skeleton and guts. Instead, everything inside it looked like ground meat, as though its insides had been blended before it was cut open. No bone, no organs, just bloody, pulverized meat. The next closest animal was one of the cows. He held a hand over his mouth and examined the wreckage of the creature. Rupert had chopped this thing into nearly a dozen chunks. Its head was sliced in half, down its face, and it was here that Joseph forced himself to look. He should have seen pieces of skull, brain, things like that. They'd studied biology in science at school and every kid learned at a pretty early age that all creatures have skeletons and brains. Okay not *all* animals had skeletons but cows certainly did. They were supposed to anyway. The inside of this cow's head looked exactly the same as the contents of the horse's torso; bloody mush.

That was enough. Was this what the farmer meant when he'd told Joseph that they weren't complete? He turned and came face-to-face with Delilah. She had been shoved onto a rusty hook on one of the barn beams. The hook protruded through her bosom. Her lower half was missing, as was one of her arms. Her blouse was covered in blood and Joseph guessed that her midsection had been cut open as well but he didn't dare look. He spotted her lower half a few feet away and, though he tried not to look, his eyes betrayed him. Her insides looked the same as the animals'.

He ran out of the barn just as Rupert came out the front door of the house. The farmer marched toward Joseph, holding a bloody bundle under one arm. He spotted Joseph, dropped the bundle, and sprinted after him.

Joseph turned and ran to the empty cattle pen.

"We are incomplete!" the farmer shouted.

Joseph vaulted over the fence surrounding the pen and sprinted through the trampled grass and mud. He shot a look over his shoulder, tripped, and landed hard on his cheek. Rupert reached the pen as Joseph scrabbled to his feet. The farmer threw open the gate and stalked toward him.

"Please don't." Joseph stammered.

"Are you complete?" the farmer growled. "I have to know."

Joseph put everything he had into running. He vaulted over the fence on the other side of the pen and sprinted for the hill closest to them. Its base was some two hundred yards from the pen. He ran for it without a glance back to see where the farmer was. He had no choice but to outrun the man. He hit the slope running and climbed as high as his legs would allow him before screaming for a break. Ducking behind an evergreen that grew out of the slope, he allowed himself a look back. The field below was empty. The farm yard too. The crazed farmer had apparently given up, perhaps in favor of performing more unspeakable acts on his son.

Joseph allowed himself a few minutes to catch his breath, never taking his eyes from the barnyard below. He'd never make the mistake of overstaying his welcome in a place like this again.

It took him almost twenty minutes to crest the top of the

hill. When he reached the peak, he saw that more hills climbed ahead of him, eventually giving way to rocky slopes that led up to the snow-covered peaks of the mountains forming the valley. He surveyed the farm, which looked much smaller from here. Still empty. He looked across the valley to the place where he had come into this world. He couldn't make out the strip of cloth he'd tied to the sapling from here. It didn't matter. He wasn't going back to that school, no matter what happened in this place. It was insane to think it but between outrunning crazed farmers and enduring Lachlan's abuse, he'd take his chances with the farmers.

He had to find another way out, another painting to escape through. But how? The place he'd come into this world was barely visible when he was standing a few feet in front of it. He'd have to comb these hills, this whole world, inch-by-inch if he was going to find another one of those shapes to go through. He'd worry about where it came out when he got there. Wherever it was, it couldn't be worse than St. Theodore's.

With no better place to start, he inched along the plateau of the hill he'd climbed, squinting and relaxing his eyes, trying to shift his focus as he went. He thought about Hasty and wished he'd had more time with her. Wished he could have gone with her back into the painting in the church basement. She could have showed him everything she knew about getting along in paintings and he never would have wound up at St. Theodore's in the first place. He allowed himself to be upset with her for a minute before reminding himself that he had *tried* to get into the painting and hadn't been able to. What had been different then? It couldn't have been his age, it wasn't that long ago. Maybe his desperation to escape Lachlan had triggered something. A fight or flight response of sorts. He didn't think that was exactly it though. According to Hasty, she had gone into a painting completely by accident, in pretty non-threatening circumstances by the sound of it.

An animal sound, unlike anything he'd ever heard, pulled him from his thoughts and stopped him short in his tracks. It was a rumbling cry that originated from somewhere nearby, echoing across the valley. He'd seen a documentary not too long ago about whales and how they call to each other in long, melancholic notes. This sounded like a deeper, more throaty version of that sound. It raised gooseflesh on his arms. He scanned the hills around him, searching for the source of the call.

When he spotted it, he threw himself to the ground, flattening himself against the grass. It crawled along a neighboring hilltop and, at first glance, Joseph took it for some kind of giant salamander. It was long and black, its flesh glistening in the sunlight. It crawled in a slithering, writhing motion that made it look almost as though it was swimming over the grass. This had to be what Hasty was talking about when she told him to watch for eels. To Joseph, who had spent a good deal of his life watching nature documentaries, this thing looked more like a salamander than an eel but he could see where Hasty got the idea. It crawled over the surface of the hill and lifted its bulky, arrow-shaped head. It sniffed the air and opened its maw to reveal a mouth full of huge, pointed teeth. Though its legs were little more than stumps sticking out from its belly, it moved swiftly and gracefully over the grassy hill. Its tail reminded him of a crocodile's, long and pointed. It did look more like a combination of salamander and crocodile than an eel but he found himself thinking of it as an eel anyway. An *eelamander*. It was hard to tell how big it was from where he lay; definitely much bigger than him—at least eleven or twelve feet long.

Something moved behind the beast. It turned and bellowed in its bizarre, chilling voice. A second eelamander crawled its way to where the first lay. As the new creature sauntered up, the first hissed at it. The newcomer gave one of those chilling calls and that appeared to end their dialogue.

Joseph stayed flat against the ground while the creatures, the eelamanders, slithered around the top of the hill for some time. The first one stuck what Joseph thought of as its snout in the air and sniffed in his direction. Convinced the thing saw him, Joseph began plotting an escape route. Nothing but grass and hills for miles. He had no idea how fast these things could move and had no desire to put them to the test.

The thing whipped its head toward the farm. It uttered a low bark in its whale voice and took off down the side of the hill. The second followed close behind, both winding a serpentine path down to the farm. As soon as they were over the crest, Joseph shot to his feet and fled deeper into the hills.

He trudged for what felt like an eternity over grassy slopes. It was impossible to tell exactly how long he'd been walking since the sun remained unmoving as ever. He trekked toward the mountains but they never grew any closer. It was just hill after hill.

Head down, feet aching, he may not have noticed the change in scenery if it hadn't been for the pine needles covering the ground. There was no telling how long his exhausted mind had translated the bedding of needles as just more grass. When he finally realized what he was looking at, he raised his head to find himself standing in the middle of a forest of evergreens. How long had he been walking on level ground? He turned in a slow circle. Towering pine trees on every side of him. No sign of a hill or mountain in any direction. The ground didn't even rise or fall in the slightest. There was no way he'd traversed all those hills *and* the mountains with his head down. This had to be some magic of the painting. He kept turning in a slow circle, expecting to catch a glimpse of one of the snow-capped mountains. What he saw instead made his heart skip a beat.

He almost missed it. Certainly would have if he hadn't turned in another circle to re-examine his surroundings. It hovered between two pine trees; a shimmering square space. An exit? It had to be. That explained the sudden change in scenery; he was no longer in the painting in Lachlan's office. At least he hoped not.

Exhaustion forgotten, he jogged toward the shimmer, stopping a foot away. Something flickered within the square space but he couldn't tell what it was. He didn't care. This was his way out of here and away from St. Theodore's and its evil headmaster for good.

He stuck one hand through the shimmer and felt himself being pulled in. He yanked his hand back. What if this new place was worse? What if this wasn't an exit frame at all but some twisted part of the artist's imagination, like the incomplete farmer's son?

It didn't matter. He couldn't stay here forever.

He stuck his hand in the shimmering frame once more. This time he gave in to the pull, which quickly gave way to the sensation of falling.

20

Joseph hit the ground on his knees, ducking into a roll and tucking his injured hand to protect it at the last second as he crashed into something that clattered to the floor. He stood and strained his eyes in the gloom to make out where he'd landed, heartbeat racing while he considered the possibilities. According to Hasty, he could have been spit out anywhere in the world. He blinked his eyes until they started to make sense of the shapes around him. The only light came through the small, square window of the door across the room. It was a dull, flickering glow; that of an old bulb. It was a glow he'd grown used to over the last few months. Sweat broke out on his forehead as more details emerged from the dimness. He picked up the chair that he'd knocked over upon falling out of the painting and placed it behind the desk it belonged to. The desk was one of twenty or so, all facing a blackboard at the front of the room. Joseph couldn't make out the writing on the board. Not like that was necessary to know where he was.

He turned around and squinted at the painting he'd

emerged from. It was hard to make out much detail in the limited light but it was very obviously the depiction of a dense forest of evergreens. He got up close to the painting and was able to discern the shape of a far off deer, partially obscured by a tree trunk. The light was too dim to make out a signature, if there even was one.

A shadow passed over the room. Someone in the hallway.

Joseph ducked behind a desk. It looked like it was just someone walking past but he didn't want to take any chances. He counted to one hundred, forcing himself to do so slowly, then crawled out from behind the desk. He crept to the window, peered through it. An old electric sconce flickered on the wall across from him, providing the meagre amount of light this room received. He couldn't see who had passed by but, judging by how dark it was, it must have been one of the brothers patrolling the halls.

Joseph put his back against the door and sunk to the floor. All that time spent in the painting of the farm had been for nothing. He'd escaped Brother Lachlan for a short amount of time but he had no doubt that his situation would only worsen once the headmaster discovered he was back. How long had he been gone? Two days? Three? He couldn't recall exactly. It had certainly felt like at least a couple of days but, given that the sun never set in that particular valley, it was impossible to be sure. He was exhausted, he knew that much. Were they still looking for him or had they assumed he was long gone by now?

He was stuck with a difficult choice; head back into the painting and risk running into those things again, or try to sneak out of the school through one of the doors. How he'd get past the dogs, through the woods, and past the fence surrounding the property, he wasn't sure. He had no idea where the school was, only that it was far removed from the city. He'd been willing to risk an escape attempt once before, months ago, but he'd since had time to think fully through his foolhardy plan. If he *had* managed to escape the school, he would no doubt have become hopelessly lost or picked up by the police. Or someone worse. That left the painting. If he could orient himself properly in the forest, he could keep moving in the opposite direction of the farm and try to find another painting to escape through. He desperately wished he had Hasty here to guide him or that she had given him more information about traveling through paintings. She was confident in her ability to travel around through them; there must be some trick to it.

He went back to the painting of the forest. His eyes had adjusted to the light and he could make out a bit more detail. Half a dozen deer were camouflaged among the trees. One of them flicked an ear, a subtle movement, barely perceptible but enough to tell Joseph he wouldn't have any trouble getting back in. He took a deep breath. He would have to start searching for another painting to escape through right away; he didn't want to risk having the deer turn on him the way the farmer had. He didn't even want to think about the eelamanders. He shook his hands out at his sides and reached for the canvas.

The door crashed open. He was was bathed in light as the overhead lights came on.

"So here's where you've been hiding," Brother Lachlan said from behind him.

Joseph turned to face the headmaster, who stood in the doorway, hands folded in front of him. The man wore a grin behind his beard that reminded Joseph of the cunning wolf in cartoons finally catching up to its prey. And this man was indeed a wolf.

Brother Lachlan took a step into the room. "When you disappeared this morning, some of the other staff were convinced you had run away. I knew better. I could still smell you in these hallways."

Joseph had no idea what to say. Defending himself or coming up with an excuse was far from his mind. He wanted to ask Brother Lachlan what he meant when he said *this morning*. He had been missing for days, certainly for at least one full day. Had the friar misspoken?

"Well?" Lachlan took another step toward Joseph.

"Sir?"

"Brother Casper and I spoke at length about how you could have made it past him and he swears to Almighty God that the door to my office never opened. So either you slipped through a window, squeezed through the two inch gap in the iron bars, and dropped over thirty feet to the ground below, or," Lachlan threw his hands up, "Brother Casper is lying to me."

Joseph's head spun. He had no idea how to respond to any of this.

Lachlan closed the gap between them so that he stood only a couple of feet from Joseph.

"Did he let you out of my office, I wonder?" Another step toward him.

Lachlan's hand flashed out and snatched a handful of Joseph's hair. He threw Joseph toward the door and delivered a swift kick to his backside. Joseph stumbled out the door and into the hallway.

From behind him, Lachlan said, "Perhaps it's time you

learned how your actions affect others. How your little schemes could hurt those who aid and abet you."

Lachlan raised a hand and Joseph flinched away from it. The headmaster chuckled, a sound like river stones being thwacked together, and pointed up the hallway. Joseph started walking.

Brother Lachlan led him to a smaller classroom, close to the main hall. He bade Joseph to sit and then left the room, perhaps testing him to see if he would attempt another escape. If it *was* a ruse, Joseph saw through it. He took a seat at one of half a dozen long tables in the room.

While he waited for Lachlan to return, Joseph unwrapped his bandaged hand. The gore underneath the cloth made him wince. The wound had healed slightly, enough to tell Joseph that it had certainly been more than a day since injuring it. Dried blood crusted around the gash in his palm and a redness surrounded it. No puss yet. He let out a sigh of relief at that. He'd seen a nasty infection take root in one of the kids, Wendel Highgrove, at school. Wendel had rubbed his hand on a wood bench and got a tiny sliver stuck under the skin. That tiny sliver had caused an infection that had ultimately turned the boy's finger into a horror show. It had swollen to twice its size, taken on a grayish-green tinge, and leaked puss constantly. One day at recess, when the wound was at its worst, Wendel convinced Joseph to smell it. The odor was something he would never forget; a pungent, sweet stench that stuck in the back of his throat. Wendel's fingernail had fallen off in class and Ms. Hendrix called his parents to take him home. When Wendel came to school the next day, the swelling had gone down and the finger was wrapped in a bandage. At lunch that day, Wendel had described to all the kids how the doctor had taken a scalpel and jabbed it into the infected finger. The boy claimed that blood and puss had shot all over the office. Joseph wasn't sure how true all of that was but he certainly did not want anyone, especially at St. Theodore's, jabbing anything into him.

Brother Lachlan returned to the classroom as Joseph was re-wrapping his hand with the dirty bandage. Brother Casper scurried in behind him, head held down.

"Be seated." Brother Lachlan gestured to the seat next to Joseph.

Casper sank into the chair, his eyes down, staring at the table. Lachlan took a seat across from the two of them and placed a large, heavy book down in front of him. It had a hard cover with gold writing embossed on it that read *St. Theodore's Academy Code of Conduct*. Brother Lachlan rested a hand on the cover and traced the golden letters as he stared at Joseph from behind his round bifocals. The only light he'd turned on was directly behind him and the shadows of the room made his face even more menacing than it normally was.

"I am going to give you each a chance to tell me what happened this morning," he said, voice calm and mellow. "Punishment will be handed down accordingly."

Next to Joseph, Brother Casper was trembling enough to shake the table. Joseph forced himself to maintain eye contact with Lachlan.

"The Code of Conduct here at St. Theodore's is quite thorough, if not somewhat archaic. I do confess, it has little room for the discipline of faculty in cases where they have forgotten the role they play in the development of our wards." He lifted the cover of the book as though to show what he meant.

"Please, Brother Lachlan," Brother Casper said in a shaky voice, "None of this is necessary."

"I'm sure you are correct. Now please shut up." Lachlan flipped through the book and stopped a third of the way through, smoothing out the pages with a large, bony hand. "In the case of a young man who attempts to flee the grounds, and I should note that this code was conceived of prior to St. Theodore's admitting girls to the academy but the rules apply to both sexes, the young person in question shall undergo a period of grounding wherein he shall be confined to his room for a period of time to be determined based upon prior behavior et cetera, et cetera. I'm sure you understand what this means, Mr. Ward."

Joseph nodded. His hopes rose slightly. If he could get out of this simply by being grounded to his room, that would be the best possible scenario. He allowed himself to fantasize about being left alone in his quarters, not being bothered by any of the faculty or students. He would miss Odilon, of course, but the reprieve from the goings-on of the school would be welcome.

Lachlan flipped to the back of the book and held up a finger. "In the case of an unruly faculty member, I'm afraid the code is somewhat nebulous. Simply put, a zero-tolerance policy has always been the way at St. Theodore's, with disciplinary action to be determined by the headmaster. Which," he slammed the book shut and Brother Casper jumped in his seat, "Leaves the burden of meting out punishment for faculty misconduct up to me."

He alternated his gaze between them and raised his eyebrows as if to indicate it was their turn. Joseph had no idea what to say and allowed Brother Casper to take the lead.

"Please, Brother Lachlan," the friar stammered, "On the Word of God I promise you that door remained shut the entire time I was on post."

Lachlan smiled. "Thank you, Brother Casper. Now all we need is for the slippery Mr. Ward to elucidate how he managed to get out of my office without opening the door."

Both men stared at Joseph. Brother Lachlan's eyes laughed at him from behind his glasses. Brother Casper's eyes, in contrast, pleaded with him. Joseph found it more difficult to meet Casper's gaze than Lachlan's. What could he possibly say that would absolve them both? Obviously neither of the men would believe that Joseph had slipped into a painting and travelled through it to another room. Attempting such a story was likely to worsen the punishment for both of them.

Joseph locked eyes with Brother Lachlan. "I snuck out the door."

Lachlan smiled as though this was exactly what he expected to hear. "And what was Brother Casper doing when you slipped out?"

Beside Joseph, the trembling friar shook his head back and forth. He stared down at the table, breath hitching in his chest. His anxiety wore on Joseph, casting doubt in his mind that Lachlan would believe him. But why shouldn't the man believe him? He obviously thought this is exactly what happened anyway. Joseph didn't want to condemn Brother Casper for anything the man was innocent of but could think of nothing else to tell his interrogator.

Joseph sent a mental apology to the trembling man next to him and hoped he could hear the remorse in his voice. "Brother Casper had his back turned. I watched from a crack in the door and snuck out when he turned away."

"That's a lie," Brother Casper said, splaying his hands out on the table as he leaned forward to plead his innocence.

Without warning, Brother Lachlan scooped up the *Code of Conduct* and slammed its spine onto the fingers of Casper's left hand. The friar howled and fell backwards, out of his chair, onto the floor. He writhed on the ground and held his hand out in front of him. His fingers poured blood and at least two of them looked bent crooked, clearly broken. Joseph felt sick with guilt.

Brother Lachlan was on his feet. "I'm quite certain I told you to stop talking, Brother." He turned to Joseph. "Where have you been since this morning? Certainly not where I found you, classes were taking place."

Joseph shrugged. "All over the school."

Brother Lachlan leaned close to him, quickly enough to cause Joseph to flinch. Disgust overcame him from having Lachlan so near. All of his instincts screamed at him to flee the room. He didn't dare budge from his seat though, for fear it would provoke the headmaster further.

"You're not lying to me?"

Guilt weighed heavily on Joseph. Lachlan would never buy the truth about being in the world of a painting for several days, especially since it seemed like only a day had actually passed. Did time move differently in paintings or had he only perceived it to be going by faster than it actually had? His head spun. He looked at Brother Casper, who sat up on the floor, cradling his mangled hand in his lap, shoulders shuddering. He reminded Joseph of a toddler who'd lost his favorite toy. It was pathetic and heart-wrenching.

"I'm telling the truth," Joseph said.

Brother Casper moaned at this but said no more to contest Joseph's story.

Lachlan sat back down and looked from Joseph to Casper. "Mr. Ward, you will receive eleven lashes, one for each hour you were missing from my office. Brother Casper, you will administer these lashes now. Mr. Ward, we *will* continue the conversation we started before you disappeared from my office, another day. Soon."

The promise from Lachlan to continue their "conversation" was much worse than the stripes. He expected Casper to whip him extra hard but the friar apparently did not have the strength to do so. When Joseph checked his back out in the mirror later on, he saw that the man hadn't even broken the skin.

Laying on his stomach in bed later that night, Joseph struggled to find sleep. His mind was divided between plotting his next escape attempt and dwelling on the guilt he felt over Brother Casper. Lachlan had commanded him to stay behind after Joseph had been dismissed. It may have been his imagination but Joseph was certain he heard the man crying out again as he headed down the hall to the stairs. Perhaps the eelamanders and psychotic farmers weren't the scariest things he'd come across during his time here.

21

———

THE NEXT DAY WAS SATURDAY AND JOSEPH AWOKE feeling untethered. His disorientation grew during mass, as Brother Lachlan worked himself into a frenzy at the pulpit. He was still having trouble reconciling with the fact that he had, apparently, only been missing from the grounds for a handful of hours. He kept expecting to catch other students looking at him and whispering to one another. He'd been gone for days, after all. He wondered again if time move differently in every painting, or just this one.

At breakfast, he took his seat next to Odilon, eager to tell his story but equally wary of the amount of ears in the room. It wasn't until he was seated with his food in front of him that he realized how hungry he was. When was the last time he'd eaten? At the farm house? How long ago was that, actually? Had it even been real food? There was a doozy. Would he poop paint? The thought made him nauseous but didn't stop him from devouring his breakfast.

"You seem extra hungry this morning," Odilon said as Joseph crammed a full strip of bacon into his mouth.

The boy had a nasty purple bruise high on his cheek.

"Lachlan give you that?" Joseph asked around his mouthful of bacon.

Odilon looked down at the table, as if he had something to be ashamed about.

"We should call the cops."

"The police are just as bad. I can deal with a few bruises."

This felt like it was going to be another conversation with Odilon that would go nowhere. It was frustrating to be friends with someone so willing to accept the role of victim. Still, it was hard not to admire his backbone.

Joseph suppressed a belch with the back of his hand. "What are you doing for free time after breakfast? Walk me to the infirmary?"

Odilon raised an eyebrow at him. "What for?"

Joseph raised his bandaged hand. The wrapping was filthy and tattered, dark with dirt and dried blood. "I need this changed. And I need to tell you something. About where I've been the last couple of days."

Odilon clucked his tongue and made a sound of exasperation that sounded like he was saying "cheese" without any of the e's. "Couple of days? You mean supper last night? I have seen you every day since you arrived here."

"I'll fill you in on the way to the infirmary." Joseph scooped an egg onto half a slice of toast and shoved the whole thing in his mouth.

Joseph told Odilon everything as the pair meandered through the halls, taking the longest route possible. He managed to get out all the major points without too many interruptions from Odilon by the time they reached the infirmary, where Sister Nina occupied the front desk, jotting something in a file folder. Joseph stopped talking as soon as he saw her, not that he thought she would believe any of what he was saying. He wasn't even sure Odilon believed him; his friend was skeptical, questioning every element of his story.

"Ah, Mr. Ward," Sister Nina said, looking up from the folder, "I was wondering when you'd—my word, child! How did that bandage become so filthy? I'll have to clean out your wound, make sure we keep infection away. Mr. Mercier, since you appear to be Mr. Ward's escort, would you please take him to bed number three? I'll be there in a moment, I have another patient to check on."

The boys made their way to one of six beds surrounded by white curtains as Sister Nina bustled across the room to another bed. As she pushed the sheet aside, Joseph caught a glimpse of a boy he vaguely recognized, laying with eyes closed on a cot. Joseph took a seat on his own cot while Odilon sat on the stool next to it.

"You think this farmer and his family all went crazy because you were there? In a painting?" Odilon asked, doubt dripping from his voice.

"It's like Hasty told me," Joseph said, "The paintings degrade or something."

"The girl who jumped out of a painting at your mother's funeral."

"I think that when a real person is in the painting, the whole reality of it gets upset. Like a sliver in a finger," Joseph said, thinking again of Wendel Highgrove. "The painting tries to push the foreign body out."

"Like an infection."

"Exactly."

Odilon waved his hands at Joseph. "I think maybe you are playing a joke on me."

"Let me show you. The classroom should be unlocked. I'll prove it to you."

"Prove to me that you can disappear into a painting and come out from another one?" Odilon smiled. "This I would like to see."

Sister Nina burst through the curtain just then. She must have read guilt on their faces; her eyebrows raised and she scrutinized them for an eternity before letting the curtain fall closed behind her.

"You boys aren't getting up to mischief, are you?" She grabbed Joseph's hand and stripped off the dirty bandage.

"No, sister," they said together.

She held Joseph's hand up, turned it toward the light, poked it with a wrinkled finger. "Mr. Ward, this is healing remarkably well."

Out of the corner of his eye, Joseph caught Odilon's eyebrows raise.

Sister Nina made short work of Joseph's dressings, dousing the cut with iodine and wrapping it tightly in clean bandages. Work done, she sent the boys off with a warning to go straight to their rooms or the library for the rest of their free time. Both promised they would do just that and both kept their fingers crossed behind their backs.

Joseph led the way to the classroom with the painting of the forest, stopping every so often to allow Odilon to catch up.

Odilon acted hesitant, as though he suspected Joseph was pulling a prank on him. And who could blame him? He'd been through enough in his life to justify the distrust. Joseph only hoped he could make this work again so that Odilon would have his faith rewarded. And, of course, to work out a way to get out of this place.

The room was unlocked and, after a glance up and down the hall to make sure they hadn't been spotted, Joseph shut the door behind them. Odilon stood just inside the door, fidgeting and peeking out the window into the hall every so often. Daylight illuminated the room enough that they didn't have to worry about turning on the lights. The painting hung directly in front of them, a serene forest setting, painted in shades of grey, blue, and white. In spite of Joseph's pleas, Odilon wouldn't get any closer than he already was, as though afraid of being sucked into the painting in spite of his disbelief.

"Try to focus on the painting, at least," Joseph said as he approached the canvas. "I want to know if you're able to see any movement in it. Or if you can see me in it when I go."

Odilon crossed his arms and leaned back against the wall. Joseph tried his best not to be frustrated with his friend. He could understand his doubt up to a certain point but did he really think Joseph was sinister enough to lead him all the way here just to laugh at him?

"Okay, watch closely." Joseph reached a hand out toward the painting.

Before anything could happen, the door flew open, slamming against the wall opposite. They both screamed and Odilon actually ducked behind a desk with his hands over his head, as though gunfire had just erupted in the classroom.

Brother James stood in the doorway, a surprised expression on his tanned face.

"You boys know you shouldn't be playing around in here. What's going on?"

Odilon pulled himself up off the floor, looking sheepish as he did so. Joseph's mind raced as Brother James folded his arms, clearly expecting a legitimate answer. His mouth started to open on its own, wanting to offer some kind of explanation but having nothing to say that would make any sense.

Odilon spoke up. "Can you tell us about this painting?"

Joseph's eyes widened involuntarily and he found himself glaring at Odilon, trying his level best to channel Luke Skywalker's force powers to make the other boy shut up.

Brother James chuckled and nodded at the picture. "That old thing?"

Joseph caught Odilon's eyes with his own. The other boy shrugged as if to say, *What else was I supposed to do?*

The friar gazed at the picture for a long minute and Joseph thought that perhaps he had seen movement within the painting as well. He forced himself to be quiet and wait for whatever conclusion the man would draw about why they were in here.

"Joseph was telling me about it," Odilon said, clearly avoiding Joseph's look. "He told me I have to see it. That it was magical."

Joseph was on the verge of strangling Odilon. How could he just blow their cover like this? What would the friar say about Joseph's claim to be able to dive into paintings? What would he tell Brother Lachlan?

Brother James said, "You really think my painting is magical?"

Joseph found himself beginning to shake his head when the friar's words sunk in. "Your painting?"

The man nodded, a small smile, one that showed a deeply buried pride, appearing on his face. "This and every other painting in St. Theodore's, few as there may be these days."

"You painted the farm landscape in Brother Lachlan's office?" The question was out of Joseph's mouth before he could stop it.

"He still has that old thing hung up?" James asked, eyebrows raised in surprise. "It's been a while since I've been in there."

Odilon took a seat at one of the desks, as though this were a class being taught.

"You created every painting in the school?" Joseph asked.

"Any you see hanging up, sure." James read the confusion on his face. "I was one of the first people hired when Brother Lachlan took over as headmaster. The existing artwork in the school had been liquidated to recover funds back in the sixties. Some good pieces were housed in here from what I heard. Anyway, Brother Lachlan knew that I had a bit of a penchant for the arts and asked if I had any work I'd be willing to part with. I made a good bit of extra money back then selling my existing work to the school and then painting a few more on commission."

Joseph's mind raced as he considered everything Brother James had just told him. He realized that, if what the man said was true, he could have a problem.

"You sold *all* of your artwork to the school?" Joseph said, unable to keep the incredulity from his voice.

Brother James smirked at him. "Pretty much. Not a bad way to make it as an artist, right?"

"You don't have work anywhere else?"

The friar raised an eyebrow at him. "If I do, I have no idea where it would be. You boys sure love this stuff, don't you?"

Joseph's heart sank. Despair made his limbs heavy, draining the energy from him. If all of Brother James' paintings were in St. Theodore's, as he said they were, Joseph would only be able to use the paintings to travel within the school.

Odilon said, "How many of your paintings are here?"

"Oh I can't recall," Brother James said, "There are plenty more kicking around, though I have no idea where they're all hung. I know a lot of them were stored downstairs."

"Downstairs?" Odilon pressed.

"In the basement. It's really a dungeon more than anything," the man said dismissively. "It's strictly forbidden for students to go down there. Don't get any ideas either, it's completely sealed off. Are you okay Joseph? You look a little peaked."

Joseph forced himself to smile. "Sure. It's just a shame that anyone would hide your work in the basement. I really like your paintings."

Brother James' face lit up. "Well, thank you."

"I had a question. About the farm," Joseph said.

"Shoot."

Joseph knew he was treading on dangerous territory but he had to ask. "Are those three people the only ones living on that farm?"

"What makes you ask something like that?" Brother James' expression became serious.

Joseph was afraid he had crossed a line but he couldn't turn back now that he'd started this line of inquiry. "I mean, it just felt like, maybe there could be someone else living in the house."

Brother James stared hard at Joseph for a long, uncomfortable moment. Joseph was about to tell the friar to forget he'd said anything when the man smiled and clapped him on the shoulder.

"You either made one lucky guess there or you are incredibly perceptive. Okay, you got me. Old Rupert, that's the name I gave the farmer, did have a son at one point."

"He was in the picture?" Joseph asked.

"Sort of. I started painting him but couldn't ever get him to look right. I don't know what it was, he just always looked deformed to me, like I couldn't quite nail it." The friar chuckled to himself. "In my imagination he was always the ignominy, the shame of the family. I often pictured him being hidden away by the farmer in one of the rooms of their house. Cruel, I know, but that's how the imagination works sometimes."

Odilon stared across the room at Joseph, eyes wide. Brother James noticed the unspoken communication between the two.

He put a hand behind Joseph's back and guided him to the door. "Okay, that's enough of the art history of Brother James McCurley. Head back to your rooms until lunch. I don't want to get myself in trouble for fraternizing with the inmates, as it were." He frowned and shook his head. "Sorry, cruel joke."

The boys were silent until they reached the turret stairs. Once the door to the staircase was shut behind them, Odilon spoke up.

"I apologize, Joseph," he said, "I did not believe you. I thought you were playing a joke on me. What brother James said, his description of the deformed boy, it was exactly what you told me."

"The farmer's name too," Joseph said, "I don't know if I told you but he told me his name was Rupert. The name Brother James gave him."

Odilon sat down on the stairs. "But if what he said is true, if he painted everything in here and if all his work is in the school, there is still no way out."

"He said there might be other paintings out there," Joseph said, "It doesn't really matter where they are, as long as it's not here."

"What if you come out somewhere dangerous? Like a volcano?" Odilon was smirking but his eyes remained serious.

Though the idea of a painting being in a volcano was ridiculous for a number of reasons, Joseph caught the other boy's point. He hadn't given it much thought himself. Sure, he'd known he might wind up somewhere he didn't like but he could always go back the way he came. Of course there was no way he'd come out in a volcano but what if he came out of a painting in a building that was on fire?

"I just need to go through slowly," he said after a minute, "And if it's somewhere really dangerous, I can go right back into the painting. I don't think we have to worry about volcanos."

Odilon stood and continued up the stairs. "What will you do when you get out?"

"Maybe try to find Hasty," Joseph said after a long moment. "I could live like she does, hopping from painting to painting. Make my way to L.A. and find my uncle."

"You will go from being a prisoner of this place to being a prisoner of those paintings."

"No men in robes to beat me in there."

"Just the monsters you told me of."

The eelamanders. Joseph had almost allowed himself to forget about them. He figured that as long as he limited the amount of time he was in a painting, they wouldn't be able to find him. Hasty had said they feed on the insecurity of the artist or something like that. Joseph wasn't even sure they were a danger to him, terrifying as they appeared.

"At least I have somewhere to run from those monsters," Joseph said as they stepped out of the stairwell and onto the fourth floor landing.

The rest of the day passed in a blur. Joseph went to the library for his study time after lunch. He browsed through art books, not quite certain what he was looking for. Many spoke of the lives of artists or their techniques but none mentioned, at least not in their index or table of contents, anything about the world *within* paintings. The closest thing he could find was Oscar Wilde's *The Picture of Dorian Gray*, which didn't come at all close to Joseph's experience. The only way he was going to figure anything out was by going back into the painting. At least he had access to one that he could practice in.

At supper that night Odilon, who had read *The Picture of Dorian Gray*, gave Joseph the run down of the plot. Hearing what the story was about, Joseph wished he had taken the book out to read. He saw some similarity in that Dorian Gray's picture aged while he stayed young but that wasn't a time disparity as much as it was a plain old curse. Maybe Mr. Wilde had experienced something like he and Hasty had, and had decided to write about it in his own way. The more Joseph dwelled on the story, the more plausible the whole thing seemed. If life could be infused into these paintings by imagination and if someone could travel through or live in one of them, wasn't it possible that an artist with this gift could arrange to have his painting take on his physical pain and sickness? And if that sort of thing was possible, couldn't any manner of science fiction be real? Thoughts of aliens and werewolves swirled about in his head.

Brother James took the podium at the front of the room, demanding the their attention and saving Joseph from his own thoughts. He announced that there would be a movie that evening, *Raiders of the Lost Ark*. The room erupted in applause and even Joseph found himself cheering for the picture, having seen it half a dozen times already. His excitement for the movie swiftly evaporated as a plan formed in his mind.

"I am excited to finally get to see this movie," Odilon said as they piled out of the dining hall with the other students.

"You'll love it," Joseph said, glancing around to make sure nobody was paying attention. "I'm going to skip it."

Odilon gave him a knowing look. "I will miss you if you find a way out."

Joseph's heart skipped a beat. He may actually be free of this place that very evening. He would miss his friend dearly but the prospect of getting out was too great to pass up. *If* he found a way. He didn't want to think of the possibility that there may not be a way out through Brother James' paintings but it wouldn't do him any good to get his hopes up. At the door to his room, Odilon reached out a hand for what Joseph assumed was meant to be a handshake. It amused him to be doing something so formal but he supposed others might find it suspicious if he hugged his friend farewell. He reached out his own hand and only realized it wasn't meant to be a handshake when Odilon stuck something cool and wet in his palm. He grimaced and looked down to see a thick slice of roast beef that his friend had stashed from his supper. He didn't have to tell Joseph what it was for.

"Thank you," Joseph whispered as he pocketed the meat.

He watched Odilon walk up the hall and disappear around the corner, then closed his door, sat on his bed, and waited.

22

Less than two hours later, Joseph stood in front of the closed door to the classroom that housed Brother James' painting of the forest. His hands shook, palms slick with sweat. He couldn't help but recall his attempted break-in at the church. He was about to repeat the exact same action that had gotten him into all of this trouble in the first place, but his desire to escape this place vastly outweighed any reservations he held.

Sneaking out of his room had been a lot easier than he'd imagined. He'd forced himself to wait thirty minutes after hearing what sounded like everyone on his floor thud down the hall before risking a look out his room door. The hallway was empty. He had no idea how often the faculty patrolled the halls up here during movie nights. He took his chance and slipped out of his room, sprinting to the turret staircase. If he was caught on his way down, he would simply claim that he had changed his mind about watching the movie. The classroom with the painting was down a hallway off of the main hall though. If he was caught there, he wouldn't have any solid excuse to offer.

As it turned out, he'd had nothing to worry about. He hadn't even needed the slice of roast beef Odilon had slipped him after supper but kept it in his pocket anyway, since he couldn't be certain when he would get the opportunity to eat again. The only person he saw on his way to the main hall was a younger student who had legitimately changed his mind about wanting to see the movie. The boy raced past Joseph without a word, glancing up at him only to see who he was. All Joseph could do was hope the kid would not find a reason to tell anyone about seeing him in the hall.

Standing in front of the classroom door unimpeded, he realized he didn't even know if the room would be unlocked. Doubt wormed its way into his mind. What if he could get into the room but the painting didn't work this time? What if it did and he wound up in the house of a psychopath, someone even worse than Brother Lachlan? The potential for such things was almost enough to turn him back. He might have done so, may have simply gone down to the dining hall and joined the other kids to enjoy the bulk of Indiana Jones' adventure, if he hadn't heard the door to one of the rooms up the hall opening. Without thinking anymore about it, he twisted the knob of the classroom door. At first his hand only slid around it and he worried that the room really was locked and that he would be caught red-handed by Lachlan himself. He wiped his hand on his pants and, sweat removed, turned the knob easily and slipped inside just as someone stepped out of one of the rooms up the hall. He stood in the dark with his back to the door for over a minute before checking the hallway through the window. All clear.

He crept across the room to the painting, casting glances over his shoulder every few steps to make sure he wasn't being spied on. Enough light seeped in from the hallway that he could clearly make out the painting. At least he wouldn't have to turn on the lights to see it. Did he have to be able to see the painting for this to work? He made a mental note to try it blind one day, when less was at stake.

Tall evergreens towered in the picture, all of them with their tops well beyond the edges of the canvas. Joseph focused on the tree trunks, the pine needles, the sleek fur of the deer hiding among the trees. At first there was nothing and he was once more struck with almost debilitating doubt. For a split second, he was convinced that he'd imagined all of his previous experiences with the paintings; Hasty, the painting in the church basement, the farm painting in Lachlan's office, all had been part of some bizarre fantasy he'd conjured for himself.

Then the pine boughs of one of the trees bounced up and down as though waving at him. A breeze blew through the forest within the painting and now all of the trees were waving. Inviting him in.

Come play, they called, *Come wander our forest. Come meet its inhabitants.*

He placed a hand on the canvas and it went through without any resistance. That falling sensation took over and then he was landing hard on his butt. He mentally thanked Brother Casper for not hitting him harder the day before, during Lachlan's interrogation. He'd have to work on these landings.

He pulled himself to his feet, brushing pine needles off his pants, and took in his surroundings. Trees spread as far as his eye could see; an endless forest. He remembered clearly the direction he had come from, off to his right, on his last foray into this forest. Though there was no sign of the end of the trees in that direction, he knew it eventually led to the mountainous valley where Rupert and his family resided. If he went back, would he find them working on the farm again as if nothing had happened? Did things reset when he left a painting? It was not something he was eager to discover first hand, at least not on that farm. He would find a way to check it out with another painting. He snapped two branches off a nearby tree and placed them in an X on the forest floor where he'd come through. Standing in front of the spot, he could see the air shimmer in a vaguely square shape. His exit frame. It would become harder to see the further he moved away from it. Having no bearing in this forest, he put his back to the shimmering space and started walking. At least this way, if he stayed in a straight line, he could find his way back.

He couldn't be sure how long or far he'd been walking by the time he allowed himself to rest. He had been following the sun, which remained exactly where it was, just above and ahead of him, for the entire time he'd been here. Legs sore, feet blistered, and mouth dry, he sat against the rough trunk of an enormous pine too tall to know the true height of. He stared up at the canopy of branches and needles and saw that he couldn't make out the tops of any of the trees around him. He hadn't been paying much attention before but he couldn't remember seeing any treetops since entering this forest. Did the trees stretch on forever or was there an eventual end to them? Was this another thing that Brother James had left unfinished, like the poor son of the farmer in the valley? He couldn't imagine it being anywhere near as terrifying. Still, he had no desire to see what was at the tops of these trees.

Several dozen feet in front of him, a deer emerged from behind an evergreen. It stepped from behind the tree in a cartoonish fashion, seeming to come out of thin air from behind the trunk. Its ears twitched as it extended its neck and nibbled at the foliage on the forest floor. Joseph clicked his tongue and the deer's head shot up, looking directly at him. He held out an empty hand, not quite sure what he hoped the animal would do. The deer took it as a threat. It turned and dashed off in the direction Joseph was headed. It hopped over a small branch and then disappeared into thin air. There was no tree trunk this time. The deer was simply there one instant and gone the next.

Joseph scrambled to his feet, keeping his eye on the spot where the deer had disappeared. He inched toward it, careful to stop ahead of where the animal had vanished. There was no shimmer to indicate this was the painting's exit but there hadn't been any such thing when he was running from the farm and the eelamanders, not that he'd been paying attention. He stretched a hand out and pulled it back before anything happened. Odilon's warning echoed in his mind. He had no idea where this would lead. For all he knew it was a battle zone or a house fire. Neither was likely to be the subject of one of Brother James' paintings but he'd only seen two of the man's pieces. He looked behind him at the endless forest and tussled with the idea of walking back through the monotony of it, searching for where he'd come back in, trying to avoid that farm all the while.

"There's no escape that way," he told himself.

Hearing his own voice break the silence of the forest gave

him the motivation he needed. Whatever the next painting was, it must be wholesome if it was allowed to be hung up in St. Theodore's. He took another minute to bolster his courage, thinking about where the exit of this next painting could lead.

"Don't get your hopes up," he said.

He shook out his hands, took a breath, and stepped forward.

Rain.

He was soaked the instant he stepped through the place the deer had disappeared. There was no sign of the animal but Joseph couldn't see much of anything at all as he fought to keep the sudden barrage of water out of his eyes. All around him the world was grey with rain and heavy cloud cover. It looked like, somewhere beyond the depths of the clouds above him, the sun might be shining. What little light came through the clouds didn't matter much, considering the sheer volume of rain made it next to impossible to see anything farther than his hand in front of his face. He started forward at a slow walk, cautious of unseen hazards, loafers sloshing in rain-soaked grass, sinking into the soft earth. Without a tree, or anything that could provide shelter in sight, he had nowhere to go but straight ahead. He faced an instant's temptation to go back the way he'd come but couldn't bring himself to give up so easily. A little rain never hurt anyone, as he'd often heard said.

Then the world lit up and exploded.

A bolt of lightning, huge and blinding, struck the ground some fifty yards or so ahead of him. The air crackled with electricity and the hairs on his body stood upright in spite of the rain weighing them down. The crash that followed deafened and disoriented him. The air around him collapsed in on itself as thunder boomed and echoed. He felt the noise of it in his bones. And then it was gone.

A faint glowing spot in the ground remained for an instant where the lightning had struck and then it was as if nothing had happened. The rolling echo of the thunder dissipated with the glow from the lightning strike and all that remained was the rain.

But that *wasn't* all. He'd seen something that his brain had ruled out as obsolete at the moment of the lightning strike but that was now vitally important. There had been a structure of some sort, just beyond where the lightning struck. He'd seen it silhouetted against the horizon of an endless grassy plain. At first his mind recalled the structure as a barn, the same size and shape as Farmer Rupert's. That wasn't right though. The shape he'd seen was much smaller, more like shed. It had a gabled roof but that was the only resemblance it bore to that barn. He hoped.

He stumbled over the grass in the direction of the shed. With no way to gather his bearings, he was walking blind, at least until another lightning strike took place. He pointed himself in the direction of the spot the lightning had hit but stopped himself before he could go more than a few steps toward it. He'd heard the adage about how it never struck twice in the same place, but he'd learned paint-logic didn't often reflect reality. It was safe to assume the lightning would strike in the exact same place that it had a moment ago. A couple of minutes later, his theory was confirmed when the lightning hit again with the same ferocity, accompanied by the same sonic explosion. Though he had no way of telling for certain, the placement looked close enough to the previous strike for him to feel confident it was the same spot.

He'd been paying attention during the second strike and saw that he had closed the distance between himself and the shed enough that he could sprint the rest of the way to it with confidence. A third bolt of lightning struck just as got close enough to the shed for it to be visible through the rain. The lightning lit the small structure up like a castle in a horror movie. It loomed in front of him, the only bastion in this field of rain and thunder. He put a hand on the door and hesitated. What if Brother James had conceived of some poor victim to be tormented by this storm? A madman or another half-finished creation could be lurking inside.

He pounded on the door. Stuck an ear to it. The rain made it impossible to hear anything inside except for the percussion of each drop landing on the roof. Deciding he would turn tail and flee if anyone was home, he pushed the door open.

A sigh of relief escaped his lips and was carried away into the storm as he stepped into the dryness of a cozy little cabin. The place was empty but had the appearance of one that had recently been lived in. Rain pounded on the roof and sluiced through the open door. He shut it, doing nothing to mute the drum of the rain, but thankful to be out of it.

An ancient wood stove stood against one wall, a stack of what looked to be dry wood piled up next to it. He knelt in front of the stove and arranged wood in a rough teepee. He struck a match from a wooden tinder box he found on the floor and set the small pyre ablaze. Within seconds of the wood catching fire, smoke began to build up in the small cabin. He coughed and held his soaking shirt in front of his mouth and nose. The flue was still shut! In a panic he scanned the stove and chimney for a handle or a lever. If he couldn't get it open, the place would be full of smoke in less than a minute and he'd be right back out in the rain. He crawled up close to the stove, ignoring the growing heat of the fire, and spotted a small lever on the back of it. He wrenched the handle down and it gave under the pressure. The room began to clear immediately. He kneeled on the floor, keeping as low as possible until the smoke evacuated.

Five minutes later, he was naked with his clothes and shoes drying out in front of the fire. He rummaged through the cupboards next to the stove, finding nothing but a couple of tin plates and a dented tin cup. He wasn't hungry yet but hoped to find a couple of things he might be able to take along with him. He considered cooking the hunk of meat Odilon had given him but decided to save it for when he absolutely needed it. As long as it didn't rot in the meantime.

Lightning flashed outside the cabin, presumably in the same place it had struck previously. He turned his clothes over to dry the other side, knowing full well he would have to step out into that torrent once more if he hoped to get out of this place. Still, it would be nice to have dry clothes on for even a few minutes.

A small cot fitted with a rough looking blanket sat in the far corner of the cabin. He was chilly in spite of the fire, being completely naked, and decided to hop into the bed until his clothes were dry. The bed was warm and the blanket much softer than it appeared. He snuggled in and watched the fire, the warmth making his eyes heavy. He dozed off staring at the flames and thinking of his mother.

He had no idea how much time had passed when he snapped awake. The fire had dwindled down to nothing more than glowing embers, which meant he must have been out at least an hour, maybe more. The rain beat down as heavy as it had been before he fell asleep. He was surprised the thunder hadn't disturbed him, he didn't think he'd been that tired. As if on cue, a flash came from outside followed by the familiar boom.

He crawled out of the bed, shivering against the relative coolness of the cabin, and pulled on his clothes, thankful they'd dried thoroughly and that they retained a small amount of warmth from the fire. Fully dressed, he lay back on the bed and tried to come up with some sort of strategy. Without any way of knowing how to find his way out of this place, he was only delaying stepping back out into the rain storm. The only chance he had to find his way out was to keep moving; he wasn't sure what would happen if he remained in this particular painting for too long and had no desire to find out.

A thought occurred to him and he shoved off the bed, going to his knees in front of the stove, and using the brass poker he found leaning against the wall to coax a blackened chunk of wood out of it. After giving it a minute to cool down, he held the piece of charcoal like a pencil and sketched the rough shape of the exterior of the cabin out on the floor. He drew the zigzag of a lightning bolt next to it and regarded his work. If the painting was made with a front view of the cabin, he imagined this would be roughly how it was laid out. He would walk in the direction of the perspective one took when looking at this place as a painting and hope that the exit would make itself apparent as he got close.

Stepping back out into the rain was harder than he imagined. There was nothing for him in the cabin other than dry warmth, which was almost enough to keep him from leaving. But eventually he would grow hungry and that chunk of meat in his pocket wouldn't keep him going for long. He stepped out into the deluge.

After several minutes of walking nearly blind, he turned to check how far he'd come. He had to wait for the lightning to flash and saw that the cabin was some two hundred yards away. Without knowing how far the structure was in the painting, there was no way to know where to look for the way out. He wasn't even sure he was walking in the right direction. The cabin being surrounded by nothing but plains meant that the picture could have been painted from any angle and any distance. The picture itself could be of a tiny cabin, perched on the edge of the horizon, in which case he could be walking for hours without getting anywhere.

He had the lightning pretty well timed out by this point. He would count to one hundred as he walked, turning around as he hit ninety-nine, and would be just in time for the lightning to strike and illuminate the cabin. He would check his distance every third or fourth strike, using the light of the other strikes to check his surroundings for any sign of a way out. He tried not to think about the eelamanders and their haunting call. With every other step he expected to hear that low, grumbling whale song that would signal their arrival.

And then the world changed. One second he was walking through a grassy plain, being pounded by history's most vicious rainstorm, and the next he was basking in warm sunlight. The switch was so sudden that he cried out when the rain gave way to sunshine. He squinted against the daylight, disoriented in the brightness. This must be how vampires felt.

He took a few steps in place and laughed when no water sloshed around his soaking wet loafers. He kicked off his shoes and socks and sank his toes into the soft, vibrant grass, digging them into the cool soil it grew from. His skin was already drying off under the comforting heat of the sun. He pulled his shirt halfway off, paused, and tugged it back down. He should figure out where he was before taking off his clothes.

He'd come through a copse of deciduous trees, lush and green. Beams of sunlight shone down between them; no sign of the stormy plains he had just come from. He stood in a vibrant meadow surrounded by a peaceful looking forest. The meadow was big, the size of at least a couple of football fields, covered in soft grass and speckled with groups of wildflowers. Smack in the middle of it was the bluest body of water he'd ever seen. Moments ago he wanted nothing but to be dry; now he ran to the edge of a small lake—or a really big pond, rolled up his pant legs, and waded in up to his knees. The water was the perfect temperature, just cool enough to be refreshing. A silver fish darted past his feet. Joseph cupped his hands, scooped up as much of the water as he could hold, and slurped. It was sweet and refreshing, slaking his thirst and at the same time driving him to drink until his belly felt close to bursting.

He stripped off his clothes and swam out to the middle of the lake. The sun warmed his scalp while his body stayed nice and cool underwater. He treaded water and turned in slow circles, checking out every angle of the lake. He was alone, that much had been obvious soon after arriving. There was no sign of life other than the occasional fish that swam by him. Perhaps he had scared off all other wildlife when he'd arrived.

"Move that cabin next to this lake and I could live here," he said to himself.

He decided that he would not attempt to find a way out of here until he'd spent at least as much time next to this lake as he had trapped in the perpetual storm of the last painting. He swam to the shore opposite of where he'd left his clothes and perched on a large, flat rock that rested by the water's edge. The stone was hot against his bare skin and felt divine. He lay back on it, feeling like an iguana basking in the sun, and closed his eyes. He stayed like that until he was completely dry then rolled off the rock, enjoying the cool grass on his feet. He imagined himself as Adam in the Garden of Eden, naked and with the world as his kingdom.

His imagination was drifting toward the notion of his Eve showing up when he spotted the unmistakable shimmer of an exit pane in the air less than a dozen feet in front of him. Suddenly he was conscious of the fact that he was standing nude in the middle of the field. He was fairly certain nobody else could see him in the paintings but the notion that someone might be staring at it this very moment made him self-conscious enough to jog around the lake and put his clothes back on.

For the first time since jumping into the world of a painting, he felt the urge to return to this place soon. Assuming it was one of the paintings still in St. Theodore's, he was thrilled to have a place to retreat to on occasion. If he'd found a way out of the academy, he would have to hope this picture was somewhere accessible, like an art museum.

His stomach reminded him that he hadn't eaten in some time. That was enough to coax him toward the exit pane on the other side of the small lake. He'd probably lingered long enough anyway. The last thing he wanted was to ruin this paradise with a visit from the eelamanders.

He knew as soon as he stepped through the shimmer that he was still in St. Theodore's. He'd known it was more than likely he'd end up back here but that didn't stop the disappointment from feeling like a basketball-sized lump in his gut. He felt sick and angry at the same time. Picking himself off the floor, and reminding himself again to get better at his landings, he took in his surroundings. Another classroom. Desks neatly arranged in four rows of five, board still covered in white chalk, words written in a neat, looping hand. Between the light coming in from the hall and the moonlight streaming in through the window, he was able to see clearly.

The painting he'd come from looked much like he'd expected it to; small lake in a meadow surrounded by trees. It was unremarkable to look at, especially when compared to the others. Maybe this was an early work of McCurley's. Joseph was fascinated by the notion that the quality of the painting had nothing to do with the quality of the world within it. It appeared to be all about content and the imagination of the artist. He wished he could see Hasty again so that he could talk about these things with someone who understood, who had experienced it themselves.

He crept to the door and pressed his face against the window, looking up and down the hall. Satisfied the way was clear, he eased the door open and stepped out of the classroom. He headed to the stairs, ready to sleep in his own bed, and halted at the turret door. Someone had painted it white. It had always been a plain, unfinished door that he'd been going through to get up to his room, but now it was white. Why paint it during movie night? He touched a scuff mark, one of many, on the edge of the door. He must have come out of a second floor classroom. He seldom visited this floor so it made sense that he had no memory of the color of the door. Why it stood out so much this time through, he couldn't be sure.

He sprinted up the stairs, noting he had indeed been on

the first floor, and inched the door open at the top. Seeing no one in the hall, he stepped out of the turret and froze. The walls were painted a light shade of lavender. Everything else looked fairly similar. It didn't make sense that someone would or *could* repaint the entire school in one night. He realized his mistake a second before the door to his right opened.

23

A FAMILIAR FACE STOOD IN THE DOORWAY. FAMILIAR because he'd seen this person gabbing to Caroline, Blue, since he'd first noticed her in the dining hall. He couldn't remember the girl's name but he knew she was one of Caroline's friends. She had reddish-brown hair that fell around her face and shoulders in thick curls.

"How did you get into the girl's wing?" she demanded in a shrill voice.

How could he have not made the connection sooner?

He held a finger to his lips, grinned at the girl, trying to look embarrassed. "Took a wrong turn, I guess. I'm still getting used to these halls."

She crossed her arms. "There's a monitor at every entrance. You're in big trouble."

"Who is that, Bronwyn?" a familiar voice called from behind her.

The girl, Bronwyn rolled her eyes. "That boy who stares at you all the time."

Caroline, dressed in baby-blue flannel pajamas, appeared behind Bronwyn. Her eyes widened as she saw it was, in fact, a boy standing in the hallway. She shoved Bronwyn back into the room and pulled the door closed behind her.

"What are you doing here?" she whispered.

"I came to see you." It was all he could think to say.

She laughed and twirled a strand of hair around one of her fingers. "And you were just going to stand out in the hall until I came out?"

"I hadn't really thought it through."

She laughed again. It was a pretty sound, like bells jingling.

A door opening down the hall made his back go rigid. He looked around for a place to hide, not quite believing he could make it back to the turret door on time. Before he could move, Caroline grabbed a handful of his shirt and yanked him into her dorm. She shoved him behind her and poked her head out the door.

"You can't bring a boy in here," Bronwyn whined from one of two twin beds in the room, "Bad enough he's in our wing."

"Shush up, Bron," Caroline snapped from the door.

Bronwyn fixed Joseph with an ice-cold stare. "You're going to be in so much trouble."

Before Joseph could respond, Caroline pulled him to the door. "Just someone going to the bathroom. Coast is clear. You'd better get out of here."

He stepped out into the hallway. Turned to face Caroline, who still had a grip on his arm.

"Meet me tomorrow night?" He almost clapped a hand over is own mouth. The question came from out of nowhere, dredged up by pure adolescent instinct. He'd never spoken to a girl like this. Directly. Making plans together. Trying to, anyway.

Her eyes lit up. "You're going to come back?"

"I know a secret way. I can show you."

"Tomorrow night?"

He nodded. "In the stairway. The turret. Ten o'clock?"

She bit her lower lip and nodded, releasing his arm. His heart fluttered, flipped over, and turned inside out. Had he just made a date? With a girl?

"Go," she whispered, "Before Bronwyn has a hissy fit."

She craned her neck out and planted a peck on his cheek. It was brief, barely holding contact for a second, but it was her lips on his skin. His face flushed. Then she was gone and the door was closed behind her. He resisted the urge to skip down the hallway to the stairs, forcing himself to take slow, quiet steps.

The downstairs hallway leading out of the girl's wing was silent. He crept along the wall, ready to duck into a classroom if he heard anyone coming. He was halfway down when a bestial growl stopped him in his tracks.

Julius.

The huge German Shepherd stalked toward him out of the shadows, looking more like a predator than a guard dog; head lowered, teeth bared. Joseph was frozen in place. He scanned the hall but found nothing to hide or shield himself from the dog. Running would do no good; Julius could easily overtake him. The beast was less than half a dozen feet from him and slowly closing that gap. Joseph kept his hands flat at his sides, pressing them hard against his legs. His right hand touched a lump in his pocket. The meat! According to Odilon, Julius couldn't be bought off with treats but a lump of beef to any dog had to be tempting. It was the only shot he had.

He fished the meat from his pocket and the dog stopped mid-step, one front paw frozen in mid-air. Julius sniffed and growled again, continuing his advance. Joseph held the meat up and, though the dog didn't slow, its attention was zeroed in on the morsel. He waited for the dog to be within touching distance then lobbed the meat back the way he'd come, down the girl's corridor. In his panic, he neglected to put much effort into the toss and the meat landed only a few feet away. Julius looked from Joseph to the meat, torn between duty and a tasty, if slightly spoiled, snack. The dog took another step forward and Joseph knew he'd blown his chance. Maybe if he'd tossed it directly to the animal he could have at least distracted it for a second. Would it actually bite him or simply bark and keep him in place until one of the brothers or sisters showed up to investigate the noise?

Lips pulled back from his teeth, Julius extended his neck and sniffed Joseph's fingers. Another growl. Then the dog was trotting over to the meat. Joseph waited for him to sniff at the beef and slowly backed away. When he reached the entrance to the boy's corridor, he turned and ran.

A woof came from behind him as he pounded down the hallway. He looked over his shoulder and saw Julius bounding across the main hall, coming straight for him. He poured everything he had into making it to the end of the hallway. The door to the turret was dead ahead. The machine-gun clicking of Julius' claws on the wood floor sounded like it was directly behind him. He leaned into his run. Julius' breath was right in his ear. He burst through the door to the stairs and slammed it shut behind him. A heavy thump came from the other side. The dog barked once and scratched at the door.

"Goodnight, Julius," Joseph said, climbing the stairs to his room.

24

————

AT BREAKFAST THE NEXT MORNING, JOSEPH SAT NEXT TO A smiling Odilon.

"I am sorry you are still here but I am glad to see you," he said.

Joseph started in on his breakfast right away. He was famished. However much time had passed in the real world, it had been much longer for him since his last meal. He slurped his eggs up in two big bites and started in on his toast.

"Are you going to try again?" Odilon asked.

Joseph nodded and swallowed. "I need to map out the pictures. I don't know if I'll find a way out but I don't want to keep getting lost."

"I don't understand."

"Each picture leads to another one, right?" Joseph said.

Odilon shrugged.

Joseph lowered his voice and said, "The picture of the farm in Lachlan's office led to the forest painting in the classroom. That painting leads to another one that I think I was lucky to get out of."

"This sounds dangerous," Odilon said, taking a minuscule bite of egg.

"You should see this place. It's a constant thunderstorm. Can't see a thing. But," he bit a piece of bacon in half and spoke as he chewed, "It leads to this beautiful lake. It's perfect. I wish I could take her there."

He stared across the dining hall. Caroline was saying something to Bronwyn, who was talking at the same time. Both of their hands were flying in excited gestures, trying to emphasize whatever it was that girls got so excited about. Bronwyn caught Joseph looking and her smile disappeared. He looked away. What had he done to make her dislike him so much?

"Her friend does not seem to like you," Odilon pointed out.

"I visited her last night."

Joseph almost *heard* Odilon's eyes widen. His friend grabbed him by the arm enough to hurt a little bit.

"You are insane, Joseph. If you get caught, you will both get in trouble. You should not make life worse for her here than it already is."

He was right, of course. Joseph had thought about that. But she also wanted to see him. She knew the risks and had agreed to meet with him that night. Joseph decided he would keep that to himself for now. He didn't need Odilon acting as his conscience all the time.

"Have you ever read the story of the Minotaur?" Odilon asked, stashing a couple of slices of bacon in his pocket.

"Greek mythology, right? Ms. Hendrix just started

teaching it before I was brought here. I was looking forward to it."

"The story is about a man named Theseus," Odilon explained. "He went to fight a Minotaur, a half-man, half-bull. The monster lived in a labyrinth, a maze, and, in order to find his way out, Theseus brought a ball of yarn to let out as he made his way through."

"Like Hansel and Gretel."

Odilon nodded.

"So all I need is a big ball of yarn or a loaf of bread," Joseph said.

"Didn't birds eat up the bread crumbs Hansel put down?"

"For a foreign kid, you sure know your fairy tales."

"Hansel and Gretel are German. Theseus is Greek. They are more foreign than I am," Odilon said with a hint of defensiveness.

"Point taken," Joseph said. "You're right though. Bread crumbs may or may not get eaten by birds in the paintings but I know for sure they won't last in the rain."

Kids were starting to clear out of the dining hall and it wouldn't be long before the staff came around to nudge out the stragglers. Joseph didn't want to catch the attention of any of the faculty if he could help it. He stood and stretched.

"Keep brainstorming," he said to Odilon.

Lunch and supper passed without inspiration. To Joseph's frustration, Odilon appeared to have become bored with thinking of ways to blaze a trail through the paintings. By the end of the night both boys had grown irritable with each other. Joseph went straight to his room after supper to kill time until he could sneak out to keep his date with Caroline.

At nine-thirty that evening, Joseph, with his hair groomed

and teeth brushed, peered out the door of his bedroom and felt his heart sink. Brother Iain, one of the friars Joseph didn't yet know very well, sat in a chair in the middle of the hallway, reading a book. Just his luck. It was rare that one of the faculty actually remained in the hallway. He quietly closed his door and lay back on his bed.

At two minutes to ten, he peeked out the door to see Brother Iain had left his post. Joseph forced himself to count to one hundred before slipping out of his room and through the door into the turret stairwell.

A few minutes later he was stepping into the classroom with the forest painting. A while after that he found himself wishing he'd thought to bring an umbrella along as he slogged through the sopping fields of the plain plagued by rain. Trudging through the wet grass, he vowed to pack a raincoat, or maybe an umbrella, the next time he came here. At the lake, he stripped his clothes off and laid them out over the flat rock, giving them some time to dry. It took about an hour but, by his rough estimate, only a minute or so would have gone by in the real world. He got dressed while his clothes were still a little damp, then slipped out of the painting and into the girl's wing classroom that housed it.

In the girl's turret, he tiptoed up the stairs, every creak and groan of the old steps beneath him sounding loud enough to wake the whole school. The top of the staircase was empty. Caroline was nowhere in sight. Joseph sighed, plunked himself down on the top step, and put his face in his hands. He couldn't blame her for not showing up. It was risky to be stepping out of your room, even to make a trip to the bathroom, let alone sneaking into a staircase to meet a boy.

He stood and stretched, deciding that he'd head back to the

lake painting and hang out there for a while before having to face the rain once more on his way back to his own side. He wished desperately that he knew of another way around and made a promise to himself that he would map out as many paintings as possible, as soon as possible. He could go in with a sketchpad and make a rough map of each one he visited.

He was so distracted with the notion of plotting out routes that he didn't hear the door to the stairwell open, or notice the figure who stood watching him. When a hand landed on his shoulder, he screamed at the top of his lungs. Another hand clamped over his mouth and Joseph struggled, breaking free of the grip and stumbling down half a dozen stairs before turning back to face his assailant.

Caroline stared down at him from the top of the stairwell, wearing a look of surprised amusement that Joseph may have found funny if his heart wasn't fighting to escape his chest. She covered her mouth and giggled.

"Sorry I'm late," she whispered down to him. "Are you okay?"

He pulled himself up and dusted off his pants, forcing himself to smile. He'd already made a fool of himself.

"What's this secret path you promised to show me?" She came down a couple of steps and took a seat just above him.

"If I tell you, it has to be our secret. You can't tell anybody. Especially your roommate."

"Bronwyn's cooler than she seems."

Joseph shook his head. "I can't tell if you're going to spill to her."

Caroline huffed and pooched out her bottom lip. "Okay, whatever."

He held out his pinky finger.

"Really?" she sneered.

He raised his eyebrows and smirked.

"Fine." She clasped her pinky around his and they shook on it.

Joseph felt chills at even this casual contact. Would they hold hands by the side of the lake? Would she let him kiss her? Would he have the guts to? His hands started to sweat and yanked his pinky back before she could tell.

"Why are your clothes damp?" she asked as he took his hand back.

"I'll tell you on the way. Come on."

He started down the stairs, almost forgetting he was in forbidden territory. He forced himself to move slowly down the steps so as to not alert any hall monitors or either of the dogs to the intrusion. He gave her the short version of his experiences in the paintings as they crept down the stairs and then through the hall to the classroom.

Within minutes they stood at the door.

"Is this a prank?" she whispered at him as he held the door open.

He shook his head and put a finger to his lips, waved her in.

She crossed her arms. "I'm not going in there until you tell me what it is you're showing me. And how you actually got wet." Her eyes lit up. "Did you sneak outside? Is it raining?"

"It's exactly like I told you," he said.

"You got sucked into a painting. Right."

"Whether you believe me or not, we should get out of the hall before someone spots us."

Caroline rolled her eyes and took a step into the classroom. She stopped just inside the door and darted her head back and forth as if she expected someone to jump out at her from the shadows.

"It's just an empty classroom," she said. "I'm not going to make out with you in here, if that's your plan."

Though it was not his plan, Joseph did feel stung by her remark, partly from the accusation and partly because that likely meant she wouldn't let him kiss her as they sat beside the lake. He tried to keep his frustration at bay; he'd be skeptical too if he was in her position.

He crossed the room to the painting of the lake.

"I've seen that painting before," Caroline said. "I have class in here three times a week. There's nothing special about it. It's not even that good."

She still had her arms crossed and appeared adamant about not stepping any further into the room.

"Just come a bit closer and I'll show you. Then you can decide if you want to try it or not. Please?" He held his hands out in front of him, folded in a pleading gesture.

She blew out a long, dramatic sigh and spun a hand around. *Get on with it.*

Joseph grinned. Once she saw him disappear into the painting she'd have no choice but to believe him. And then she'd absolutely want to join him by the lake. Who *wouldn't* want the chance to enter the world of a painting?

He rubbed his hands together like a magician preparing to dazzle his audience of one.

"Don't take your eyes off me as I go in, alright?"

She gave no response. This was a lot harder than Joseph had anticipated. He'd imagined she would be excited about such a magical prospect. The initial skepticism was, of course, understandable but wasn't she even curious? Even if he was pulling one over on her, didn't she want to see what was going to happen? Debunk it with her own eyes?

"Here goes. Keep your eyes on me."

He turned away from her, trying his level best not to be discouraged by her lack of interest. He tried to do it slowly but as soon as the tip of his finger was through the canvas, he was sucked right into the painting and into the warm glow of the sun. His spirits rose when the sun hit his face. He couldn't wait to show Caroline.

He made himself walk around the lake twice, to give her at least a few seconds in the real world to verify that he had indeed disappeared from the classroom. He wished she could see him walking around the lake. What would she think when she got here? She might freak out. What if she wasn't able to go through with him? He hadn't really considered the possibility. He was basing everything he knew about the paintings off the brief education he got from Hasty and none of it really covered bringing other people along.

"Guess we'll find out," he said to himself as he stepped through the wavering exit frame and into the real world.

The room was empty. Joseph half-heartedly checked to see if Caroline was hiding by one of the desks but knew as soon as he got back that she was gone. He ran to the door and stuck his head out into the hall just in time to see her disappear through the door to the turret staircase.

"Caroline!" he hissed.

If she heard, it made no difference. He pulled his head back into the classroom, closed the door, and shuffled back to the painting. He was mystified and frustrated. She'd *seen* him go in. What could have possessed her to take off on him like that? Did she think he was pulling an elaborate prank on her?

Maybe she was scared. The thought hadn't really occurred to him before but he supposed something so incredible could very well frighten some people. He had known a girl who was scared to death of birds of all shapes and sizes. If birds could scare someone, he supposed anything could. He'd have to apologize to Caroline when he saw her next.

He slipped into the painting to make his way back to his room.

25

AFTER THAT NIGHT, SECURITY TIGHTENED IN THE hallways of St. Theodore's. Even a trip to the bathroom in the middle of the night became a trying ordeal. Obviously Caroline had squealed after Joseph had tried to show her the world within paintings. She had taken to ignoring him completely. Could he really blame her? It was easy to see how she interpreted the whole thing as a prank. It worried him, though, that the headmaster hadn't yet confronted him about it.

Before he knew it, November was almost entirely past and Thanksgiving dinner was being served in the dining hall. Joseph hadn't made a single trip into the world of the paintings since his failed date with Caroline. The classroom doors were now locked at night and any other time they weren't in use.

A feeling of melancholy had overcome him, one which seemed to delight the faculty, especially Lachlan. Whenever Joseph passed the headmaster in the halls, he would keep his eyes on the floor and try to make himself as small as possible, dreading when he would be called back into the office.

Lachlan would invariably stop and watch Joseph until he was out of sight. There was a triumphant look to the man's gaze, as though he knew exactly what Joseph had been prevented from doing, unlikely as that was. Caroline may have ratted on him for sneaking over to the girl's wing but there was no way anyone would believe he could travel through paintings.

Odilon had done his best to keep Joseph's spirits up, trying to help him see the bright side of being at St. Theodore's. His attempts were without much enthusiasm though; even Odilon, in his perpetual state of optimism, had a hard time finding things to like about this place.

"At least you no longer have to deal with your father," Odilon had reminded him on more than one occasion.

For all Joseph knew, his father was dead and buried in an unmarked grave. As much as he despised the man, the thought made him sad. He felt sorry for him, wasting away by himself with only his beer to comfort him. He may have met someone, Joseph tried telling himself. There was even a chance he'd quit drinking. Though it was far from likely, this notion made Joseph more upset than the idea of him being dead. If he had given up drinking, that meant that he didn't want Joseph around even when he was sober. This drove Joseph even deeper into his depression and by the time he sat down to Thanksgiving dinner, he was lower than he'd ever felt in his life. Even after his mother had died, there'd been some hope for a brighter future. Now he could see nothing ahead but the walls and bars of the academy.

"Happy Thanksgiving," Odilon said with a smile as Joseph dropped into his seat next to him.

Joseph bit his tongue—he didn't trust himself to say

anything kind in return. There was nothing happy about celebrating Thanksgiving in this place.

It didn't seem like his attitude could affect Odilon's spirits today, for which he was glad. He didn't want to make other people miserable, he just didn't want to share in their misplaced joy. Not behind these walls.

He barely tasted the dry turkey beneath the mounds of cranberry sauce he had to pile on in order to make it palatable. He ate mechanically, half-listening to Odilon talk about Thanksgiving on the street and how it was his favorite time of year, next to Christmas. The boy prattled on about soup kitchens and how, on those days, it felt like he truly had a family.

Pumpkin pie was set out and Joseph had a piece only to keep his stomach from complaining later on. He watched Odilon sequester a couple of slices of turkey in his pants pocket and marveled at how the boy kept his spirits up the way he did. He felt guilty for not sharing in Odilon's enjoyment of the holiday but he couldn't muster the energy to even return a smile.

"I have something for you," Odilon said after supper.

"For me? Why?"

His friend clapped him on the back and Joseph fought the desire to throw his hand off.

Odilon must have felt him stiffen because he removed the hand on his own. "It is a present. For Thanksgiving."

"You're getting your holidays mixed up," Joseph said. "Christmas is when you give presents. Thanksgiving is about being thankful."

"And I am thankful."

Joseph looked at him. "For what?"

Odilon smiled. "I am thankful the Lord sent me a friend in this place."

Joseph felt sick with shame. He'd spent months feeling sorry for himself when Odilon had it much worse than him inside and outside this place. Odilon was always smiling and Joseph took it for granted, as if the other boy owed it to him. And now Odilon wanted to give him a present because he was thankful for him.

"Sorry, Odi," Joseph said. "I've kind of been a butthole, I guess."

"This place is hard to get used to," his friend said.

Joseph's throat tightened and he had to look away.

"You're a good friend." Joseph forced himself to smile and put an arm around Odilon. "So what'd you get me, chum?"

"You'll see," the other boy said with a grin, "When you get back to your room."

It took no small amount of effort for Joseph to keep himself from sprinting back to his room after supper. Sister Eustice had announced there would be a movie that evening, which the entire student body had anticipated anyway. She declared that anyone who chose to skip the movie would have to stay in their rooms. That suited Joseph just fine, now that the classroom doors were kept locked he had little desire to roam the halls as he once did.

Marching up the turret stairs to his room, he tried to guess what Odilon may have got for him. How had he managed to sneak it into Joseph's room without his key? Had he picked the lock? He was touched once more by the thoughtfulness of his only friend in this place. He made a vow with himself to somehow get them both out of here. He imagined them hitch-hiking back to civilization, living on the streets together, forming their own posse. They would work their way west and track down his uncle Edgar. They'd spend their days basking in the pool and at night they'd roam the streets of Los Angeles. He shoved open the door to his room, smiling at the fantasies he'd cooked up.

He was so lost in his daydreams that he almost forgot about Odilon's present. The gift leaned against the headboard of his bed; large, flat, and rectangular, wrapped in plain packing paper. He checked to make sure his door was shut tight then allowed himself to approach the bed. He gripped an edge of the packing paper and tore. Tried not to look until all the paper had been pulled off but he could feel the edges of the frame and the raised paint on the stretched surface of the canvas.

Either he was developing an eye for art or Brother James' style was distinctive enough to pick out. The man certainly did love landscapes. Joseph turned the frame so that the painting was right-side-up, and noted James' signature in the bottom right corner. The painting depicted a gently winding dirt road that ran from the base of the frame up to a distant horizon near the top. Lining each side of the grassy shoulders were large, leafy trees, perhaps maples or oaks. The sky through the trees was the light blue of a clear, sunny day.

He reached a hand out without thinking twice about it.

A knock on the door made him yank his hand back, as though he was about to be caught in the act of something heinous. The door opened an inch and Brother James' head poked through.

"Sorry to interrupt." He raised a hand either in greeting or surrender. "Just wanted to make sure you got your present. Odilon had me help him out and open the door to your room. I hope that wasn't too much of an invasion of your privacy."

"It's okay," Joseph said, not quite trusting the man's apparent altruism.

"May I?" The friar placed a tentative foot in the room.

Joseph nodded.

"It's nice to have someone interested in my work," James took a seat in the chair at Joseph's desk. "I know it's the only art around but, still, it's nice to know someone values it enough to give it, and to receive it, as a gift."

Joseph leaned the painting against the wall. "I really like it."

"I'm glad you do," James smiled at him. "Your friend was pretty desperate to get it to you. Strange, so long after your birthday and a full month before Christmas. He just couldn't wait."

Joseph wasn't sure what to say to this so he simply smiled at the friar.

Brother James stood and stretched. "He would've done just about anything to get this to you. It seems like you really mean a lot to each other."

"He's a good friend."

"A friend, is he?" James went to the door and casually turned the deadbolt.

Gooseflesh rose on Joseph's arms. His stomach tightened and he told himself to calm down; Brother James was a co-conspirator in a sense. He just wanted to talk. For some reason, though, Joseph couldn't help but think of his encounter with Lachlan in his office last spring.

"He might be more than a friend. Isn't that right?" The man sauntered over to the bed.

"I'm not sure I know what you mean, Brother."

James reached behind his neck and fiddled with his cassock. "You know what I mean. He's your little fag friend. Your bum buddy."

He slipped out of his cassock so that he was dressed only in a white tank top and briefs and took a step toward Joseph.

Alarm bells went off in Joseph's mind.

"No," he said, "Nothing like that."

"Come on," Brother James took another step toward him. "Good looking guy like you. Little gay-boy like that must find you attractive. Look, he's buying you presents. *Art.*"

"He's not. It's not like that."

"You may want to ask him about that. The stuff he did to earn that painting. He's got a reputation around here, you know."

Joseph's mind raced. What did Brother James mean by a reputation? With the faculty? He didn't want to believe it but it sounded like the friar was talking about something sexual. Were they all interested in the students in that way? He refused to believe the man was undressing for his benefit, because he expected something from Joseph. Lachlan had forced himself upon him, grabbed him violently. James was behaving almost as though he was trying to seduce Joseph. Had Odilon really done what James was saying, just to get a picture for him? There had to be more to it than that. Joseph had only a schoolyard education in sex and all of that stuff and he'd certainly heard the words *gay* and *faggot* tossed around. Had even been called those things himself, amongst a litany of other names with meanings kids his age didn't understand. But that didn't mean he *was* gay did it? Did Brother James really get that feeling from him? Did Lachlan? Either way, he was just a kid. So was Odilon. Something about this rang very wrong with him. Brother James was supposed to be one of the good ones. He had thought so anyway. Had Odilon known the man was capable of this behavior?

"I think I want to go watch the movie." Joseph backed up a step, mindful not to step on the painting.

"No you don't." James took another step toward him. He held his hands out as though expecting a hug.

Joseph shot a look behind him, at the painting leaning against the wall. Almost imperceptibly, the leaves of the trees swayed in a gentle breeze.

"I just want you to show me how much you appreciate my work," James said, closing the gap between them.

Without another thought, Joseph spun and dove toward the painting. A finger disappeared into it and then he felt Brother James' hand on the waist of his pants, pulling him backward. Joseph lunged forward with all his might, stretching both arms out as far as they'd go. The friar held on tightly but Joseph felt himself sliding forward, into the painting.

It was his best landing yet. He tumbled onto the dirt road, rolled, and shot up to his feet, looking around to see where he'd come in. Directly behind him was the shimmering exit frame where he'd come through. Beyond it, the road stopped in a round cul-de-sac.

"What the hell is going on? Where are we?"

Brother James lay sprawled out on the dirt road at his feet, darting his head back and forth, seeming to try to make sense out of where he was. Joseph took several steps back to create a safe distance between them.

"This is your painting."

Why lie to the man? James would recognize this place was

at least similar to the road he painted. Even if Joseph had wanted to lie to him, he wouldn't have had the faintest idea of where to start. There was no reasonable explanation for them being here.

Brother James pushed himself up to his knees, a bewildered look in his eyes. He scooped up a handful of dirt from the road and watched it stream out of his open hand. With shaking legs, he brought himself into a standing position. It was almost funny to see this frightened man in his underwear standing in the middle of the road.

"It's exactly the same." Brother James turned in circles, eyes wide. "Even the spots that aren't in the actual painting. They're exactly the way I imagined them."

"I know," Joseph said. "I met Rupert's son."

At this, the friar's head snapped to face him. A strange look passed over him.

"You were there? You met the unfinished son? You met my family."

Joseph was stunned. "Your family?"

Brother James appeared to stand taller, to find his footing. "Well, a representation of them. My real family all died in a barn fire. Same barn as in the painting, in fact."

"That's why Rupert brought them all there. The unfinished son—that was you."

Brother James' eyes widened then narrowed to slits. "Smart kid. I was going to include myself in the painting but thought it might be bad luck." He inched closer to Joseph. "You said he brought them to the barn?"

Joseph took a step back. "He slaughtered the whole family and every animal on the farm. Dragged their bodies to the barn."

"He didn't set it on fire?"

"I didn't stick around to find out. Why would he?"

James smirked. "Because that's exactly what I did once I'd dragged their useless corpses in there."

Realization hit Joseph so hard it was like being punched in the stomach. James had painted the farm *after* murdering his family and burning their bodies in the barn. For what? To preserve the fond memories he had of the place before they died? He decided he didn't want to know. He had to get away from this man. The way out was only a couple more steps behind him.

"Why would Rupert, your father, have killed them?" Joseph wanted James' attention to be diverted enough for him to run. He was almost within arms reach and wouldn't stand a chance if the friar suspected he was going to flee.

"He may as well have in reality as well. He brought our family to ruin. Turned my mother into a spineless cow and my sister into a shell of herself. He frittered the family's money away on booze. Turned my mother and sister into slaves of the bottle. I did them all a favor."

Joseph could hardly believe what he was hearing. This man had murdered his entire family, had apparently gotten away with it, and now he was in charge of hundreds of children. He had actually thought of James as the nice one, the one they could trust. Turned out he may be the worst of the bunch. Or perhaps everyone in this place was just as corrupt. What secrets was Brother Lachlan holding? What about the rest of the faculty at St. Theodore's? Were the sisters just as culpable?

He'd heard enough. Joseph pivoted on one foot and made to leap for the exit pane. He was stopped by a powerful hand on his shoulder. Brother James flung him onto the road and he hit the ground hard. James grabbed him by the foot and dragged him up the road. Joseph's shirt pulled up and the road bit into his back as he was dragged, shredding his skin.

The traitorous friar let him go after he'd hauled Joseph a dozen or so feet from the way out.

"Where did you think you could run to?" Brother James said. "This place is straight out of *my* mind. I know every inch of it inside and out." He stood over Joseph, breathing heavily, surveying the world he'd conjured.

Joseph's mind raced. He could try to run for it but Brother James had already proven to be quicker than he was. He wasn't sure he'd even make it to his feet before the man stopped him.

A familiar howl, like a low, rumbling whale song, drifted through the trees toward them.

Joseph shot to his feet, suddenly heedless of Brother James.

The friar grabbed him by the arm. "What was that?"

The sound came again, closer this time. It was impossible to tell which direction it came from. Joseph's heart jackhammered in his chest as James jerked him around, spinning in circles in an attempt to discover the source of the sound.

"What in God's name?" Brother James muttered, staring up the road.

Joseph followed the man's gaze.

There were two of them again. One of the eelamanders had crawled out into the middle of the road, twenty yards ahead of them. The other was just off the shoulder, sniffing at a tree. The one on the road had spotted them and issued a short, barking version of its call. The second creature whipped its head around and fixed its gaze on them.

"What the hell are those things?"

"We need to run," Joseph whispered.

Brother James threw Joseph to the ground and sprinted down the road, away from the approaching eelamanders.

Joseph sprung back to his feet, having half-expected such a move. He darted off the road, into the trees, and leapt at the first reachable branch he came across. He scrabbled his feet up the trunk of the tree, clinging onto the branch for dear life. He managed to pull himself up and climbed higher, refusing to look down. He had no idea if these things could climb trees and really didn't want to find out. He rested on a thick branch two thirds of the way up and scanned the ground below him.

No sign of the creatures or James. He allowed himself to feel a modicum of relief though he was far from safe. Why had the eelamanders showed up so quickly? Was it because there were two people here instead of just himself? Because the creator of the painting was present? Or did they migrate throughout paintings? Maybe he and Brother James simply had the misfortune of going into a painting the creatures already happened to be in. Whatever the answer, all that mattered was escape. Since he had no idea where the border to another painting might be, the best bet was to make for the exit, where they had come in. He could just make out the spot on the road where the dirt was very clearly disturbed; the spot they'd landed when they got here.

He scanned the ground around his tree; the coast was still clear. It would be an easy run from the tree to the exit frame. He took a deep breath and climbed down to the lowest branch.

"Joseph!" Brother James shouted from the ground.

Joseph teetered, nearly fell, corrected his grip. Brother James appeared below the tree and Joseph pulled himself up just as the man made a grab for him.

"Joseph, help me!" James shouted. "Get down here!"

The man jumped with hands outstretched but Joseph was clearly out of reach. James snagged the lowest branch, which bent under his weight, and pulled himself halfway up, folding himself over it. He was swinging one leg up when the first eelamander appeared from around the tree.

It was like watching a crocodile pull an unsuspecting gazelle off the shore in one of the nature documentaries on television. The creature leapt up, keeping its stubby back legs on the ground, and snatched Brother James' dangling leg in its gigantic maw. It yanked him off the tree branch like he was just another leaf. The man's body slammed into the ground below. As soon as he landed, the eelamander shook its head back and forth, shaking James' body like a rag doll until his leg separated with a nauseating rip. Blood shot from the stump, just above the knee. James screamed and began to crawl away while the creature swallowed his leg whole, slurping it up like a noodle.

The second eelamander was waiting for him. Brother James had managed to crawl perhaps three feet from the first creature when the second appeared from around another tree trunk. The friar's scream disappeared forever into the jaws of the second eelamander as it bit down over his head and shoulders. When its mouth came away, the top third of Brother James was gone. Blood flooded the grass as the first creature joined the second.

Joseph made himself turn away as they devoured the rest of the body. He crouched in the tree with his hands over his ears and his face in his knees. Even through his hands he could hear them slurp and chew.

The slurping went on forever. Joseph allowed himself a

glimpse and immediately wished he hadn't. The eelamanders were nose-to-nose, lapping up the man's blood from the grass where they'd torn him apart. They were leaving no trace of him behind. Brother James McCurley had been completely erased from the world.

Joseph started to shake. It began in his hands, which he clasped tighter over his head, then moved to his arms and shoulders. Soon enough his entire body had joined the dance. He felt like he'd vibrate right off the tree if it kept up. He tightened himself into a ball, leaning back against the tree trunk for support, thankful the branch he was on was so large and sturdy.

I'm responsible for the death of a man. I let him die. I watched him die. It's my fault.

The thoughts flashed through his mind, one after another, a loop of guilt and terror. Intellectually, he knew Brother James brought this all on himself. Joseph had done nothing more than try to flee someone who intended to do him harm. Someone who had taken advantage of his friend.

"He murdered his entire family," Joseph said to himself.

He realized he could no longer hear the eelamanders. Apparently they'd finished cleaning up everything that remained of their meal. He peeked over the branch.

The eelamanders lingered at the base of the tree, staring up at him. They were motionless and could have passed for statues if it wasn't for the glisten of their skin or the blood around their lipless mouths. They were waiting him out. At least they couldn't climb the tree. Could they? Anything that was capable of making a man disappear so quickly shouldn't be underestimated. He craned his neck to survey his surroundings. There was no way he'd be able to make it to the exit frame with those things sitting right at the base of the tree. He needed a way to distract them. He patted his pockets but already knew there wouldn't be anything useful in them. He reached up, snapped a branch off the tree limb above him, and threw it with all the force he could muster. There was nowhere for it to go. It got caught up in the leaves of the tree and tumbled to the ground below, a couple of feet from the creatures.

A sob slipped out of him. He would either waste away in this tree or be devoured by strange amphibians. Possibly both.

"Leave me alone!" he shouted at the top of his lungs.

The eelamanders were as unfazed as they had been by his tossed stick.

"Go away!"

His shout turned into a cry. Angry, frightened tears slid from the corners of his eyes. He yanked another branch off the limb above him, heedless of his balance, and threw it at the eelamanders with all his might. He might as well have been throwing tissues for all the reaction he got out of them. He continued his barrage, tearing every branch and twig within reach off the tree and raining them down upon the monsters.

In unison the eelamanders turned their attention to another direction, like two dogs who had just heard their master's call. They lumbered off together, as though Joseph had simply ceased to exist.

He watched them vanish into the trees. Were they really leaving him alone? Were they capable of trickery? He swiveled his head back to where the exit frame was. It wasn't that far. He could make it. Assuming they'd really left. He breathed deep, trying to force his shaking limbs to relax. All he had to do is climb down a few branches and he'd be able to drop to the ground. From the base of the tree it was a quick sprint back to the road and the way out of here. He took a final deep breath and shook out his arms.

Lowering himself to the next branch, he scanned the ground below. Four more branches and he'd be low enough to drop to the ground. Thankful he wasn't afraid of heights, he dropped down one more branch and froze. Something else was moving down there, from the opposite direction the eelamanders had gone. Was there a third creature? He held his breath and listened. Nothing. He let his breath out slowly, looked down at the next tree limb, and lowered himself so that he was dangling from his current branch. His feet barely touched the next one down. Apparently his fear had given him an extra inch of reach on the way up. He centered his feet on the branch below and let go with his hands. His feet landed solidly. For half a second.

There was a loud crack and then he was falling.

He landed on his back and, for a second, everything went black. Movement nearby snapped him back to consciousness. Everything in his body hurt. For a moment, he didn't think he'd be able to stand up. The snapping of a branch and the rustle of nearby foliage forced him into a sitting position. He was dead if he didn't get to his feet this instant. He steadied himself on the tree. Managed to stand for a second before his knees buckled and he collapsed. Breathing directly behind him. Like a gasp. Like a monster opening its mouth to take a bite out of a helpless boy. He squeezed his eyes shut.

"Well I'll be a horse's mother!"

That voice. Dripping with southern twang as though the speaker had deliberately exaggerated it for his benefit. He opened his eyes.

26

"Hasty!"

But the woman standing in front of Joseph only looked like his one time friend. This person could very well have been Hasty's mother; she had the same dirty blond hair and the same smile that went from ear-to-ear. The difference was that she was an adult. Her hair was beginning to show grey and she had pronounced wrinkles under her eyes and around her mouth. But she grinned at him as though she recognized him. Did Hasty have an older sister who she'd told about him? How else could she know who he was?

"You haven't changed a bit," the woman said. "I suppose I've been out of the world a lot longer than I realized." She offered a hand out to him.

Joseph took it and allowed her to help him up. He winced as he got to his feet.

"You took quite the fall, there," she said. "I was worried you mighta broken something. Yer made of sturdy stuff."

She clapped him on the back and it was all he could do not

to yelp. The pain from the fall was still fresh and her gentle slap felt like being hit with a baseball bat.

"Are you...have we met?" he asked.

"Why, if I didn't just watch you fall out of a tree I'd have half the mind to be insulted, young man."

"Hasty?"

She threw her head back and laughed. "Do I look so different?"

"You were a lot younger when I saw you last."

"Your momma never teach you not to say such things to a lady?"

At the mention of his mother, his mood darkened. It must have shown; Hasty wrapped an arm around him and hugged him tight.

"Hey," she gave him a little shake. "Sorry I mentioned her. That was dumb. It's been a long time since that day. For me anyway."

She pulled her arm off him and only now did he see the hand was missing. He hadn't been paying much attention to her hands when he'd first met her but he was fairly certain she'd had both of them intact. This woman only had her right.

She saw him looking. "Tell you bout that later. Right now we need to get somewhere safe. Come on."

Before he could protest, or even register what was happening, she scooped him up in her arms and carried him to the road. She put her back to the place where he'd come into this world and jogged away from it, making what he at first thought to be a random right turn. Then he caught a glimpse of a small, black X spray-painted onto the base of a tree trunk. Hasty ran swiftly, holding him tight to her chest in a solid grip despite being short one hand. He noticed that her arms practically bulged with cords of muscle.

Another X and another turn, after which she slowed to a jog and then a walk. A few minutes after she'd taken off running with him, she set him down gently.

"Sorry if that was a little presumptuous. We needed to move fast and it didn't look like you were much up to running."

Joseph stared at her, unable to close his mouth. "It's really you."

Her smile was sad. "Good to see you again, kiddo. Take three steps forward. I'm right behind you."

Ahead of him was what looked like endless trees. As he walked toward them, they disappeared, different trees taking their place. All at once he was walking out of a much denser forest into a familiar meadow surrounding a small lake.

"I know this place." He spun around in time to see Hasty appear out of thin air between two trees. There was a black X spray-painted on each one, clearly marking the gateway between paintings. Why hadn't he thought of that?

She led him down to the small lake, to the rock he'd basked on when he first came here. He washed his face in the cool water while she lay back on the rock and shut her eyes. He stared at her while his face dried in the sun. Her hair was chopped shorter than when he'd first met her. Gone was the vest with the Iron Maiden patch. In place of it she wore a plaid shirt with the sleeves torn off, showing off muscular arms that he couldn't help but stare at.

She sat up and looked him in the eye. "Suppose we oughta chat a bit. See where each other's at. Who was that man I saw got eaten up by them *eelagators?*"

"I've been calling them eelamanders."

She laughed, snorted, and spit something semi-solid into the water. "That's pretty spot on. You ever see anything like a salamander do that to a man though? Or this?" She held up the stump of her left hand.

Eelagators did make more sense.

"Now," she put her intact hand on his shoulder, "Tell me what I missed."

He told her everything, beginning with the death of his mother. A weight left his shoulders while he told his story and he realized he hadn't really spoken to anyone about what he'd been through in the last year. With the exception of Odilon, nobody at the school knew about his mother or how he'd wound up there. And even Odilon only had vague under-standing of what Joseph was experiencing in the paintings. He cried as he talked about his mother and again when it came to being sent to St. Theodore's.

"I've heard of places like that," Hasty said, rubbing his back. "Boarding schools, training schools, those sorta places. They're all the same kinda hell. Most of em have been closed down, like, from what I've heard. Turns out people don't actu-ally want abusive clergymen taking care of their kids. What rattles my pony is that so many of these places are guilty of mistreating their kids. I wonder if them places attract the worst sort of people or if they're bred to become monsters once they're in charge of someone. Makes you wonder what other kinds of devils are out there masquerading as respectable indi-viduals."

Hasty's bottom lip quivered for just a second. Though he barely knew her, Joseph felt a deep affection for her. He trusted her completely.

After a long silence he said, "How'd you get so...you know."

She squinted at him. "You weren't about to say old, were you?"

He opened his mouth to deny it but couldn't bring himself to lie to her.

"Just joshin. Course I'm old." She leaned back on her elbows and stared up at the sky. "I suppose it's sort of addicting, especially to a wayward soul such as I. Traveling the paint, I mean." She glanced at her wristwatch, pulled it off, tossed it to Joseph. "Keep an eye on the time for me. When that timer hits zero, we've gotta go."

Joseph caught it and glanced at it. It was a digital watch on a sport band. On the display a stopwatch was running down; there was just under an hour left on it.

"What happens when time runs out?"

"They'll be coming."

"The eelamanders? Gators. Whatever."

She nodded. "Takes less time when there are more than one of us in a picture. I used to think they were just a part of each painting, the dark edges of it. But now I believe they're more of a cleanup crew. Sorta like a suckermouth catfish."

"To clean what?"

"Stuff that don't belong. Impurities. You and me. From what I can tell, the only thing they don't go after is paint. That's how I blaze my trails." She reached into her knapsack and pulled out a can of black spray paint.

"How did you find me?"

She shoved the can back into her bag. "Wish I could say it was deliberate, little man."

"Where've you been? How did," he nodded at the stump of her left arm, "That happen?"

"That, partner, is a long yarn that'll have to wait for another time. You said you know this painting?"

He nodded. "It was one of his."

"That nasty man who got himself eaten up? And his are the only ones left in that prison of yours, huh?"

"Yeah. You'll show me the way out of here, won't you?" He couldn't help the pleading tone in his voice. He wanted so desperately to be free from the walls of St. Theodore's.

"I'll take you right now if you got everything you need," she said.

"There's just one thing."

She stuck her hands on her hips. "Come on then, out with it."

"My friend. Odilon. I want to bring him with me."

She considered this a moment then pulled her backpack on and stepped off the rock she'd been laying on, onto the soft grass of the meadow.

"I reckon those things have moved on," she said. "Or disappeared into the ether or whatever it is they do when their job's done. They'll be looking for us here before too long."

"The place you found me leads back to my room. If you think it's safe."

***

Twenty minutes later, the two of them emerged from the late Brother James' painting in Joseph's room at St. Theodore's. He set to packing some things up right away. He hadn't been granted a backpack at this place, since there was really no reason for anyone to carry anything more than what was needed for the next class, but he did have a canvas book bag that he was able to cram a couple of things into. As he picked through his meagre belongings, deciding what was important enough to bring, Hasty smoked a cigarette and eyed the cassock laying in a heap on Joseph's floor. When Joseph looked up at her, she wore a grim expression, cigarette dangling from her lips.

"We're not allowed to smoke in here."

She looked up as though startled to see him there. She grinned in a way that reminded him of the younger Hasty he'd first met a year ago and shrugged.

She pointed at the cassock. "That belong to Father Supper, back there?"

"Brother James," he suppressed a shudder.

"He do anything to you?"

He shook his head. What if the painting hadn't been in his room when the friar had barged in? What if he'd had nowhere to run? How many other kids hadn't had the chance to escape his hands? He tried not to think of what had been done to Odilon.

Then there was Lachlan. How many kids had he hurt? The more Joseph thought about his visit to the headmaster's quarters, the more he realized that he'd been lucky the man's attention had been diverted. What if Brother Casper hadn't knocked on the door when he did? Against his will, he remembered the feeling of Lachlan's hand squeezing his privates. As bad as that had been, he was grateful it didn't go any farther, though he couldn't even imagine what that would mean.

"Joseph?"

"Hm?"

"You sure he didn't do nothin?"

He shook his head. "I think he did something to Odilon though. Said he did, anyway. Lachlan was the one who...you know."

"The guy in charge."

Joseph nodded.

Hasty spit on the floor. "Can't even trust the fuckin church anymore. Pardon my language."

"Aren't they supposed to follow God? I thought they were all supposed to be good and wanted to help kids." Joseph didn't know a lot about the Bible but he was absolutely certain God didn't want any of his people touching children the way Lachlan had touched him, and the way it seemed James had wanted to.

Hasty put her good arm around him and gave him a squeeze. "Monsters choose all sorts of disguises to get to us. None better than someone who you're supposed to be able to trust."

A knock on the door startled them both into silence. Hasty looked down at Joseph, a question in her eyes. She glanced at the painting, then at Joseph, eyebrow raised. He held up a hand.

"Joseph," Odilon whisper-shouted from the other side of the door.

"He came to us," Joseph whispered to Hasty.

He pulled open the door, ready to embrace his friend, to tell him that they didn't have to worry about this place anymore. He couldn't wait to show him the wonders within the paintings. They'd travel the world together without ever having to get on a plane. The episode with Brother James proved he could bring others into paintings with him.

The sorrow in his friend's face told Joseph something terrible had happened. Then he registered the bruises on Odilon's face and the black cloth taking up the hallway behind him.

Brother Lachlan shoved Odilon through the door, into Joseph, then barged in and slammed the door. The headmaster glared at Joseph with triumph in his eyes. His gaze shifted to Brother James' cassock on the floor and then to Hasty.

His eyes narrowed. "And who might you be?"

Hasty darted toward the painting and Lachlan stepped between it and her.

"Mr. Ward, you know you are not permitted to have females of any age in your room?"

"Only grown men are allowed any privacy with these here boys, that it?" Hasty said.

"What happens here is none of your concern."

"Get the hell out of our way." Hasty took a step toward him.

The strike took everyone in the room by surprise. Lachlan, who had been standing with his hands folded in front of him, punched Hasty square in the face. Blood exploded from her mouth and she collapsed to one knee. Lachlan raised his own knee into her chin and sent her crashing to the floor.

He knelt down next to her and stroked her hair. "I will show you exactly what we do with disobedient children. I think you'll enjoy it."

Hasty rolled and jabbed the stub of her left hand into Lachlan's face, grabbed his hair with her good hand, and smashed his head into the dresser. She pushed herself up, swiped blood from her face, and kicked hard into his chest. He went all the way down, gasping for air.

"Let's get the hell outta here," she said.

Both boys nodded.

Joseph stepped over Lachlan, who was writhing on the floor, and grabbed the canvas bag he'd packed.

"Right behind you," he said to Hasty.

"Don't doddle." She blew him a kiss, knelt down, and slipped into the painting.

The canvas shimmered behind her, like the surface of a pond.

"Let's go," Joseph said, pulling Odilon toward the painting. "You'll have to hang onto me."

Odilon's arm slipped out of his grasp. Joseph stopped and turned back.

His friend stared at the painting with trepidation and then at Lachlan, who had caught his breath and was rousing himself.

"I do not know if I can."

"It's easy. Hasty will show us the way out and then we'll be free. I can show you where I live. We can go to Hollywood and find my uncle Edgar."

Odilon shook his head violently. "You have told me of the monsters in there."

"There are monsters out here, Odi." He reached out his hand to Odilon. "Please. I can't leave you."

Odilon reached out his hand, slowly, still unsure but apparently willing to trust Joseph to get him through it. They turned together and stood hand-in-hand in front of the canvas. The road in the painting stretched on infinitely to the horizon and beyond. The road out of here.

"On three," Joseph said.

He didn't even get to say "one" before they were yanked

backwards, away from the wall, and sent crashing into the bed frame. Then Brother Lachlan put a foot through the canvas.

"No!" Joseph screamed.

He rushed at Lachlan as the man stomped on the frame, shattering it into pieces, grinding the canvas underfoot. Joseph grabbed at his cassock and tried to pull him away. Lachlan's fist came around, into the side of his head, and the world went black.

27

———

Cold. Dark. Damp.

Joseph drifted through darkness that wasn't quite darkness. Colorful shapes drifted past him like ghost ships. He tried to focus on them as they went by but they lingered just out of the center of his field of vision. He opened his eyes.

Consciousness oozed back to him and he sat up, head throbbing. He was on hard, damp ground. His face was sore and cold from being pressed against it for however long he'd been out. It was so dark. What little illumination there was came from a crack along the floor, a short strip of yellowish light. A door.

He scrambled to his feet. Dizziness washed over him and he stuck a hand out, resting it on a cold, wet wall that felt like rough stone. Where was he? The room smelled of wet earth and rotting wood. He groped along the wall, knocking something leaning against it with his toe. Whatever it was shifted and he skirted around it. As he reached the shaft of light, his hands brushed against the hard wood of a roughly hewn door.

He felt around until he touched a mottled iron handle. He yanked on it and then tried shoving against the door. It didn't budge either way.

"Hello!" he hollered.

He pounded on the door then stuck his ear against it, listening for any movement. Nothing. Panic was just out of reach, creeping in closer and closer. He shut his eyes and leaned his forehead against the door. Forced himself to take long, slow breaths.

Where was Odilon? He assumed his friend would have answered him if he'd been within earshot. Hasty had escaped and Lachlan had destroyed her only way back. At least she was safe, even if he may never see her again.

How did Lachlan know about the painting? He'd been out cold when Hasty had gone through. At least, he'd had his head down and had been writhing in agony. There was a chance he'd heard her take off but would a grown man really assume that a woman had just disappeared into a painting? Would he believe it? Joseph almost hadn't when he'd seen it first hand, and he was a kid.

The door burst open, smacking him in the head and sending him reeling backwards, tumbling onto his backside. He landed on his tailbone and bit his tongue at the same time. He barely felt any of it.

Lachlan stood in the doorway, silhouetted by dim yellow light shining from behind him. Joseph could see what looked like an ancient, unfinished basement behind him. He was in a barren room with rocky walls that dripped moisture. The heavy wood door had a padlock hanging off the outside of it. He'd been locked in a dungeon. To his left, a painting leaned against the wall; that must have been what he'd kicked. The canvas depicted some sort of distant landscape that was too difficult to make out from where he sat. It appeared to be a red plain or desert, with silhouetted structures in the distance. Black blotches dotted the landscape. Why had it been left in here?

"Do you like it?" Brother Lachlan adjusted his glasses, watching Joseph.

"Where's Odi?"

The man pulled a pocket watch from his cassock and glanced at it. "Your friend is enjoying some time to himself. If things go well here, you can both soon be having breakfast with the rest of the students."

"You mean prisoners," Joseph said, trying not to think about what Lachlan meant by things going well.

"Everyone at St. Theodore's is here by choice."

"Bullshit."

Lachlan stepped into the room. "You chose to commit a felony, as did the majority of the students here. In doing so, you made the choice to forfeit the life of sin you were living and to instead dwell under my roof and abide by my rules."

Joseph cast a glance over at the canvas.

"Please, admire it to your heart's content."

Joseph pulled himself up from the floor and crossed his arms.

Lachlan threw his head back and laughed. "The very picture of defiance, you are, Mr. Ward. Now please," he extended a hand to the canvas, "Take a look. Tell me what you think. I'm told you appreciate fine art."

Joseph remained rooted where he was. He wouldn't play this man's game with him, whatever it may be.

Brother Lachlan held up a finger and stepped out of the

room. The sound of him rummaging through something echoed through the door and he returned a moment later with a wooden chair, which he set down just inside the door. He smoothed his cassock behind him and took a seat, blocking any chance Joseph had at escape.

"Someone told me a funny story not too long ago. I admit, I had a hard time believing it at first. I thought this person was attempting to gain favor, or to besmirch the reputation of one of our cherished students. Recent events have led me to believe this person was telling the truth." He snorted in what may have been laughter. "You'll never guess who told me."

Joseph kept himself as still as he could, focusing on his breathing. In through the nose, out through the mouth. He kept the painting in his peripheral vision, trying not to let Lachlan see him eyeing it. How far was he from the canvas? Eight feet? Lachlan was just slightly farther from it than he was. If he could somehow distract the man, he could make it to the painting and dive through.

"No guesses?" Lachlan said, intent on seeing this game through. "I'll help you. A certain friar under my supervision allowed a certain child under *his* supervision to slip away."

He must have been talking about Brother Casper. But what could he have told Lachlan that would matter to Joseph?

Lachlan pulled a tobacco tin from his pocket and started on rolling a cigarette. "Brother Casper had been duped by a child and deserved the punishment he received." He licked and sealed the cigarette. "The poor man was sent to the infirmary thanks to this lapse which, with my current perspective, seems providential. Wouldn't you agree?"

"I don't know what that means." Joseph didn't want to talk

to him but he had to bide his time until he could figure out a way into the painting.

Brother Lachlan lit the cigarette and crossed one leg over the other. He smoked and watched Joseph. The silence stretched on for a minute or more.

"I think you know more than you let on, Mr. Ward. I think you have tapped into something truly special." He blew thick blue smoke through his nostrils. It floated around his head, making him look all the more sinister. "Brother Casper was in the very next bed while you and your filthy friend were discussing your little magic trick."

Joseph's guts liquefied. Lachlan didn't have to tell him any more for Joseph to know what he was talking about. How stupid could he have been to blab about it to Odilon without knowing who was around them? It was all too incredible. He knew Odilon would have trouble believing it and hadn't even considered that anyone else would, let alone a grown man. He'd told everything to Odilon that day. How much of it had been said in the infirmary? How much of it had Brother Casper told Lachlan?

"What do you want?" Joseph turned away from the headmaster, taking the opportunity to gauge the distance between himself and the painting.

"You don't need to sneak glances at it, Joseph." Lachlan got up, grabbed the canvas, and hung it on a tarnished nail sticking out of the wall. "I want you to use it."

So that was it. There was no sense denying anything anymore. Joseph shook his head.

"You're going to use it. You're going to show me how all of this works." Lachlan took a step toward him. "Or I'm going to start breaking bones in your body. I'll only break, say, a dozen.

Fingers and toes, mostly. Then, if you would still like to disobey me, your friend will be brought down here to join us. I think I'll start with his arms. He'll be a paralytic before I return my attention to you. I'm a patient man."

Joseph shook his head. His heart pounded in his chest like a captive animal struggling to escape its cage. Maybe he could convince the man it was all an elaborate game he and Odilon had been playing.

Lachlan's patience was a lot thinner than he'd let on. He practically leapt toward Joseph and wrapped an arm around his chest. He grabbed Joseph's left hand, his strength immense. Joseph writhed, tried to slip out of the hold, and Lachlan used the momentum to bring him to his knees. He wrenched Joseph's hand back, grasped his pinky finger, and twisted it backwards with an animal grunt.

The pain was instant and all encompassing. Joseph felt the bone of his little finger twist then snap in several places. Agony like nothing he'd experienced lanced from his finger up his arm. He screamed and scrambled across the floor. Lachlan let him.

Joseph clutched the wrist of his mangled hand with his good one and forced himself to look at the injured finger. His pinky was already swollen and canted to a severe angle, away from the rest of his fingers. Lachlan was saying something over his screams but Joseph didn't care, wouldn't listen. He was on the verge of vomiting.

The headmaster grabbed him by the throat and put his lips to his ear, the spidery whiskers of his beard felt like they were trying to burrow into Joseph's ear canal.

"Show me now or I will double that pain. Then I'll let you stew in it for a while before I come back and try again. Cooperate and I can have you up to the infirmary within the hour. They have some lovely pain killers."

Joseph forced himself to calm down. He breathed deeply and tried with all his might not to focus on the pain in his hand. The amount of physical agony he'd endured under the roof of St. Theodore's was beyond anything he ever imagined having to deal with in a learning environment, or what claimed to be one. In that moment, he promised himself that he wouldn't allow Lachlan, or anyone at St. Theodore's, to injure him, or Odilon, any further. If Lachlan wanted to see how the paintings worked, so be it. Joseph would disappear into it and find a way out, assuming that whoever painted this had done anything else in their lives. He was no art critic but the red landscape looked like it had been painted by an experienced hand. Looking closely at it, the picture appeared to have been painted from high above the ground, as though the artist was looking down at it from a helicopter. Large groups of the dark spots were scattered around the landscape, all seeming to be coming from the dark, strangely shaped structures far off in the distance. The thought of stepping into a world like that made the hairs on his arms stand up.

"Do I need to provide further motivation?" Lachlan asked.

Joseph shook his head and stepped up to the painting. "I'm going."

Lachlan grabbed hold of his shoulder. Joseph struggled but the man was strong and held him in place.

"You didn't think I'd let you go in there alone, did you? No, Mr. Ward, I will be going with you. I want to see your little trick first hand."

Panic threatened to overwhelm Joseph. His little finger throbbed and ached with a ferocity that wouldn't be ignored.

He wanted to cry but refused to give his tormentor the satisfaction. If Lachlan wanted to go into the painting, fine. He hoped there was something out of frame that he'd be able to use to hide, otherwise he'd be stuck trying to outrun the man until he found an exit. Or until the eelamanders showed up. His plan was to stick his landing and run as fast as he could. Lachlan didn't know what to expect when they went through; it was reasonable to assume he would fall when he landed, just like James did.

Joseph grit his teeth. "Ready?"

In response, the headmaster gave his shoulder a hard squeeze.

Joseph took a breath, stuck his hand out, and slipped into the painting.

He barely managed to land upright. He stumbled but managed to keep his feet under him. He could no longer feel Lachlan's hand on his shoulder. Without wasting anytime looking back at him, he took off running.

The first thing that struck him about this place was the heat. It felt like it was well over a hundred degrees without any sort of humidity. Hot air wafted up from the ground, which was formed from some sort of red rock. Joseph ran in spite of it.

The next thing he noticed was the moaning. It came from everywhere. Without slowing his pace, he searched for the source and discovered he was far from alone. Ahead of him was a crowd of people, perhaps two dozen dark figures silhouetted against the red light that came from everywhere. The crowd shuffled about, moving in his general direction. They moaned in what sounded like pain but could have been exhaustion from the heat. What was this place? Joseph wasn't sure he wanted to find another painting to slip into if it was anything like this.

"I need help!" he shouted at the crowd.

No one in the group responded or even looked in his direction. They all had their attention focused on the sky behind him. Many stretched their hands upwards, as if in prayer.

He came within a few feet of the crowd and stopped dead. It wasn't shadows that made these people look dark and indistinct. They were all blackened, charred, burned beyond the point of mobility for any normal person. They gave off a pungent odor of meat burned to a crisp. Bits of them crumbled as they shambled onward, giving Joseph none of their attention. They moaned together in agony as they marched toward whatever it was that drew their attention. Other groups of charred people marched toward the same goal for as far as he could see, none of the crowds bigger than a couple of dozen people.

Joseph turned to follow their collective gaze.

It was Lachlan. Laughter boomed from the man's mouth, echoing across the vast desert and Joseph realized who had painted this picture. He'd been duped.

28

———

"Where were you running to, Mr. Ward?"

The voice was like thunder, shaking the very ground he stood on.

Brother Lachlan towered before Joseph and all the crowds of burned people, who continued their ceaseless march. Joseph was a big fan of the old Godzilla movies and knew the monster to be around a hundred and fifty feet tall. He thought that may have been close to the height Lachlan reached.

The picture hadn't been painted from the perspective of a helicopter or skyscraper, it was from the perspective of a giant Lachlan, painted by the headmaster himself. He'd known exactly what went on in these paintings and had fooled Joseph into stepping into a world he'd created, one in which he ruled as a monster-sized version of himself.

With nowhere to run, Joseph tried to hide behind the group of burned people closest to him. It did little good since they continued to march toward the giant robed figure. Lachlan's voice boomed through the air again, rattling his eardrums.

"If you wish to serve your god," he pointed a gargantuan finger directly at Joseph, "Tear him to pieces."

The shambling and moaning stopped at once. For a breath, the world stood still. Lachlan's giant fingertip was like a moon crashing toward the earth, eclipsing any light that slipped around his body.

The charred people turned toward Joseph, crispy skin crackling.

And then they were coming toward him, much faster than they'd been moving a moment ago. They still shambled but did so with urgency, eager to please the giant.

He ran, hoping Lachlan wouldn't decide to simply bring a colossal foot down and crush him like an insect.

With nothing else to give him any sense of orientation, Joseph ran toward the structures far off in the distance. From here it looked like it would take days for him to reach them but it was the only place he could think to go, and the only thing visible in the vast desert of red.

He glanced over his shoulder. He was outpacing the closest group of burned people but there were two more groups up ahead, crowding in on him in a pincer formation. He dodged to one side and managed to skirt around one of the groups, narrowly avoiding dozens of blackened fingers stretching out for him. The moaning became more animal, hungry, as the shambling figures got closer to him.

A brittle hand reached out for him. He ducked, stumbled, rolled, managed to shake off a second hand that barely caught hold of his shirt. He regained his footing and dashed away from the crowd.

A dark mass formed in the horizon. It came from the strange city in the distance, like smoke or fog. It stayed low to the ground and was very clearly getting closer. Seconds later he recognized the cloud for what it was; hundreds, thousands more of the burned people. Pitch black, they poured from the city, like ants evacuating a colony. They spread along the horizon as far as the eye could see. There would be no sanctuary in that direction. His only hope was to get out of here the same way he came in; presumably, directly behind the towering man with an army of scorched zombies at his command.

For a moment, time moved in slow motion as Joseph accepted the circumstances. He was going to die in this place if he couldn't get out soon. He turned back from the legion of blackened bodies marching toward him and faced Lachlan.

The group he'd just avoided were closing in on him. He jogged just out of their reach and scanned the area behind Lachlan. The landscape around him was just as barren as the rest of this place. There was literally nowhere to run, no place to hide. Even if there was a rock he could scurry behind, Lachlan was watching him like a hawk and would see wherever he went.

Joseph felt as though his insides were hollowing out. Hopelessness weighed him down, turned his feet to lead. Suddenly he didn't want to run anymore. Didn't care if Lachlan's army of crispy people caught up to him and tore him apart. At least he'd die at their hands and not Lachlan's, even if they had been created by him. How painful was it to die? Would they torture him first or make it fast?

He'd almost given up and stopped jogging altogether when he noticed two of Lachlan's minions behaving oddly. At least, it was odd compared to the rest of them. The first one he noticed was a shorter version, almost child-sized, moving off to the side and behind Lachlan's giant foot. All of Joseph's pursuers, that he'd noticed, were adult-sized. This one didn't shamble either, it ran. And it was on its own, separate from any of the others. As Joseph watched, it jumped and waved its arms. As he was puzzling over this new development, the second figure ran around the other side of Lachlan. This one didn't look burned at all. It waved its arms around and pointed at the shorter figure.

Recognition dawned on him, lifting the weight of defeat and giving him renewed energy. He bolted in the direction of the shorter figure, the one who was not scorched at all, whose skin was naturally dark, and who had been his friend ever since this nightmare chapter of his life had started.

Odilon jumped and waved Joseph toward him as Hasty busied herself with something around Lachlan's other foot.

The giant friar watched Joseph, apparently not having seen the two newest arrivals. Lachlan laughed and it was like thunder.

"Where will you run?" his voice echoed across the red plain.

Out of the corner of Joseph's eye, he saw Hasty running around Lachlan's foot. She stopped every so often before continuing around it. Joseph kept his eyes focussed straight ahead so as to not give her away. It didn't matter because seconds later, Lachlan was made very aware of what was happening.

Joseph poured everything he had into reaching Odilon. He ducked under grasping hands that flaked bits of charred flesh on the ground as their crumbling digits clutched at the air around him. Out of the corner of his eye, he saw an orange flickering and had to turn. Lachlan turned his attention to his foot at the same time Joseph did, feeling the heat of the fire Hasty had started on his robe. She'd been running around him, lighting bits of cloth on fire while Lachlan was busy watching Joseph. By the time Lachlan noticed what was going on, the fire had climbed up to his knee.

The headmaster roared in agony and surprise. Whether he'd spotted either of the two newcomers was unclear; he was entirely focussed on his burning leg.

Joseph reached Odilon and grabbed him in a hug that made the other boy cry out in surprise.

"We have to go," Odilon said as he pulled himself from Joseph's grip. "This way."

Odilon ran off in what seemed like an arbitrary direction.

"Wait!" Joseph called. "That's not the way out. We came in from behind him."

All at once Joseph was grabbed from behind and propelled toward Odilon.

"Just trust us, kiddo," Hasty shouted in his ear.

Lachlan bellowed and smacked at the fire that rapidly engulfed his cassock. Joseph looked over his shoulder at the same time the friar spotted them. A snarl appeared through the huge man's beard. He appeared to forget about the flames. He took a giant step toward them, shaking the ground as it landed and closing the distance between them by more than half.

Up ahead, Odilon had stopped running and was searching the ground for something. Joseph was about to call to him when he spotted what the boy must be looking for, a black X spray painted on the ground up ahead and to Odilon's right. Joseph kept up his momentum, grabbed his friend by the shirt, and pulled him past the X.

The world shifted from red to grey.

Momentum kept Joseph moving even as he registered the dramatic change in tone and landscape. He needed to be as far as possible from that red plain ruled by a colossal Lachlan. The grey sky that took over the stark redness of the previous painting almost blinded him, skewing his depth perception. He stumbled as the ground beneath him changed from red rock to grass that barely counted as green. Ahead of them was a vast body of water which he ran toward at top speed, desperate to escape the heat of the hellish world he'd just come from.

His foot stepped into empty air and he realized, too late, the water wasn't only ahead of him but far below as well. So this was how he would die. His mind switched to a state of acceptance as the inevitability of his doom became apparent.

And then he was yanked backwards by his shirt, hard enough against his momentum that the collar strangled him for a brief second. He fell back on the ground and heard an "oof" as he landed on something that moved underneath him.

He rolled off Odilon and sat up.

"Thanks."

Odilon waved a dismissive hand at him. The boy's eyes were wide, his face ashen.

Joseph stood and brushed bits of grass off his pants. He inched up to the edge of the cliff he'd almost taken a dive off and peered down. Waves from the dark sea surrounding them crashed against the rocky bluffs hard enough that Joseph imagined he could feel the rumble of them through his shoes. Far below, scattered amongst the rocks were dark shapes that Joseph's mind at first refused to accept for what they appeared to be. He lowered himself to his belly, hoping that closing a few more inches of distance between himself and what he was seeing below would show it to be an illusion. One of the shapes was looking up at him, or would be if it was alive. He pulled himself back from the ledge.

"There are bodies down there," he said to Odilon. "At least a dozen, all caught on the rocks."

Odilon didn't look like he'd heard. He was staring out at the sea, mouthing soundless words.

"Odi?" Joseph knelt down in front of his friend and put his hands on the other boy's shoulders. "We should be ready to move once Hasty gets here. How did you guys find me?"

Odilon kept his eyes glued to the sea. "After Lachlan hit you, he locked me in your room. The woman, your friend, came back soon after. From a connected painting. She picked the lock and we followed you to the basement. She saved my life."

"I wonder what's taking her so long." Joseph stood and offered a hand to Odilon, helping his friend to his feet.

Odilon looked at him now. "She found the way out and marked it very quickly. You could learn from her."

"That's been the idea all along, chum."

"Why are there bodies at the bottom of the cliff, Joseph?"

Joseph shook his head. "I don't want to think about it."

"I could offer a bit of an explanation."

The boys turned at the sound of the voice and Joseph felt the blood drain from his face. It took everything he had to keep from bursting into tears.

A normal-sized Lachlan stood in front of them looking like something from a nightmare, or perhaps like a resident of the place they'd all just come from. The left half of his clothing was in tatters, the skin beneath it blackened and burned, spots of pink flesh glistening where the flames from the fire Hasty set had done the most damage. Half his beard was scorched and the pale face underneath it reminded Joseph more of a skeleton than flesh. The man had a wild look in his eyes that scared Joseph more than his size in the previous painting had. He dragged something behind him and now he threw it down in front of them.

Hasty, body broken in a dozen places, landed at Joseph's feet. A low moan was coming from her as she lay motionless, barely breathing from the looks of it. Her good arm was bent in several places, both legs were a twisted mess, her jaw canted on an angle that horrified Joseph more than anything he'd seen over the last year.

"Hasty," he said, holding himself back from running to her with every ounce of his will.

"Is that her name?" Lachlan kicked her hard in the abdomen. "Turns out she wasn't hasty enough to avoid a giant shoe. Like an ant." He kicked her again.

The moaning continued from Hasty, uninterrupted by the kicks.

Lachlan looked around, as though seeing where they were for the first time. He grinned, which only served to make the exposed part of his face look more like a skull, and strolled toward the bluff. He peered his head over, laughed, and clapped his hands.

"It's good to be home, boys."

He strode back to Hasty, grabbed her by the hair, and dragged her toward the edge of the cliff. He dropped her and she turned, slowly, almost as though she was trying to escape him.

Joseph's heart broke as he watched her. He wanted to go to

her and to hold her but Lachlan would toss him over the edge in a heartbeat if he got close enough.

"I was never much of an artist," the friar said, looking once more over the bluff. "This was a college project I remember well. A young man I was, when I painted this. Perhaps eighteen. This was my favorite place to spend time. Occasionally I'd bring a friend."

"You killed all those people down there."

The realization horrified Joseph. He knew Lachlan was a bad man but he hadn't imagined he could be a mass murderer.

"It's not easy to conceal one's self when one lives on an island, even one with a few million people on it. But people trust a man of the cloth, it seems."

"You joined the church so that you could kill people?" Joseph took half a step forward, putting himself between Lachlan and Odilon.

"Nothing so deliberate. My profession was chosen for me long before I reached college. You know how fathers are, don't you, Joseph?" He cast another glance over the cliff. "I wonder if we could spot mine down there."

As Lachlan admired his work, Hasty turned her head so that she was looking directly at Joseph. The bottom of her jaw was twisted away from him so that it appeared as though she had an extreme overbite. One of her eyes was swollen shut, the other red with broken blood vessels. The eye that worked found Joseph and, somehow, conveyed an affection that reminded him of his mother on her best days, before the medicine had become a daily ritual. Her eye closed slowly and crinkled at the edge and he recognized it for what it was. She was winking at him.

Lachlan turned from the edge, saw Joseph staring at Hasty,

and chuckled. He nudged her with his foot so that she was on her back again.

"It's a pity I didn't know about any of this when I painted this picture. I may have pursued a career in art if I'd only known. And what better place to bring my friends?"

A guttural cry came from Hasty as she twisted and managed to wrap her handless arm around Lachlan's leg. Cracking sounds came from somewhere within her as she locked her arm around him and twisted toward the edge, clearly trying to roll over it. Her body was too broken to do much more than hold onto the leg. Lachlan looked down at her as though he'd just stepped in shit and had it stuck to his shoe.

"Your friend is tenacious." He grabbed her by the hair. "It's unfortunate she wants to die so badly."

He took hold of Hasty with his other arm, lifted her, and heaved her over the edge like a bail of hay.

"Hasty!" Joseph screamed.

He ran at Lachlan, shaking off Odilon's hand as his friend tried to stop him. The man batted him away with one strong blow, sending him crashing to the ground. He stayed prone, unable to control himself anymore. He sobbed for Hasty and for Odilon. He'd brought them to their deaths in a vain attempt to escape St. Theodore's. He had their blood on his hands.

Lachlan pulled him to his feet by the hair. "You'll be allowed to join her just as soon as you explain to me how it is you manage to enter paintings at will."

Joseph stared out at the grey sea before them. He wanted Lachlan to throw him over. He'd had enough of what existence had in store for him. Why continue to try when life wanted to make him miserable at every turn? His mother had told him

God watches out for children and drunks but looking at his own life expectancy he thought perhaps only the latter group benefited from His protection. He didn't want any part of a life where he would have to watch the lives of people he loved, those who had cared for him, beaten and tossed away like garbage. Let him be tossed out just like his mother and like Hasty. If Lachlan didn't throw him into the sea soon, he would take the leap himself.

Lachlan yanked Joseph back from the edge and threw him back to the ground. "I can practically hear what you're thinking, Mr. Ward. Fear not, you will have your respite. Of course," he started toward Odilon, "You'll have to wait your turn."

A sound familiar to Joseph stopped Lachlan in his tracks. All three of them froze as the haunting call drifted up over the hills and across the cliffs. It melted into the crashing of the waves and at first Joseph couldn't be sure he'd heard what he thought he had. A second cry came on the heels of the first.

"What was that?" Lachlan snapped.

Joseph looked to Odilon who stood frozen, looking so pale he may have passed for a well-tanned caucasian. He stood and scanned the cliffs. No movement that he could see. Where were they?

Lachlan stormed back to him and grabbed him by the shoulder. "Answer me."

"It's nothing," Joseph said quickly. "I mean, I don't know."

"Liar." Lachlan marched back to Odilon and grabbed the boy by his neck.

Odilon did nothing to resist as Lachlan dragged him to the cliff's edge. The headmaster held him over the precipice and looked back at Joseph.

The cry came once more, closer. From below them.

"Fine," Joseph said. "But let Odi go first. You can do whatever you want with me."

He needed to buy some time.

Lachlan smirked and shoved Odilon toward Joseph.

"You know he has no hope of surviving in this place once you and I are through."

The headmaster turned his back to the sea. Joseph put himself between Odilon and the mad friar.

"Well?" Lachlan said. "I eagerly await enlightenment, Mr. Ward."

The cry hadn't repeated itself. Joseph hoped his hearing was accurate. Who knew how these cliffs and the sea itself distorted sound.

"They live in the paintings."

Brother Lachlan looked around, hands raised, burned cassock flapping around him. Did the man realize how badly burned his flesh was? Standing on the edge of the bluff, grey sea and sky behind him, he looked like a wraith, an agent of death. It wasn't far off from the truth.

Joseph struggled for something to say that might buy them some more time when a black hand with four clawed digits grabbed the cliff's ledge. Another appeared after it, followed by several more. *Three* eelamanders pulled themselves over the edge of the cliff. Three more followed behind them. A new terror rose up in Joseph. Where had they all come from? All this time he'd foolishly assumed there were only two.

Lachlan turned, having seen the look on the boys' faces.

"What—?"

It was the last word to escape the man's mouth. Two of the eelamanders slithered toward him with frightening speed and immediately bit and clawed at him. A third joined in as Lachlan struggled to shake them off, screaming at the top of his lungs. A fourth, smaller eelamander, leapt onto his torso, forcing him backwards. For a moment his arms pinwheeled, as the horrors scratched and gnashed. Gravity fought against them and Lachlan tipped over the edge of the bluff, taking the four beasts with him.

Joseph turned his attention to the remaining two eelamanders. They watched their brethren fall to what Joseph hoped would be the death of them and their prey.

"What are they?" Odilon whispered from behind him.

"Never mind," Joseph said. "Let's just go back the way we came."

He put a hand back and tried to pull Odilon with him but the boy yanked his arm back.

The eelamanders turned from the cliff and took slow steps toward them, once more reminding Joseph of crocodiles.

"I can not go back to that place," Odilon said, his voice shaking.

Joseph turned toward his friend, pulling him as he did so. "It's the only way out. You have to trust me."

Odilon resisted for only a second more and then gave in.

They sprinted for the place they'd all come into this world. The eelamanders picked up their pace and Joseph heard them shuffling swiftly after them. They passed through the spot where they'd entered from the red plain.

And continued running along the grass, under the grey sky.

Joseph stopped. "It was here!"

He spun around, looking for any sign of entry. There, on the grass, right where they'd passed, was a spot of blood, likely

Hasty's. They were in the right place. Had the window disappeared with Lachlan's demise? Why hadn't the same thing happened with Brother James' painting?

The eelamanders were almost upon them. There was nothing to do but run. Joseph grabbed Odilon's arm, and tugged his friend along with him.

They ran down a gentle slope that gave way to a short, rocky drop.

"Jump!" Joseph shouted.

They leapt together, landing on the grass a few feet below. The bluff continued to slope down and the boys followed the grade onto a bumpy path that wound down, around the cliff, and to what looked like a rocky beach. Joseph glanced over his shoulder to see the eelamanders crawling down the drop they'd leapt over. They'd bought themselves a few seconds but what good would it do them? What if Lachlan hadn't painted anything else in his life? Even if he had, how would they find it?

"Where are we going, Joseph?" Odilon said between quick breaths.

Joseph pointed toward the small beach. "Looks like they have a bit of trouble on the rocks."

They stumbled onto the rocks of the beach as the eelamanders closed the gap between them. Sure enough, the creatures' bodies were too low to the ground and they had to slow down to navigate the craggy boulders.

The boys had almost as much difficulty as the eelamanders. The rocks were slick with sea water and did not make for easy footing.

As they sprinted and leapt along the beach, Joseph caught something out of the corner of his eye that he could hardly believe. He swiveled his head to check, unable to be certain of what he'd seen. And then they were past it. The eelamanders were keeping up, if not catching up to them at this point.

"Odi!" he called. "Get back up to the grass!"

Joseph was afraid his friend might argue but the boy simply changed directions on the fly and leapt across the rocks to the edge of the grass, where he turned and waited for Joseph. Behind them, the eelamanders were gaining ground. They would have to use every second of lead time they had to put distance between them.

"We need to run back," Joseph said as he leapt off a rock onto the grass.

Odilon only nodded. Joseph was grateful he didn't have to explain himself.

As the eelamanders got closer to the grass, the two boys raced back in the direction they'd come. Joseph glanced to his left every so often to check their position. He looked behind them. The eelamanders had reached the grass and were speeding toward them at an alarming pace.

"Back onto the beach!" Joseph banked left.

"What are we doing?" Odilon called as they leapt across rocks.

Instead of answering, Joseph tugged his friend's sleeve and changed direction again, back to the path they'd just navigated along the beach.

The eelamanders caught on and followed their progress along the grass.

Joseph stopped suddenly and grabbed Odilon by the arm, nearly causing him to lose his footing. They turned toward the eelamanders, who had stopped with them. The monsters faced the boys. Joseph and Odilon had their backs to the sea. The beasts watched them from the grass with hungry eyes.

"I need you to trust me." Joseph said, staring straight ahead and reaching a hand out to Odilon.

Odilon took his hand. "I have so far."

Joseph gave his friend's hand a squeeze and ran along the rocks, toward the eelamanders, dragging Odilon behind him.

One of the beasts bellowed and both started toward the boys, maws opening to reveal rows of jagged teeth and long, black, slathering tongues.

The gap between them closed quickly from twenty feet to fifteen, to ten. Odilon started to pull his arm back, clearly regretting going along with the plan. Joseph gripped his friend's hand harder and pulled him closer to the monsters.

Five feet. Four. Three.

The monster to their left leapt at them.

And the world changed once more.

29

———

Joseph managed to land on his feet, loafers slapping on what he barely registered as white linoleum. He dodged to one side just as Odilon came spilling out of a small, framed painting hanging from a powder-blue wall. Joseph grabbed him by the shoulders, just keeping his friend from tumbling onto his face. His broken finger, dark purple and swollen to at least twice its normal size, jammed against Odilon's shoulder and he had to bite the inside of his cheeks to keep from screaming. He clutched his wrist and doubled over, breathing deep to keep from passing out. After a couple of minutes, he stood upright and gave Odilon a weak thumbs-up with his good hand.

The picture they'd come from was held in a plain, wooden frame. It was a well-done but simple painting of the bluff they'd just come from, painted from the perspective of someone looking up at it from the rocky beach. Scrawled in the bottom-right corner: *L. Kelly*.

"His mother," Odilon whispered.

Joseph made himself tear his eyes away from the picture. They were in a hospital room, that much was clear by the smell alone. It reeked of disinfectant and something else, something sour that lived underneath all other smells in this place.

An old woman lay sleeping in a cot in one corner of the room, next to a window with heavy curtains drawn across it. Her chest rose and fell in shallow breaths, a thin wheeze whispering out of her nostrils. Her hair was so white it was almost transparent and had thinned to non-existence. She was the oldest person Joseph had ever seen. Next to her head, on a small night table, was a framed photograph. In it, the woman on the bed looked only a bit younger but much more vital. Towering over her, with his arm around her shoulders, stood Brother Lachlan, frowning at the camera.

"Do you think he visits her?" Odilon asked, voice hushed.

"Doubt it."

He definitely won't be anymore.

Joseph tiptoed to the window, keeping a close eye on the old woman. It didn't seem likely she would stir since they hadn't already disturbed her when they'd spilled into the room, but better safe than sorry. He peeled the curtain back and glanced outside. It was daytime but that was about all he could tell; the sun was hidden behind a thick cloud cover that almost blended in with the snow blanketing the ground. They were in the middle of what appeared to be a small town, much smaller than Philadelphia anyway. They could've been anywhere; Canada for all he knew.

Voices in the hall made him snap the curtain back into place.

He held his breath and caught Odilon's eyes with his own. The other boy's eyes were so wide Joseph thought they might pop out of his head. The thought was too much for him and he felt his mouth twitch in what desperately wanted to be a smile. Odilon saw what was happening and shook his head, eyes growing wider still. It was too much for Joseph. He burst into a fit of laughter so violent it caused spasms of pain in his side. Odilon rushed to him, threw his hand over Joseph's mouth, and wrestled him to the floor, which made him laugh even harder. Tears streamed from his eyes.

"Joseph, be quiet," Odilon hissed.

His laughter was uncontrollable. He hugged his friend's arm, embracing the hand clamped over his face and laughed with every part of his body. It was more than laughter, it was release. Months of torment, desperation, and nightmares flooded from his soul. It was impossible to tell when the laughter stopped and the crying started. All he knew was that Odilon cried with him, holding him in his thin arms on the cold linoleum floor of that hospital room in an unknown, snow-covered town.

After the laughter, after the tears, when they'd both regained their breath and composure, they sat with their backs against the wall. They watched the old woman's labored breathing for a long time, no longer concerned with being caught. No one came to check on her anyway. It broke Joseph's heart.

"We need to go back," he said, breaking the silence. "We need to tell someone what happened."

Odilon nodded. "But not everything."

"Not everything."

Joseph helped his friend up from the floor and led him by the hand to the painting on the wall. He reached for it and paused, hand held in mid-air.

"What is it?" Odilon asked, worry creeping back into his voice.

Joseph reached into his shirt and pulled out the cross of nails Odilon had given him. He looked at Odilon and didn't have to say a word. The other boy nodded, a smile that made him look thirty years older playing over his lips.

Joseph crept across the room and draped the twine over the woman's head, placing the cross on her thin chest. He didn't know why he wanted her to have it so badly; it just felt right.

"I'm sorry," he whispered.

Without knowing he was going to do it, he bent and kissed her on the forehead. She didn't stir. When he looked back to his friend, he saw fresh tears in Odilon's eyes.

"Let's get out of here," he said.

Joseph stood facing the painting and held out his hand. Odilon's dry palm slid into his own and gave it a squeeze. Joseph took a deep breath, heard Odilon do the same, and once more reached a hand out to the sketch.

They passed from the hospital room into the painting of the bluff, wary of any lingering eelamanders. There didn't seem to be any sign of the beasts. Did they just vanish when the boys left the painting? There was no way to know.

The landscape was quiet save for the rush of the ocean as it broke against the cliffs. Knowing they would have to go back through the scorched plain, Joseph was almost tempted to suggest to Odilon that they return to the hospital room and try to call someone from a payphone. How would they explain themselves though? And to whom? It occurred to him that they may not have a choice in the matter; the exit frame hadn't been where he thought it should be when they'd last tried to flee this place.

They picked their way up to the top of the bluff, where they'd faced off against Lachlan. Where they'd lost Hasty. It seemed like so long ago that Joseph had first met her in the church basement, when she'd only been a teenager. Maybe it was because when he next met her she'd been so old, but he felt like he'd known Hasty for most of his life. He wished he could hug her one more time.

Odilon startled him from his thoughts by placing a hand on his shoulder.

"Do you see it?"

It turned out Joseph needn't have worried about finding the exit frame. He looked to where Odilon was pointing. A square, shimmering space hovered directly in front of them. Hasty's blood, thankfully, was gone from the grass; either disappeared with their exit or sucked up by the eelamanders. He didn't want to think of them lapping up her blood, as he'd seem them doing with Brother James'. The thought of them devouring what was left of Hasty made him sick.

Neither boy moved toward the exit frame. Did they really want to face the charred, shambling masses again? Would the burned people remember Lachlan's order to kill Joseph? It didn't seem likely. Joseph was pretty confident now that things reset whenever they left a painting.

They had to move; the longer they hesitated, the more likely it was the eelamanders would return. It worried Joseph that so many of the beasts had set upon them last time they'd been here. And so quickly. It could have been because four of them had been intruding on the world of the painting. Or maybe it had to do with the creator of the painting being present. But only two had shown up in Brother James' painting. It bothered Joseph not knowing. Either way, he didn't want to put off leaving this place any longer.

Joseph held his hand out to Odilon. "Ready?"

Odilon took his hand without a word.

The heat struck them as soon as they passed through the shimmering space, suffocating in its intensity. The land seemed even more barren without a giant looming above them. Without their master to guide them, the few scorched beings visible in the painting simply shambled about, not seeming to notice the boys. The relief Joseph felt was almost enough to make him laugh. Fear of drawing the hoard out of the black city kept him from giving in to that impulse.

The boys put the city to their backs and wandered in the opposite direction, moving slowly so as to not miss the shimmering space where they had first come into this world. They spread an arms-length apart and inched forward, scanning the air in front of them. Ten minutes passed. Then fifteen.

After what felt like half an hour Joseph swore under his breath. "We're running out of time."

"How long do we have before the demons come for us?"

Demons. That was as good a word for them as any. And they'd be right at home in this place.

"I'm not sure exactly," Joseph said, rubbing his eyes. "An hour? I wish I had a watch."

He was positive they hadn't yet been in this place for an hour but every minute that passed brought them closer to the arrival of the eelamanders. The demons. Didn't matter what you called them; they would devour both boys in an instant, the way they'd gobbled up Brother James and, presumably, Lachlan.

"Is that it?" Odilon asked.

"Where?"

Joseph squinted, peered at the air in front of him. Nothing. He looked to Odilon and saw the boy was pointing up. Way up.

30

It was barely visible from where they stood but
when he caught a glimpse of it, it was impossible to un-see.
The exit frame, that shimmering square space that would take
them out of here, hovered high above them, over a hundred
feet up. Right where the giant Lachlan's eyes would have been.

"Shit!" Joseph screamed at the top of his lungs.

"How will we get up there?" Odilon asked.

Joseph wheeled on him, furious. "How the hell should I
know? Do you see a ladder around here?"

Odilon shrank back and Joseph immediately regretted
yelling. He knew he should apologize but found every ounce
of his energy consumed with figuring out how to escape.

Okay, so they couldn't go back the way they came. They'd
have to go to plan B then; back to the hospital and call
someone to come pick them up. Even if they had to call the
police.

He said as much to Odilon and both boys turned back
toward the border between this place and the bluffs. Joseph

had a rough idea where they'd come through and was confident they'd make it back easy enough.

Then he saw the shapes speeding toward them. They didn't shuffle like the charred people. And they stuck much lower to the ground. Beside him, Odilon whimpered. He'd seen them too.

Three eelamanders snaked their way toward the boys, moving like alligators on the attack. Two of them came from the direction of the only other exit from this place.

"We need to run," Odilon said, his voice quivering.

"We can't outrun them. We need to distract them or get around them."

The beasts weren't far off. They would reach the boys in less than a minute. Joseph's mind raced.

"Can't you do what Lachlan did?" Odilon nearly shrieked.

"What are you talking about?" Joseph tried not to be frustrated, which was easy only because he was so afraid. He desperately wanted Odilon to have an answer. As it turned out, he did.

"How did he make himself a giant? How did he call the army of burned people?"

Joseph's panicked mind couldn't grasp onto whatever Odilon was getting at.

"I don't know," he stammered. "He created the painting. He made it from his own perspective."

Odilon grabbed him by the shoulders and turned him toward the exit frame. "He's not here. It wasn't his perspective."

Joseph was about to scream at Odilon to explain what he meant when it clicked. Lachlan hadn't painted himself as a giant. He had somehow *become* a giant when he'd entered this place. How had he figured it out so quickly? Even in his panicked state, the answer came to him. At least he hoped it was the answer. He glanced over his shoulder. The beasts would be upon them any second now.

Unless.

The earth shook. Odilon screamed at the top of his lungs, apparently believing this was the end. The eelamanders were less than fifty feet away, scuttling across red earth to devour the boys. They paused for only a moment when the tremors began. Seconds later, the beasts were forced to come to a complete stop.

Between the boys and the monsters, the red earth rose up in a great crimson wall. Red dirt rained down on them as the barrier skyrocketed upwards ten, twenty, thirty feet high. There it stopped, a great wall separating the eelamanders from their prey, stretching as far as the eye could see.

Odilon leapt high in the air, pumping a fist in a show of enthusiasm that Joseph had never seen from him. He wrapped Joseph in a bearhug.

"That was you!"

Joseph was dumbstruck. It had been him. He'd barely had to think about it and the land had bent to his will. He was certain he could have made the wall even higher if he'd wanted to. Had he been able to do this the whole time? Could Odilon pull off the same trick? And why hadn't Lachlan used a similar technique to save himself on the bluffs? Unless he had to be touching Joseph for anything like it to work. That would make sense since, presumably, the man hadn't been able to travel into the paintings without Joseph leading the way. In all likelihood, Lachlan hadn't even known he'd been tapping Joseph's ability to make himself a giant. They would have to test his theory. He opened his mouth to tell Odilon to try something similar.

A chorus of deep whale-songs cut him off. A shape appeared at the top of the wall, followed by another, then several dozen more. They scuttled down the wall like lizards. All along the red wall, more and more of the things appeared.

"They're drawn to any kind of change in the painting," Joseph muttered.

If Odilon heard, he didn't respond. His mouth opened and closed without making a sound.

"Run!" Joseph shouted.

He turned Odilon around by the shoulders and pointed him in the direction of the exit frame.

"Oh shit," Odilon whimpered.

Dozens, hundreds more of the eelamanders charged toward the boys from their side of the wall, seeming to appear from nowhere.

"Go!" Joseph pushed Odilon toward them.

His friend dug his heels in, understandably not wanting to run toward the hungry mouths of those things. Joseph shoved at Odilon's back, forcing him forward.

The earth shook once more and all at once they were stepping up onto a large red stair. From the first stair rose another and more after it, climbing skyward to the exit frame.

Odilon stopped resisting and sprinted up the steps. Joseph followed close behind, risking a single look over his shoulder. The eelamanders had leapt onto the staircase twenty steps or so below them. Their only advantage was that the anatomy of the beasts made climbing stairs difficult. Not that Joseph found running up them an easy task.

They were less than a dozen steps from the top when an

enormous eelamander climbed up the wall of the staircase and planted itself in front of them. It hissed at Odilon as the boy skidded to a stop, nearly falling back into Joseph. The creature took a step down toward them. Joseph spun around; the stairs below were packed with an advancing army of the things.

He grabbed hold of Odilon's waist.

"Odi," he whispered into his friend's ear, "Do what Lachlan did. You can be giant."

"I can't do it," Odilon said in a voice that was nearly breathless from shock.

"You can," Joseph moved his hands to the boy's shoulders and squeezed. "You can do it if that bastard could."

The monsters howled a chorus of their low whale-song as they closed in from behind. The eelamander at the top of the stairs took another step toward the boys—and cried out as something shot out of the earth, impaling it through its belly. Blood, only slightly darker than the red of the stairs, poured from its underside. A bloody spear protruded from the thing's back, then retracted itself back into the stair. The beast wheezed, rolled off the side of the staircase, and plummeted to the red earth below.

The horrifying cry of the eelamanders closing in on them from below was deafening. Still holding Odilon's shoulders, Joseph looked behind him to see they were only a few feet away. Too close. They'd never make it.

And then, out of the sky, a gigantic boulder crashed to the staircase behind Joseph, missing him by an inch. The staircase shook with the impact. The boulder rolled down the stairs, crushing some of the beasts underneath its weight and sending many more of them flying over the edge.

Joseph looked back to Odilon, who wore a grin that took up his entire face.

"*Raiders of the Lost Ark*," Odilon said.

Joseph laughed. It felt good. Triumphant.

"Let's get out of here, Indiana."

Odilon didn't need to be told twice. They darted for the exit frame as the boulder tumbled the rest of the way down the stairs behind them, crashing into Joseph's conjured wall. A wall he was nowhere near as proud of as he had been only minutes ago.

They returned to chaos.

31

IT WAS OBVIOUS FROM THE MOMENT THEY RETURNED that something was going on in the school. They emerged from the dank room Joseph had woken up in...how long ago now? It was impossible to say. Odilon led the way out and up a set of ancient but sturdy wooden stairs. From above came shouts and the stomping of feet. Some steps clomped across the floor above them in strong, purposeful footfalls. Others seemed to sprint, as though students were running around in a panic.

As it turned out, that wasn't a far stretch from what was actually happening.

The first thing the boys saw when they emerged from the basement were police, dozens of them, milling about the main level. Staff, friars and nuns alike, ran amok throughout the main foyer. Among all the grownups, kids from every grade were either being escorted out of the hall by uniformed officers or appeared to be engaged in some form of rebellion. A couple of younger kids ran up and down the main staircase as though it was the first time they'd seen it. At the top of the stairs, half a dozen older kids had broken into Lachlan's chambers and were being chased out by a female officer who looked like she'd already had her fill of children for one lifetime. Another group of kids were singing at the tops of their lungs just in front of the dining hall.

"*On top of aaallll smooo-keeey,*" they belted.

Joseph looked to Odilon but, from the expression on his face, the other boy had no idea what was going on.

"You call the police?" he asked anyway.

Odilon shook his head.

Finally someone they recognized whizzed past.

"Bronwyn!" Joseph called.

The girl skidded to a halt and whirled around. When she spotted them she came running over, curls bouncing in rhythm with each step.

"What is happening?" Odilon asked before Joseph could get another word out.

She shrugged. "Cops, obviously. They stormed in here and everyone went crazy. Nobody can find Brother Lachlan. Someone said Brother James is missing too."

She narrowed her eyes at them and, for a brief moment, Joseph was positive she knew he was at least partially responsible for both of their demise.

"Where have you two been? Sneaking out again?"

Caroline appeared from out of the crowd and stood next to her friend, arms crossed in front of her.

"Hey," Joseph said, trying to forget about their botched date. "Cool, right?"

Caroline sniffed. "They'll just send us to another place that's just as bad or worse than this one."

"Yeah," Joseph muttered.

How had he once believed this girl to be perpetually happy? The opposite had seemed true ever since he'd started to get to know her.

It looked like Caroline was about to say something else when Joseph heard his name called from across the hall. He recognized that voice.

Uncle Edgar, of all people, jogged across the floor toward them. It was exactly as Joseph had imagined it happening so many times before. He had to be dreaming. First the police, then this. Maybe he was still unconscious in the musty room in the basement, with Brother Lachlan standing over him, waiting to unleash torments on his body that he would remember forever.

And then his uncle swept him up in his arms, hugging him tightly. It was strange to be embraced so intensely by someone he barely knew.

"I'm sorry, Jo. Sorry I couldn't come sooner. Sorry for all of this," Edgar said.

After several long seconds he ended the embrace and held Joseph at arm's length.

"Did the police call you?" Joseph asked, his voice husky from emotion he could barely suppress.

"I called them." Edgar's voice dropped a bit when he said this.

"How...?"

His uncle sighed. "Your father called me last night."

Joseph had never been so caught off guard in his life. Even returning to all of this, to Uncle Edgar showing up with the police. Even traveling through magical worlds of paintings.

Edgar went on, "He was very upset with himself, Jo. He told me you shouldn't be here. Asked me to take you away. He was the one who told me to call the police, he said he knew there were some bad things going on in this place and that you don't belong here. I didn't even know if they would listen to me but it turns out they've had their eye on the school for some time."

"But the police brought me here!" Joseph would have shouted were it not for his throat tightening up and the tears beginning to fall. It came out as barely a whimper instead.

"Unfortunately not all cops are good cops," Edgar said. "Just like apparently not all priests are good priests."

"Friars," Odilon corrected from behind Joseph.

Edgar smirked at that. "I stand corrected—Jesus, Joseph! What happened to your finger?"

"Horsing around," Joseph said, breathing deeply to take control of his emotions. "I want to introduce you to Odilon, my best friend. He saved my life."

His uncle's eyes widened at this. The man introduced himself to Odilon.

From a dozen feet away, Caroline stared at Joseph with a look he couldn't place. It may have been jealousy. Or hatred. It wasn't nice, whatever it was. He smiled at her as warmly as he could manage and she turned away quickly, but not before he noticed the tears soaking her cheeks.

"Did my dad come with you?" Joseph asked Edgar when he'd finished quizzing Odilon on his accent.

Edgar only shook his head.

"It's okay," Joseph said, "I guess I have to go back to him now."

"Well, only sort of." Edgar knelt down in front of him. "Business has been changing quite a bit for me and I've been looking into relocating, settling down a bit. On the east coast."

Now it was Joseph's turn to stare. "You mean you're moving here?"

"Not here exactly. Boston." Edgar held his gaze for a full ten seconds. "Would you want to live there with me?"

Joseph threw his arms around his uncle's neck and squeezed so hard the man actually had to pull him off. Joseph was powerless to stop the tears from falling. He'd thought he'd cried all of the tears of relief that he could in that hospital room housing Lachlan's mother but they came again in torrents.

"What about Odilon?" Joseph asked, looking to his friend, whose eyes were cast down at the floor.

Edgar's mouth opened but no sound came out. He looked around at the chaos taking place in the foyer of St. Theodore's and then cast a look at them that told Joseph he was thinking hard on something.

"Let me make some calls," was all he said.

It was enough for Joseph. He wrapped Edgar in a hug again, then pulled Odilon into it. Odilon fought him only for a second. The three of them embraced while St. Theodore's unravelled around them.

A thought came to Joseph and he pulled back from the group hug. "What did you mean that I *sort of* have to go back to my dad's?"

Edgar gave him a sad smile. "Just to get your things, Jo. I'll put us up in a hotel until I can sort out where we're going to live."

The three of them walked out of St. Theodore's and to Edgar's car together without anyone bothering to stop and ask them where they thought they were going. Apparently Edgar had already spoken to everyone who needed speaking with.

Odilon hung back when Edgar opened the rear door of the car for them.

"You can wait here if you'd like," Edgar said to him, "But I don't think it'll be much fun."

"I am a criminal," Odilon muttered, barely able to meet Edgar's gaze.

The man smirked and jerked a thumb at Joseph. "So's he."

Joseph stretched his good hand out to Odilon. "You did your time, Odi."

Odilon still looked doubtful, but he climbed into the backseat of the car nevertheless.

"First stop, hospital to get someone to look at that hand." Edgar put the car in gear and piloted up the long laneway, passing cruisers as even more of them paraded toward the school.

They passed through the open rolling gate entirely without ceremony. Edgar pulled out onto the rural highway that had brought Joseph here and, just like that, they were free of St. Theodore's.

They stopped at a little hospital in a small town about twenty miles away. While they sat in the waiting room, Joseph wondered if this could be the same hospital Lachlan's mother had been kept in. Something told him it wasn't.

The doctor who set his finger asked Joseph a few times how it had been broken. Joseph maintained it had happened wrestling with another student. The doctor cast suspicious glances at Edgar and Odilon but didn't press any further. Joseph couldn't be sure why he didn't tell the doctor, or Edgar, the truth. He suspected it was because he'd already given Lachlan more attention than he deserved.

32

<hr>

JOSEPH WAS YANKED OUT OF A DREAMLESS SLEEP IN THE backseat of his uncle's car. Edgar was shaking his shoulder and whispering his name. Night had fallen, though it was far from dark outside the car. The lights of downtown Philadelphia, lights he had never thought he could miss until now, cast their yellow-orange glow on the street. Passing headlights washed over them, illuminating the interior of the car. Across the road, McLaren's florescent Open sign was a beacon to the thirsty and the lonesome.

"My dad's probably not home," Joseph said after he'd rubbed the sleep out of his eyes. "I don't have my key."

"That reminds me," Edgar said as he dug around in his coat pocket.

Next to Joseph in the back seat, Odilon slept on. No sense waking him. It's not like Joseph wanted to show off his apartment. He could still hardly believe he was going to live with Uncle Edgar after all. It felt surreal. It felt right.

Edgar held a closed hand out to Joseph and said, "I got

your stuff from the police station. Your backpack's in the trunk."

Joseph stuck out his hand and two things fell into it; his apartment key, something he hoped to be using for the last time tonight, and his Mickey Mouse watch. His throat tightened and he swallowed against it. He'd cried enough for one day. He muttered his thanks, not wanting Edgar to hear the thickness in his voice, and fastened the watch onto his wrist. It seemed so long ago he'd last worn it that he was surprised to find it was still keeping time.

"Want me to come up with you?" Edgar asked.

Joseph shook his head, still not trusting himself to speak, and shoved out of the car. His feet landed in a bronze pile of slush but he hardly noticed the cold wet soaking through his loafers. He stared up at the apartment building he'd lived in for his entire life, save for the time spent at St. Ted's. In all likelihood, his father was across the street, sidled up to the bar in McLaren's, drowning himself in beer. Joseph considered walking across the street to check but decided against it. If his father was home, he would deal with it. He'd certainly gone up against worse over the last seven months.

"I'll pop my head in across the road and see if you're dad's in there, just in case. He'd want to see you're okay," Edgar said through the open window, seeming to read his mind.

Before Joseph could put up a word of protest, Edgar cut through the late evening traffic, to the tune of a couple of angry horns, and parked his car in front of the bar. Joseph trudged toward his building through the thin layer of filthy snow that covered the sidewalks.

The door to the main entrance was still broken, not that he'd expected it to be repaired while he was away. He let himself into the lobby and recoiled against the smell. Had it always been this bad? Perhaps one of the only things St. Theodore's had going for it was that it had at least been clean. This place smelled like a mix of piss, garbage, and stale cigarette smoke. He called the elevator which, thankfully, was already on the main floor. The doors dinged open and the smell of urine grew stronger, as if it originated from within this car. He ignored the tackiness of the floor and jammed the button for the eleventh floor.

The ride up didn't take nearly as long as he'd hoped. He realized he'd been dreading coming up here after all. What if his dad *was* home? What if he'd changed his mind and wanted Joseph to stay with him? What if he decided to send him back to St. Theodore's? It seemed like that place wouldn't be around for much longer but, like Caroline had said, there must be others like it, staffed by people just as insane as Brothers Lachlan and James and whoever else in that place dealt with children in a similar manner. The elevator doors dinged and started to close again right away. At the last second, Joseph tapped the Door Open button and stepped out onto his floor. He forced himself to put one foot in front of the other until he stood outside his apartment for what might or might not be the last time.

He put his key up to the lock and hesitated.

Should he knock? He didn't want to surprise his father and suffer whatever wrath may come out of that. At the same time, wasn't his dad expecting him? He'd never imagined it could be this hard to come home. It all felt too good to be true, going to stay with Edgar and leaving this dingy hole behind.

He shoved the key in the lock and turned it. The clunk of the deadbolt was deafening in the hallway.

"Dad?" he called through a crack in the door.

Through the opening, he could just make out the arm of the couch his mother had lived and died on. His stomach folded in on itself at the sight of it. He missed her so much.

He nudged the door open another inch and now he could see the couch in its entirety. It was so quiet in the apartment.

"Dad?"

Another inch or so and he could see the hallway that led to the bedrooms and the bathroom. He gave the door a good bump and it opened enough to reveal a boot, kicked out in front of his father's easy chair. The boot was attached to a jean-clad leg that he recognized as his dad's. He pushed the door open the rest of the way and saw why it was so quiet.

His dad was passed out, empty beer cans crowded on the end table next to his chair and strewn about on the floor. Joseph wondered for a minute why it felt so strange to see his father there, since the man had often been passed out in that exact same position.

He wasn't snoring, which explained the eery silence. Had he stopped snoring as soon as no one was around to hear it anymore? Joseph briefly considered sneaking past his dad; trying to get his stuff and get out of here before—

Something wasn't right. Beyond the silence. The way his dad's head was tilted, mouth closed in a grim line, lips blue as the colored chalk Ms. Hendrix used sometimes on the black-board at school. An empty prescription bottle sat on the edge of the end table, front and center among the beer cans, almost as if put on display.

All at once, a roaring, like static, erupted in Joseph's ears. He felt frozen in place.

A brown stripe of puke ran down his father's shirt, flecked with blood.

He blinked and then it was nothing more than a damp patch from what might have been spilled beer or whatever had been in the thick glass bottle at his father's feet.

The roaring static in his ears was so great that he didn't hear Edgar and Odilon rush in behind him. He didn't even realize it was Edgar who was pulling him out of the apartment, saying something over and over in his ear. One second he was standing in his living room and the next he was floating backwards. He just accepted it, thinking he must be dreaming. He was still asleep in the car. He'd wake up any second and try all this again in real life.

Edgar set him down in the hallway and pulled the apartment door closed. When Joseph looked at Odilon and saw his friend's face broken with pity, he decided he must not be dreaming.

"I'm sorry, Jo, I'm so sorry. I should've come up first," Edgar was saying.

"The man at the bar said said your father gave him this to get to you," Odilon held out something that glinted in the hallway light.

It was so much to process. Joseph collapsed into Edgar's arms. Odilon wrapped his arms around him and the three of them kneeled in the hallway, embracing. Edgar repeated his apology over and over, stroking Joseph's hair all the while. Odilon pressed something cold and solid into his palm. Joseph brought his hand in front of his face, within the huddle the three of them had made, and felt his breath catch.

The Purple Heart. The one he and his mother had smashed the frame to.

He closed his palm around it and wrapped his arm around Odilon, his other already clutching Edgar. They stayed like that for some time; this new family, born out of death and misery, but also out of kindness and compassion. He realized how lucky he was, which seemed like a strange thought to be having right now. How many people got a second chance at family though? Not only did he have a new guardian in his uncle, he'd also gained a brother, something he had never hoped to have in his life.

After a while, two bored-looking paramedics showed up and pronounced his father dead at the scene. Two police officers arrived on the scene soon after and took all of their statements then left to go across the road to question the staff at McLaren's.

Uncle Edgar went into the apartment to get Joseph's things; books and clothes mostly. Joseph didn't want to have to step foot in there ever again. It was as dead to him as his parents now were.

After much too long spent in the grimey hallway of that apartment, having to dodge the questioning looks of the other tenants who had drifted out into the hall to watch the latest drama, they were allowed to leave. The three of them took the elevator to the ground floor in silence and found Edgar's car double-parked in front of the building. And then they were on the road, headed to a new life together.

The funeral took place in the same church as his mother's. Joseph didn't feel even the slightest urge to venture into the storage room in the basement. With Hasty gone, the painting down there meant nothing to him.

Far fewer people attended Joseph's father's funeral. He wasn't sure how to feel about that. One thing he was glad for was that there were blessedly few people who he was obligated to speak to. In fact, no one approached Joseph for the duration of the service. A couple of men, presumably from his father's work or the bar, muttered their condolences on their way out.

When everyone had gone, Edgar took Joseph aside, leaving Odilon to munch on church lady sandwiches.

"This was with the Purple Heart your dad left for you," Edgar held out a folded sheet of paper. "I don't know why I held onto it. I should've given it to you a lot sooner. Sorry, kiddo."

"It's okay," Joseph muttered.

He didn't have to ask for privacy; Edgar left him there and joined Odilon at the food table.

Joseph took a breath and unfolded the sheet of paper. He was so caught off guard by what was written on it that he allowed himself to cry for the first time all day. He couldn't remember ever having seen his father's handwriting, would have sworn the man was illiterate, yet he knew in his heart that this was his. The letters were all capitalized and written with a shaky but firm hand. His father had pressed the pen so hard that the letters were practically engraved into the page; if he flipped the note around, the words would be mirrored in raised paper on the back of it. He read and re-read the letter, as he would do on an almost daily basis for the rest of his life. It read:

I'm sorry, Joseph. I love you.

EPILOGUE

Joseph woke with a scream on his lips. He was barely able to catch it before he roused Odilon, and possibly Edgar, for what would be at least the third time this week. The nightmares were becoming less frequent since they'd moved into the new house on the outskirts of Boston, but they weren't any less intense. As with the other nightmares, the details of this one were already slipping away from his memory now that he was awake. It had taken place in St. Theodore's, he could remember that much. And Lachlan had been there.

Odilon slept across the moonlit bedroom, the subtlest of snores escaping his lips. He looked completely at peace. The haunted look had gone out of his eyes within a few weeks of moving here and now he was just another kid. Joseph was almost envious at the calmness Odilon gave off now more than ever. If he had nightmares like Joseph had been having, he said nothing about them. He'd been unreasonably tolerant of Joseph waking him up in the middle of the night with his screaming. At first it had been every night. Just over a month later and it was now only a few times a week that Joseph woke the house up with his shrieks. Odilon and Edgar were both more patient with him than he thought anyone had ever been. Except, perhaps, Ms. Hendrix.

Joseph slipped out of bed and followed the glow of the bathroom light down the hall. It was Odilon who insisted the light be kept on at night. He'd never liked the dark. Blamed it on his experience sleeping on the street, under the glow of street lamps. Joseph never complained.

After he'd drained his tank, a term he'd picked up from Edgar, Joseph crept down the hall to the kitchen where he poured himself a glass of ice-cold milk. He sipped it and stared out the kitchen window at the darkness of the backyard. Their house was in a residential neighborhood unlike any he'd visited in his life. With the exception of St. Theodore's, Joseph had only ever known the city. This neighborhood was all quaint houses with large front yards and even bigger back yards, many backing onto a forested area, as theirs did.

He was rinsing his glass in the sink when he heard it. A faint clicking noise that, for a terrifying moment, reminded him of the sound Julius' nails made on the floors of St. Theodore's. He quickly dismissed the idea that it could be a dog; these were heavier sounding, and accompanied by a scratching. It was almost like a heavy rake being dragged across the linoleum. The sound was faint but continuous. It came from the basement.

He considered waking Odilon up but decided against it. He did that enough without meaning to; he should let his friend sleep. No doubt there would be another nightmare to do the trick before the week's end.

Padding to the basement door, Joseph held his breath,

listening. There definitely seemed to be something down there. A rat? Sounded too big. Maybe a raccoon had somehow gotten in through the basement window. There was a solid foot of snow on the ground outside and it had drifted even higher against the ground-level window; he couldn't imagine a raccoon being able to get the window open through all that. They were animals known for their cleverness though so he didn't dismiss the idea entirely. Besides, if it wasn't a raccoon, he wasn't sure he wanted to know what it was.

He flicked the light on at the top of the stairs, expecting the sound to stop when he did. It kept going. That was reassuring —it meant it was most likely something mechanical making the sound, probably the furnace. They hadn't been in this house for long enough to get to know all of the noises the place made at night. Emboldened, he figured he'd better check on it, in case it was something that needed immediate attention, not that he knew what to look for.

He inched down the stairs to the first landing, where they curved around to the left. Once he reached the landing he'd be able to see into most of the basement. He took a breath and tip-toed down, around the corner. Nothing. The basement looked empty.

The sound was indeed coming from where the furnace was, so Joseph skipped down the rest of the stairs to check on it. He froze when he reached the last step. What he was seeing was impossible. He rubbed his eyes, a gesture he might've found funny at another time; it was something he would have thought only happened in movies. It was still there when he looked again, plodding around the basement in a circle. It had just stepped back into view when Joseph reached the bottom step. It didn't seem to notice he was there at all. It marched in a slow, tedious circuit around the basement, the claws of its feet scratching at the tiled floor. Joseph wished it had been Julius after all.

The eelamander opened its maw and bellowed its mournful cry.

ACKNOWLEDGMENTS

Words, for all their power and mystique, can be a paltry means of showing appreciation. But they are all I have to offer so I hope those to whom I am thankful will accept my gratitude with the assurance that each word of it is tethered to my heart.

The first and most passionate of my thanks goes to my love, my best friend, mother of my children, tamer of our many beasts, and my lifeboat in stormy seas, Annie. If it wasn't for her, I may not have even worked up the courage or *chutzpa* to take the leap and write my first novel. It was Annie who suggested I take a break from my careers in restaurant management and event entertainment to write the book, even with our first child on the way. I didn't stop working entirely but I certainly worked far less than I ever had in my adult life. The practical sacrifice she was making is obvious; not only was she carrying—soon to deliver—our son, she would also be bringing home the majority of the proverbial bacon while I futzed about in my imagination or did whatever we writers tend to call "work". This novel has taken about two-and-a-half years to complete and Annie has encouraged me every step of the way. More than that, she hasn't let me feel small or like a non-contributor to our family, even as my subconscious was screaming at me that I'm a deadbeat husband and father for locking myself in my office for several hours a day to write. She didn't encourage me through false platitudes, which I probably would have seen right through, but by helping me feel needed, giving me purpose, while also talking about my writing and my book as though they were real parts of our life. Even though I've been doing it all my life, my passion for writing and storytelling has often been something I've been mildly ashamed of, something I always thought was considered by much of the world to be a waste of time. She saw me the way I wanted to see myself, as a writer, and helped me to embrace that identity. Thanks, Annie. I love you.

Both of my parents have also been huge supporters of my work. I owe thanks to my dad for being vulnerable and sharing his experiences with me, but also for trusting me to use them as the setting for Joseph's story.

My mom was hugely instrumental in the technical development of this book and has read it more than anyone. She donated her own time and effort to perform a couple of in-depth edits and saved me from looking silly by catching dozens of errors that I may or may not have noticed on subsequent read-throughs.

Big thank you to one of my greatest supporters, my grandmother and "Super Oma", Sandra. She's encouraged me to take steps with my writing I never would have imagined taking and has been supporting and encouraging my writing since I was about eight years old.

Huge thanks to Thom, my writing mentor, without whom this story would be a third of what it is in terms of content and quality. In the years I studied under him and worked with him, Thom has dramatically changed the way I write and how I approach story. He's challenged me to try things I would never have dared to and has taught me to tickle the ol' vagus nerve in all the right places.

Thanks so much to my early readers: Elliott, Mel, Michael, Jason, Laura, and Sue for all the constant read-throughs and amazing notes and insight.

Josh Brine is not only a good friend but a stellar designer and without him, the book wouldn't look as great as it does. Big thanks to him for all the hard work and for putting up with countless notes and requests for revisions that I dumped on him.

And for the encouragement, belief in my abilities, and general "being there-ness", a big thanks goes to Carol, Donny, Jack, Peter, and Trevor. I'm blessed with having a lot of really great people in my life who not only set stellar examples but who go out of their way to encourage, support, and teach me. These five are the cream that rise to the top in that group of people and I couldn't be more thankful for them.

And you. Thanks for taking a chance on my debut novel. I hope you enjoyed it. I want to say I hope it wasn't too upsetting but I think some things in life need to shake us up a bit, without being gratuitous. I hope you'll be back for the next one. I've got lots to share.

Until next time, adieu.

-C.S.

ABOUT THE AUTHOR

Christopher Sweet has worked as a freelance writer, m. waiter, bartender, event DJ, actor, children's entertainer, driver, shopkeeper, call center operator, concierge, c assistant, barista, and a campground manager. He loves bo movies, the outdoors, and baseball.

He's written several dozen short stories and multiple screenplays. This is his first novel.

He lives with his growing tribe of humans and beasts in New Brunswick, Canada.

You can catch him online at: www.authorchristopher-sweet.com